UNCHAINED PASSION

"I'm tired of your laughing at me," Anna said angrily. "There is nothing wrong with my wanting you. How long will it be before you even kiss me? I'm tired of waiting."

In the next instant, Prince had his huge black arms around her, pinning her arms to her side. He had waited a long time too—too long. "Do you know what I am going to do with you?" he said.

Anna shook her blonde head.

"I am going to lie down with you and show you what men and women are meant to do." His lips found hers, pressed hungrily. If they were discovered it would be the end for both of them—and as his body flooded with passion he could also feel the nearness of his own death. . . .

To Joan
and David —
To acquaint you
with the old St.
John Thomas —
Eleanor
Herbert

MUSCAVADO

ELEANOR HECKERT

A DELL BOOK

To My Beloved GARCIA

Published by
DELL PUBLISHING CO., INC.
1 Dag Hammarskjold Plaza
New York, New York 10017

Dell ® TM 681510, Dell Publishing Co., Inc.

Reprinted by arrangement with
Doubleday & Company, Inc.

Printed in the United States of America

Previous Dell Edition #6155
New Dell Edition
First printing—August 1975
Second printing—November 1975

1698

Chapter 1

On the morning of September 20, 1698, a long line of Negroes shuffled down the waterfront street in the port of Charlotte Amalie, St. Thomas, Danish West Indies. There were two hundred and fifty-seven slaves in the procession, their chains clanking in a solemn rhythm of defeat and weariness. At intervals the procession stopped, and a fallen slave was unlocked from his shackles and rolled from the line. Then the other slaves were prodded on, moving past the unconscious bodies that lay in the parched weeds beside the hard dirt road. Their destination was the Royal Danish West India Company on the west side of the harbor.

The street was lined on both sides by a noisy, disorderly group of white men. Their well-tailored dress, representing what was fashionable in each of their varied homelands, gave an aura of importance to the gathering. These were the Danish planters of the island and the prosperous slave traders from surrounding Spanish and French possessions. The delayed arrival of the ship had exaggerated their anxiety about the condition of this shipment of slaves.

A drum rolled. As the white men fell silent, a crier stood up on a rum barrel and made the following announcement in a monotonous, bellowing voice as the slaves filed past:

"By order of Governor Johan Lorentz. Owners are reminded that slaves are forbidden to hold feasts or drum-dances. Slaves will be at home on Sundays by sunset and all other evenings at drumbeat. Punishment for violation of these laws will be as follows . . ." A pause. The even cadence of the chains echoed ominously on the street. "For the first offense he is to be whipped . . ." A pause. "For the second offense he is to have his ears cut off . . ." Pause. "For the third offense, he is to be hung and his head placed on a stake."

As the line of slaves neared the company building, the onlookers surged forward to inspect and lay claim to their pick of the human cargo. Spanish, French, Dutch, English, and Danish erupted in a harsh babble. Wide-brimmed hats, some with colorful plumes, were knocked awry in the melee and polished silver-buckled shoes scuffled in the dust, raising it like a shroud over the entire scene. Greedily the buyers yanked and pulled at each other to get a closer look at the prime male slaves. Some of the men reached out and crudely handled the females.

An ebony-black, half-starved child straggled along at the end of the line, unattached by chain. Her brown eyes, squinting against the bright tropical sunlight, were fixed upon the ground in front of her. Up ahead, the noise increased. She halted and could make out a dusty haze in front of a large building. As the noise of the foreign voices built in volume, the girl panicked and threw herself against the woman in front of her, only to stumble and fall to the ground. With a final burst of energy she grabbed at the woman's leg and held on. The woman continued to walk, dragging the child forward in the dust. Annoyed, she grabbed the child's arm and pulled her to her feet. "Walk, Bahbu. They will beat me if we fall behind."

Clutching the waistband of the woman's skirt, Bahbu stumbled along obediently. By the time they reached the building the white men had moved aside and were hastily placing their bids on the male slaves. Bahbu moved into the coolness of the shaded room without receiving the glance of interest or the appraising pat that most of the other female slaves had gotten.

Inside, Bahbu was led into a crowded stall where she maneuvered into a corner and sank down on the cool tiled floor. "Mama," her mind cried out. "Oh, Mama, I am afraid and I am sick. Why do these white men, these evil gods, torture us like this?" She put her hand on her shoulder. It was only now healing from the hot iron that had seared her flesh and left its strange markings there forever. That seemed like such a long time ago.

When they had left their village home, Bahbu's mother was sobbing. She told Bahbu that her father, the chief, had sold them because of his greed. The trip down the river was comfortable enough. Late at night they reached a gathering place. Here there were hundreds of people, all writhing and moaning with fear. Bahbu and her mother

6

were put in a crowded hut, one of many beside a great stone house that was bigger than anything Bahbu had ever seen before. Inside they were lined up. There a man put the hot iron on their shoulders. Bahbu's mother was bent over crying with pain when they placed the iron on Bahbu's tender skin. Bahbu thought she would never hurt as much or cry as much as she did that night. But the worst was yet to come.

The next morning they were moved by canoe to a very large ship. Aboard it they were taken to a dark, smelly room and chained together in pairs at the ankles. They were packed together side by side, so close that it was difficult to stretch out or ease the pain in their aching bones. A rod was put through their chains, holding them to the floor. Time seemed endless as days ran into nights. Then the storm came. The boat pitched and rolled violently. They were thrown against each other with such force that Bahbu's body pained. In that dark hell, Bahbu thought she was being torn apart. She could feel herself retching, adding her vomit to the slimy mess that was all around her. Finally she fell to the floor, feeling about to burst with the strain of the convulsions that wracked her. When the storm had subsided, the white men came down and unlocked the rod that held Bahbu and her people in place on the floor. Instantly, hundreds of black, chained feet thundered up toward the light and air. Yelling, "Kill the white man," they stampeded on deck. A gaunt-faced black man lifted Bahbu up and placed her out of the way against the side of the ship. Bahbu screamed for her mother and shrank back against the wall. In the confusion, she thought she saw her mother being lifted up along with the mass of people. Above her there were howls of fright and moans of death. Finally part of the group was forced back, most of them falling down the steps. The cover was thrown into place and they remained locked in the darkness, without food or water, until this morning. Then the white men came cautiously down the steps. Three men stood guard while four others went around securing all of the people by a common chain. They ignored Bahbu.

Prodded by the cautious guards, the prisoners filed up the steps, the moaning increasing with their fearful uncertainty of what was ahead. Bahbu sat and stared at her people, searching in vain for her mother. By slow, painful degrees the belly of the ship was vacated. Finally, Bahbu was alone. She looked at the bloated, lifeless forms that were left behind. Carrion fumes clogged her nose. Slowly Bahbu began to crawl on her hands and knees to the steps. Then she pulled herself up the ladder, trembling with fear that she would be separated from the other black people.

Now, here on the factory floor, she was again surrounded by the nervous shuffling of many black feet. Would it never end? Bahbu raised her bony knees and rested her head on them. Around her, the screaming of foreign voices and the tension that filled the room passed over her unnoticed. To an eight-year-old African girl it did not make any different whether the slave trading was good or bad at the Danish West India Company that day.

Aboard the slave vessel *Copenhagen Bourse*, Captain Innes Petersen breathed a sigh of relief now that his strange cargo had reached the security of the company. He looked at the Danish flag flying over the bastions of Christian's Fort and thanked God to be alive to see it. For Captain Petersen and Bahbu alike it had been an evil voyage of violence and death, a voyage begun with five hundred and six black bodies in the hold and now almost half that number strewn in a bloody chain on the bottom of the sea from the Guinea coast of Africa to these sandy white shores of the Virgin Islands. Even now he estimated that thirty or forty of the Negroes at the company were close to death from scurvy.

The captain felt uneasy at this thought. Already he had been summoned by Governor Lorentz to give an explanation of the heavy losses. He looked over at the town. It was clean and orderly. Small, one-story brick residences were built side by side on the road between the harbor and the imposing company building, or factory, as it was called. There were, however, no more than fifteen houses, all grouped closely together. To the right, on the road between the factory and the limits of the town at Christian's Fort, there were several other small buildings, mostly shops of the trades people. Here there were two tailors, one hotel keeper, one blacksmith, one shoemaker, a fisherman, one washer and ironer, a tavern, and one cotton ginner.

The settlement was on a strip of flatland. Behind it a mountain loomed upward, the top a ridge of green cutting a long line across the clear sky. The captain was still amazed that he had endured so many hardships on this crossing only to find his destination to be a small mountainous island lifting out of the Caribbean Sea. And yet it had to be an important market, for here in the harbor were eight other ships of varied classes, representing Denmark, Spain, Great Britain, Holland, and France.

On the dock were hundreds of puncheons of rum and hogsheads of muscavado, the brown sugar with which he'd return to Copenhagen. There were spices, cotton and tobacco. Campeachy and Brazil woods would provide ballast in the recently emptied hold. With any luck he would be able to load his ship in the next four days and set out for Denmark to complete this triangle of trade.

Rumors spread quickly of the violence that had befallen the *Copenhagen Bourse* on her maiden voyage from Africa to St. Thomas. For over a week now, these men had been gathered at Charlotte Amalie, awaiting the largest shipment of slaves ever scheduled to arrive. Seeing the slaves, they were disappointed and angry at their weakened condition and diminished numbers. Jan Henderson, owner of the island's most productive sugar and rum plantation, leaned against the wall of the factory building and listened to his young brother spend his anger.

"These damn savages gave the captain and his crew a bad time of it," Lars said. Above Lars's full lips was a thin blond mustache. His blue eyes did not show the emotion that his voice carried. "Mutinous bastards," he added. "The captain should have thrown a few more into the sea." Lars removed his heavy, ornate hat and wiped the perspiration on his forehead with a soiled handkerchief. He wore his hair in the current European style, with a heavy crop of curly blond hair spilling over his shoulders. "Damn, it's hot today," he complained. "I hate to dress for town in weather like this." He lifted the bottom of his black brocade vest and shook it. "You don't look like the heat is bothering you," he said, looking enviously at Jan.

"You worked up a lather running around getting the bloodier details of the crossing—in the saloon," Jan replied.

"And what of that?"

"I just doubt that these stories being passed about in the streets have much to do with what really happened on that boat. After all, the ship's crew was armed—and the slaves were not." Jan pushed his wide-brimmed straw hat down lower on his forehead to shade his eyes from the blinding tropical sunlight. Tall men, the brothers stood eye to eye. Jan, too, had blond hair—but his was straight and shorter, cut well above his shoulders. Unlike his brother, Jan had not dressed in his finest clothes today. He was wearing a loose-fitting white shirt that was open at the neck and a pair of thin black trousers. Jan looked like a plantation owner. Lars, who acted as his overseer, could have been mistaken for a prosperous slave trader or a visitor.

"One day you will stick up for these savages once too often," Lars said. "From what I hear, this is the most savage group ever to be brought here. It won't be easy to tame them. Why shouldn't I find out what I can? We owe it to ourselves."

"But what is the truth of the matter?" Jan said. "From what *I* hear, the ship had lost some of its crew from scurvy before the mutiny ever started—they weren't really killed by the slaves. Some say that when they hit that hurricane the slaves were smothered and crushed from being packed too tightly in the hold. You can't blame a lot of frightened people for fighting their way out of hell."

"Can't blame them?" Lars snorted. "I can blame them for mutiny. And if I have any trouble from our slaves, they'll know soon enough where the blame falls. You listen to only one side of the story, the slaves' side as always. You know, Jan, there must be some times when the trouble is the fault of the slave."

"Many terrible things happened on that ship," Jan said quietly. "All I'm saying is that we'll never know the truth of it. The only version of the story we're going to get is from the ship's captain, but he's in trouble already with the King's company and will be sure to place the blame elsewhere. It does look strange to me, though, and to some of the other planters, too, that almost half the slaves died, got killed, or jumped overboard on the voyage here. It never happened like this before."

"Let's forget it," Lars replied. "Come on, let's go to the tavern. God, I'm hot."

"You go on. I'll secure our bid on that young buck we selected. He looks as good as any of them look right now."

Bahbu had just raised her face and was looking through tear-swollen eyes at the tall white man who had halted and

10

was staring down at her. Bahbu was frightened because the man had eyes like a clear blue sky and hair like a leopard's skin. Bahbu had never been close to such a man before. She shrank down, hoping he would not look her in the eye. She thought he must be a witch and if he looked her in the eye she would go blind. She pulled her legs up tighter and buried her face again.

Jan felt a desire to put a comforting hand on the girl's head. Don't be a fool, he cautioned himself, she is frightened out of her wits and may bite. Poor devil! He moved on to the next room where the male slaves were kept.

"Jacob," he called to the man in charge. "I have put my mark on this young buck here." Jan pointed to a young, muscular black. "I will pay for him now." The smell of the slaves, still in the filthy rags they had worn since their capture, oppressed him. He walked to a table where another employee was collecting money and making notes in the company's journal. Since there was now a line in front of him, Jan moved restlessly from the room. As he passed Bahbu, still crouched in the corner, he stopped.

Suddenly, Lars was at his side.

"I thought I'd take a look at the wenches before I left," Lars said. "There might be a good strong one, for breeding later on." He glanced down at Bahbu. "My God, Jan. What are you looking at her for?"

"I have been thinking I might buy some females for kitchen work."

"If they gave her to you, you'd have no bargain. She looks sick. She couldn't carry a load of wood to the fire. Come on." Lars pulled on Jan's arm. "Look, here's a strong, healthy wench—and not bad-looking, either."

Jan jerked his arm from Lars's grip. "Keep your hands off me. *I* pick the slaves for the Hendersen plantation." He turned and called to Jacob. "I'm putting my mark on this young girl in the corner."

"We don't need an ugly female like that," Lars persisted.

"I'm paying for my new slaves now, and we're leaving," Jan shot back. "The stench in here makes me sick."

11

Chapter 2

They had climbed the narrow mountain path quietly. Now the path fanned out and a breeze stirred the brush. Jan nudged the golden Palomino he rode, knowing that the gates of Hendersen were just ahead. Behind him the new male slave and Bahbu rode on a broad mule. Lars brought up the rear, sitting loosely in the saddle with a loaded musket resting in the crook of his arm.

They came out of the plateau, facing the gates of Hendersen Estate on Fortuna, the highest mountain on the west of the island. The buildings of the cane plantation were silhouetted against the bloodshot blue of the evening sky. On the south was the mill, a massive circular stone building, tapering to a flat top. An arched door on the front of the mill opened onto a path that broadened into a sizable clearing. On one side of this were the factories: the boiling house, the curing house, and the distillery. On the other, a cluster of small wooden huts with thatched roofs: the slave quarters. From the clearing in front of the huts puffs of smoke raised lazily off the ground, then, caught by the trade winds, disappeared. A heavy odor of charcoal hung in the air.

On the north side of the plateau the greathouse sat on a gentle slope, commanding a view of the working village. A wide stone staircase led up to a shaded porch and an open archway just beyond it. Behind the greathouse the lush green forests fell away from Fortuna to Botany Bay, where the land eased into the Caribbean Sea. Out there the sun was a bright orange ball hanging on the surface of the sea, outlining the hazy shapes of other, smaller islands.

As the group moved through the gates, the only noise was that of the horses' feet plopping with a muffled thud on the earthen path.

Bahbu, who had spent the trip with her head against the muscular back in front of her, suddenly tensed and sat up.

Somewhere in the distance she heard a sound that had a familiar ring. There—yes, she heard it again. Far off, from somewhere below this mountain, she heard the hollow booming of a drum.

Lars straightened in his saddle. "They are at it again, down at Bordeaux. Damn savages! The minute they stop working they creep away to beat those drums."

"It's little enough for them to have to look forward to," Jan said. He was about to continue when a movement on the veranda of the manor house caught his attention. His wife Christina was standing there. She was a tall woman, with broad shoulders, full hips, and an ample bust. Her hair, once a pale blond, was now of a rusty tone, like the feathery tops on the cane stalks. She wore it in a soft bun piled high on her head. Christina stepped forward and waved. The skirt of her long white cotton dress moved around her ankles.

"Take the new slaves to Mary," Jan called back to Lars. He spurred his horse and rode toward the house. Christina was coming down the steps as he ran up. Meeting halfway, they embraced. Jan dropped his head into the place on Christina's neck where the clean, flowery scent seemed to come from.

"Oh, Jan, I've missed you," she said. "What took you so long?" She cradled his head.

Slowly Jan straightened. "The ship was delayed. A lot of things happened. But that is a long story. I want to have a bath. Then we'll sit down and I will tell you about it." He put his arm around her waist and they walked up the steps.

"Mary, get out here!" Lars yelled out as he approached the slave huts. By the time he dismounted, a young woman appeared at one of the doors. Her skin was a dull black, making the whites of her large eyes a startling contrast. She wore a calf-length, loose-fitting cotton dress of a faded red print. A brighter red scarf was bound around her head, wrapped to form a flat pad on top of it. Her hips moved gracefully under her garment as, barefoot, she moved noiselessly into the clearing.

"Get these people cleaned up and fed. See if you can talk to them. If not, find someone with their dialect. Tell them that they are here to work for us and if they behave, they

13

will not be harmed. Tell them if they don't behave, I will beat them to death!"

Bahbu sat with her head down, shyly rolling her eyes to look over at Mary. In the momentary silence that followed, the drum sounded again in the distance. Mary spoke in her native tongue.

"Hurry, girl, get down and come over here."

Bahbu pushed off the back end of the mule, bounced on the ground, and ran to Mary. She threw herself against the woman and sobbed. Between the sobs she mumbled, "The white men took away my mother."

Mary held the thin body close to her. "Don't cry. You are safe here. The drum tells us now that the ship brought more of our people to the island today."

"What are you talking about?" Lars demanded.

"She has lost her mother."

"Tell her to forget it. Tell her why she is here. And see if you can talk with this one." Lars nodded toward the slave on the mule.

Still holding the child protectively, Mary looked at the newcomer. "What is your dialect?" she asked.

He stared at her. "The same as yours. I am Amina."

Mary smiled, showing even white teeth against her full lips. "You will not be harmed here if you listen to what I tell you to do. Soon you will understand their language." Mary looked cautiously at Lars. "This man is evil. The other, who bought you, is a good man."

"What are you saying?" Lars demanded.

"I told him that you are a good master and he should learn your language. He will listen to me."

"What tribe is he from?" Lars said.

"Amina," Mary answered.

Lars was irritated by the note of pride in Mary's voice. "You might know it," he said bitterly. This means more trouble, Lars thought. My dear brother certainly can pick the worst ones. "Well, Mary—get moving. Take him in to the others."

"Come," Mary grunted at the newcomer.

The slave slid from the mule. Squaring his shoulders, he walked to Mary's side. He was very tall.

"He looks arrogant enough," Lars said. "Probably thinks he is a chief's son. Yes," he laughed, "we will call him Chief. We already have a Prince."

With that, Lars turned his horse. He looked back and

said, "Make sure you get all the stink washed off them. And send Prince to stable the horses—now!"

Lars's voice carried to the other side of Mary's hut, where Prince heard it. Putting down the two pails of water he was carrying, he jumped closer to the back wall of his mother's hut and waited there. He felt trapped. Prince hated the sight and sound of Lars and always reacted fearfully to his presence, although he tried not to show it. He knew he had to go out and do as the master commanded, yet he found pleasure in trying to hide from him.

It had never occurred to Lars that a slave woman whom he summoned to his bed could give birth to a child so obviously his. And when she did, Lars was determined that no Negro would make a claim on Hendersen birthrights or expect special favors. The child was a slave, and that was that. Lars resented the family resemblance in the child and did everything to show the other slaves that some white blood did not change their status.

Undeniably, Prince was a Hendersen. At eight years of age he was already tall and lanky, like the Hendersen men. The combination of his mother's broad features and Lars's thin ones had given Prince a handsome, angular face. His eyes were a golden amber and his skin a rich, light tan.

To the other slaves, Prince was an accepted by-product of the services Mary was forced to render to their master. Everyone knew that Lars would punish any one of them who stood in his way when he wanted Mary to come to his room. Mary had arrived with a mate, Watsu, who had made the mistake of trying to keep Mary from Lars. One morning they found Watsu in the sugar mill, dead. His arm had been chopped off and he had bled to death. Lars told Jan how Watsu had gotten his arm caught in the grinding paddles and how he had to use an ax to try and save Watsu's life. But everyone wondered why Lars had not called Christina to tend to Watsu before it was too late.

After Prince was born, Mary tried to protect him from Lars, but it was a useless effort. As soon as the boy could walk, Lars was making demands of him and as the boy grew older, Lars sought ways to punish him whenever he could.

Now Mary led Bahbu by the hand around the back of

15

the building. Prince, hearing the crunch of footsteps, turned suddenly. Seeing Mary, he smiled.

"Go, my son," Mary said. She nodded her head toward the front of the hut. "Put the horses away."

Prince dropped his head.

"Hurry! Then come back and meet Bahbu. She is afraid. They have taken her mother from her."

Prince looked at Bahbu. She pushed against Mary, dropping her eyes.

"Go!" Mary commanded.

Prince ran around the hut. When he came into the clearing, he saw Lars getting off his horse in front of the one-story square white building between the slave huts and the greathouse which was Lars's separate home as over-seer of the plantation.

Lars dismounted and looked around, searching for Prince. He saw the boy running toward him. Prince caught up and reached out eagerly to take the reins. Lars shoved his hand away.

"That beating taught you a lesson about being slow, didn't it?" Lars grinned as he talked. "Now, maybe I should teach you about not being rude." Lars saw fear rise in Prince's eyes. "The next time you grab anything out of my hand, I'll cut your ears off!"

Frightened, Prince moved slowly backward. Lars fol-lowed, step by step.

"Stand still," Lars said menacingly.

Prince froze in place. While Lars stared at him, the expression in Prince's eyes changed. The wide-eyed, fear-ful look was now replaced by a calmer stare. The lids of Prince's eyes drooped, showing two vivid amber slits that held Lars's gaze, unwavering.

Slowly, Lars raised his hand and offered the reins to Prince. As Prince reached out to take them, Lars let them fall to the ground. Cautiously, Prince crouched down on one knee. Keeping his eyes upraised, he reached out and groped on the ground for the reins. Lars spit in front of him. Then he turned his back and walked through the gate to his house, whistling.

Prince stared after him, letting some of the hatred that was boiling up inside him spend itself in the contemplation of his plan. Yes, some day, when he was grown and strong enough, he was going to kill Lars. Then he would run away to Crab Island, off to the west, where he heard other slaves had gone and found freedom. Right now he could easily jump on Lars's shoulders and with one arm pull his head back and with the other hand slit his throat and glory in the blood that pumped his life out on the ground. But Prince knew he wasn't quite strong enough yet to hold Lars—for Lars was a very big man—or to go to Crab Island on his own. Instead, Prince ran one of his long, thin fingers across his own throat as he looked after Lars. Reaching the steps, Lars paused. Prince hastily pulled the horse around and hurried it toward the greathouse, where the other horse was tied. His thoughts continued on. Maybe his mother's witchcraft would work soon. She certainly tried hard enough to put a spell on Master Lars. But his mother had often said that Lars was such an evil devil-man that he could tell what to do to keep the other spirits off.

Now that Prince was older he had to sleep in one of the huts with five grown male slaves. This made him feel good because he was a step nearer to being a full-grown man and strong enough to carry out his plan. But, thinking about it, he missed those exciting nights when his mother assembled the twigs and herbs and old patches of cloth to hold the forbidden ceremonial tribal rites that were meant to cast a spell on Master Lars. The other female slaves loved the ritual too. Everyone wished for Lars to have a terrible death at the hands of a demon. Even though it had not worked to date there was a certain satisfaction in those frequent, hopeful attempts. Useless as it seemed the witchcraft against Master Lars was something that always gave him comfort, some kind of inner anticipation that carried him through many days.

When I am a man—when I am sixteen—I will kill Master Lars. That is, if the witchcraft does not do it before, Prince told himself as he walked along. It was the same thing he told himself every day.

After he was bathed and freshly dressed Jan joined Christina on the porch. Immediately one of the house slaves appeared, bringing him his evening portion of rum. Relaxed, Jan carefully related the tale of the delayed arrival of the ship and the deplorable condition of the Negroes it brought to St. Thomas.

"The slaves must have suffered very much," Christina said.

"Yes, I believe they did. But this has made the rumors

17

of their savagery all the stronger. It grieves me that Lars believes them. He hangs out in the tavern exchanging gossip with the sailors and the rowdiest of the planters. There is a meanness in him that disturbs me, Christina. Do you know of what I speak?"

Christina nodded.

Jan continued. "I don't want to be disloyal to my brother. But if anything should happen to me, Christina, I am afraid he would abuse the slaves until all of them would run away. I have always tried to pick the proudest of the Negroes. They work harder and respond better to fair treatment. But if they are abused, that pride will force them to try to make their escape. My investment in our Negroes is heavy. Without them, Hendersen plantation could not produce. Why is it that Lars cannot see this? He insists that they are savages who can only be tamed by the whip. All around him here at Hendersen is evidence that this is not true."

"He is a young man, Jan."

"Ah, but old enough to upset me. Everyone in town knows that he does not stand behind my policies at Hendersen. That's the trouble with one's brother as an overseer. I cannot dismiss him—there is no place for him to go now that our mother is dead. No roots elsewhere. You know he has been siding with Wilhelm Bodker. He knows that Wilhelm speaks against me at the council. This is disloyal." Jan slammed his hands down on the arm of the mahogany rocker. "How I long to be rid of him."

"He needs a wife. A woman would soften him."

"Huh! As scarce as women are on this island, you think one is likely to settle so quickly on Lars? They are more likely to tell stories about his latest fist fight than think of him as a husband. Women here want a respectable man."

"Perhaps he will settle down. Living on the island is very difficult for a young man. There is not much social life here."

"That is what you always say, Christina. How much time do you think we should allot for him to settle down?"

"I do not want to speak against your brother, Jan. Will you excuse me? I'll go and see if our dinner is ready."

Christina moved from the porch, leaving a faint, flowery scent behind her. Jan leaned back in his chair and closed his eyes. Yes, Christina was a devoted wife. Sometimes her devotion was so great that Jan was overwhelmed by it. It was only two years ago that she had remained by his side when the island was threatened by attack from the Spanish fleet. The Spaniards, at war with Louis XIV, regarded Denmark's neutrality as sympathy with France. Using this excuse, they planned an attack on St. Thomas. The Privy Council, a group of St. Thomas planters, met and decided that their families should be sent to the Leeward Islands for protection. It was only common sense that the colony could not withstand the attack of a force as strong as the Spanish fleet. There were also rumors that the Spaniards planned to use the slaves, turning them against their masters, to assist them in taking the island.

Christina refused to leave. Jan agreed because he was certain that Hendersen slaves could never be turned against them. It was Christina, with her gentle manner and kindnesses to them, who had won their confidence. They repeatedly vowed loyalty in case of attack. Fortunately, the French fleet, under Pointis, sailed into the Caribbean, and the Spanish fleet withdrew to Havana. Later, thinking the French were no longer on the alert, the Spanish fleet sailed again for St. Thomas. But Pointis was waiting.

Between Puerto Rico and Santo Domingo, the Spaniards were met by Pointis commanding a squadron of six French men-of-war. There, a raging battle took place in which the Spanish vice-admiral, three hundred men, and fifty-four guns were captured by the French. The colonists of St. Thomas breathed a sigh of relief, and went back to the planting of cotton, tobacco and cane. But during the early summer, the English, at war with France, accused St. Thomas of siding with the French and sent out three or four privateers in an effort to break up St. Thomas' sea trade. But this threat was short-lived. By fall, peace between the French and English was reached and St. Thomas had nothing to fear on the Spanish Main except the pirates.

Recalling this, it seemed to Jan that his problems with Lars were small by comparison with the struggles the island settlers endured to hold onto their plantations and make them produce.

Chapter 3

Aroused by the hollow tone of the conch shell Bomba sounded each morning, Prince leaped off his straw mat and ran outside. It was still dark. Prince paused, waiting for the tropical darkness to become light from the early morning stars and a sliver of moon. Seeing Bahbu, he ran forward. They wrapped their arms around each other and danced in a circle.

"Today you make sixteen," Bahbu chanted, "today you make sixteen." Round and round they danced. As they whirled about, Bahbu noticed a light flicker up from Master Lars's house. "Stop! He is up. He will beat us if he sees us dance."

"It would be the last," Prince whispered gleefully. Then they stood quietly side by side. "Tonight," he dropped his voice, "tonight when they are all asleep, meet me beside the mill. Just think, Bahbu," his voice rose in volume, "tomorrow we will be free!"

"Shhh," Bahbu cautioned, pulling away. "Be careful. Now I go to the house. Master Jan will be getting up."

"Don't forget to put the salt meat and potatoes at the hiding place. I will bring the sugar cane," Prince whispered after her. She turned. Holding a thin finger against her full black lips, she nodded.

Prince walked to the cane field where the harvesting was taking place. It is good that everyone is working so hard, he thought. They sleep well at night. Deep inside he felt some remorse. Now he would be leaving Hendersen plantation without killing Master Lars.

The first in the field, Prince went directly to work, chopping at the tall stalks with his cane knife. He felt grateful for the hard work that had developed his muscles. Now he knew he was man enough to protect Bahbu and care for her once they reached Crab Island and freedom. This day had been carefully planned for the last three years. Even now a canoe was hidden on the beach at Botany Bay. The drums had confirmed it last night. By tomorrow, St. Thomas would be out of sight forever.

Later, Bahbu and Mary came into the field, bringing the breakfast of corn bread, salt meat, and sugar cane juice. Prince put his knife in the rope belt that held up his trousers and walked toward them. Bahbu handed him a piece of corn bread. They were about to speak when they heard an approaching horse. Prince took the bread and moved away from the cluster of slaves.

"Prince!" Lars yelled out as he approached. Prince stopped. Every slave in the field froze into place. Lars reined in his horse. "Go to the mill and work. They are moving too slow, as usual. And work!" Prince looked at the corn bread in his hand. "Take that with you and eat it on the way."

Lars kept his eyes on Prince until he was out of sight. Then, turning to the others, he shouted, "Eat, you fools. There is work to be done."

On the way to the mill, Prince passed seven unloaded donkeys being led up to the cane field by their young slave handlers. Each nodded, passing by silently. Now that Prince thought about it, there was an unusual stillness hanging in the air today, as if any talk or laughter might betray the night's plan.

As he entered the mill, the same silence met him. The two slaves who were feeding the cane stalks to the churning wooden cylinders did not halt or look up. They feared this job of feeding the noisy machine, and with good reason. If a hand got caught in the grinding cylinders, there was no way to stop the crushing pressure. Jan had chosen a good place to build the mill and there was always a strong wind turning the great wooden paddles that powered the noisy machine. Prince looked at the sharp ax against the wall. This was the means by which a mangled limb could be chopped off to save the slave from inevitable death. He quickly turned from the sight of it.

Chief was in charge of the mill. His job had not been appointed by coincidence. From the day of his arrival, he and Mary had the common bond of being Aminas. It was not long before they were in love. Though they were cautious about their relationship, they knew Lars was suspicious when he put Chief in charge of the grinding, for he was a powerful man, capable of heavier work in the field. Chief was always aware of the ugly cylinders and trained himself never to be startled by the sudden tap of Lars's whip. Chief knew that Lars hoped to catch him unaware and force an accident.

Prince moved into position and concentrated on feeding the cane. Long cautioned by Mary and Chief, he kept his mind on the work and the long hot day passed quickly. All around, the making of sugar and rum moved at a fast, well-organized pace. The juice from the cane ran down a trough out of the mill and ran into large copper kettles in the boiling house. Each batch had to be transferred to fresh kettles for three or four cookings before it was properly crystallized. While it was boiling, the foam was skimmed off and taken to the distillery. The crystallized sugar was taken to the curing house to cool. Later it was emptied into molds. From there, the molasses drained off and went to the distillery for making Hendersen rum. Jan was in charge of the distillery and supervised each process from the time the cane juice poured into the copper kettles until the muscavado and rum were delivered to the waterfront. His rum was known to be the best on the island and each season the barrels of Hendersen rum brought the highest prices on the wharves of Charlotte Amalie.

At dark, when the slaves could no longer work in the fields, the grinding stopped. Leaving the mill, Prince automatically continued the work that had to be done at this time of the year. He and the other male slaves had to carry enough wood to keep the fires going under the copper kettles, bring water from the cisterns for the distillery, and feed the livestock: the goats and cows, the horses and mules. The women began preparing the night meal, some gathering beans, cassava and sweet potatoes from the garden. Others started charcoal fires in front of the huts on which to cook the food.

Later, as they ate, the slaves continued their silence. The punishment for a caught runaway slave depended on the master. Lars had often enough let them know that he would settle for no less than death. So far, no slave had tried to make his escape from Hendersen plantation. They were fed, clothed, and housed better than any slaves on the island, and they knew it. But none of them felt that Prince was wrong to take Bahbu and find freedom. They knew— or had felt themselves—the sly cruelties inflicted by Lars when Master Jan or Mistress Christina could not see.

They knew, too, that Prince was the one upon whom Lars inflicted the most pain and humiliation. Escape, then, was a natural plan, even with so much risk involved. Still, they could not help feeling fearful.

Mary squatted on the dirt beside the fire. Her skirt hung loosely between her legs, touching the ground. The amber light of the fire reflected on her black face and yellowed the whites of her eyes. Around her neck was a finely carved wooden amulet, polished to such a sheen that it appeared to absorb the heat and light of the fire and take on a life of its own. Bahbu squatted beside Mary, a miniature, frailer image in every detail, with the exception of the necklace. Mary's loose-fitting cotton blouse hung low on her broad shoulders and billowed out over high, firm breasts. Bahbu's blouse, with the same thinness from wear, the same faded red color, hung on her bony shoulders and puffed out in front, with a sudden accent, as if a matched pair of small round fruits had been placed there. Both wore scarves of cotton wrapped tightly around their heads. The upward pressure of the scarves pulled at the sides of their faces so that their eyes took on an oriental slant and the skin on their high cheekbones shone like two round patches of polished ebony.

Prince scooped out a generous portion of salt meat and beans from the pot over the fire and squatted beside Bahbu.

"Eat, Bahbu," he said gently. "Tonight we have a long walk."

Bahbu shook her head. "I am sick. Here." She put her delicate hand on her stomach.

"I am making bush tea for Bahbu," Mary said. "It will give her strength for the trip ahead."

Prince put the red clay pottery plate on the ground beside him. "Do not be afraid, Bahbu. We go over the plan again." He edged closer to her. "The only danger is if we are caught before we reach the boat. If this should happen, then we are to say we went off to be alone for the night. They cannot kill us for running away if we say we are not running away. We say we did not know how far we were walking. Master Jan knows that we are good slaves. He will not kill us."

Bahbu stared into the fire. "My heart will be sick for Mistress Christina. She is good to me."

23

"And would you stay here to serve Mistress Christina and have to make babies with Master Lars?"

"I would pick to die," Bahbu answered solemnly.

"Then think of it! This is why we go tonight."

"Do not talk of that," Mary commanded in a sharp voice. "You will be free by morning. All of our people will be silent. They know I will put an evil spell on the first who talks. They would prefer a beating by Master Lars to the torture I would put on them."

Mary turned to Bahbu. "This I have made for you." She put her hand on the wooden ornament. "You will wear it, Bahbu. It carries a curse for Master Lars. Should he harm you in any way, he shall be killed," she paused, "by the hand of his son." Mary raised her eyes and fixed them on Prince. Solemnly, Prince nodded. Mary removed the amulet and placed it around Bahbu's neck. The carved face was pointed at Prince. Yes, it was smiling at him. But there, when the light flickered, the face moved. The mouth fell down agape, and the eye sockets grew deeper, sucking in the round little eyeballs until they disappeared. An ugly, sightless face grimaced at him, like the face of death.

Prince was frightened, but he could not take his eyes from the thing. Bahbu moved, bending her head forward to look down at the gift. The face changed again. The eyeballs came forward, filling the sockets; the gaping mouth closed and raised up at the corners. The face of life smiled at Prince. He felt his body relax. Until now he did not realize the tension this idol of witchcraft had put upon him. Prince looked up at Mary and smiled.

Mary nodded. "The power of all that my people taught me is in this gift. You go tonight, my son, with no fear of Master Lars."

Bahbu rubbed the piece of wood. It had a satisfying feel. Where it rested on her chest she could feel a warmth from within it. Suddenly Bahbu was not afraid. And the pain in her stomach was gone.

Chief came over from where he had been sitting with another group of slaves, and crouched down behind the three of them. "Tonight I will tend the fires. If Master Lars rides off, I will signal Bomba, who will be hiding in the field. He will beat the drum. If you hear the drum tonight, you will know that you are in danger. Every slave on the west of this island knows not to touch a drum on this night." Chief rested his big, calloused hand on Prince's

24

shoulder. "You are as my son. Go—and find happiness. The gods are with you tonight." He then put his hand on Bahbu's arm. "And you, my child, do not be afraid. You go with a man who will protect you from harm."

A silence followed. Everyone stared into the fire. Bahbu wanted to throw herself against Mary and cry. But she was not a little girl any more. She could not. Prince felt himself grow still taller than his present height of six feet, and could feel his body fill out substantially, as with the fullness Chief had acquired with maturity. Mary hurt deep down inside, where she had once carried this young man. The gods had chosen that no other children had ever spawned in there, but this one was child enough to fill her with pride. The gods had been good to her.

Chief felt his love for those before him swell up inside of him. This was his family. Here on this wind-swept piece of land they had shared both their joys and sorrows and had been united in a tight circle by that sharing. He did not know how to show his love. As head of the family, he could not let the pain which was burning in back of his eyes, wanting to flow out, be shown. He stood up. With his head held proudly erect, he walked away, his large silhouette fading quickly into the darkness.

Immediately Mary stood up and lifted Bahbu by the arm as she did so. "Come. You will drink the tea and rest until it is time to go."

Prince also raised up off the ground, his eyes settling on his mother's face. Mary returned his gaze, the two of them unable to move or speak. Bahbu, seeing the pain of the unspoken message in their eyes, raised her hand to her mouth to hold back a sob and ran toward her hut. Mary did not move. "Happy journey, my son," she finally brought herself to say. And with that she turned and walk away.

Bahbu lay on the hard straw mat, aware of all the noises around her. She knew the other women were not asleep. There were none of the noises of deep breathing or turning that were usually there at night. In the dark, stuffy room she could feel their tension. Only a few minutes before, Mary had left the hut. When she returned, after making sure that Master Lars was in bed, Bahbu would have to leave on her journey to freedom. She squeezed the wooden amulet. Her hand was numb from the pressure.

25

Oh, why, why didn't it bring her more comfort? Her stomach was hurting again.

The door opened and closed. Mary was whispering beside her. "Go now. It is quiet over there."

Bahbu sat forward and grabbed Mary. "I am afraid!" she sobbed against Mary's breast. Mary stroked her shoulders. "No, my child, there is nothing to fear." She pushed Bahbu away from her. "Go," she commanded, and threw herself over onto her own mat.

The door opened and closed as quietly as it had a few minutes before and suddenly Bahbu was standing in front of the hut, looking toward Master Lars's house. Seeing it, she became alert and ran noiselessly around the side of the hut toward the mill.

Prince was suddenly beside her. He took her hand and they ran off toward the foot path that went to Botany Bay. He stopped. "Now we will walk. There is no reason to run. You will hurt your feet. Bomba has put our food down beside the path. He said he would put a stick across our way so we will find it. Come, Bahbu, we are free."

Around them were the noises of night, cheeps and chirps, and the rustle of the wind in the tall cane stalks. Ahead of them they could see the wooded area that ran between Hendersen land and Botany Bay Estate. They walked swiftly toward it. Overhead, the sky was filled with tiny, sharp bits of blinking light. As they walked down the path, hand in hand, freedom encompassed them and they moved with a light, easy step that sang of it.

As they were about to enter the woods, Prince stumbled. "Bomba traveled a long way tonight to hide our food. See, here it is." His voice was low, not because of fear, but because the whispering noises of the night demanded it. He looked around, knowing that somewhere out there Bomba was hiding with a drum. It was reassuring.

He put his arm around Bahbu's shoulders and drew her to him. Bahbu wrapped her arms around his lean waist and rested her head on his chest. Hugging her, Prince said in a hoarse voice, "I am going to build a house for you, and we will have our own earth to plant. And we will make many children to help us with the land." Bahbu clung to him, so tightly that he could feel the amulet push against his bare chest. An overwhelming passion weakened his legs. Deliberately he pushed her away. "Come. We have far to go." He raised the pole from the ground. On each end of it

26

was tied a large sack. He balanced it carefully on his shoulder. Taking Bahbu's hand, he led her into the woods.

Lars could not sleep. What was it that gave him this feeling of uneasiness? It began this morning, when Prince walked out of the cane field. Had sixteen years of taunting this slave finally made him, Lars, the complete master? No. Prince had too much pride. And something had been wrong around the plantation today. The heavy, sweet odor of sugar and rum, the pungent smell of sweat, and the oily charcoal fumes had all been the same. The click-clack of the windmill, the hollow thud of the cylinders squashing cane, the braying of thirsty donkeys, the crackling of fires, and the gentle swish of falling cane were all familiar and comforting. It had all been there—but something *was* missing. What was it? Lars stared into the semi-darkness of his room, trying to find the answer. Outside, the fires under the boiling copper kettles in the workhouse sent a soft glow through his bedroom window. The wind whined through the locked paddles of the mill. But there was something else out there, some sort of silence that put him on guard. Yes, that was it. A silence from the slaves—no drums. Something had to be wrong.

Mary lay on her straw mat. Around her the others had now gone to sleep. Prince and Bahbu have a good start, she thought. It should not take them more than an hour to reach Botany Bay. The path is good. They have been gone for almost an hour now. Soon they will reach the boat and be safe from the island. Why is it, then, that my heart pounds like a drum? Lars cannot beat me if I hold my tongue. And I am not afraid, even if he does beat me.

The door of the hut slammed back against the wall. Beneath the fiery light of a torch, Lars stood glaring at Mary. She was already sitting in an upright position on the mat. "Where is she?" he screamed at her, grabbing her up by the arm. He pulled her forward, until her face was just under his. "Where is she?"

"I do not know," Mary said. Her calmness added to Lars's anger.

"Tell me where she is, or I will cut your black tongue out!"

"Please, please," Mary begged. "If I knew, I would tell you. I did not know that she was not here beside me. I woke up when I heard your footstep. In the dark I did not see anything." Her voice was persuasive.

Lars threw her back on the mat. "Stay there."

He ran out of the door, torch flames leaping all around his head as he ran toward the male huts. Mary leaned over and watched him enter the hut in which Prince had lived. He ran out immediately. "Chief—saddle my horse!" Lars ran back to his house, clumped up the wooden steps, and jabbed the torch into a holder before disappearing inside. Soon he reappeared, carrying his musket and a whip. Another slave came running across the clearing, bringing a saddled horse. From a narrow window in the mill, Chief watched.

"Where is Chief?"

"He feed the fire tonight." The child's eyes were wide with fear. Lars grabbed the reins, knocked the youth aside, and hoisted himself onto the horse. As he rode directly to the mill, Chief appeared at the doorway. Lars rode slowly up the ramp. Drawing to a halt only a few feet from Chief, Lars pointed his musket down at the slave's chest.

"Where are Bahbu and Prince?"

Chief calmly raised his eyes to look into Lars's face. "I do not know, Master. I have not seen them."

Lars stared. Chief held his gaze. Suddenly, Lars spurred his horse around and rode up the hill to the high field.

Hurriedly, Chief ran into the mill. Picking up Bomba's conch shell, he went to the small window in the back of the mill and put it to his lips. Even as its hollow tone echoed out into the night, a drum began to boom, a loud, evenly measured beat. Now the plantation came to life, slaves running in all directions as had been planned. Lars came galloping down the path, riding into the group of milling slaves who had to fall back to keep out of his way. "Who sounded that alarm?" He looked at the sober faces. The drum had ceased to beat. Where had it come from? From here—or farther down toward Botany Bay? Lars knew he could not find the answer without wasting more time. Botany Bay would be the logical place for a planned escape. Yes, he would take that path.

Jan came running across the clearing, still buttoning his shirt. "What has happened here?" he demanded.

28

"Prince and Bahbu are trying to run away!" Lars yelled at him.

"What makes you so sure of this?"

"It has been planned all day. I could tell. Tonight I went to the huts. They are both gone. And someone has sounded an alarm for them. They have to be trying an escape, or it would not be planned so well." Lars paused. "I'll take this path, the one to Botany Bay. You take the one to Bordeaux." Without giving his brother a chance to reply, Lars kicked his horse and galloped off.

Jan looked at the black faces surrounding him. He addressed Chief. "Saddle two horses. Ride with me."

Bahbu and Prince were out of the wooded area and crossing Botany Bay Estate when they heard the drum. "We must run!" Prince whispered. He threw the pole with the food to the ground. "We must reach the boat before he finds us." He took Bahbu's hand and pulled her along.

Lars's horse galloped easily across the path cut in the cane field, but when they entered the woods, Lars had to slow the animal down. It would be too easy for the horse to stumble over a fallen tree or rock. He let the horse move at its own pace while he peered into the night for objects that could cause them harm. There was such an intense eagerness for speed within him that Lars loudly cursed the animal when it stumbled and almost fell.

Ahead, Bahbu and Prince ran toward the beach. Bahbu's lungs ached and her breathing was labored. But she was determined to get to freedom—and the determination forced her on.

Jan was on the path to Bordeaux, with Chief following behind. The two estates ran together and were under cultivation right to each boundary line. After a short distance, Jan signaled Chief to halt.

"If you know where Prince and Bahbu have gone, you have to tell me. If Master Lars finds them first, he may kill them."

Chief looked at his master, and was silent.

"If we find them, I will not harm them. I give you my word. We will say they were out here making a baby. Do you understand?"

Chief remained silent, looking at his master.

"Speak up, Chief," Jan said angrily. "You have to trust me!"

29

"I do not know," Chief said flatly.

Jan turned his horse around and rode off toward Bordeaux. Chief followed, thinking of what Master Jan had said. Chief knew that the master would not give his word and then betray it. He had often enough proven that to all the slaves. He knew Lars had a good chance now of catching Prince and Bahbu before they reached the boat. But what if he and Jan did not reach there before Lars overtook them? Then Prince would surely die. And what if he, Chief, told of their plans now, and they did escape from Lars? Then he, Chief, would be punished for knowing of the plan. Master Jan did not say anything about that.

"Master," he called. "Wait!"

Jan pulled his horse around and stopped.

"They have gone to Botany Bay. There is a canoe waiting there for them."

"Come, then," Jan shouted, spurring his horse. "We have no time to waste."

In single file, they galloped back up the mountain side toward Hendersen Estate and the path to Botany Bay.

Prince and Bahbu reached the beach at Botany Bay. Ahead of them, a canoe was by the water's edge. Exhausted, Bahbu fell on the sand, gasping for breath. "Do not stop," Prince urged her, pulling on her arm while he, too, heaved for air. "We have to get away from the beach." He pulled on her arm, but she could not raise herself. She remained slumped there, trying to make her breathing less painful. "Get up, get up," he pleaded, tugging at her limp arm. Bahbu tried to raise herself, but fell back immediately.

"I will get the canoe in the water. I will be back." He dropped her arm and ran toward the canoe. Above the surf, Bahbu heard the crashing of dried palm leaves. Simultaneously, she saw the horse and rider on the sand. She opened her mouth to scream—but no sound came out. Prince, hearing the rider approach, turned. Lars galloped toward him, a whip in his hand. Prince turned to face him, raising his arm to protect his face from the whip. In that instant, Lars halted the horse and pulled the musket from his saddle. Taking careful aim at Prince's chest, he pulled the trigger.

The impact of the shot threw Prince backward on the sand. Dismounting, Lars walked toward the sprawled body. Blood flowed over Prince's chest, making a dark spot on the sand beside him. Lars lowered himself on one knee and carefully lifted Prince's head. Prince's eyes and mouth were open, his head weighed heavily in Lars's hand. Lars looked into the eyes that stared blankly at the sky.

"You've killed him. You've killed him." Bahbu's hysterical voice rang out. She threw herself on Lars, her sharp nails cutting into his face. A sudden enormous anger filled Lars as they rolled in the sand. He forced her under the weight of his body, and sat astride her, striking vicious blows at her face. She struggled fiercely for a time, then went limp beneath him. Panting, Lars stopped.

Bahbu, almost unconscious, reached for the wooden amulet around her neck. With her last energy she raised the strap over her head and threw it in the sand.

Lars stared at the ugly wooden carving for a moment, then grabbed it. Pulling Bahbu by her hair, he raised her head and placed the charm around her neck. "You will wear the damned thing," he commanded. "You savages and your gods." He yanked at the carving pulling it so hard that the leather cord jerked Bahbu's head back and forth. "You will wear it, always. Go back and tell that witch that your gods don't protect any of you." He hit her again. Bahbu moaned. "Wear it, wear it," he shouted, ripping pieces of cotton cloth and throwing them on the sand. Finally she was nude, a crumpled heap on the sand beside Prince's body. Lars walked back and forth in front of her, his anger and hurt exploding into a greater passion. He undressed hastily and threw himself on top of Bahbu. Forcing her limp legs apart, he pushed himself into her. In the heat of his passion he could feel the wooden necklace digging into his chest. He hated the ugly thing so much that he pushed harder, in violent jabs, letting the charm dig into his chest each time he came down.

By the time Jan and Chief rode onto the beach, Jan could see only two bodies sprawled on the sand. Lars's horse stood nearby. Dismounting, Jan ran toward the forms on the sand and crouched to look from one face to the other. Prince's eyes were fixed on the gray clouds of dawn above. Bahbu's swollen eyes were closed. Jan reached out to feel Prince's heartbeat. His hand rested in the cold, sticky blood on Prince's chest. Slowly, Jan withdrew

31

his hand. Bahbu moaned as Chief picked her up in his arms.

"She is alive," Chief said.

Dazed, Jan stood up. Before he could speak, he saw a form rising out of the water. Slowly, Lars appeared.

"They attacked me," Lars said casually, rubbing the water off his body with his hands."

"Attacked *you?*"

Lars put his head down and rubbed the salt water out of his long hair. He saw that Jan's hands were doubled into fists. "Look at my face. She clawed at me like a mad animal."

A long silence followed. Finally Jan relaxed his hands and raised his head. "Put your clothes on, Lars," he said quietly. "And then you will put your dead son in that canoe and you will take him out and bury him at sea. He longed for freedom from you. Now you will give it to him."

Bahbu felt the hardness of the straw mat beneath her. She smelled and heard familiar things. She opened her eyes, to find herself back in the hut. Squatting beside her was Mary. Was it a dream? Had she and Prince yet tried to escape? "Prince—" she muttered the name through swollen lips.

"He is dead." Mary's face was expressionless, her eyes dry, her voice firm.

Bahbu closed her eyes and rolled her head aside. It was not a dream. It *had* happened. That terrible hole in Prince's chest. The open eyes staring past her at the sky. Bahbu grabbed at the wooden carving.

Viselike, Mary's hand gripped Bahbu's. "Stop. Do not remove it, *ever.*" Mary put her face close to Bahbu's ear. "Did he take you, Bahbu?"

Bahbu nodded her head.

"Then you will bear his son. Do you hear me? You will bear Lars's son. And when *he* is grown, he will kill his father. All of this is in my carving."

Bahbu rolled her face toward Mary's. "I do not want his son." It was painful to talk, but she spit the words out forcefully.

"Look at me," Mary commanded. Her eyes lowered into fine slits, the whites lit by a hidden fire. "I hate him more. He has killed my only son. But you, Bahbu, you will have another Prince. For us." Mary reached out and took the smooth wood carving. "And he will kill his father. You will live to see that day." She caressed the carving and then placed it squarely in the middle of Bahbu's chest.

Chapter 4

The full moon that soared over the ridge of Fortuna Mountain and hung just over the top of the mill cast an eerie light on both the group of slaves who squatted on the dirt in front of Mary's hut and the three white people who sat on the porch of the greathouse. Mary emerged from her hut and picked her way silently through the group of slaves as she approached Christina sitting on the porch.

"It will be soon, mistress," she said. In response, Christina picked up the satchel that was beside her and moved off the porch. The swish of Christina's long skirts hung in the uneasy silence that followed.

After a time, Lars broke the silence. "It is a pleasant night. I am going to ride to Bordeaux." He got up from his chair. He stretched. There was an effort about the gesture that appeared false to Jan. Jan did not speak. Lars walked lazily down the steps. Jan noticed that Lars did not approach the group of slaves. Instead, he went directly to the corral. In a few minutes he rode across the clearing, bareback, sitting erect. He maneuvered his horse at an easy gait. Jan thought his brother was only pretending disinterest. Under the pose, Jan sensed his brother's fear. But fear of what? Ever since the slaves had started to gather in front of Bahbu's hut earlier today, Lars had been uneasy. Births were a routine part of plantation life. But tonight was different.

Jan tried to identify it. Agitated, he rocked back and forth in the caned-back mahogany chair. The rockers moved on the wooden floor in a succession of short, regular taps. Why were the slaves so positive that a son would be born to Bahbu tonight? For the last six months, whenever mention was made of the child that was to be born, it was referred to as "he." What did the birth of this child mean to them? When they spoke of it, there was awe in their voices. And who had fathered it, Prince or Lars? Jan suspected Lars. He had, ever since he had known of Bahbu's pregnancy.

These people and their superstitions will always have me bewildered, Jan thought. There is a connection with their witchcraft and the birth of this child—I'm sure of it. There must be, else they would have talked more of it to Christina. They gossip easily with her. A faint smile crossed Jan's face. He loved Christina all the more for her gentleness with the slaves. That they responded to Christina's love was apparent in their manner when they were around her. They always ran to Christina like frightened children when they were ill. Yet tonight was something special. Mary was a good midwife and had delivered all the slave children born on the estate. What was special about this child that had caused Mary to ask Christina to deliver it?

Inside the hut, Christina sat on the mat beside Bahbu. It was humid and extremely hot. Christina swabbed Bahbu's wet, pain-ridden face with a damp cloth. With close regularity, Bahbu tensed up, often emitting a high-pitched moan of pain. Then the veins in her neck swelled so that Christina could easily see the rapid beat of her heart.

"It will be over soon," Christina said gently.

Bahbu fell back on the mat. Christina put the cloth in the pan of water and squeezed it until it felt cool again, placing it then on Bahbu's forehead. In the center of the hut, Mary squatted in front of a fire. The heat was beginning to make Christina feel dizzy. Christina looked at Mary's face. Her eyes were rolled back, trancelike. She spoke aloud in her native dialect and threw a powder into the fire, making it puff up in bright blue-white flames that added more heat to the already stifling room. It seemed to Christina that Mary knew how many more pains Bahbu had to endure before pushing out the baby, for now Mary became very alert and concentrated on the task of flicking powder on the fire in rapid motions, making a continuous series of flames dance out of the pot. In preparation, Christina stood up and pushed her own damp hair off her forehead. In the poorly lit hut, Christina seemed like a great white goddess to Bahbu, who watched her for confidence between pains. Mary took the piece of cotton cloth in which the powder had been wrapped and tossed it onto the fire. Christina stared at it, noticing its resemblance to a piece of fine shirt fabric, such as Jan or Lars wore on

Sundays when they went on the long trip into Charlotte Amalie to services at the Fort. Briefly the cloth smothered the fire. Then it exploded into a solid mass of flame. Christina heard the movement beside her. Bahbu leaped up on the mat into a squatting position. Her thin arms wrapped around the top part of her protruding stomach and she pushed downward, straining and grunting. Christina could do nothing but stare at the child's face. Bahbu's head was back, the light of the fire shining on her sweaty features. The nostrils of her flat, broad nose flared back and forth. Her mouth stretched as if a scream were forcing it, but no sound came forth. Her agonized brown eyes looked up at the ceiling, imploringly, as though beyond there she called on one of her own gods to assist. Then, as suddenly as she had sat up, she fell back. There, between her legs on the mat, was the child.

While Christina finished the delivery, she could hear Mary's deep voice mumbling over the fire. Not until she had the child washed and wrapped in a cotton blanket did the mumbling cease.

Christina placed the baby in Bahbu's arms. "You have a fine healthy son, Bahbu," she said.

"I know," Bahbu answered. She turned to the bundle beside her and gently raised the blanket. Bahbu's eyes moved carefully over every feature before she murmured, "He is Prince."

Mary came to the mat and bent down to hold the amulet around Bahbu's neck. Her incantations reached a pitch and then subsided. Watching this strange sight, Christina felt, for the first time among the slaves, a certain fear of their strange rites. She took up the satchel and hurried from the hut. Outside the door, Chief was standing with his arms crossed on his chest. Christina, hoping he would speak, searched his face. He remained silent.

"It *is* a boy," Christina said.

Chief acknowledged her only with a nod and moved aside, allowing her to pass through the group of slaves who were sitting in front of the hut. As word was passed from one slave to the other by a nod, a chain reaction set in. Mumbling began. By the time Christina reached the steps to the porch, there was a joyous air of excitement behind her among the slaves.

Jan met her at the top of the steps. "A boy?"

36

Christina paused. Looking up, she said, "Did you doubt that it would be, Jan?"

Jan shook his head no.

"It is a boy. A brown-skinned boy with soft, fine hair. He resembles Prince." A pause. "And where is Lars?"

"He has gone to Bordeaux."

Christina walked past Jan. "Please stay here. After my bath, I would like to sit out here and watch them dance."

"Christina—" The moon lit up her tired face, the paleness of its rays giving her pink-white skin a delicate sheen. But there was always a delicate quality about Christina. Even though she was tall, she seemed to Jan very feminine and frail. Perhaps it is the fresh white dresses she always wears that make her appear so, he thought. He moved close to her and took both of her hands. He bent forward and kissed her forehead. "I love you, Christina."

She raised her eyes. "I love you, too, Jan, very much."

Jan dropped her hands and turned away. "Did you find out anything in there?" he said. "What does it mean, now that Bahbu has had a son?"

"Mean?"

"Yes, mean," Jan said. "You know that there has been something behind the birth of this child." He walked back and forth. "I cannot help but feel that this child is like a . . . like a savior to them, Christina. You must know what I mean. Have you not felt it all along, as I have?" He stopped in front of her, searching her face.

"Yes, Jan. All the more in the hut tonight. But I do not honestly know what the child means to them. They have not said anything in front of me."

"What did they name this child?"

"Prince."

They stood quietly for a moment, then Christina turned and went into the house.

Later, Christina and Jan sat side by side watching the celebration. When, earlier today, Chief had asked permission to hold a drum dance after the birth of the child, Jan agreed. In addition, Jan gave them a goat to roast. On one side of the clearing two youths turned a spit over a smoldering fire. Great torches, fanned by the trade winds, sent flames darting toward the sky. Drums boomed out a hollow resonant tone to which the people leaped and twisted with fluid gyrations.

37

In the middle of the clearing, a large fire sprang up. When it had taken hold, the flames reached the direction of the manor house. Four drummers lined up on the east side of the fire, facing the women's huts. Then the individual dancers fell back, crouching in a circle, clearing the area around the fire. Other noises faded, accentuating the boom of the drums. Jan stood up and walked to the railing of the porch.

"Come here, Christina." Jan half turned and reached his hand toward her. "They are going to have a special dance."

Christina walked to the rail and took Jan's hand as they leaned against the rail and watched. There was a pattern in the slow, even cadence of the drums that held their attention. The slaves fixed their eyes on the door of Mary's hut. Then, suddenly, the door opened. Christina gasped.

Mary stood in the doorway. For the first time since the day she was purchased, Mary did not have a scarf tied on her head. Her hair was combed upward, an astonishing wiry mass. She paused—then her hands darted up and out, her long fingers stretched wide. She was wearing her usual loose skirt and bare-shouldered blouse, but the blouse hung so low on her large breasts tonight that there was a sensuous quality about her. Around her neck was Bahbu's amulet. Even from the distance between the huts and the manor house, Christina and Jan knew what she was wearing. There was a glow from the fire that shone on the wood and emphasized the oblong outline of it.

Mary stepped out, gracefully lifting one leg up and out to the slow beat of the drums. Finally, she was very near to the heat of the fire. The beat of the drums softened. Mary stroked the amulet by slapping her hand on her bare chest above it and letting that hand pull down across it, then following with the other. The tempo of the drums increased. Each time one of Mary's hands hit her chest, the slaves clapped, until finally there was a hypnotic beat pounding through the whole plantation.

With a great leap, almost into the flames, Mary twisted in the air and landed facing her hut. She raised her arms, and the pounding ceased. When the drummer began again, it was with a lighter, faster beat. Mary broke into a wild, energetic dance, a series of twists and shakings that raised her skirt and shook her breasts fiercely under her thin blouse as she ran around the blaze. She brought vivid visions to Christina and Jan of the ceremonial dances that were rumored to take place in the jungles of Africa. Jan moved closer to Christina and put his arm around her protectively. Christina found herself leaning against Jan, but she could not take her eyes off the dancer before her.

On and on, around the enormous bonfire, Mary continued with her frenzied dance. Then, at one point, when she reached the area with the opening toward her hut, she leaped once more into the air and came down on both feet. She dropped her bushy head so low that her hair dragged in the dusty ground around it. Rising, with the same step she had used to make her entrance, she backed up. She moved her legs, one by one, up, out, and down—up—out —and down—until she disappeared into the hut. The drums stopped.

"Ai-yee!"

The night air was pierced by a savage, deep-throated scream from within Mary's hut. Jan was running across the clearing toward the noise before Christina was over the shock of hearing it. From the doorway of Mary's hut, Bahbu came running into the circle of slaves. In her arms she held the child, bare of its blanket.

The slaves milled in back of Bahbu, forming a barrier against whatever it was that she was escaping. Bahbu continued running toward Christina and the manor.

Christina lifted her skirts and ran down the steps. She opened her arms for Bahbu, who ran into them for protection. "He was going to kill him! He was going to kill him!" Bahbu cried in terror.

"Who?" Christina demanded.

"Master Lars. He tore the blanket from my son and grabbed him. Mary came and took the boy from him."

"Come inside," Christina commanded. "The night air is too cold for the child."

Putting her arm around Bahbu's shoulders to guide the girl up the stairs of the great house, Christina could feel the raised flesh where Bahbu had been branded. "Come, Bahbu," she said gently.

Jan already guessed the reason for the sudden change in the festivities. Now he feared for Mary and Chief with the same gnawing apprehension he had known for Prince last summer. He ran into the open doorway of the hut to find Mary crouched against one wall, a sharp cane knife in her hand. Chief and Lars were struggling on the floor.

"Stop!" Jan commanded.

Chief went limp at his master's command. Seizing the opportunity, Lars pulled himself upward and raised a fist. Before the blow could be struck, Jan pulled his brother up and spun him around so the two men stood face to face. Without taking his eyes off Lars, Jan issued a few tense commands. "Mary. You and Chief—get out of here. Close the door. Start the drums. Begin the dance again."

Mary and Chief eased toward the door. After Jan heard it close, he let go of Lars's shirt. Lars squared his shoulders and tried to control a drunken sway. "I was only trying to see the new slave. That savage attacked me." His voice was high-pitched. It also brought the smell of rum into the room. Outside, the drums began to beat and the activities of the feast renewed. With his left hand, Jan grabbed the ruffles on the front of Lars's shirt. Simultaneously, he drove his right fist into Lars's mouth. He felt his brother's teeth resist. Again and again he pounded, with left and right, until Lars, who was trying to protect his face with his arms, fell to the ground.

"The Privy Council will hear of this," Lars hissed, looking up over one upraised arm. "You cannot hit me because I protected myself from a slave."

"Take this to the council," Jan said, "and I will bring witness against you for the murder you committed at Botany Bay. I promise you that. Even on this island, slaves cannot be killed on the whim of an overseer."

Lars, about to speak further, hesitated. The council invariably took the part of the planter against the slave, that was well known. But what of planter against planter? Especially Jan Hendersen, who was the most respected of them all.

Jan stared down at his brother. "The only reason I have not reported you before is that you are my brother. But what you have done to many of my slaves, and especially to Prince, is worse than anyone should tolerate. I will not protect you again. Get up."

Slowly, Lars got to his feet. He shoved his unruly blond hair back off his face and spat some blood on the floor.

"Put your hat on," Jan said in an even voice. "We are going to walk out of here together."

Lars carefully smoothed his hair and placed his hat on his head so that it would shadow his face. Jan opened the door and they walked around the circle of dancers. When they reached the steps of Lars's house, Jan halted and turned to face his brother. In a husky voice he said, "You will stay away from Bahbu in the future. And her son."

Nervously, Lars swiped the back of his hand across his mouth and glared at his brother. "There's no sense in my saying again that I did not bother them. You always take the part of the blacks against me. But listen to me, Jan. When the rumors of revolt become a reality, I hope you will be the first they attack. They take a gentleman's kindnesses as a sign of weakness and fear of them. I tell you they plan cruel things for us—and your weakness only encourages them."

"That's a chance any planter has to take on this island. But as long as I am master at Hendersen, these people will be treated properly. If there *is* a proper way to treat a man in bondage."

"Your sentimentality is noble," said Lars. "But if it were not for you and the other plantation owners like you, there would be no market for slaves in these beautiful Virgin Islands. *You* bring the slaves to Hendersen, not me, so take your soft-hearted drivel elsewhere."

"Hold your tongue, Lars. There are things a man does in his lifetime of which he is not proud. But inflicting pain on defenseless human beings or allowing you to kill a baby because their drumming frightens you is not going to be on my conscience."

"Human beings! Jan, you know that these savages are not human."

"I suppose you think that God has put half human blood, and half inhuman blood, into that boy that was born tonight?"

"What do you mean?"

"I mean that this child is part Hendersen. But whether *your* blood is human or not I don't know!"

Jan turned his back and walked away. On the way to the greathouse there was merriment all around him. Yes, he thought, they may be in bondage, but they still have the heart to express some joy. Even a free man does not always have this. A free man—who, among us, is truly free? We are all bound over, along with the slaves, to the land on this island. For God—and ourselves—by order of our King.

Chapter 5

After-dinner coffee was being served in the dining room of the greathouse. Jan sat at the head of the oblong mahogany table with Christina at the other end and Lars between them. Oil lamps on the side walls cast a soft amber glow over the room. A circular silver candelabra was in the middle of the table, giving off a bright flame that added luster to the finely polished silver place settings and flickering on the gloss of the red-brown mahogany floor.

After the house slave had finished serving and left the room, Jan was the first to speak. "Lars, I still think it best that you move to St. John now and plan to live there at least until the new plantation is under way."

"Chief knows everything there is to know about plantations," Lars replied. "Why don't you send him there to oversee it?"

"The law states that one white man must be on each plantation. You know that."

"But how many people really obey the law, Jan? We could let him oversee the clearing of the land and the building, and then I could move there when the production begins."

"Is there a particular reason why you do not want to go?" Jan asked. He watched Lars carefully. Although thirteen years had passed since Prince's death, Jan had never regained confidence in his brother's word. He watched Lars's face for the reactions that could not be hidden.

"No," Lars said. "None in particular." He took a cigar from the box on the table. "Well, nothing that we can't discuss later on. Is there a particular reason why *you* are so anxious to establish land in St. John right now? This year?"

"Many reasons. Christina and I are getting old. If Hendersen plantation is going to expand, it is best to do it while there are the two of us, Lars. This year is as good as any.

I do not believe we have to fear the English any longer."

Lars looked at Jan. "The minute we put foot on St. John they sent Marshall here to warn us off. That English man-of-war, *Scarborough,* was enough to scare me," he said.

"It's been over a year since our settlement there has been under way and there has been no further threat from the English. If they were serious, they would have driven us off the island before we got such a stronghold. Now the fort on the harbor is almost finished and we have nine cannon there to guard it."

"How long do you think it will take to get a plantation in working order?" Lars asked.

"Three or four years. They have found fresh water. We will be permitted to use as much lime and wood as we will need to build. With the additional land taxes the King has levied on our colony this year, many of the planters will move to St. John. The eight-year tax exemption for St. John is enticing to all of us. We are smart to choose our land before the best is taken."

Lars nodded. "Yes, and the land is said to be very fertile. I suppose I will agree to go. However, there are some things we should discuss." He lit his cigar. The smoke drifted toward Christina. He looked at her over the candles and said, "We can do that on the porch."

Christina put her napkin on the table and pushed her chair back. "It is warm in here tonight. I will meet you on the porch." As she stood up, the room turned around her. Feeling weak, she fell back in her chair.

Jan ran to her side. "Do you feel all right, Christina?" He put his arm around her shoulders.

"I'm a little faint, that's all. I'll be better when I'm out in the air." Her voice was frail.

Jan pulled her gently to her feet. "Come, let me help you." He put his arm around her waist and walked her from the dining room.

"You may clear the table," Christina said to Bahbu as she passed her.

Bahbu stared at Mistress Christina. She looks very old and very tired tonight, Bahbu thought. Unconsciously, Bahbu trailed along behind them. At the front door Jan turned and said, "Your mistress is weak from the heat, that is all. Go back now, Bahbu, and finish your work."

Slowly Bahbu walked back to the dining room. Seeing

Lars coming out of the room, Bahbu dropped her eyes and passed him. Her concern for Mistress Christina was forgotten. This was Prince's birthday, his twelfth. On each of his previous birthdays an omen from the gods had appeared. Three years ago it was the great wind that destroyed their gardens and the cane fields. Last year it had rained, bringing an end to a long drought that had again threatened to destroy their food. But today, with only five more hours until the day was past, the sign had come again. Master Lars was going across the sea to another island!

In her hut, Mary was preparing for a ceremonial rite.

"Do not ever forget that these white men forced your mother from her tribe and put her in chains when she was younger than you are today," she intoned to Prince.

Prince sat beside Mary, on the dirt floor of the hut. In front of them was an unlit heap of straw and wood shavings. When was it he had first been told about his mother's sad voyage from Africa to St. Thomas? He had been five— or maybe six. It had saddened him so much that he had put his head on Bahbu's lap and sobbed. Mary had pulled him from his mother's lap and stood him on his feet in front of her. "You, Prince, are the young man whom our gods have sent to free your mother and all of our people from these cruel white men. Do not cry. Be a man."

"What gods?" Prince had asked.

"Our gods," Mary answered. "The gods that give us sun and rain for good harvests. And the windstorms that sometimes ruin the crops. Our gods give us everything, depending on whether we please them or not. They give us life—and death—and pain."

"Our gods sent you to us, Prince," Mary continued. "On this twelfth year of your birth we will thank them again. We will let them know that we have not forgotten their gift."

Prince pushed himself up from the floor and strode around the hut. His legs were so long that he circled the hut in twenty steps. He counted them, as Mistress Christina was teaching him to do. But even this did not take his mind off the excitement that was inside him. For, after all, he was a special gift of the gods. Didn't all the other slaves treat him with a special manner that constantly reminded him that he was the one chosen by the gods to free them?

"When will I save our people?" Prince asked Mary, stopping to look down at her.

Mary raised her face to him. "When you are a grown man. They will give us a sign when they are ready. But you must be patient, Prince. The gods move slowly. We cannot try to move before they are ready. Do you understand?"

"But how will we know when they are ready? What do you think the sign will be?"

"I do not know what the sign will be. But it will be a very strong one. You could not save our people if they are not shown to follow you. When the time comes, all the slaves on the island will know that they must rise up against the evil white people and follow you."

Prince crossed his arms over his chest as he often saw Chief do. Standing like this, Mary was aware of how much Prince resembled his namesake. She knew the gods had given this young boy her son's image to ease her longings. In fact, to Mary this Prince had taken on the exact identity of her dead son, and was in every detail and mannerism, identical. In reality, Prince did resemble the former Prince. It was not a strange coincidence, however, for they both had the same father, and though the mothers were not related, they were each Amina. Tribespeople held strong resemblances to one another in any event. This Prince's skin was a darker tan than his namesake's, and he had promise, at twelve, of being taller. But he had the same yellow-green, almond-shaped eyes and fine, even features of his dead half-brother.

"Tell me," Prince said to Mary. "Why is it that Master Jan and Mistress Christina are not evil?"

"They are one of us. Their gods made a mistake when they colored their skin, that is all."

"Do you think they will join us when we rise against the white men?"

"No, I do not. They have their own gods. They have never been taught to follow ours. They will not know when the sign appears. We will have to protect them, for they will be very old. But *only* Master Jan and Mistress Christina. Do you understand that?"

Prince closed his eyes and thought about it. "Are all the other white people as evil as Master Lars?"

"All of them. Listen to the drums. What do our people on other parts of the island tell us? They are all in misery and suffering."

45

Although Prince did not know the language of the drums, Mary translated for him, and the messages were so frightening that Prince shuddered every time he heard them. A slave has had his tongue cut out. A slave has had his ear cut off. A slave has had his foot chopped off. A slave has had his head chopped off and placed on a stake for all the other slaves to see. The messages, more times than not, were originated by Mary to impress Prince with his mission in life. The drums always stirred fear and determination in the youth.

The door burst open and Bahbu ran to Mary and crouched down next to her. "The sign appeared tonight in the manor house. Master Lars is going to St. John to live." Bahbu searched Mary's face. "What do you think this means?"

Mary squinted her eyes at the unkindled pile of debris in front of her. She said, "I do not know. I must ask the gods."

For over an hour Bahbu and Prince squatted silently on the floor beside Mary while she mumbled and glared into the flames. The sacred powders that she threw on the fire fogged the small hut and made such an increase in the heat that their faces were slick with sweat.

Finally, Mary leaned her head back and closed her eyes. In a firm, trancelike voice, she said, "Master Lars will not go to the other island. But across the water I see a great plantation with many slaves." Her voice stopped and she squinted her eyes harder. "I see Prince crossing the water in a canoe. He is a grown man. He is going to the other island. There beside him is his mother."

"And you," Prince interrupted eagerly.

"Ahhh, yes—I will cross the water in a boat. Very soon." Mary's face took on a painful grimace. "And there—on the other island—I will die."

Prince remained motionless, terrified at the thought of Mary's death.

Bahbu was wondering why the gods had not shown her a sign in the fire tonight. She clutched the wood carving at her neck and continued to search the flames. Although she often saw visions in the fire, tonight she had seen nothing. It was most unsatisfying. So many things about Mary's vision were still unanswered. What about Prince? Was he also to die on the other island? And of herself? If she lost Prince, she would have nothing to live for. He was the one who gave purpose to the hard work and hated confinement on this island. He brought her hope for freedom. Bahbu vowed that if Prince were to die in the uprising that she, too, would join him. It would be better to be on the other side of the moon, the sun, and the stars where they went after death than to stay on this side, alone.

"I will go to Chief, now," Mary said. "He has a drum hidden in the field. He will tell the others about the omen."

The hollow drumbeat was put out into the night air with a strength that frightened Lars. It seemed to him that a tension always preceded the drumming and tonight that unusual silence had surrounded the slave quarters. Lars was about to mention it to Jan when the drum began. Lars sprang to his feet.

"It is right here on the hill," he said, pointing to the crest of the mountain on the east side of the mill.

"Sit down," Jan said. "Today is Prince's birthday. They are celebrating, that is all."

"I hate those drums," Lars growled. He paced in front of Christina and Jan. "If we only knew what they were saying to each other. There are always so many rumors about a revolt."

"And there always will be," Jan said. "It is something that everyone fears. But we cannot pay attention to all the rumors on the island."

"You must not take the drums so seriously," Christina added. "You should be accustomed to them by now."

"I'll never get used to them," Lars retorted. "We should put an end to it, once and for all." He paused and cocked his head to one side. In the distance another drumbeat rumbled back. "Hear that!"

Christina laughed.

"Laugh," Lars said. "But you won't be laughing when they have us tied to a stake and beat the drums while they set us on fire."

"You have a sharp imagination," Christina replied. "But if the rumors of a revolt were a serious threat to us, do you think King Christian would have recently appointed the company's officials as judges to supervise the punishment of the difficult slaves, instead of leaving it to the individual planter as it was done before?"

Lars sat down on the edge of his chair. "You know that

47

law has not really changed anything. The council will always take the word of the planter against the slave."

"Not if I were on the council," Jan said.

"That is why you were not appointed," Lars said. "There isn't a planter on this island who does not know that you are too lenient with your slaves. Even your neighbor, Wilhelm Bodker, voted against you."

"Wilhelm Bodker—huh! He would have twice as much cotton to sell if he didn't beat his slaves so much."

"Poor Madame Bodker," Christina said. "She would take her two daughters and leave, no doubt, if it were not for the King's order that the island's unmarried women cannot go."

"Do not be so foolish," Lars broke in. "Madame Bodker is very happy at Estate Bordeaux. There is not a finer greathouse on all of St. Thomas."

"It should be the finest on the island. It's furnished with booty from the sea robbers," Jan said.

"And why shouldn't he barter with the pirates?" Lars asked.

"Because the governor does not want it so. We only aggravate the other countries whose ships have been robbed. Why should we risk being warred against because planters like Wilhelm Bodker are greedy?"

"Is it wrong for a man to want his wife and daughters to have the finest things available to them on this miserable island? There is probably not a woman in all of Copenhagen who is better dressed than Madame Bodker."

"My Christina makes them look like charwomen," Jan said. "Madame Bodker is much too small to wear such heavy silks. She always looks very warm. Haven't you noticed, Christina?"

"It is of no importance," Christina answered. "Madame Bodker has a great amount of time to worry about clothes. Wilhelm forbids her to spend any of it with their slaves. I must admit, she is very clever with her hands. Her youngest daughter, little Anna, looks like a doll when she is dressed up. When we are at services, I find it difficult to take my eyes off that child."

"It is too bad you did not have children of your own," Lars said. "Then, maybe, you would not keep the kitchen full of those little black savages."

"Hold your tongue," Jan said curtly.

48

In the silence that followed, the drumbeat suddenly disappeared.

"They have finished," Lars said. "Now I'll take a ride down to Bordeaux. Tonight I'm calling on Johanna."

"Johanna," Jan gasped. "What are you trying to do? A man of your age courting a girl who is barely in her teens."

"It was Wilhelm who first brought the matter to my attention. He believes that his daughter should marry an older, established man!"

"Wilhelm Bodker would only sanction this because of his own drive to get power of the west," Jan said.

"Don't say that," Christina interrupted. She put her hand on Jan's arm. Turning to Lars, she said, "It does not make any difference that she is young. The news is a surprise, that is all. You know, Lars, Hendersen needs another woman here. And you need a wife. Jan and I are very happy for you."

"Thank you," Lars said. He got up and faced Christina, directing his words to her. "I will ask her to marry me tonight. If she says yes, which I am sure she will, since Wilhelm and Victoria are in favor of this marriage, then we will have to make further plans." He turned to look at Jan. "Then we will discuss St. John. I do not want to take Johanna there until we are certain it is safe. And there is the matter of building a decent house. Johanna has been accustomed to living properly."

Stunned, Jan sat quietly. Lars bowed to Christina. "Good night," he said to her evenly.

Johanna Bodker slowly eased herself down onto the brocaded settee. Mama had pulled the strings of her girdle much too tight. Why had she eaten the banana pudding after so much of the stewed chicken?

Across the formal parlor, her mother sat down. "Johanna," she said sternly, "must you perch yourself so clumsily on the edge of the settee? Sit properly. Raise your shoulders, carry your head high. You are small enough, without hunching over. Fold your hands on your lap. No. Not like that. Gently, one in the other, palms up. Now, knees together, cross your ankles and keep your feet on the floor. Arrange your skirts. You are allowing too much of your shoe to show."

Madame Bodker had a pinched, pale face which foretold

that she was a prim little woman. She had a thin-lipped mouth that was tight set, the skin around it creased with dozens of wrinkles. There was a plainness in her coloring that gave no contrast to her dull brown hair which was pulled up into a tight bun. A twitch at the left corner of her mouth was persistent when she was nervous—and Madame Bodker was, by nature, a nervous little woman. When she was not sewing or fussing with one of her daughter's hair styles, she sat in the parlor tatting, her mouth twitching all the while. "Idle hands are the tools of the devil," was her favorite expression.

Johanna, fixed on the settee, leaned forward and said, "Do I look pretty, Mama?"

Madame Bodker looked at her daughter. Her mouth twitched a little faster. How can anyone say she is pretty, she thought. Her face is too small. And her eyes, why did they have to be so round and little, like her mouth? And her chin is much too weak.

"Yes, my dear, you look pretty," Madame Bodker said. To herself she added, at least your dress is *very* pretty, if I must say so myself. But why couldn't she have had a full bustline? It is impossible to create a proper décolletage for such a flat chest.

Johanna swung one foot back and forth.

"Sit still," her mother said gently.

Johanna squared her shoulders again and sat fixed. From behind her, a breeze stirred through the open louvers of the window. It felt good on the dampness behind the large cluster of blond curls that hung on her neck.

"Close the louvers," Madame Bodker added. "It took me hours to arrange your hair. We can't have it blowing all over your face."

Johanna eased slowly around. With one finger she pushed up on the bar that controlled one half of the window louvers, then repeated the move with the other half and turned back into position. She moved like a robot.

"Now, let us hope that Mr. Hendersen has enough sense to notice your new dress when he calls on you," Madame Bodker said. "You know, my dear, Madame Hendersen is much too conservative in her manner of dress. Why, I have yet to see her in anything but white. White cotton in the daytime, white cotton with lace trim on Sundays, and, with rarity, a white silk for one of the government balls. However, she is such a big woman, I suppose conservative clothes call less attention to it. She is no doubt envious of petite women, such as we are. I hope that Anna will not be a tall woman. For a ten-year-old, she is very tall now. She takes after her father. You, Johanna, are fortunate to resemble my side of the family. Englishwomen are not such Amazons."

"For an old woman, Madame Hendersen always looks very beautiful. I sometimes think, Mama, that the heat does not bother her. And she is so straight and tall, she looks like a queen."

"Nonsense. The white dresses make her *look* as though she does not mind the heat, that is all. And don't be so childish. Queens are not tall women."

Dismayed, Johanna slumped against the bones of her girdle.

"Sit up, Johanna. When a girl reaches seventeen, it is time she knew how to receive a caller. If you want to catch this man, which I am sure you do, you cannot let him think you are still a child."

Johanna sat up.

Madame Bodker continued her monologue. "With all the wealth the Hendersen family has, I should think that Madame Hendersen would insist on having finer fabrics. Why, all the women on the island say her husband is not very generous with her." She stopped talking. Another idea had just come into mind. Her mouth twitched. "Why, come to think of it, they must have an enormous horde of gold."

"Mama," Johanna leaned forward. She pursed her round, pink mouth out and stretched her eyes open, appearing startled. "I have heard some of the slaves say that the master of Hendersen spends a great amount of his money on the slaves."

"Jan Hendersen is a fool. Thank God that Lars Hendersen is a sensible man. Without him, there would be no discipline there. Just as I have told you, some day, very soon, Lars Hendersen will be master of that estate. And a good thing it will be for the west of the island. Jan Hendersen gives his slaves too many liberties. Why, just tonight, those drums again."

"Why is it that you and Madame Hendersen have not been friends, Mama? You never go to call on her—and she never comes here."

"Because your father does not like their attitude about

51

the slaves. Lars Hendersen is the only sane one on that estate."

"When I marry Mr. Hendersen, do I have to go there to live? I would be afraid, Mama."

"Shhh. Be quiet! There is nothing to fear. Those old people are harmless." Victoria lowered her voice. "Remember what I told you. Some day you will be mistress of Hendersen. Every woman on the island will envy you."

"Mama, I hear a horse."

"Pinch your cheeks and bite your lips. Hurry! Get some color in your face. Shake your skirts. Now remember, do not be too shy. And smile. You are much prettier when you show the dimples in your cheeks."

Johanna heard the heavy footsteps cross the porch to the front door. Her heart pounded and a lump came up in her throat. She clenched her teeth and tried to swallow. Oh, dear God, let me look pretty and be able to say amusing things like Mama does, she prayed silently.

Johanna was determined to marry Lars Hendersen. For months, her mother had been telling her of the virtues connected with the marriage. Mama had led Johanna to believe that if she did not catch Mr. Hendersen, she might end up being an old maid, for there were very few men on the island who were prosperous enough for one of Wilhelm Bodker's daughters. Now that she could hear Lars moving into the house, she gave a final fluff to her skirts and sat staring at the door.

Lars, familiar with the Bodker house, walked directly into the parlor. He looked at both women.

"Good evening, Lars," Madame Bodker said. She moved her hand out gracefully. "Come in."

Lars removed his hat and strode in large steps across the room to Madame Bodker. Johanna noticed that his knee-high riding boots and tight trousers fit well on his long legs. Thinking he might notice her boldness, she dropped her eyes.

Lars bowed to Madame Bodker. While bent forward, he picked up her hand and kissed it. "Good evening, Madame Bodker. It is nice of you to allow me to call on your daughter." He straightened up. "You look beautiful tonight, as always."

Madame Bodker reached for a lace fan that was in the chair beside her. Fanning it open with a movement of her wrist, she raised her face and smiled. Candlelight flickered

52

in her brown eyes. The smile broadened her pinched face and it took on a sudden attractiveness that otherwise remained hidden in her perpetual expression of boredom. "You flatter me, Lars Hendersen. And I like it."

Lars squared his broad shoulders causing his cutaway coat to fall in place, exposing a proper amount of black vest and white ruffled shirt.

Madame Bodker stood up. She closed the fan. Keeping her eyes turned flirtatiously up at Lars, she moved forward. "If you will forgive me, I must go see that Anna is safely in her bed. You and Johanna don't want a foolish old woman sitting here with you. Now, do you?"

"A beautiful woman such as you, Madame Bodker, should not take herself so lightly."

Madame laughed. It was a musical, excited laugh that Johanna made a mental note to copy.

After kissing Johanna's hand, Lars had difficulty sitting beside her. His pants were so tight that he had to sit on the front of the settee, slightly sideways on one buttock with his legs stretched out behind him. Thus settled, Lars looked at Johanna. There was a rosy glow in her cheeks, but he suspected that this was only an attribute of youth. She, like her mother, will eventually have a sallow complexion, he concluded.

Lars had watched Johanna grow from a thin child who reminded him of a nervous hummingbird, into a fairly personable young woman who in the last four or five months was giving him glances that Lars knew were not of a neighborly nature. Her attention stimulated his desires. Perhaps it is the pinkness and white of her that does arouse me, he thought. Clumsily, he picked up Johanna's small hand.

"Johanna—" His voice came out very hoarse. Johanna stared blankly at him. "Johanna—" his voice was firmer. Johanna's little eyes opened wide. "Johanna. Will you marry me?" His voice was firm and loud.

A silence followed in which she remained looking at him wide-eyed. Finally, she said, "Why, Mr. Hendersen, I don't know what to say." She could not take her eyes from his mustache. The tips of it were stained brown from the cigars he smoked and Johanna found the two tones of it fascinating. As she stared, rivulets of water rolled down his cheeks and caught in his mustache. He cannot take too much of my shyness, she warned herself. Why, oh why, didn't Mama tell me what to say at this precise time? She wet her round lips with a swipe of her tongue and blurted out, "Yes, I'll marry you, Mr. Hendersen." A deep pink flush crept up her neck into her face.

Lars wanted to kiss her. Instead, he stood up.

"Well, then, now that you have accepted my proposal, my dear, I will go summon your mother and father so our wedding arrangements can be made. I, naturally, want to marry you as soon as possible." To himself, he said, I wish I could take you to bed right now.

Johanna watched Lars move out of the room. As soon as he disappeared, she sprang to her feet. Hugging herself, she danced in circles. I am going to marry the wealthiest man on the island! Oh, how jealous all of my friends will be, she thought.

Wilhelm Bodker, returning from a useless search of the cotton fields for the drummer, walked up onto the porch of the greathouse. Frustrated, he slammed his shoes against the wooden boards of the porch floor. When he reached the arched open doorway to the parlor, he stopped.

Wilhelm was quite paunchy, an evidence of the luxuries with which he indulged himself at table. He looked peculiar in his dinner clothes, for it was not customary for a planter to return from the field dressed in such fine attire. But the drums had angered him so that he had not taken time to change, hoping that his speed might enable him to catch the culprit who had disobeyed him. Now, he began to feel the perspiration accumulate under his heavy silk vest and around the tight waistband of his trousers. He drew a fine lace handkerchief from the sleeve of his coat and wiped at his face. The sun had never tanned Wilhelm. He was so fair that his complexion only reddened from the tropical sun. At Victoria's insistence, he was always clean-shaven, giving his face the taut, shiny appearance of a wax carving painted with a deep pink enamel. His strawlike hair was bleached to an orange-blond, and the two colors of face and hair did not go together.

Seeing his daughter dancing about the room, Wilhelm forgot his disappointing search. His eyes darted around the room, taking in every detail of Johanna's performance and the ornately appointed room. Ah-ha, he congratulated himself, it appears that wedding plans are to be made.

Imagine Lars Hendersen and Wilhelm Bodker. What a combination to control the west of the island. And Johanna will have all her heart desires.

Upstairs, Madame Bodker stood by her daughter Anna's bedside. Even in sleep, Anna was an angelic-looking child. Considering that neither her mother nor father was a handsome person, some fate had been kind to Anna, bestowing on her an unusual beauty. Her hair was heavy and silky, of the palest blond color. She had strong features, all of them evenly balanced. Her eyes were large and deep blue. Around her shoulders, the fat long curls that Madame Bodker gave so much attention to had fallen carelessly on the layers of tatted lace on Anna's nightgown. You, my child, will be able to have any man on this island, when you are grown, she thought. And, thank heaven, it looks as though your sister has made a good catch, too. She reached over to take one of Anna's curls in her fingers and twisted it until the curl was perfectly cylindrical and smooth. There, now. Sleep well, my precious.

"Victoria, Victoria—" Wilhelm's voice carried up to the room. Hurriedly, she tiptoed from the room and closed the door behind her. She went to the head of the steps. "Yes?"

"Come, my dear," Wilhelm said. "Lars would like to discuss the wedding plans with us."

She raised the hemline of her skirts and moved down the carpeted stairway. She felt as if she were floating.

Chapter 6

A rooster crowed. The misty gray light of dawn crept through the tilted louvers of Jan's and Christina's bedroom. Christina could hear familiar noises in the kitchen behind the manor house. Carefully, she eased down onto the stool beside their high four-poster mahogany bed. All night she had suffered with a pain in her chest, and even now her arms were numb. Maybe some of Mary's bush tea would make her feel better. She put her foot out to step on the floor when a searing pain ripped through her chest.

Jan heard her fall. As he reached Christina's side, she gave a deep gasp. Quickly, he sat on the floor beside her and took her head into the crook of his arm. Christina looked up at him. She appeared to be holding her breath, for she was turning gray in color and her mouth was outlined with a blue shadow. A great breath escaped her with a rush of air and a sigh of relief.

"Christina," Jan sobbed. He gathered her closer in his arms and pulled her head against his chest.

In the kitchen, Bahbu dipped boiling water from the black kettle that hung over the Dutch oven. Making coffee was one of her favorite chores. Master Jan repeatedly told her that she made the best coffee on the island. Aside from that, it smelled good, as good as it tasted after she had heaped it full of brown sugar until it was syrupy. She moved about her work in an organized manner, with an air of authority that the other two slaves who shuttled in and out of the kitchen respected. Prince poked his head through the open door.

"Mama. The coffee. Is it ready?"

"No," Bahbu answered flatly. "Gather the eggs. Then it will be."

Mary came into the kitchen with a pail of water balanced on her head. It rode steadily on the flat, padded scarf. She put one arm up and swung the pail down onto a brick shelf beside the Dutch oven. "I will cook the eggs," she said.

"I boiled a pot of pawpaw and sugar," Bahbu said. "Mistress Christina will have some." Bahbu spooned the thick yellow fruit onto a dish. "Mistress Christina likes all the food we eat. She says we are better cooks than she is."

"We are," Mary grunted. "They do not know what spices are for. Everything they eat is very plain. Too flat."

Taking the dish of jam with her, Bahbu walked from the kitchen. The custom of balancing heavy weights on their heads gave most of the slaves a very erect bearing. They had, however, a shuffle to their gait, as though searching with their bare feet for obstacles. In the silence that followed Bahbu's departure, Mary dipped boiling water into a smaller pot in which she would cook the eggs. The shuffle of feet took her attention and she turned, expecting to see Prince with the eggs. Instead, Bahbu was back.

"They are not downstairs yet," Bahbu said.

They were both puzzled. What could be wrong? Mistress Christina and Master Jan were always downstairs in the dining room by now. Mary shuffled past Bahbu to the opening between the kitchen and the house. The sky was getting red and the sun would soon be up. "Come," she said to Bahbu. She walked on into the house, entering the dining room. Bahbu followed.

It was not the custom of Master Lars to take breakfast at the greathouse. He was in the field at daybreak when the slaves began their work. Later, when they took their breakfast, which was carried to the field for them, he returned to the kitchen. There he had breakfast prepared by one of the younger girls. Alone in the kitchen with one of the black girls he particularly favored, he could pinch and pat without interference. Bahbu and Mary knew this, for they had both gone through their apprenticeship in the kitchen with Lars. But since that night when Prince had died, neither of them had been appointed by Lars to cook for him.

In the dining room, the table was set. A sliced orange was on each plate. At Mistress Christina's end of the table, a dish of pawpaw jam was in front of her plate. Mary stopped and closed her eyes, listening for a noise from above. Hearing nothing, she padded toward the staircase. At

57

the bottom of it, she stopped and listened again. Bahbu, who was still following, moved up closely. "There is something wrong," Mary said. When they reached the top, Bahbu was so close to Mary that Mary could feel the heat from her body. The door to the bedroom began to open. Mary felt for Bahbu's hand. Clutching it, she watched the door open further. Jan, still in his long white nightshirt, stood in the doorway, dazed.

"Mary—Bahbu." His voice was gentle. "Your mistress . . . Mistress Christina is dead."

Bahbu gave out a heart-rending scream—"Nooooo" —and threw herself against Mary. Mary swayed, holding Bahbu in her arms. Mary began to chant in her native dialect. Tears flowed down her face. Jan, watching the strange, mournful sight, felt his own eyes burning.

"Go to her," he choked out. "She loved both of you very much." He moved off down the hall. It was a sight Mary was never to forget: her master running away. His white shirt flapped around his legs. His silvery head was bent forward. His face gleamed with his tears.

The great four-poster bed was framed in the doorway. Mistress Christina lay flat in the bed, her head on a pillow. Holding Bahbu with both arms, Mary moved cautiously with her into the bedroom until she could see Mistress Christina's face. It appeared that she was asleep. They moved closer. Her white hair had been combed into a smooth, soft bun on the top of her head. Mary thought of Master Jan's large hands patiently combing it.

Held by the sight in front of them, with arms wrapped around each other, they stared at their mistress. There was the silence of death in the room. Suddenly Bahbu broke from Mary's grasp. Lifting the mosquito netting, she threw the upper part of her body on the high bed. Her slender, long arms fell across Christina's body. "My mistress, my mistress," Bahbu moaned. Overcome, Mary, too, fell beside Bahbu. Together, their noise filled the household.

Lars, entering the dining room, immediately noticed that the breakfast table had not been used. He heard the mournful wailing from above him. Taking the steps two at a time, he reached the open doorway. There he saw Bahbu and Mary thrown over the waist-high bed, their arms flung across Christina's body. Over their prostrate forms, he saw Christina's peaceful face.

He ran to the bedside. Grabbing each of the slaves by an arm, he jerked them off the bed and threw them to the floor behind him. "Let the dead rest in peace," he threatened.

"What's happened here?" he shouted at Mary. The normal tan color had faded from Lars's face, and his skin appeared yellow.

Mary shook her head. "I do not know. She was dead when we came here."

Lars raised a shaky hand and wiped the corners of his mouth, pulling slowly down through the bristly hairs of his mustache. "Where is Jan?"

Mary shook her head.

"I am here," Jan's voiced startled Lars. His brother was standing at the end of the bed, looking at Christina. "She died a short time ago. It must have been her heart . . . it was very quick." He reached up and touched one of the feet that made a rise in the white coverlet. "Thank God for that."

Jan's eyes were mottled with pink streaks and his face was drawn. Lars was suddenly aware that Jan was becoming old. "Why don't you come downstairs and have some coffee? Let Mary dress Christina for viewing," Lars said. His voice was unusually gentle.

"No, Lars. We will bury Christina as she is dressed now. She has only gone to sleep. I want her to be comfortable." Jan spoke in a soft monotone, keeping his eyes on Christina's face. "Ask Chief to come to me. I will show him where to dig the grave. I want her resting close to the house—out in the open sunlight—where the trade winds can cross her grave. Christina loved this land at Fortuna, and these people. I want her to be where she can hear the noises of Hendersen." He took his hand from her foot and turned to Lars. "Only our slaves will view her. Today. Tonight before supper we will put her to rest."

"But Jan—what of the neighbors. Surely they will want to see her. Why, Victoria and Johanna and Wilhelm—and . . ."

"Only the slaves," Jan said firmly. "Christina had no other friends on this end of the island. The Bodkers did not call on her when she was alive to greet them. Why should they see her now?" He turned back, looking again at Christina. "Please, Lars, do not argue with me about this. My Christina will be buried as I know she would

59

want to be." Hearing Lars walk from the room, he said, "Mary, go tell the women, and have Chief tell the men, there will be a day of mourning today. You may do this in the manner you are accustomed to. Those who want to say good-by to Christina may do so. Tell them to come through the parlor. They may call at the house until noon. I will spend the afternoon with Christina, alone."

Mary left the room. Jan, hearing Bahbu's muffled sobbing, walked over to her and raised her from the floor. "Come, Bahbu. You must not grieve like this. Your mistress has gone to heaven—to the other side of the sun and moon. The place you talk about." He put his arm around Bahbu's frail shoulders. She has never fattened up, he thought. She is almost as thin as she was the day I bought her.

"Will Mistress Christina go where the black people go?"

"Your mistress believed that. And so do I. Yes, Bahbu. She will go where the black people go."

"Then she is already with our dead Prince. She is not alone."

"No, Bahbu, she is not alone."

All morning the slaves moved one by one through the room. Bahbu and Mary stood at the head of the bed, one on each side. Each of them had their black hands resting against the white sheet on either side of Mistress Christina's pillow. As each slave passed through, either Mary or Bahbu talked to them. Each, when talking, sounded as if Mistress Christina were alive and had appointed them to speak for her. "She has gone to join Prince, on the other side of the sun and moon," Bahbu explained. "Yes," Mary confirmed it, "our mistress believed in our gods. She has gone where she is happy. When we die, we will see her again."

Some of the female slaves emitted a deep-throated sob or groan when they first entered the room. Several fell down on the floor before they reached the bed. Bahbu and Mary patiently guided them to the side of their mistress's bed and soothed them with the explanation of her departure. All of the slaves were frightened when they first saw the white vision of death before them in the room. They halted at the bedside in a terrified manner, and their footsteps quickened when they turned to leave the room.

Prince was the last to enter the room. He was confused

that Mistress Christina could be up "there" with his name-sake and yet here, too, in this house. He was more hesitant than any of the others to go close to Christina. For a long time he stood with his amber eyes fixed on the bed. There was a furrow between his eyes that saddened his face.

"Come," Bahbu said. "Do not be afraid. Mistress Christina was a good woman. Only the evil harm us after death."

Prince moved a few steps closer to the gigantic bed.

"You are a man," Mary said irritably. "Go to Mistress Christina's side."

The command moved Prince and he approached the bed. Awed, he rested both of his hands on the coverlet and looked at Christina's face. She did not appear dead. She was whiter than she usually looked, as if she had been coated with a new layer of skin. As he stared, the finely curved lines at the corners of her mouth suggested that she was smiling at him. Prince moved one hand forward and rested it on Christina's hand. Carefully, he worked his fingers under the palm and raised her hand, keeping his eyes fixed on her face. She approved. Prince leaned forward and dropped his head until his cheek rested against Christina's hand. She seemed very cold. He pressed his cheek against her hand and said aloud, "Good-by, my mistress." Then he put her hand back as it had rested before. Without looking at Bahbu or Mary, he turned and walked from the room.

The drums began during the late afternoon. Lars, trying to control his anger, walked back and forth in the parlor, occasionally halting at the stairway. At one point he sat in a rocking chair and tried to compose himself. He pushed the chair violently back and forth. No, that would not do. Sitting down made his head ache. What would the Bodkers say? They knew nothing of Christina's death. And when they did find out, they would most certainly be angered that they had not been invited to view her. By now they would have heard the drums. Maybe he should ride to Bordeaux and explain to them. There was nothing for him to do here at Fortuna. The grave was ready—right at the side of the house, where they would never be able to avoid it. And Jan was locked in the room with Christina and would in all probability stay there for the remainder of the day. And the slaves, those barbaric animals, were outside, leaping and gyrating and mumbling in their individual dialects until he thought he would lose his mind. He picked up his black dress hat and stormed out of the house.

Jan sat on a straight chair beside the bed holding Christina's hand in both of his. His head was dropped between his arms, resting on the coverlet.

It will be better if I go to St. John instead, he was telling Christina. There are so many memories of you at Hendersen, I would not find a minute's peace. Lars will be getting married next week. And as you always said, responsibility will settle him. It will solve the problem of a proper house for Johanna. Oh God, Christina, I cannot bear to think of another woman in your house. He wiped his eyes on the sleeve of his shirt and looked up at Christina's face. You know, Christina, when I am in St. John I can pretend that you are here at Hendersen awaiting my return. Eagerly, as you always have. Christina seemed to smile at him. He put his head down again and sobbed.

Chapter 7

The day after Christina's death Jan sat down with Lars to discuss his plans. They were on the porch, looking out at the slaves in the field.

"I'm leaving Fortuna," Jan said softly.

"Leaving! Where are you going?"

"To St. John."

There was a long silence. Lars felt the loss of Christina and his brother's grief more than he wanted to admit. He had always taken her for granted. Now that she was gone he felt more grieved than he had when his mother had died. Perhaps that was it. Jan and Christina seemed more like his parents than his brother and sister-in-law.

"I want to discuss the financial arrangement with you," Jan said. He glanced at Lars. "You are the only family I have now, Lars. The plantations will be yours when I die. In the meantime, I will share evenly with you the profits of Hendersen at Fortuna. When I have the plantation on St. John in operation we will meet and work out a plan to make your share even greater."

"That is generous of you," Lars said. "I will do my best to keep the plantation in order."

"Yes, I believe you will. Christina always said that a woman would soften you. Now that you are getting married, I'm sure you'll do what is best to secure your fortune."

Lars remained silent, crossing his legs and looking out over the high field.

"I'm not going to lecture you, Lars. Or tell you how I want you to run this plantation. You're on your own now. Tomorrow I'll ride into Charlotte Amalie and file with the company for land on St. John."

Lars turned toward Jan and asked, "How soon do you plan to go?"

"Before the week is out."

"Why so soon? I'm getting married on Friday."

"I know," Jan said gently. He stood up and walked to the porch rail. His hand gripped the railing. "I don't want to be here when another woman comes to Hendersen. Oh, this has nothing to do with Johanna. Only with Christina."

Lars closed his eyes and leaned his head back against the chair. He swallowed hard. The swift rush of events had drained him emotionally.

Jan spoke again, his voice stronger. "I'll take ten of the slaves. Chief, eight young men, and a woman. The men will have a difficult job clearing the land and building there. The woman will take care of the garden and cook our meals. Before the harvesting begins here, you'll be able to buy replacements for the ones I take." He looked straight at Lars. "I'll take Mary. She's used to my ways."

Lars stood up to go. "I wish you luck, Jan." He turned and walked swiftly down the steps.

Jan watched Lars ride away. He seems different today, he thought. Christina was right. A woman will soften his ways.

Mary was confused when she heard that she was going to St. John. Although glad not to be separated from Chief and Master Jan, she did not want to leave Prince, who was still a child. During the years ahead he had to be made ready for his mission. Who would show him the way? One night, as she sat stirring the fire in her hut, the flames answered her question. Every day Master Lars would remind Prince of his mission. The gods told Mary that Master Lars would not change with marriage and would turn his hatred toward the boy as soon as Master Jan departed. And Bahbu would carry on the rites.

Now on the morning of the departure for St. John, Bahbu and Prince sat in the corner of Mary's hut watching her arrange her few possessions in a large square of cloth. "Remember," Mary said, "the gods told me that it is my duty to lead our people in St. John. It will take many years to organize them. Our separation will be a long one. But we will be together when the time comes. The gods have described it."

"I do not see how," Prince said. "You are taking a long journey."

"It is not that far," Mary said sharply. "Do not ever question what the gods tell me. They have said we will be

64

together—and we will be. You will see. But be patient, my son. Do not rush the gods, or we will fail." Having tied her things securely, she stood up and looked at him. "Prince, go. I will talk with your mother. See if Master Jan needs help."

Reluctantly, Prince left the hut. Mary turned to Bahbu. "I hurt in here," she put her hand on her chest, "for what is ahead." Mary squeezed her eyes together, recalling the vision. "Prince will have much suffering. But when he suffers, Bahbu, rejoice. It is by the hand of his father that Prince will learn to value his mission."

Bahbu nodded her head. It was all very clear to her and she raised her hand to the wood carving. Time had darkened the wood to a glowing patina and the edges of the carvings were worn. They did not speak about the idol. Talk was useless, for they both knew the fate carried by the carving for Lars and Prince.

"So much is happening today," Bahbu said. "You and Chief and Master Jan, all leaving. And tonight we will have a new mistress at Hendersen. They say she is very young. The slaves at Bordeaux have suffered very much from their master there. How will it be without Master Jan to look after us?"

"It will not hurt you to suffer. When you do, you will grow strong for the job ahead. Remember that. Mistress Christina gave you love. Master Jan gave you food so your belly did not hurt when the rest of our people on this island were hungry. With them, you would forget that we are to lead our people against the evil white men—you forget that he is really one of us. Now you will learn what it is like to live under the hand of the *cruel* white man. When you are beaten, when you are hungry, when you are lonely or frightened, when you long for the freedom you had in Africa, remember that what you feel is what all of our people on these islands feel every day of their lives. If you find you cannot hate the white people, think of that night at Botany Bay."

"I will never forget it," Bahbu promised.

The sun was directly overhead when the procession lined up to leave the plantation. Jan walked up one side of the group and down the other. He stopped to test a rope that held two cages of chickens slung on either side of a mule. There were seven mules in all, two heavily loaded with straw baskets holding roots, seeds, and cane cuttings, and three others laden with crates of brown sugar, dried meat, and preserves from the cellar. Chief and Mary each rode a mule and at the rear, eight young men, bare to the waist, stood with their individual cargoes on the earth beside them.

Satisfied that the group was properly assembled, Jan, seeing Prince and Bahbu standing together, walked to them. He put both his hands on Bahbu's shoulders. "Good-by, Bahbu," he smiled at her. She dropped her head. He pulled her chin up. "Here. Look at me. You and Prince will take good care of things in my absence, won't you?" Bahbu kept her eyes turned up into Master Jan's and nodded her head up and down. "That's good. I will rely on you." He turned to Prince and took up his hand. Firmly shaking Prince's hand, Jan said, "And you, young man. I expect you to take Chief's responsibilities, do you understand?"

"Yes, master," Prince said. He felt himself grow taller again. Over the years, it had become apparent to Prince that Chief was, indeed, given a good share of responsibility. Everyone said that Chief knew the way to make sugar and rum as well as Master Jan. At a plantation such as Hendersen, Prince knew this was a compliment for a slave. His hand was limp in Master Jan's.

Jan hardened his grip. "When a man offers you his hand, shake it firmly." No other man, black or white, had ever offered Prince his hand. However, Prince squeezed.

Jan mounted his horse. He could still feel the pressure of Prince's parting grip. He will be a strong man, Jan told himself. Good. It will not be easy to abuse him. He spurred his horse and moved to the head of the group. The slaves at the rear of the line lifted baskets or crates up on their heads. Others who had gathered to see them off scurried around collecting the ropes of the animals that were to go and handed them to the young men. Then the procession began. When Jan reached the gate of Hendersen he stopped and turned in his saddle to look at Christina's unmarked grave. Turning back, he went on through the gate. The noises of the chickens and goats and the hollow thud of the mules' and horses' hoofs were drowned in the sudden burst of noise that sprang from the slaves who stood behind. They yelled and waved and ran a short distance after their friends. Bahbu and Prince stood long in the same spot, watching them disappear around the side of the mountain.

The sun had just dropped below the sea behind them when Lars and Johanna rode up to Fortuna. Standing in back of the kitchen Bahbu saw them approach. Johanna, in her white wedding dress, rode sidesaddle on her horse. The wind caught her veil and whipped at the heavy, billowing skirts. Bahbu thought of Mistress Christina—a vision of white death riding into Hendersen. As the woman got closer, Bahbu saw that she was a small, young girl, not at all like her mistress.

Bahbu ran through the dining room, into the parlor, and out onto the porch. Timidly, she moved against the wall. Lars swung from the horse and walked over to Johanna. Raising his arms, he said, "Jump, little one." She let herself slide down the round side of the horse into Lars's arms. Lars clumped up the stairs, easily carrying his bride.

Bahbu moved out from the wall. "Master Lars. Supper is ready when the mistress would like it."

Lars turned so that Johanna could look at Bahbu. "This is Bahbu. She is a house slave."

Johanna's small blue eyes moved in Bahbu's direction. Noticing only that the slave was very black, Johanna turned back, looking into the open archway. "Oh, Mr. Hendersen, the parlor is lovely," she said gleefully. "Mama said . . ." She blushed and fell quiet.

"No supper tonight," Lars growled over his shoulder to Bahbu. "Go back to your hut!"

Moving off the porch, Bahbu heard Lars's heavy footsteps going upstairs and, above that, a high-pitched giggle from the new mistress of Hendersen.

"What is the new mistress like?" Prince whispered to Bahbu as he set a pail of charcoal down beside her.

"She is a child," Bahbu answered, busying herself with the twigs. She looked up at the greathouse. It was strange to see it in darkness at this hour of the night. Bahbu felt a dull ache, deep inside her, so deep bush tea could not cure it. The lights of the greathouse had never seemed important until now.

The cooking fires sprang up around them. Prince and Bahbu sat silently in front of their fire, brooding over the dark greathouse.

"It is very strange not to have Mary here," Prince said, breaking the silence.

"Yes," Bahbu agreed.

"Do you think they are in the boat by now?"

"No," Bahbu answered. "They do not plan to get in the boat until tomorrow. Mary said that Master Jan told her they will sleep in a field outside of town tonight."

"Mary is in the field now? Cooking supper for them, as we are?"

"Yes."

"Do you think she is cooking corn meal? As we are?"

"They took some with them."

"Is there no food on St. John, Mama?"

"There is food. But only a little. That is why they took the seeds and bulbs. It will not be long before Mary and Chief have a good garden." Bahbu stirred the pot. "Get your dish, Prince. You ask too many questions."

Later, in the hut, the emptiness of Mary's mat beside her was a reminder to Bahbu that everything about her former life at Hendersen had suddenly changed. Why was it that the things she had loved most—with the exception of Prince—had swiftly gone from her life? Truly, this was an omen from the gods—this could only mean the beginning of the mission ahead of them. Maybe if she lit a fire and put the powders into it, she could see better what the future held for them. Bahbu felt that she needed direction now.

Outside, the clearing was deserted and quiet hung over the estate. The greathouse was still in darkness. Bahbu ran toward the mill where she knew she could collect some straw and twigs to begin a fire. A movement in the mill startled her. From the darkness there she saw the figure of the old Bomba staggering out into the night. Bomba, seeing her, stopped. Bahbu noticed that his face was wet from his tears.

"If Master Lars catches you here, he will beat you," Bahbu whispered. "Go to your hut. Hurry!"

The Bomba tried to fix his eyes on Bahbu but his head rocked uncontrollably. "Beating not hurt me," he mumbled at her. "Maybe old Bomba need beating." He staggered closer. Bahbu could smell the sweet fumes of rum. "You hurt like you been beat, Bahbu?" He waited for an answer.

"Yes," Bahbu said. "We all hurt for what the gods have

taken from us." Her voice got firmer. "But the gods have hurt us for a reason. We could not know what the rest of our people suffer if we lived at Hendersen with Mistress Christina and Master Jan for the rest of our lives. Don't you think our gods know this? We had love and full stomachs when our people on other parts of the island had pain and empty stomachs. We do not grieve for what we have lost. We prepare ourselves for the mission ahead of us. Do you understand?"

A grin broke across his face. Toothless, he smiled at her. "I see, Bahbu. The gods make us ready."

"Yes. Now go to your hut."

Quickly Bahbu gathered some straw and twigs from a box outside the curing house. Returning to her own hut, she closed the door and set about lighting the fire. Mary had given Bahbu careful instructions regarding the powders that were to be sprinkled on the fire. One powder, a peppery color and consistency, was the most powerful of all. This one Bahbu chose tonight to evoke the gods. When the fire was burning properly, she said aloud, "Gods of our people, I ask you to give me an omen, an omen of what is ahead for us. Show me, gods of our people." She threw a small amount of the powder on the fire. The flames leaped up. A billow of black smoke filled the hut. Bahbu squeezed her eyes tight as Mary had taught her to do then opened her eyes to look into the flames. At that instant, the door flew open.

"Get up, you black heathen!" Lars screamed at her. "Now that my brother is gone you people will not practice these savage rites at Hendersen."

Cautiously, Bahbu raised up from the floor. Lars stared at her, his heavy-lidded eyes drooping. "Don't look so frightened, Bahbu," he said in a low voice. "I wouldn't touch you. Not with my hands. Tomorrow morning you will be tied to a post and beaten. When the rest of the blacks see you punished they will know I mean to run the estate according to the laws of the colony."

Lars turned and walked from the hut. A moment later he returned with a pail of water and threw it on the fire, making it hiss and smoke. "Now, stay in here and breathe this stench," he said. "I will get another slave to come cook for my bride and me."

Bahbu looked at the pile of smoldering ash. Most certainly the gods had given her the omen. She trembled inside.

Before dawn Bahbu crept out of her hut and went to Prince. Carefully she shook him awake.

"Mama," Prince exclaimed. "What is it?"

"Shhh—come. Meet me outside. I talked with the gods and they have given us a sign."

Prince sprang up from the mat. "What did they say?"

"Come outside. I will tell you. And then you must see that our people know."

Standing in the clearing with Prince so she could keep an eye on the greathouse, Bahbu explained the omen.

"When I threw the most powerful powder on the fire and asked for a sign of our future here at Hendersen, Master Lars came into the hut, at that very minute! He has said he will beat me today, at a post, for our people to see."

"Mama. No . . ."

"Shhhhh. You will awaken Master Lars. Listen, my son. The gods have done this to show our people what is ahead for them here at Hendersen. It will be good for our people to see, before them, what is happening to the other black people on the island every day. Do you understand?"

"Why does it have to be you, Mama? I won't let him hurt you!"

"He will not hurt me, Prince. Now that I know our gods have called on me to show our people how evil the white men are, I can stand the pain. We must learn, Prince. And you must not try to stop him or he will hurt you in some way that will hinder you with your mission. Master Lars only waits for the chance to chop your foot off, or your ear, or maybe have your head. If you strike him or try to stop him he will go to the other white men and they will vote to have you beheaded. Promise me, Prince, that you will not move."

Prince was silent. What his mother said made sense. He could not fulfill his mission if he were killed or crippled before the time was ready. Hadn't Mary, many times, cautioned him about being patient, until he was a grown man? Hesitantly, he said, "I promise, Mama."

"Go back to your hut. When Bomba sounds the time to get up, you move to our people and tell them that today when Master Lars beats me it is an omen from our gods.

70

It is a gift. From it we learn how evil the white men are."

The whipping post was erected directly in front of Bahbu's hut. Although the drums from other plantations had often told them of a slave being whipped at a post, no Hendersen slave had ever received this punishment. An occasional blow from Lars suddenly seemed light punishment compared to a methodical lashing that tore the skin off one's back and took months to heal. Now they gathered around the post, watching two slaves put it in place as Master Lars directed them. Finally, it was finished and Master Lars went back to the house. When he appeared again, he carried a long black whip in his hand.

"Every slave on Hendersen is to gather here this morning," he shouted. "Prince, go see that all are here."

Prince broke from the crowd and pretended to search the buildings surrounding the clearing. He already knew that every slave had gathered in front of the frightening post, for he had told them of the omen Bahbu had received from the gods. Each black face in the crowd was solemn. Certainly the gods had worked swiftly. Not only had their beloved Mistress Christina been taken from them, but Master Jan and Mary and Chief and eight of their strongest men had been sent off to another island. And here, before them, was a whipping post. And soon Bahbu would be beaten on it. Bahbu, such a thin woman, a frail house slave; their witch doctor now that Mary was gone.

"Bahbu, come out here," Lars yelled sternly.

From her hut, Bahbu appeared with one hand folded on her chest, squeezing the amulet. She walked to the post with head erect, her eyes looking out toward the gates of Hendersen.

On the porch, Johanna stood by the rail, looking down at the crowd that was gathered before her in the clearing. How brave Lars is, she thought. With all those blacks standing around him, he risks his life to keep his position here on this estate. I wish Mama were here to see it. She always said he was the only one who would make a move to stop their heathenish ways. It occurred to Johanna that the slaves just might revolt. Hurriedly, she ran into the house and locked herself in the master bedroom. Here she could watch and feel much safer. Trembling with anticipation, she stood at the window and peeked out.

Lars jerked Bahbu around, facing her to the post. With

pieces of hide, he strapped her wrists to the wooden arms. Bahbu pressed her face to the rough wood, the amulet around her neck digging into her chest. She pushed harder, comforted by its presence.

Her eyes found Prince's, and mother and son gazed helplessly at one another. The gods, she was thinking. They had brought this omen. Remember your promise, my son. It cannot hurt me. It can bring you death if you do not remember your promise. She stared hard into Prince's eyes, sending the message.

The whip came down across Bahbu's back, causing her body to arch against the post in pain. Prince's face was contorted with anguish and rage. He opened his mouth as if to scream out and moved forward, clenching his fists. Bahbu thought he would spring out of the crowd. She relaxed against the post and let her eyes settle intently on his. She saw him flinch and knew that the whip was about to descend again. This time, she prepared herself. When it cut into her flesh, she did not move. Now she could feel the two individual places where the whip had landed. She was reminded of the night another fire had been placed on her flesh and put those markings there. "I hate you, white men," she whispered through clenched teeth.

Again and again the whip landed. Each time the whip struck her, the pain shot from Bahbu's back to her stomach and possessed her whole body. She began to retch uncontrollably. Unable to support her own weight, but still conscious, she sagged against the post. The unimaginable pain descended again and again. Finally, it was over.

"This time I am lenient," Lars's voice broke the deadly silence. "If I catch any of you practicing your witchcraft again, or putting hand to a drum, I'll beat you until you wish you were dead."

The slaves remained fixed in position, each too frightened to release Bahbu until Lars commanded, "Take her down. Then get to work."

He wound the whip into a circle in his hand, moving slowly and heaving from the energy he had spent. No one moved. Lars glared at the group, his eyes moving from one to the other. His mouth was curled down at the corners in a defiant leer. "Go on," he snarled when his eyes met Prince's burning stare. "Take your witch off the post!" He turned on the heel of one shoe and walked away.

Prince leaped forward from out of the group. He ran

to his mother and reached up to untie one arm. Then he saw her back. Where the whip had landed, lines of white flesh puffed in mounds across her back. Blood leaked out of the welts. Unconsciously, Prince pulled back, still holding his arms upward. Bomba pushed Prince aside and began untying Bahbu. Another slave took hold of Bahbu's weakened body and supported her while both arms were untied. Bahbu felt the pressure holding her up. Leaning against the strong arms, she turned herself. Prince, who had now dropped his arms beside him, stood helplessly staring at his mother's drawn face.

"Mama," Prince sobbed. He fell on his knees in front of her. Wrapping his arms around her waist, he put his head against her and cried, "Mama, Mama, I hate him."

"Go, Prince . . . to the field. Bomba will bring the pain healer for my back," she whispered.

"Let me get the pain healer," Prince begged.

"Then go. But hurry."

Bomba and another male slave, Tando, helped Bahbu to her hut. "We kill him some day," Tando said.

Bahbu stopped. Weakly, she said, "No, Tando. *Prince* will kill Master Lars—when the time comes. You and Bomba will kill other white men. But Master Lars is for Prince to kill."

Chapter 8

Anna Bodker hugged the trunk of the tamarind tree and looked out around it at the slaves in the field. She had been looking secretly for some months now at Hendersen slaves —ever since Johanna had married Lars. With the exception of the light-skinned boy with the yellow eyes, she could see no difference between Hendersen slaves and those at Bordeaux. Though time had lessened her fear of discovery, the game was still exciting and she came several times a week to watch. The object of the game now was to locate the light-skinned slave that fascinated her so and watch him at work.

Behind Anna, the leaves moved from a heavier touch than that of the wind and she swung around, her eyes wide with terror. An iguana skittered away and she heaved a sigh of relief. Along with the muffled thud of the hoe blades hitting against the dirt, Anna felt the heavy pounding of her heart echo in her ears. This apprehension was the very thing that made the game so much fun. Her parents would be furious at finding her in the fields. She picked a tamarind from the ground, cracked the thin shell, and popped the fruit into her mouth. The sourness of the gummy pulp drew at the muscles in her jaw, causing her mouth to water and relieving her thirst. Then a sharp crack of a breaking twig cut the silence and she leaped to her feet again.

Cautiously, Prince pushed the leaves aside and put his head through the opening to find the white girl directly in front of him. Her mouth fell open and her blue eyes were fixed on his. Suddenly, the girl turned and ran off through the brush. When she was gone, Prince was not sure that she had ever been there. It had been like this every time he caught a glimpse of her in the last five or six months. He knew that she was a young girl, almost as tall as he, with long thin legs, pale blond hair, and big blue eyes. He knew she must belong to one of the nearby plantations. But why she spent her time dodging behind the trees and bush to look out at him, he did not know. And he was curious. He was so curious, in fact, that catching her some day had become an obsession. Prince knew that he could not be bold with a white child, but this was not his intention. If he could surprise her, maybe he could find out where she came from and who she was. And possibly look at her more closely. It was only curiosity, part of his game. And it made the weeks and months pass quickly.

Anna did not stop running until she came to the path that marked the boundary between Hendersen and Bordeaux. There she slumped down on the grass beside the path, panting for breath. In this sheltered haven the air was very hot and still. The wet, heavy mass of hair on the back of her neck was weighty, and uncomfortable. Perspiration trickled down the sides of her face. She ran her hands across her chin and shook the hair loose from her neck. What difference if she was uncomfortable? She was safe, safe on Bordeaux. She had escaped, that was the important thing.

Escaped what? The slave had looked as startled as she had felt when their eyes met. And hadn't she been studying him carefully for a long time? He looked harmless enough. Maybe they could become friends. Maybe he was as lonely for someone to play with as she. Now that she thought about it, there was nothing frightening about the boy at all.

Standing up, she wiped the dust from her white stockings and walked down the hill, through the cotton fields of Bordeaux. "As soon as I can, I'll go back to Hendersen again," she said aloud. Anna often talked aloud to herself. It was part of the game of pretending she wasn't really alone.

Prince was working in the field on the mountain top, pulling weeds from between the rows of tall, almost ripe cane. He had purposely moved up here because it was the highest point on the west of the island and he could look east and see St. John. Now that he was sure Lars was not in the field, he stepped from between the cane rows and stood on the edge of the cliff.

It had rained earlier in the morning and the small outlying islands appeared very close, as if they had, under cover of the rain mist, crept closer to St. Thomas. The sandy shore line of St. John looked as if it touched the east end of St. Thomas. Did Prince imagine it, or was someone walking on the beach, there, in front of the cluster of palm trees? He stood on his bare toes and waved. "Mary! Master Jan! Here I am! Do you see me?" Prince was sure the brisk wind would carry his voice. "Mary! Master Jan!"

He listened for an answer. The wind rustled through the briars on the face of the cliff. A donkey brayed down near the mill.

"Mary, Mary, I am here," he shouted.

Close by, he heard a giggle. He hastily bent down and pulled at the weeds. Beside him there was a crunch on the loose dirt. Prince looked up and saw the white girl tiptoeing through the rows of cane toward the mountain top.

"Stop," he commanded.

The girl froze in place.

"There is a cliff in front of you. You'll fall," he said. The girl stared at him. "I will not hurt you," he said more gently.

They stared at each other.

"Who are you?" she said in a thin voice.

"I am Prince."

"I know you live here," she said, dropping her head.

"Yes. I am a Hendersen slave."

Prince noticed that her long, silky curls were tied in a cluster at the back of her head with a big bow that was the color of her eyes. Her eyes matched the sky and the sea. He summoned enough courage to ask, "Who are you?"

"I am Anna."

"Anna," he said softly. "That is a nice name."

"Who were you calling?" she asked, raising her face and looking directly at him.

Prince was embarrassed. Yes, she would have heard him. Reluctantly, he said, "I was only playing a game."

"What kind of game?"

"I pretend that my other mother—she has gone to live on St. John—I pretend that she can hear me call her." He laughed nervously. "I know she really cannot hear me. I just pretend that she can."

"Do you really have two mothers? Or do you just pretend that, too?"

"I have two mothers," he said sternly. "Bahbu, who lives here, and Mary, who lives on St. John."

76

"Two mothers," Anna sighed, admiringly. "I never knew anyone with two mothers before."

Prince cocked his head and closed his eyes. "Neither have I," he said. His eyes opened and he pulled himself erect, looking down at Anna. "I am very special," he said flatly.

Anna appraised him carefully. He must be special, she thought. He doesn't look like other slaves. He has very strange eyes and skin. She took a step forward. Then, hesitating, she said, "You must be special. You even have funny-colored skin. It's different."

Prince looked at Anna's skin. She was the prettiest color he had ever seen. She was not white, like most white people. She was a soft, glowing color, like the pink-white flowers that sometimes bloomed on the wild trees on the cliff below them. He raised his arm and compared its color to Anna's. "I am different," he said.

"How did you get so different?"

"I do not know," he said. "I suppose our gods colored me like this."

"Gods? How many do you have?"

Prince crossed his arms on his chest. "Many."

"My mama says that slaves are not Christians, that they don't believe in God."

"Gods," Prince corrected her. "Your mama is wrong. Slaves believe in gods. Why, they bring the sun and the stars . . . and this wind. Who else but the gods could bring all of this?"

Anna sighed. "You're just pretending. I like to play make-believe too. I do it all the time. And anyhow, Mama says that slaves don't have a God like we do and that they don't have souls like we do—and that they—"

"Your mama is wrong," Prince said angrily.

Frightened by his abruptness, Anna stepped back. "I didn't mean to make you angry," she said. "Mama honestly told me that."

Prince kicked at a clump of dirt and said quietly, "Do not talk about it."

Cautiously, Anna moved toward Prince. Her eyes were very big now, and she raised her hand timidly toward him. "Can I touch you?"

"If you want to." He put his arm out toward her.

Anna grabbed a piece of flesh and pinched. As Prince jerked his arm away, she leaped back.

77

"Do you have to hurt me?" he said. "You are very young to be hurting the slaves. You are like all the other white people."

Anna was staring, her mouth open. "But Mama said that slaves don't feel pain," she mumbled, astonished.

"Your mother is wrong in everything she has told you." He looked directly into Anna's eyes. He saw there a sad expression that reminded him of the look Mistress Christina often had had when she tended to a sick slave. "But I do not care," he added more gently. "It did not hurt that much. Beside that, Mary told me that a man does not cry or complain about small pain."

Anna wanted to run home. Was it true that all these things Mama had told her were wrong? She just saw for herself that this boy felt pain. But she couldn't ask Mama, or Papa either. They'd punish her for talking with the slaves, and especially a Hendersen slave. And if she ran, she wouldn't be able to make friends with this boy. Having a friend was more important than finding out who lied. She said, "How old are you?"

"Twelve," he said. "How old are you?"

"Ten. I ran away today. I came here from Bordeaux."

He unfolded his arms and looked at her. "Why are you running away?"

"Oh, I just came up here to see where my sister Johanna lives."

"Mistress Johanna is your sister?" Seeing Anna nod, he said, "She lives down there."

"I know. But I don't want her to know I am here. It would spoil my game of running away. Mama wouldn't let me come up here alone, I'm sure. And I like it up here. We live by the sea. I can't see much from there."

"Look," Prince said, pointing toward St. John. "See that island? That is where Mary lives. And see there," he turned and pointed to the west. "That is Crab Island, and Puerto Rico, where slaves can go if they run away and want to find freedom."

"Then why don't you run away?" she asked.

"I can't tell you that. I just don't want to run away."

"You're afraid," she taunted. "Papa says that runaway slaves are always caught and have their foot cut off."

"I do not worry they will cut my foot off," Prince said sternly. "I cannot tell you why. I just do not want to run away now. But when I am a man, when I am a full grown man, then I will think about it." He looked solemnly at her. "You believe me, don't you?"

"Yes, I do," she whispered. "I can tell by the way you say it that you mean it."

Prince smiled.

"Can we be friends?" she said, blurting out the words before she knew where they came from.

"Friends?" he said thoughtfully. What if Master Lars found out he was friendly with a white girl, he thought. He would surely beat him at the post, or maybe cut his tongue out—or kill him.

"Why do you look so frightened?" Anna said, interrupting his thoughts.

"Go home. If they find out you were here, they'll beat me. I do not want a beating. That is why."

Anna stepped closer. "I will not tell. We have a secret. If I told, I would get punished too." She took another step forward and looked up at Prince. "I'd like for us to be friends, I don't have anyone to play with. I will run away often and we can come up here and play. I'll never tell."

He concentrated on Anna's serious face. He wanted to be her friend but he didn't want to appear too anxious. "If you promise you will never tell a white person about our secret, you can be my friend," he said.

"I promise," Anna said eagerly.

"Then we are friends."

"Can I touch you again?" she said softly, putting her hand out.

"Why? So you can hurt me again?"

"No. I want to feel your skin. I like the color of it." She stepped closer, reaching her hand out. Hesitantly, Prince moved his arm toward her. Anna stroked it. "You feel smooth, like you look." Suddenly, she pulled her hand away. "Come on, let's wave at your other mother." She ran to the top of the hill and waved. "Here we are. See Prince? See me?" Laughing, she looked at Prince. "Come on. Jump with me." Prince took her hand and jumped beside her. They popped up and down, both waving their hands. "Mary, Mary," their voices called out.

Suddenly Prince tugged on Anna's arm, pulling her to the ground. Still laughing, he said, "They might hear us."

"Who?"

"Master Lars and Mistress Johanna. If we are going to

be friends, if we are going to play, we will have to be more careful."

"I know what we can play," Anna said eagerly. "Let's pretend that we are both slaves and that we are running away to Crab Island. Then we will have to be very quiet."

Just then the hollow tone of a conch shell drifted up the hill. Prince turned quickly to Anna. "They call me. If I do not go, Master Lars will come looking for me. Hurry. Go back to your house."

"Do you have to go?"

"Yes, I must." Prince was already moving down the hill.

Anna followed him. "Will you come back?" she pleaded.

"Not today. After I eat I will work at the mill. We are repairing the sails. It will soon be harvest." Seeing Anna's disappointment he said, "But I'll come here tomorrow. I pull weeds until we eat at midday. I'll look for you," he said over his shoulder as he moved hastily away.

The next morning, when Bomba sounded the noise for the slaves to arise, Prince sprang out of bed and hurriedly pulled on his trousers. He tied the rope which held them to his waist in a loose knot and ran out of the hut before the other slaves were off their mats. Bomba watched, bewildered, as Prince ran up the road to the high field.

Maybe she is there now, Prince was telling himself. All night he had been restless. Each time he awakened, there in the darkness of the hut he could visualize the soft pinkness and white of Anna's skin—and remember the gloss of her plump curls and how tall and thin she was, like him. Today he would ask her if he could feel her curls. Agile, he disappeared out of Bomba's sight. He continued running as fast as his feet would go. The morning wind was cold on his face. Above him, beyond the mountain top, it was still dark, while behind him, the dawn was pushing back the black sky. "Anna—Anna—" he called as he ran along. It was very silent around him. The tree toads were still making their night noises. He was reminded that it was too early for Anna to have reached the mountain. He would hurry and pull weeds so they could have more time to play. Today they would play escape to Crab Island.

The sun increased its heat on Prince's bare back. He knew from the warmth of it that it was getting close to the time for Bomba and Bahbu to bring breakfast into the field. Below him he could hear a movement. He knew this

80

would be Tonda, pulling weeds in his designated area. Each of the male slaves picked a special plot of ground to work. The women worked closer together, weeding a larger plot of ground in common and whispering back and forth in dialect when they knew Master Lars was not in the field. Sometimes they even called out to the men by their names and made jokes.

"Prince—Prince," he heard the whisper. He turned around. There was Anna, crawling toward him down the row between the cane. His heart leaped when he saw her. Quickly he got down on his hands and knees and crawled toward her.

Anna stopped and looked up at him. Today she had on a dress that was a pale pink, matching the color of her skin. Her curls fell on either side of her shoulders. Prince stopped. Face to face, they stared at each other. "Can I feel one of your curls?" he asked when he could find his tongue.

Anna nodded. Prince scurried forward. Sitting sideways, he reached out and held one of the curls. "It is very soft," he said, rolling it between his fingers.

"We are going to be slaves who are running away. Remember?"

"Of course I remember. I thought about it a lot last night. We will crawl very carefully right to the top of the mountain. Then we will follow the ridge, keeping Crab Island in sight. That way we cannot miss it."

"You go first," Anna said.

Prince swung over on his hands and knees again and began moving carefully up the hill. Below him, the conch shell sounded. Prince stopped. "Mary and Bomba are bringing our morning food. Master Lars will come into the field. He always does when we are eating. He is afraid that when we are together we will talk about him."

"Let's pretend that you have to steal the food for our trip to Crab Island. See if you can escape with enough for me to eat."

"Are you hungry?"

"No, I have eaten. But I could eat some more. And we need food for our trip. We will wait until we reach the very highest point of the mountain and then we will eat."

"Be careful. Stay down. I will have to walk."

"I'll be careful. You be, too. I don't want anyone to find out our secret."

"I will be careful," he whispered. Then he stood up and ran down the hill. Breathlessly, he approached Bahbu. He had, during the trip down the hill, watched the road and found that Master Lars was not yet in sight. "Mama, let me have two pieces of corn bread. I am very hungry!"

She handed him two large pieces of corn bread. Prince took them and ran back to the edge of the field. Bahbu watched as he hurriedly looked around and then ran back. "Mama, can I have a banana leaf? I want to hide some food. Today I am very hungry."

Bahbu looked carefully at Prince. He was flushed, and his outstretched hand trembled. "Are you sick?" she asked.

"No, Mama, I am very hungry."

Bahbu pulled a banana leaf from under the bread and handed it to him. He ran back. Placing the leaf on the earth between the rows of cane, he then put the bread on it and folded the ends of the leaf over it. From where she stood, Bahbu saw that the bread was carefully hidden. The other slaves watched, smiling. Tonda said, "He has worked hard this morning. A young man has a good appetite."

"Here," Bahbu handed him another piece of bread. "Eat this."

Prince looked at the bread. He was much too nervous to eat right now, but what else could he do? He had just told them how hungry he was. He took the bread and stuffed some of it into his mouth.

"Bomba, can I have an extra jug of cane juice? I am very thirsty today."

Bomba handed Prince a clay jug. "Take what you want," he said. "You run too much in the heat." Bomba squinted up at the white sun. "Wear your hat, Prince. You get sick from this sun."

Prince turned around and ran to the spot where the bread was hidden. Hiding the jug with it, he turned around. Seeing a figure on the road below, he ran again to Bahbu. "More bread," he said hurriedly. He took the bread from Bahbu and then moved slowly the other way, away from where the food was hidden. He eased himself down on the ground and chewed slowly on the corn bread.

Lars rode up into the group and reined in his horse. Sitting up in the saddle, he looked around. Turning his head slowly, he went from face to face. When his eyes settled on Prince, Prince bit into the bread and chewed fiercely. Lars remained looking at him and Prince could feel the bread stick in his throat when he tried to swallow. He put his neck out in an attempt to get it down. He was choking when Bomba handed him a clay cup filled with sugar cane juice. Gratefully, Prince took the cup and washed the bread down with cool, sweet liquid. Finally, Lars turned away and moved his horse out of the group. He rode in the direction of the hidden food. Lars was almost at the hiding spot, going directly toward it, when he pulled his horse to the side and moved away. Prince relaxed and took another bite of the bread. This time he was able to swallow.

A mosquito buzzed around Prince's head. He did not want to swat at it because it might draw attention to himself. The sun beat down on the back of his neck. It had never seemed so hot. He should have brought his straw hat, but he had been in such a hurry today he had forgotten it in the hut. His ears followed Master Lars's course up the side of the cane field. Soon he would be on the top ridge, looking down on all of them. The mosquito whined. He raised his head and swatted at it, looking up as he did. Lars was on the top of the ridge now, directly in front of him. Anna would be hiding close by.

Prince could feel a terrible tightness in his belly. If Master Lars found Anna, would he beat her? What would Master Lars do if he tried to protect Anna from him? Should he dare risk it?

His stomach remained tight. For an instant he thought he was going to throw up the bread and cane juice. But then his ears picked up the increasing thud of the horse's hoofs and he knew that Master Lars was coming back down the mountain side. He and Anna were safe.

"Get back to your work," Lars shouted. "Do you have to take all day to eat? You have enough time to rest in the afternoon. If you sit around here sleeping all morning, we'll never get ahead of the weeds."

Prince raised his head. Around him the other slaves were returning their earthenware dishes to the basket Bahbu had tied on the mule. Prince picked up his cup and ran toward her. When he had placed the cup in the basket, Bahbu whispered to him, "Whatever you are doing, be careful!"

Prince looked innocently at his mother. Bahbu went on in a whisper, "We will talk, tonight. Go. But walk, Prince. Walk."

The words slowed him down. He began to walk up the hill. When he reached the place where the food was hidden, he turned very slowly. Lars had his back to him, talking to Bomba. Swiftly, Prince reached over and took up the banana leaf. Cradling it in his left arm, he scooped up the jug in his right hand and hurried forward into the safety of the high cane stalks.

Deeper into the cane, he moved faster. He caused very little movement of the cane tops, however, for he bent his head and carefully picked his path on the damp red earth.

"Anna, Anna," he whispered. "Where are you?"

"Here," her high voice answered. From in front of him, Anna appeared, as if by magic. She got off her hands and knees and sat in a rut between the stalks. Her dress was caked with the wet red earth. Her face, too, had great smudges on it, the claylike mud sticking to her forehead and cheeks. Her long white stockings and shoes were stained red.

Prince eased down on one knee and put the cane juice and bread beside him. "How did you get so dirty? You have ruined your pretty dress. What will your mama say?"

Anna looked down at her dress. She tried to rub the mud from off her skirt, but the stain was in the fabric. Her eyes were very wide and blue when she looked up at Prince. "I'll tell Mama I fell."

They both stared at the soiled dress. "How did you do it?" Prince asked. "Were you frightened?"

"Mr. Hendersen came very close. I threw myself down on my face. It was slippery. The earth is still wet."

"The sun does not get in here to dry it when the cane is so high," Prince said.

"Did you get the food?"

"Yes. See, we have corn bread and sugar cane juice."

"Sugar cane juice? If I drink it, my skin will turn the color of yours. Papa says that cane juice is for the black people. He never lets me have it."

"Then don't drink it," Prince said. "I don't care."

"But I am very thirsty. We will never be able to play going to Crab Island if I do not have something to drink."

Seeing that Prince had become angry, she picked up the jug and drank from it. It was cool and sweet. Her eyes moved to her arm and she watched her skin, delighted that it did not turn color. She brought the jug back to her lips and this time drank more.

Prince watched her skin, too. "See. Your papa is wrong, too. Cane juice is not only for black people. Mistress Christina always drank cane juice."

"I'm glad to know that," Anna said, looking up again at Prince. "I can tell Mama I fell when I was running in the field and explain how my dress got dirty, but I don't know how I would explain it if I turned your color." Relieved, Anna sipped again on the cane juice.

Prince stood up. "Stay down until I tell you it is safe. Master Lars is still below us. He is turning away now. Yes, there he goes. He will spend a long time in the kitchen. He eats late."

Prince threw himself down on the ground again. "Did your mama find out where you were yesterday?"

"No. I told her I was playing on the beach. Mama had a headache yesterday. She was in her room when I got home. They never knew I ran away."

"The first time they catch you will be the last time you can run away," Prince said. "Is that not true?"

"They won't catch me. Mama sews. And Papa is in the field all day. He says he has to beat his slaves to make them work." Noticing that Prince turned his head away, she said, "Now that I know you feel pain, I don't like to think about it." She put her hand out on Prince's arm. "Let's go to the top of the mountain. When we get there, we will eat."

On hands and knees they crawled through the few remaining rows of cane. There was a path to the top of the ridge. From there they could look down on another plantation, to the east of them at Perseverance Bay. "Who lives there?" Anna asked, stretching her head higher so she could see the back of the greathouse far below them.

"I do not know. It is far away. We talk to the slaves with our drum."

"What do they do there?"

"They beat their slaves and cut their feet off. The drums say so."

Anna wrinkled her nose. "I don't like to talk about that."

"Come," Prince said. Still crawling, they moved west on the ridge. "Follow me. If we are pretending that you are a slave, remember—if we get caught, we will *both* have our foot chopped off. That is the punishment for runaway slaves."

"Will we get caught?" Anna whispered.

Prince turned around and crawled back to her. "No, we will not get caught. And if we do, I will protect you."

Anna looked into Prince's face. His expression was so serious that she knew he would protect her. Without speaking they began moving west again. The ridge began to slope downward, taking a sharp drop so they were at an angle which gave them speed. Wet clay gathered in a clump at their knees as they scooted along. Prince stopped. "Look. There is a big rock. See it?" An enormous rock, almost as big as a slave hut, protruded out into space. "We can hide under it and there we will be safe. We can eat our food and plan our escape."

They crawled around the rock and entered the cool shaded area beneath it. The area was open only on the side facing the sea. "This is nice," Anna said, sitting down and scraping the mud packs from the knees of her once-white cotton stockings. "This is our house," Anna said. "Let's not pretend we are going to escape. Let's pretend that we live here. And the plantation below—that is our plantation." They could still see the beach at Perseverance and the tall, slender palm trees just behind the sand.

"I am the master of the plantation," Prince said. He crawled forward and looked out. He turned back. "No, that will not do. I do not want to be a plantation owner. I am a slave. I want to remain a slave. Until we are all free, at least."

"Free? How will all the slaves get free?"

Prince looked at Anna. He could not trust her with his secret. She was a white girl. And she was very young. He sat down to unwrap the banana leaf. "By pretending. It is just as easy to free the slaves as it is for me to become the master of that plantation." A silence followed. Prince handed Anna a piece of corn bread. Immediately she bit into it.

"This is good. I am hungry now. We have traveled a long way."

"How do you get from Bordeaux to Fortuna? That is a long way for a white girl to travel."

"I rode my donkey to the back of your kitchen and tied it there."

"But Master Lars eats in the kitchen every morning."

"Today I told Mama I was going to visit Johanna. She said I could." Anna looked at Prince. "I will come here often now that I have touched a slave . . . and found you for my friend. I don't know why Mama and Papa say those lies about black people."

"Mary says that the white men's gods teach them to be cruel to the black men."

"Why doesn't Mary ask your gods to tell our gods to be different?"

"Mary has tried. She says that evil gods belong to the white men and will not listen to black people."

"Maybe I can ask our God not to make us cruel to the black people."

"Would you do that?"

"Yes, I will ask God—next Sunday—and every night when I pray."

Feeling very satisfied, Prince leaned back against the cold, hard rock and chewed on the corn bread. In front of them, the sea was empty with the exception of a very small, barren island that jutted up, its brown flat surface breaking the monotony of blue water. A large bird, its wings spread wide, glided in front of them and quickly disappeared from sight.

"Prince—Prince," the voice of his mother interrupted their silence. Prince crawled quickly out of the hiding place. Standing in front of the opening, he peered above the rock. Then on the ridge he saw Bahbu.

"I am here," he called.

She motioned him to come to her. He ducked down and whispered to Anna. "It is my mother. I will have to go back to work. Can you find your way back?"

"Don't leave me. I don't know if I can find my way."

"Then wait here. I will be back."

Prince ran up the ridge, his bare feet slippery on the clay. He held on to the dry clumps of weeds scattered on the hillside to help him make his way up. Panting, he was soon beside his mother.

"Why have you gone from the field?" Bahbu asked sharply.

"I . . . I . . ."

"What is it, Prince? You know that Master Lars would beat you if he found you here. Why did you go so far from the field?" Prince dropped his head. "Then I will go see what you have been doing." Bahbu pushed him aside

87

and started down the sharp grade, Prince trailing after her.

At the opening in front of the rock, Bahbu squatted down allowing her eyes to adjust to the dark.

"Ay-y-y," she muttered. "A white girl."

Prince crouched down beside his mother. "It is my friend, Anna."

Bahbu grabbed her head with her hands. "Master Lars would kill you for this." She sprang up and grabbed Prince's arm. "Come. You must go back to the field!"

"But, Mama, she is afraid. She cannot find her way from here. I *cannot* leave her in this place."

Bahbu released his arm. She squatted down and looked in at Anna. "Come. I will take you to the path." She turned to Prince. "You go back to the field."

"Do not be afraid," he said to Anna. "My mother will not hurt you."

Anna put her hands over her face.

"Anna," Bahbu said softly. "I will not hurt you. But if you are the friend of my son, then you want to help him. He will be killed if his master finds him here. You do not want that, do you?"

Keeping her hands over her face, Anna shook her head no.

"She is going to ask her gods to teach the white people not to be cruel to us," Prince said, proudly.

"Go to the field, Prince. I will take care of Anna. She will not be frightened of me. Go."

"Don't be afraid," Prince said quickly into the cave. Then he turned and ran up the hill.

Slowly Anna dropped her hands and stared at Bahbu. Bahbu sat down on the ground and looked away from her, toward the sea. Bahbu could hear the girl moving up behind her. Slowly, Bahbu turned her head. Looking over her shoulder, she said, "Come. Sit by me."

Cautiously, Anna eased herself into a sitting position beside Bahbu.

"It is pretty out there," Bahbu said. "See the ship over there?" Bahbu pointed toward the west. Anna leaned forward and looked out.

"Do you think it is a pirate?" Anna said.

"Yes. It is a pirate."

"You are very black," Anna said.

Bahbu smiled. Anna liked the way her face changed when

88

she smiled. She did not look angry any more. "You are very white," Bahbu said, still smiling.

Bahbu stood up and reached down for Anna's hand. "It is getting late."

Anna leaped up beside Bahbu and gave Bahbu her hand. "Will you be my friend?"

"Yes, if you would like me to be your friend, I will be. Now come. Where are you going?"

"To Hendersen, to visit my sister Johanna."

Bahbu closed her eyes. She gripped Anna's hand tighter.

"Do not worry," Anna said. "I know she is your mistress. I would not tell Johanna."

There was a long silence. They looked steadily at each other. Bahbu finally said, "I believe you, child." Holding onto Anna's hand, she led her up the path.

Chapter 9

Both planter and slave counted time by the seasonal chores, the yearly cycle of hoeing and cultivating, planting, weeding, and the harvest; then the delivery of the rum and muscavado to the company's dock. But Bahbu counted time only by Prince's birthdays. While the slaves sweat and fought against the elements to make the harvest a good one, Bahbu looked forward only to the summer when another year would be added to her son's age and another omen would be shown.

On his fifteenth birthday a letter for Master Lars arrived from Master Jan saying that the plantation on St. John was developing according to expectations but that Chief had died of the fever.

On Prince's sixteenth birthday, the omen had been a strong one. At Bordeaux, Wilhelm had beaten one of the slaves. By nightfall, the drums told them that the slave had died. The drums resounded all over St. Thomas for the remainder of the night. They carried to St. John where the message reached Mary.

On Prince's seventeenth birthday, Tando had two fingers chopped off his left hand by Master Lars, punishment for being caught in the field while answering one of Mary's drum messages.

Mary sent messages at least every three or four months. The noise was discernible from the easternmost tip of St. Thomas. The beat was picked up by a drummer at Yerse Bay, then rotated on to Smith Bay, to Wintberg, to Canaan. From Canaan, it was transmitted to Misgen, and from there to Dorothea and Carrett Bay. From Carrett Bay to Bonne Esperance. There, when it was evening, a drummer put out the message that rolled up the mountain side to Fortuna. The messages were always the same: the slaves in St. John were horribly treated by the white men with the exception of Jan Hendersen; and Mary continued organizing them for the time Prince would lead them in revolt. Then Tando would acknowledge the messages and his drumbeat traveled eastward to St. John passed along by the same hands. Tando continued drumming despite his wounds.

On Prince's eighteenth birthday, there were several omens. Early that morning Lars and Johanna rode from Hendersen to Charlotte Amalie. This started the day on a festive note for the slaves and during the midday meal Tando took up his drum and tapped out a rhythmic beat. The slaves circled him, clapping their hands and stomping their feet.

"Dance, Prince, dance," they shouted in unison. The chant grew. Hearing it, Anna went to the slave quarters and leaned unnoticed against a hut. Soon she saw Prince leap into the clearing beside Tando.

Prince strutted around the clearing, shuffling to the jerky beat of the drum. He clenched his fists and rolled them in front of his chest, laughing. Tando's hands moved faster. In the circle one of the young women swayed and rolled her hips, intermittently changing the circular hip movement to a forward, seductive thrust at Prince. The crowd yelled encouragement. She moved out, fixing her eyes on Prince. Prince walked to the beat, his legs spread apart. When he was close to the woman, he dropped back, lowering his torso in time to the music. His brown legs were spread wide, holding his gyrating torso. The girl shuffled in between Prince's legs, leaning backward, thrusting out her pelvic area. Their bodies almost touched. Each time they gave a lusty shove the onlookers squealed.

At that moment, Prince saw Anna. She was glaring at him, her mouth set in a straight line. He stopped his dancing and walked to her.

A silence fell over the crowd. Wisely, Tando hit the drum head with a fierce stroke and began an ardent pounding. Halfheartedly, the slaves shuffled their feet. The drum sounds increased. Then, abandoning timidity, the slaves gave themselves over to the drumbeat and danced.

Prince hesitated, looking back at the dancers. Anna raised her skirt and ran up the path to the high field. Prince followed. She had reached the cave before he caught her. Inside, Prince fell back on the dirt floor and rested his head on his arms. "You are jealous," he said, laughing.

"I am not."

"Yes, you are. Your face is very pink. You are angry. You are jealous."

"Why would I be jealous of such a black old woman?"

Prince sat up. "She is not an old woman. And she is a very fine color. Her skin shines."

Anna turned away. Prince grabbed her shoulder and pulled her on the ground beside him. "Don't be angry," he said.

Prince felt his heart pounding against Anna's body. His lips moved down, settling on hers.

There was no other sound in the cave except their breathing. Anna tingled from her brain down to her toes and back again.

Suddenly, a voice rang out. "Prince." There was a shuffle of feet. Closer, louder. "Prince."

Prince's head dropped on Anna's neck. Under his face he felt Anna's heart beating. He closed his eyes, clinging to her.

"You will be killed. Both of you," Bahbu said sternly. "A black man cannot have a white woman."

Still they clung to each other.

"You do not want Anna to be killed by the white men, do you?" Bahbu said pleadingly. "That is why you will stay with the black woman, Prince. You cannot make babies with Anna. I have saved your lives today. This is an omen. Get out of the cave."

Prince raised his face. Looking at Anna he said, "She is right. It is too dangerous."

Anna wrapped her arms around Prince and held him against her. "I don't care," she said. "But what about that woman?"

Prince pulled Anna's arms away and rolled over on his back. It was so quiet in the cave they could hear the wind running up the mountain side. Staring at the ceiling, Prince finally said, "I am a man, Anna. I must have a woman. But it does not change how I feel about you. You are the one I love. We cannot make babies, that is all."

Anna jumped up, shaking her wrinkled skirt. "Then have your ugly black woman. See if I care!"

"When I am free, Anna," Prince said gently, "then you will have me."

"You are always talking about when you are free. Free. You will never be free." With that she ran from the cave.

Later that night, Bahbu went to the cave to talk to the

gods. A scorpion dropped from the ceiling, landing on the fire. It foretold of death. Bahbu squeezed her face in a knot and stared at the omen. She had saved Prince and Anna today. Did this mean that she had to remain on guard whenever they were together in the future? But five months later, Mistress Johanna gave birth to a stillborn child. For the first time in that five months, Bahbu relaxed. This did not mean she stopped following Prince and Anna, to protect them from their own desires. But, she knew the omen had been fulfilled.

Now, on Prince's nineteenth birthday, Anna sat in the parlor waiting for her sister to take her midday nap. Anxious to meet Prince at their cave, she thought Johanna would never tire. Johanna rocked back and forth in her favorite cane-backed chair, fanning herself. She had become very plump. Her small face rested on a collar of fat that settled on her shoulders. She still dressed in heavy satins and silks, which made her perspire and grow tired soon after the midday meal.

"Anna," she said, her voice high-pitched and childlike, "would you like to see me to my room?" With a grunt, she pushed herself out of the rocker, having to hold her back ramrod straight because the bodice of her dress was so tight. "If only I could lose some weight. Ever since my confinement, I have been unable to eat a thing without having it settle here," she put her jeweled, chubby fingers on her stomach. Anna was reminded of her father.

"You poor dear," Anna said. "It is a warm day. Come, let me help you out of your clothes."

"You are a dear little sister," Johanna said brightly. "I don't know what I would do without you. No one else understands what I have suffered, losing the baby and never having a healthy day since then." She raised her heavy skirts and walked in small, jerky steps toward the archway.

Anna paced herself to move along with her sister. Anna had grown into a tall, slender young woman. When her mother was not there to fuss with her hair, she pulled it back, tying it with a ribbon at her neck and letting the long, tawny blond hair flow behind her.

Johanna took hold of the rail and pulled herself up each step. "You are very fortunate to be so tall," Johanna puffed out the words. "Your clothes don't bind you. Mama always said I was fortunate to be tiny, like her, but she is wrong. That is only correct if a woman remains thin." She moved on into the bedroom. The large four-poster bed was awaiting her with the sheet turned back and the mosquito netting raised. Johanna began unbuttoning her dress. "No wonder Mama remains thin. She is so nervous. I would much rather be fat—and more placid. Imagine what my life would be like, the way Lars is prone to temper when he drinks, if I were a nervous woman and could not put up with his ravings."

Seeing her sister struggle to take her arms out of her dress, Anna assisted her. As Anna pulled on a cuff, the satin stuck to the damp skin below it. She pulled again, freeing one arm. With the same process she released the other. Johanna let the dress fall in a heap on the floor and stepped over it. "Ah," she sighed, "how much cooler it is." Anna began to untie her sister's corset strings. Johanna continued, "Maybe you are right, that cotton is cooler. But Mama says you dress much too plainly for a young woman your age. But you know as well as I do, Anna, you're so pretty you don't need clothes to show you off. Sometimes I wonder if Mama's ideas that men count a woman's clothing so important is entirely right." She turned, trying to look over her shoulder at Anna. "Come to think of it, you are seventeen now, aren't you? And you still do not have a serious beau. Maybe you should be more careful of your dress, Anna. You don't want to be an old maid, do you?"

Anna struggled with a knot in the string. It finally gave way. The corset, assisted by the weighty pressure beneath it, easily unlaced. Johanna sighed again. "My, that feels good. It is hot today!"

Johanna wrapped a cotton peignoir over her frilly underclothes and climbed up on the stool beside the bed. "You didn't answer me. Did I hurt your feelings, Anna? I didn't mean to, if I did."

Anna moved up to the side of the bed. Leaning on her elbows, she rested her chin on her hands and stared at the wall. "No. You did not hurt my feelings. I don't worry about being an old maid. There are no young men on St. Thomas whom I've met that would interest me in marriage."

Johanna fanned herself with the edges of the sheet. "Well, you are too young as yet. That is why they don't interest you. You just wait, when you decide it is time to get married, you'll change your ways." She giggled. "Mama gets very angry with you, Anna. She says you are a rebel. And that you are. But I suppose if you are going to be a planter's wife, it does not make much difference that you like to ride and run through the fields all day. Heavens, a girl doesn't have much chance to dance on this island." She settled down against the soft pillow. "How long has it been since we went to the last ball?"

"A long time," Anna said. "And I didn't enjoy it one bit. Frederick von Campenhout danced all over my feet. My, he's clumsy!"

"He is shy, that is all. All young men are nervous when they dance with a girl."

"One time I saw some of the slaves dancing. Those young men don't look clumsy. They made me want to join in; they make music, it seems, instead of following it."

"Anna! What are you saying? Stop talking foolish. If Mama or Papa—or even Lars—heard you talk like that, they would disown you. Imagine. Wanting to dance with a savage."

"Johanna, some of those slaves are very handsome men. Honestly. Why don't you look more carefully?"

"Oh, Anna. Watch your tongue." She snapped her head around to be sure no one was in hearing distance. Lowering her voice, she said, "I'll never repeat what you have just said. But you must promise me that you will never say anything like it again." Anna was silent. "Promise me," Johanna demanded.

"I only say that some are handsome. Is that so wrong?"

"And what difference would it make if they really are?"

"None, not to you. You think they have no feelings, as Papa and Lars have told you."

"*Everyone* says so. Unless they are beaten, so that they know who their master is, they would kill us all. Anna, doesn't that frighten you?"

"No, it does not," Anna said. "I cannot understand why you enjoy seeing them punished. You are always telling Lars things to set him against them. Sometimes I wish you would hold your tongue. I do not like to see them beaten."

Johanna swung her short legs around off the edge of the mattress. Anna thought she was going to slide off the bed. Instead, she pointed a finger at Anna and said, "Don't you *ever* talk like this again. Do you hear me? If you do, I'll tell Papa. Then you'll be sorry for the way you talk. I'll give you one more chance, only because you have been so good to me. Do you understand?" She fixed her eyes on Anna's face, holding her index finger in the air, waiting for a reply.

Anna dropped her head and clasped her hands in front of her. "Forgive me, sister. I know what they are. It's just that I like to tease you at times. You know that."

Johanna dropped her hand and made a noise of relief. "Oh my, you are a bad girl." She fell back on the pillow. "Now promise me, Anna," she lifted her hand out toward Anna. "Here, take my hand. Now, promise me that you will never say such foolish things again, even in jest."

"I promise," Anna whispered.

"Now, then, be a good girl and run along. You know I need my rest. Ever since my confinement, I have not gotten back my strength."

Anna walked from the room and closed the door behind her. She moved with a determined step down the stairs and out the front door. On the porch she broke into a run, leaping down the steps. She ran straight across the clearing, past the factories and the slave huts, and took the path up to the high field. On the east side of her she could see the slaves bent over between the rows of cane. On and on she ran, until she came to the very top of the mountain. There she stopped, gasping for air. In front of her was the endless expanse of sea and sky. Below her lay the beach at Perseverance and the plantation behind it. Anna looked carefully to see if her brother-in-law was in the field. He was nowhere in sight. She turned west on the ridge and ran down the slope that led to the rock. She and Bahbu and Prince had agreed, long ago, that they could not walk in the same place, lest they make a noticeable path. Instead, she moved from one clump of reedlike grass to another, easing her feet into the side of each so she would not tear the grass and leave a trail. When she was at the opening, she peeked in. It was empty. There on a grass mat was a hand of ripe bananas. Sitting down and holding the bananas in her lap, she removed her ankle-high shoes. Then she rolled her thin white cotton stockings off each leg and threw them beside her. She wiggled her toes. She broke off a banana and peeled it, carefully measuring each stroke so that the peel was hanging evenly around her hand. She bit into the banana and gazed out to sea. There was a large schooner in front of her, its sails curved full of wind.

Perhaps it was Captain Kidd. He had been here before and Papa had bartered with him, running right out across the waves from Perseverance Bay in a small boat. They had all been sworn to secrecy. Anna remembered it because Mama had said the governor would not like it. What was it they had gotten? Was it the silver service, or the crystal glasses Mama treasured so?

A small stone rolled down beside the rock, making a lizard scurry into the cave. Anna moved back, pulling herself quietly by her arms. Then she saw the bare brown feet and knew it was Prince. He leaned over and peeked in.

"Come quickly," Anna said. "Captain Kidd is sailing off to Puerto Rico. Look. Maybe if we wave, he will stop and take us with him. Would you go, Prince?"

Prince reached for a banana. "Maybe. It depends on how much gold he would offer me. I have heard he pays the slaves to work for him."

"I don't think we would go. You are always saying you will not run away and get free."

"I always say I will wait until we are all free. Is that wrong?"

Anna looked at Prince. His eyes were following the schooner. "When will you tell me what your secret is?" she asked.

"Some day. It is not important now. I cannot stay long with you today. Today I make nineteen. Bahbu says we must be very careful until the omen has appeared. There is always an omen on my birthday. It is to remind our people that the gods do not forget them."

"I know—I know, Prince," Anna said impatiently. "But I wanted to talk with you. I had a fight with Johanna. She says she will tell Papa about me if I ever fight with her again."

Prince frowned. "What did you fight about?"

"It was silly. I was trying to tell her that the black people do have feelings. But she would not listen. She became very angry."

"You should know that it is not wise to talk with Mistress Johanna. She is pleased when one of us is beaten. It is clear to see on her face. Why do you try to change her mind?"

Anna shook her head. "It was wrong, I know that now. But, Prince"—she put her hand on his muscular arm—"it

97

all seems so hopeless. The white people will *never* understand. Maybe we really should run away to Puerto Rico—or somewhere—so you and Bahbu can be free."

"Do not ever talk like that. You have to believe that we will be free some day. And the day is not far off."

"But how, Prince? The plantations are armed. And they have their signals to meet at the fort if the slaves try to gain freedom from them. You cannot fight the cannon and muskets. How do you plan to get free?"

Prince took Anna's arm in his hand and gripped it firmly. "You have to believe that we *will* be, that is all. Have I ever lied to you?"

"No."

"And I will not begin now. But I cannot tell you. Not right now. I have to go back to work. Lars will be coming to the high field soon. I am to be working at the mill. Later, Anna. Maybe this Saturday night he will visit Bordeaux. Then we can come here to meet and I will tell you."

"Prince, I have a gift for you." Anna reached down in front of her dress and brought out a small bundle. She handed it to Prince. "Happy Birthday!"

He opened it. Inside were two jagged, polished teeth.

"They are shark's teeth," Anna said, proudly. "One of the slaves at Bordeaux gave them to me. He said they are very good to keep the evil spirits away."

Prince was pleased. He closed his big, calloused hand over them and rubbed their smooth surfaces. Keeping his hand closed in a fist, he raised up, bending over in the narrow space, and walked out of the cave. Outside he pulled erect and looked about him. Seeing nothing, he bent over and said, "You have made my birthday very happy, Anna. Good-by."

Anna sat in the coolness of the cave and watched the schooner sail out of sight. Reluctantly, she pulled on her stockings and then pulled on her shoes and laced them. He does not understand that the white people do not want to be taught, she thought. Even Lars says without slaves he could not make money, just as Papa says. They have bought them—they will never free them—and they will always beat them. Prince and Bahbu and I will always have to sneak to see each other. She grabbed at a pebble on the ground beside her and threw it out of the cave. It soared out over the cliff and then, caught by the wind, it seemed to stop before it dropped out of sight.

Anna had reached the path to the mill before she noticed a group of slaves surrounding the whipping post. She began to run. Before she reached the clearing, she knew what she would find. When she reached the crowd, her heart sank as she saw that her fears were confirmed. Prince was already strapped into position on the wooden arms. Frantically, Anna searched the crowd for Bahbu. She felt someone grab her arm, and turned. Bahbu stood beside her, squeezing her arm. "Do not call out," she whispered, "or he will kill Prince." Bahbu released Anna's arm and moved away. Anna continued searching the faces in the crowd. Maybe someone was there who could stop Lars. The black faces surrounding her were set, their mouths pulled into stern lines, their eyes fixed on the post. Anna turned and looked at the greathouse. There, in the second floor window, she saw Johanna, her eyes fixed on Lars. She was smiling. Anna's shoulders sagged, and she turned back and let her eyes rest on Prince's back.

Lars was still on his horse. He rode back and forth in front of Prince, looking at the gathering. He had a two-day growth of beard, and his white shirt was soiled. His pants and boots looked as though they had not been cleaned in a long time. His lids appeared much too heavy on his eyes. In his hand was the whip. His voice broke the silence in a loud blast.

"Listen to me. This slave was trying to run away. I caught him on the way to Botany Bay. Running away, do you hear? I could cut his foot off." He had come to the end of the group, pulled his horse around and walked it back. "Or I could chop his head off. The only reason I will spare him is that I need him. The harvesting is near. But when I get finished with him . . ." Now Lars had reached the other end of the group. He turned the horse around again and reined him in. "When I get finished with him, he will wish I had cut his foot off." Lars dismounted.

With the whip rolled in his right hand, Lars raised his arms and stretched them back and forth. He spread his legs and shuffled his feet into a satisfactory position. He raised his right arm high, and let the whip unfold. It rolled backward, a good length of it falling on the ground. With a great heave, he brought his arm forward. The whip came down straight on Prince's shoulder. Lars moved to a different angle and reset his feet. Putting his right arm out straight to his side, he snapped the whip into position again. Again he heaved, throwing his arm back and snapping it forward. This time the whip struck Prince's back from the side, making a great raw welt slant across his back. Prince's wrists struggled against the leather ropes that held him on the post. Back came Lars's arm—heave—forward. He continued the movement in a measured pattern that brought the whip down, over and over again until each blow brought blood, turning Prince's back to scarlet. Finally, exhausted from the heat, Lars had to stop. Prince was limp on the post.

The white glare of the sun burned Anna's dry eyes. Her ears were pounding, as if the whip were still landing on Prince's flesh. In a cold fury, she turned and walked toward the greathouse.

"Have another sweet potato," Johanna said to her father.

"Ah yes," Wilhelm answered, reaching for the dish. He spooned two large potatoes out on his empty plate. "Tell me, Lars, I hear you had a runaway today."

"Not really," Lars answered. He bit off a piece of bread and chewed it. Washing it down with a swallow of rum, he said, "You know I would not settle for the post with a runaway."

Anna picked at a piece of cubed beef. She put it in her mouth but let it remain in her cheek unchewed.

"He acted very strange. I was riding up on top of the high ridge when I saw this slave turn and run through the weeds away from the ridge toward the mill. I followed him. But he didn't go to the mill. He ran on past, toward the path that does eventually lead to Botany Bay. When I overtook him, he would not explain why he had run from me. He must have been up to something he did not want me to know about, or he would not have run." Lars paused. "Now that I think of it, I should have gone up to the ridge and had a look. Well, I didn't have time. I was so infuriated that he would not tell me what he had run from that I had him tied to the post. I told the other slaves he was trying to run away, but just to give them a scare."

"Maybe he had one of the black wenches in the weeds," Wilhelm said, grinning slyly at Lars.

"Wilhelm," Victoria Bodker said, twitching at the corner of her mouth. "Please. Anna is here."

Wilhelm wiped at his mouth with his napkin and reached

out to pat Anna's knee. "Excuse me, my dear. I did not mean to make you blush." He turned again to Johanna. "May I have more stew, my dear? Your slaves are excellent cooks."

Victoria Bodker pulled at a piece of meat, making the fork hit against the china plate in fast taps. "The meat could have been cooked longer," she said.

"Anna, your plate has hardly been touched," Johanna said. "Aren't you feeling well?"

Anna shuffled the piece of meat between her teeth and began chewing. She swallowed, forcing it down. "I am tired tonight. It has been a very hot day. Don't you agree, Johanna?"

"Yes, very hot. Why, look at the time we had taking my dress off." She giggled. "It was so warm today my dress was stuck to me."

Lars looked at Anna. For the last few years he had cursed himself for not waiting a little longer before choosing one of Wilhelm Bodker's daughters. But Anna was aloof. He felt that she would never give him an opportunity to make advances. Nevertheless, she was pleasurable to look at. He was glad that Johanna wanted her in the house so much. "Well, dear sister," he said to Anna, "I noticed you were out there to see me punish that slave. What did you think of the way I handled it?"

Anna folded her hands in her lap and dropped her head. "You were very brave," she said, her voice barely audible. It was exactly the words she had heard Johanna say and Lars had always been pleased.

"You should remain in the house when the slaves are being punished," Johanna said. "If they try to resist, they might harm you. The next time, you come in the house with me."

"Don't you worry about that," Lars said. "I would not let those savages put a finger on you, Anna."

Anna raised her head and looked at Lars. He was smiling at her. He was half drunk; his eyes were very bloodshot and some gravy from the stew clung to a corner of his mustache. Anna felt sick. She forced a weak smile and turned back, taking up her fork and putting another cube of meat in her mouth.

"Johanna was telling me you gave this savage a good beating," Wilhelm said. "I hope he doesn't die, like that

101

devil did on me last year." He bent his head closer to the plate and stuffed a large piece of potato in his mouth.

"I doubt it," Lars said. "He is young and very strong. There are a lot of good years left in him. I would hate to have them wasted."

"Yes, I suppose so," Wilhelm said. "But the council would agree with punishment of death if you stick to your story that he was running away. They'd reimburse you."

"But I didn't buy him. He was born on Hendersen . . ." He paused. "The council is very close with the money they reimburse for our legal losses. They would give me practically nothing for a young slave born at Hendersen." Lars gave Wilhelm a knowing glance and added, "As you know, if it weren't for the money, I'd be very happy to see the last of this particular slave."

Wilhelm returned the glance and returned to his argument.

"We pay our special taxes for this very purpose, Lars. You know that the two of us would be very strong with the council. We could no doubt make money on his death." He twirled the thin stem of the crystal goblet in his fingers. "Come to think of it, maybe it would be better if he died. We could present the case to the council and get enough money to buy *two* slaves when the next trader arrives."

"That's one way of getting some of our tax money back," Lars growled. "Taxes. We work our fingers to the bone out here on this miserable island to fatten the King. They tax everything. Lady," he yelled at the house servant, "bring some rum in here!" Lars looked up bleary-eyed at Wilhelm. "But you have a good idea there, Wilhelm. Why don't we pick out the poorest of our black wretches and plan to do them in, all at one time. We'll tell the council they grouped up on us and tried to attack our families. That way we can get rid of the undesirables and have enough money to replace them with new ones."

Wilhelm leaned back in his chair. "An idea, Lars. It has possibilities." He sucked on a tooth, making a loud noise. "We had better wait until your brother dies, however. A scandal of this type would spread through the islands. We would not want any opposition—especially from a Hendersen."

Lady brought another decanter of rum and put the cigar box on the table.

"Come, my dear," Madame Bodker said to Anna. "Let's

go into the parlor. I brought you a new dress tonight. It's that beautiful fabric your father bought last month. You simply must stop wearing those cotton dresses *all* the time. Why, do you want people to think I don't attend to you properly?" She walked behind Anna's chair. "Oh my, your hair is a mess." She turned to Johanna. "Can't you do something about her hair?"

Johanna looked at her mother blankly. "Well, never mind," Victoria went on, "you're as helpless as she is. It's all my fault. I've never taught you girls how to dress your hair. There, that's something we can do this Sunday afternoon. I will give you lessons in how to do each other's hair."

Johanna pushed her chair back. "Mama," she whined, "you know I have to rest in the afternoon. Ever since my confinement . . ."

"Damn the confinement and that woman talk," Wilhelm yelled. "You women get out of here so we can talk business."

Johanna's mouth fell open. Victoria stared at her husband, her mouth twitching. Anna hurriedly pushed herself from the table and walked out of the dining room. Behind her, she could hear her mother say, "We are leaving soon, Wilhelm. You know I do not like to travel at night unless we have a moon. And it has threatened rain all evening."

Instead of going into the parlor, Anna went to the porch and sat down. Below, in the clearing, there was no activity. The blazing fire over which Bahbu usually cooked her evening meal was not lit tonight. Other fires, now only embers, were dimly visible in front of several huts. Overhead, the stars faded from view—then returned—and faded again. Behind the mill, the sky lit up with heat lightning. There was a distant rumble of thunder from the direction of Puerto Rico.

Victoria, hearing the thunder, called out, "Come, Wilhelm. It is going to storm." A pause. "Anna?" Her footsteps hit the wooden floor of the porch. "What are you doing out here, child? The wind is chilly tonight. I can smell the rain. You'll catch cold."

"The lightning was terrible, Mama," Anna said. "You and Papa had better hurry. It would worry me if you were caught in a storm."

"Wilhelm, come, dear. It looks very bad out here." Victoria turned back into the house. Anna could hear her heels clicking briskly on the mahogany floors. From the dining room she could hear muffled tones. Finally, her father's weary voice.

"Yes, my dear. I am ready." He walked out on the porch, Lars following.

Lars put his hand out and supported himself against the door frame. "Johanna," he mumbled, "I am going to bed. You see your parents off. It has been a bad day for me."

Their horses were still tied in front of the greathouse. Wilhelm assisted Victoria onto the horse's back. She sat sidesaddle. With effort, he swung his heavy torso up into position on his own horse. Waving and calling good-by, they rode off.

"Now, little sister," Johanna said, "you go to bed. As tired as I am, I will have to stay with the slaves. They might break my good china."

Gratefully, Anna went upstairs. She stopped in front of the master bedroom. Lars was snoring. He must have fallen in bed with his clothes on, Anna thought.

Later, in bed, Anna could hear Johanna come up the stairs and then stop. She would be turning the lamps down, moving from one to the next, then the third and last. The door to her room opened and closed. A high wind suddenly sprang up. Anna got out of bed and closed the louvers on her windows. When she got back in bed, the room lit up with a flash of lightning immediately followed by the heavy roar of thunder. Then the rain came down in a pounding torrent, as if the clouds had aimed their full capacity at the plantation. Anna went to the window and tilted the louvers so she could look out. She could not even see the vacant overseer's house next to the manor. A flash of lightning. Raindrops pounded down on the hard dirt surface of the clearing. A rivulet of water ran from the house toward it. There was not a sign of life. Why did it have to storm? Johanna was such a coward about lightning. If she became frightened, she would come in the room and visit, maybe for hours. Anna returned to bed and pulled the sheet up to her neck feigning sleep. As suddenly as it began, the rain stopped. Waiting, listening for some noise, Anna remained with her eyes closed. It seemed to her that hours passed. Finally, she got up and looked out of the louvers. The stars were out, blinking sharply overhead. There was a streak of light in the sky directly over the mill where the moon hid behind a thin cloud.

Prince was stretched out on his stomach in Bahbu's hut. Bahbu and three other females crouched around him chanting in deep, whispered voices. Bahbu looked up when she heard the door of the hut open. Anna moved swiftly inside and closed the door. She had on a black cape over her nightdress. A heavy braid of blond hair fell down her back.

Bahbu got up and went to Anna, who stood leaning against the closed door. "He will live," Bahbu said, "if he does not die of fever. He has good spirit."

Anna looked at the three women crouched around Prince. "They are talking with our gods to bring him health," Bahbu said.

Bahbu turned around and spoke in dialect to the women. They got up from the dirt floor and left. "I will go and watch for Master Lars or Mistress Johanna. If you hear me making noise at Tando's hut, leave."

Anna moved slowly to Prince's side, horrified by the raw, bloody welts across his back. Her head felt light.

"Anna?" Prince spoke softly.

There was a silence.

"Anna, come, speak to me."

Anna dropped on the dirt floor. Putting her face next to Prince's on the mat, she sobbed. Her noise filled the hut.

"No, Anna, don't cry." Prince moved his hand until he found Anna's head. His fingers caressed her hair. She moved closer to Prince, until he could feel her wet, cool cheek against his own.

"I love you, Prince," she said softly.

His deep voice spoke out. "Anna, Anna, do not say it. When it is said, when it is out in the open, they can kill you. Bahbu has warned us. You know the law. I would not want to live if anything happened to us. And there is a mission ahead of me. I cannot leave with you until the thing is done."

"What is the mission? What is it that keeps us from being able to speak our hearts and make an escape from this horrible life?"

"It is the gods. They have picked me to lead our people against the white men. It takes a long time, Anna. For nineteen years Bahbu and Mary have been organizing our people. When the time comes, we must be ready. It must be carefully planned so the cannon and muskets are outnumbered by our black bodies. Do you understand?"

105

"Yes—yes—I can see it."

"Anna," he whispered.

"Yes?"

"If I cannot be free to live with you, I would rather die. But I must fulfill this task. I do not want to turn you against your people—not your family. When the time comes, we will save them. Bahbu and I have agreed to that." He was quiet. Then he added, "Master Lars is not your family. That is part of my mission. The gods have appointed me to kill him."

"If we can be free, I do not care who you kill. They are not my family any more. You and Bahbu are my family. I knew that today when you were beaten. As Bahbu says, the gods have colored me wrong. I do not think like the white people."

"But you are white, Anna. We cannot have each other until the black people are free."

"Prince," she bent over him again, "do you love me?"

Prince pushed himself upward on the mat. Beads of sweat covered his forehead and surrounded his mouth. He reached out and took Anna's hand. "Love you, Anna? I cut the cane for you. I plant the seeds for you. I get up in the morning with your name on my tongue. I go to my bed with Anna in my heart. I yearn for you as my people yearn for their freedom. Do you know how I suffer, not being able to touch you? Only the fear of making a baby and having you killed because of the laws is bigger than my love for you. Today," he went on, his voice thick with emotion, "when I was beaten, it could not wipe out the pain in my heart. I did not care that he beat me. I wanted the whip to stop this other, bigger pain."

"Oh, Prince," Anna moaned. "What can we do? Can't your gods help us?"

"Our love has been spoken of now. It is something the gods gave us. But we must not speak of it again, or kiss, or touch. I do not trust myself. Until the revolt is over, you must be patient about our love. For us, there is no future until we are free. I cannot betray my people. Every slave on this island knows of the omen. It is written in the necklace Bahbu wears. But when the revolt is over—when we are free—we will be together without fear. So, it is worth waiting for."

Anna moved her face closer to Prince's. "I will wait, Prince. I promise you that I am yours."

Prince leaned forward, his lips almost touching Anna's. "I am yours, Anna. I promise." Prince saw that she wanted him to kiss her. "Go, Anna," he said gently. "Walk out of the hut and leave me. Our time will come. My nineteenth birthday is a day I will remember for all of my life."

It had taken four years before the first cane was put in the earth at Hendersen Estate on St. John. First there had been the high trees and heavy bush to clear, then the dividing of the plantation into timber land, pasture, and garden, then the construction of the housing and factory areas. A large garden for food was planted. Then came the arduous work of collecting stones, carrying lime and water, and cutting planks. The slave village went up, then a simple greathouse for Jan. Stone by stone the house and then the boiling, curing, and distilling factories took shape. When the giant windmill was complete, Jan and his slaves hoed the land in even furrows, three feet apart. Finally the cane cuttings were set to grow.

During these years Jan had buried his grief beneath long hours of toil. Because he knew that a visit to Hendersen on St. Thomas would only bring back painful memories of Christina, he had made that trip only once in four years. He had stayed at the old house only one night, glad to depart after settling the necessary business matters with Lars.

It had, by Jan's accounting, cost 16,850 rigsdalers v.c. to establish this new estate. After three more years, when the cane had taken root and Jan was satisfied with the results of his investment, he sent word to Lars that he wanted to meet with him again, this time in Charlotte Amalie, to discuss further financial arrangements.

When the company's brig on which he sailed entered the mouth of the St. Thomas harbor, the three stone towers of Frederiksfort[1], the Skytsborg[2] and Christian's Fort, became visible, the red and white Dannebrog flying high from each. At this distance the red roofs and white walls of the small buildings looked like scraps of cloth left scattered on the ground when the flags had been made. Jan had mixed feelings about these trips to St. Thomas. His eyes moved west, past the town, toward Fortuna. It was

---

[1] Now called Bluebeard's Castle
[2] Now called Blackbeard's Castle

hidden behind the hills. He was sure that he had made the right decision in not going to Fortuna for this meeting with Lars. Christina was there. And yet, she was not.

Once ashore, he noticed the heavy, sweet smell of fermenting molasses hanging over the town. He looked toward Contant. It must be coming from the distillery up there. Even the smells of the island made him ache for Christina. He pulled his straw hat lower on his forehead and walked down the dusty road toward the tavern.

Blinded by the shade in the tavern, Jan hesitated at the door. There were two Danish soldiers standing at the bar. They looked curiously at Jan. "A St. John planter," one said to the other. "They all look alike. They haven't been there long enough to look prosperous." The other nodded and turned back to his drink.

Lars sat at a table in the corner of the sour-smelling room. His head was bent close to the man beside him, his back to the door.

"Then it's a bargain," Lars said.

"That it is. We sail out of the harbor at sundown tomorrow night. There'll be a long boat at Fortuna Bay, just after dark. I'll pay you as soon as the rum is loaded."

Lars sat back and raised his glass. His companion clinked his glass against Lars's. They drank.

"Am I interrupting?" Jan asked.

Lars looked up. He shoved the chair back and leaped to his feet. "Jan!" He put his hand on his brother's shoulder. "My God! I'm sorry I missed your arrival. My friend here—" He turned. The man stood up. "Captain Davis, this is my brother, Jan Hendersen."

Captain Davis smiled vaguely and stepped out from behind the table. "I'll be getting back to my ship now." He slapped Lars on the back, nodded at Jan, and walked out of the room.

"Sit down," Lars said, pulling out a chair for Jan. "You look well, brother. How are we progressing on St. John? Rumors say that your plantation there will be richer than Fortuna in five more years."

"The soil apparently likes the cane. The crop looks good," Jan said. He took off his hat and threw it on the chair beside him. Pushing his hair back off his shoulders, he glanced at Lars. "And how is the plantation here?"

"Good enough. The sugar production is holding up. I

don't know yet about this year's rum. The company has dropped its price again so I doubt if we'll make much at all. They have us cornered." He shrugged his shoulders. "But there's nothing we can do about that."

"No, I suppose not."

"Here's the accounting." Lars reached into his jacket and pulled out a folded sheet of paper. He smoothed it flat on the table and shoved it in front of Jan.

Jan's eyes ran quickly down the sheet. "Your rum production was really off last year, eh, Lars?"

"I tried a new experiment. It didn't work. I ruined some."

"Nothing wrong with the process I taught you." Jan leaned forward, putting his calloused hands flat on the table on either side of the paper. "Is there?"

Lars leaned back in the chair and looked straight into his brother's eyes. "No. Not at all. And there's nothing wrong with trying new ideas once in a while either." His mouth set in a hard line.

"You wouldn't be trading with the British smugglers, would you?"

Lars's face reddened. "Damn it, Jan. Are we going to start fighting again? You're accusing me of cheating you!"

Jan stared at the paper. Accusing him, he thought. He must think I'm a fool. He would have had to spoil fifty per cent of the rum production to come up with figures like these. Yet he bought the same number of barrels and staves as he did other years when rum figures were up. Of course he's cheating me. He glanced quickly at Lars. Lars's mouth was still set in a tight line. What difference, Jan thought, carefully scanning his brother's face. I suppose he has to keep up with the Bodkers.

He looked back at the paper. "No, I didn't come to St. Thomas to argue with you," he said to Lars. "It appears I will be self-sufficient on St. John. I didn't spend as much money on the plantation as I had anticipated. Unless by some act of God I do not harvest next spring, there is no need for me to take a share of the plantation here. You won't need to account to me in the future, Lars."

"You mean you don't want any of the Fortuna profit?"

"None." Jan raised his glass and looked over it at Lars. "You're not my young brother any more." He sipped on the drink. "My God, this rum is bad. 'Kill devil' indeed."

Lars smiled. Now the main obstacle was past. Sure, he

traded with the British smugglers. Why not? They offered a hell of a lot more money for Hendersen rum than the West India Company. He didn't actually mean to cheat Jan. But if he didn't have receipts to show from the company, how could he list all the sales of the rum? Jan was just a victim of circumstances.

"How is your wife?" Jan said.

Lars shrugged his shoulders again. "Ever since she lost the child, she has been ill. I think it is more self-pity than anything else. She looks healthy enough."

"There's enough work up there to keep her busy. She shouldn't have time to feel sorry for herself."

"Johanna doesn't do much work. Her sister is living with us now. She takes charge of the details at the house. She reminds me of Christina."

At the mention of Christina's name, Jan stood up. Taking his hat from the next chair he said, "Let's go to the blacksmith's. I have to place a good-sized order before I can harvest in St. John." He picked a coin out of his pocket and threw it on the table. "I hate to spend money on bad rum like this," he said.

It was late afternoon of the next day when Lars's strange procession came down the rocky incline to the beach at Fortuna. The mules were harnessed in pairs, carrying the casks of rum on poles between them. Lars rode in front, picking his way on the precarious path, shouting orders over his shoulders. Prince and Tando and two other Negroes drove the mules. They shouted and coaxed and yanked at the harnesses as the animals balked and kicked on the treacherous path.

Reaching the beach, Lars dismounted and walked along the water's edge, searching for the channel in the coral reef just off shore.

"Drive those mules over here," he shouted. The animals stepped clumsily on the pebbly beach. Reaching Lars, the Negroes unloaded the barrels. Then they sat down on them, knowing that it would be dark before their work continued.

When it was night, the longboat stroked toward the beach, taking a straight course for the lantern Lars held to guide them. Captain Davis leaped out on the beach as the boat ran in on a wave. Three sailors jumped into the water and pushed and tugged the boat up on the beach. There they tipped it on its side.

"Roll that hogshead over to the boat," Lars shouted at Prince.

Accustomed to the loading process, Prince and Tando set their weight against a barrel and pushed it toward the boat. At the gunnel the barrel stopped. Prince and Tando set their bare feet in the stones and sand and put their weight and muscle against the cask. It had just begun to move when Prince lost his footing and slipped back. He heard the crack of leather and then the whip crashed down on his back. He clenched his teeth and put his strength to the barrel. Slowly it rolled over the gunnel and fell into position inside the boat. The four slaves and three sailors moved into position along the gunnel and heaved the boat upright.

It was just past midnight when Captain Davis handed the pouch of coins to Lars and joined his crewmen on the last shuttle to his brig. "I will see you next year, Lars Hendersen," he shouted from the boat. "That is, if the sea robbers don't interrupt my plans."

The slaves got on the mules and walked them up the mountain. Lars followed last, a loaded musket on his lap. A strong wind moved inland, rustling the tangled bush along the side of the narrow path. An almost full moon hung over Fortuna Mountain. By its light, Lars could see the fresh welt across Prince's back, glowing white against the background of healed scars.

Prince had his eyes fixed on the mule in front of him, but his every sense was alerted to the man who rode behind him. The wound smoldered in a long ribbon across his back. The night wind blew over his skin and he felt his flesh go cold. He tensed. He did not know if it was the wind or the presence of Lars directly behind him that had made his body tremble. He pressed his elbows tight against his rib cage and took a deep breath. He looked up at the moon. Yes, my gods, he thought. When I fulfill my mission in life, Lars Hendersen will never put the whip to a black man again.

Lars saw that Prince had tensed. He knew by the slant of his head that he was looking at the moon. Damn heathen, he told himself, they really think there are a bunch of black gods up there.

111

Prince heard Lars's snort, but he did not turn. Experience told him that Lars was nervous in the field at night with the slaves, any sudden movement might cause him to raise his gun and fire. The other three felt it too, so they all drove their mules quietly, tapping their heels into the warm mule bellies.

Lars twisted in his saddle and looked back. The English brig was gliding through the Virgin Channel toward the colony of Massachusetts with her cargo of muscavado and rum.

1733

Chapter 10

The drum noises started at sundown. By midnight the pulsating noise was not that of a single drum, but of many. The one that was nearest Fortuna put out a fierce, patterned boom, while those in the background, as far as the easternmost tip of the island, rumbled like a chorus of deep male voices.

Lars rolled out of bed and lit the lamp on the table beside him. Talk of insurrection was now persistent, whispered at every gathering. Even those planters most hardened to the island's constant rumors had begun to feel their confidence undermined by the gnawing fear of revolt.

Johanna sat up. Squinting against the light, she said, "Why are you getting dressed? You're not leaving the house? I'm afraid!"

Lars tugged at his tight breeches. Time and rum had taken their toll on his physique. He struggled, trying to button the waistband. "Damn! Why don't you work on my clothes? They all need to be let out. If you got up and did some work, maybe you would not feel so poorly all the time."

Johanna threw herself back. Burying her head in the pillow, she sobbed, "You don't care if they kill me."

Lars jammed his arms into a soiled shirt. "Don't act so foolish. Of course I care."

"You don't care. You *don't!* You're going to Bordeaux and drink with Papa. I know!"

"Say what you want. I'm going to the field and see if I can't stop this damn drumming. If you're frightened, go to Anna's room. She's not afraid."

Hearing Lars's heavy footsteps go out of the room and down the steps, Johanna slid her fat body over the side of the bed and hurried toward Anna's room. Opening the door, she whispered, "Anna, are you awake?"

"Come in," Anna said.

Johanna slammed the door behind her and turned the key in the lock. "Light the lamp," Johanna whispered into the darkness.

When the glow of the lamp filled the room, Johanna, clutching at the front of her thin nightdress, sat gingerly on the edge of a chair. "I am going out of my mind, Anna. Those drums! What if the slaves mean to kill us? We're out here in the country with no protection. Papa and Lars could not hold off all those savages. Aren't you frightened, Anna?"

"Why should I be frightened? I haven't hurt the slaves. I can see no reason why they would want to hurt me."

"Nor I, Anna. You know I wouldn't harm a slave." Her round face expressed pious innocence, her mouth and eyes diminished by the white circle of fat around them.

"Don't worry, Johanna. The militia will be on guard tonight."

"Militia, indeed! Lars told me today that they were gathering at Bordeaux this afternoon, drinking with him and Papa."

Anna picked up a brush. Pulling her hair around her shoulders, she stroked it vigorously. "If the militia is irresponsible, it's half the fault of Papa and Lars. They are always encouraging the men to drink with them. Papa should have gone into politics."

"Has it occurred to you that perhaps because of their generosity to the militia we may be better protected than anyone else on the west of the island if there is a revolt?"

Anna began to braid her hair. "Then why are you so frightened? When we were young there was no militia. You weren't frightened then." Her long fingers moved deftly, twisting the three heavy strands into an even braid.

"But look how the island has grown," Johanna said. "Why, there are over one hundred and fifty plantations on St. Thomas now. When we were young, there were not one quarter as many!"

"It is a little late to be worried about the increase in plantations and slaves, isn't it?"

"Anna," Johanna raised her index finger, "just tonight Lars was saying that the company may discontinue their slave trade. I overheard him and Papa talking after dinner."

"Oh? And were Papa and Lars in favor of it?"

"Heavens no! They said they would vote against it. I'm just telling you this to point out that the company is aware of the problem."

Anna secured the braid with a ribbon and let it fall across her shoulder. "Nonsense. The company—and the planters —will only discontinue the slave trade if they find it unprofitable. No one is worried about the welfare of the slaves. You know this, Johanna."

"Well, I should hope not. Who said anything about the slaves? It is *us* we have to worry about, Anna. If they keep importing these savages from Africa in the numbers they have been bringing them here, we will be so outnumbered that they will obviously get the upper hand." She looked at her sister, who had now crawled back up on the bed. "Anna, there are three or four blacks to every white man now. Don't you find this frightening?" Anna shrugged. Johanna went on, "You've always been different, Anna. You don't worry about our problems. Sometimes I think you don't live in our world at all. Why, I have never heard you voice an opinion about anything. It's Mama's fault, always telling us that women should not have any voice in important affairs."

"What is so important that I should voice an opinion?" Anna settled back against the headboard and looked down at her sister. The drum noises filled the room and dominated her thoughts. Tonight was Prince's twenty-fifth birthday. And this is the birthday omen. I wonder what the drums are saying. They have never before been so bold— so many at one time. Anna could visualize the individual slaves crouched in the bush on many plantations, defiantly talking to their people. Tando would be out in the bush talking for Hendersen. It was a joke among the slaves that since his fingers were cut off he drummed better than he had before. Anna smiled, picturing his big black hands caressing the face of the drum.

Johanna's thin, plaintive voice broke in on Anna's thoughts. "Could I sleep in here with you?"

Anna had known her sister would ask. Johanna was afraid of everything. And no wonder. She got such enjoyment out of watching the slaves being tortured that every slave on the plantation hated her. What could she say to Johanna? Yet, Anna was determined to meet Prince tonight no matter how frightened Johanna was. She had to know what the message was. Maybe the revolt would begin soon.

"I think I'll go outside for some air," Anna said. "It is very warm tonight. And I have a headache. Would you like to sit on the porch with me?"

"No—not on the porch. Why, that is not safe tonight."

"Well, I'm going," Anna said. She jumped out of bed. "You can lock yourself in, Johanna. I won't be long. When I come back, I'll knock."

"Do you have to go outside tonight, Anna? With all those horrid drum noises?"

"Yes," Anna retorted. Throwing her black cape over her arm, she went out of the room.

Outside, Anna cocked her head, listening to the drumbeat that filled the air around her. She tried to pinpoint the direction the Hendersen drum was coming from but the wind carried the throbbing vibrations. Maybe it was coming from the high ridge. She tilted her head. Now the throbbing seemed to be on the other side of her, toward Botany Bay. She leaned to the right. No, it came from behind her, somewhere between Bordeaux and Fortuna. She ran further into the clearing so the greathouse would not block the vibrations. There, it seemed as if the noises were coming out of the half-moon that shone overhead. Behind the moon, the stars threw off uneven flashes of light, as if they were being jarred by the beat of the drums.

"Anna," a voice came out of the darkness. She turned her head. Bahbu was standing in front of her hut.

"Bahbu, where is Prince?"

"At the cave."

Anna grabbed Babhu's hand. "What do the drums say, Bahbu? Tell me."

Bahbu looked up into Anna's face. Anna was now much taller than she, as straight and as tall as Mistress Christina had been. "Go to the cave, Anna. Prince will tell you. The news is good. It comes from Mary."

The years had not changed Bahbu. She was still thin— and her face was ageless. Anna could still make out the lettered brand that had been burned on Bahbu's shoulder when she was a girl, partially obscured now by the drawn and puckered scars of the whip. Bahbu had often been beaten for practicing witchcraft. Although her most sacred rites were performed undetected in the cave, she had been caught twice boiling the herbs for special teas, three times

116

drying leaves that would be ground into powder for the fires, and once hiding a worn shirt of Lars's. Although Lars's increased drinking had relaxed his vigil in the field, when he did catch a slave at a forbidden thing, he spent his drunken anger on him more violently then he had at an earlier time. Anna put her hand on Bahbu's shoulder. "The drums are exciting, Bahbu. Do you find them so?"

"Yes," Bahbu grunted.

"Will it be soon, Bahbu?"

"You are still a little girl," Bahbu said. "Soon. But that is all I tell you. Go to Prince."

Anna put her cheek against Bahbu's. "Thank you," she whispered.

As she peeked from the window, Johanna's mouth fell open in astonishment. She continued watching as her sister broke away from Bahbu and ran out of the clearing with her great black cape flying out behind her.

On the top of the ridge, Anna stopped. A strong wind blew off the sea into her face. Below, the sea was patterned by the clouds, and Crab Island glowed in a patch of moonlight. It is an omen, she thought. It represents our freedom. Hurriedly, she ran along the ridge to the rock.

When she reached the hiding place, Prince was standing outside. "Come inside, Anna. The message is very good. We must talk. The time is getting very near."

Inside, they sat close to one another, their eyes drawn to the patterns of light and dark on the sea before them. The noise of the drum seemed louder here, as if it echoed against the back wall of the cave. "That is the drum at Perseverance," Prince said.

"How can you tell?"

"It has a deeper tone than ours."

"Where is Tando? I tried to pick out the direction of our drum, but I couldn't. It sounded all around me tonight."

"Tando is in the east field. He can watch for Lars from there."

"Tell me, Prince, what do they say?"

"Mary sends word that the slaves in St. John are organized. She says there are very few white men there and that the overseers drink too much. Mary says the revolt will begin in St. John and the gods say I will be there to lead it." He turned to Anna. "That is why the drums are busy tonight. They defy every planter on this island, to let Mary

117

know that the black people in St. Thomas are with them."

"I can *feel* it, Prince. It is all around us. Even Johanna. She knows that tonight the drums are different and is very frightened. Lars went out. Bahbu says he has gone to Bordeaux. I suppose he and Papa will get drunk again." She laughed. "When they cannot catch a slave to punish him, they get drunk."

"They will not catch the drummers tonight, Anna. When so many drum noises fill the air, they will never find the drummer."

"I know it—I know it—oh, Prince, I am so happy tonight. We are very close to freedom—and being together. I cannot believe that the time will come when we do not have to hide." Her voice dropped. "Prince, how will you get to St. John to lead them? It sounds impossible and it's so hard for me to think of you leaving me, ever." She reached out to touch him.

"Please do not make it so difficult for me." He stared back at her, his shadowed eyes burning into hers. He saw that she was about to cry.

He threw both his arms around her, rocking her against his shoulder. "Do not cry, Anna. We do not have long to wait."

"Just keep holding me in your arms," she said. "I think if I don't feel your warmth and strength, I might die."

Prince pushed her back gently and wiped the tears from her face. "Now—that is better. Come, I will let you rest on my arm." He stretched out on the hard earth and pulled Anna down beside him. With his hand, he placed her head on his shoulder. "There. Now, Anna, let us make believe. Talk to me. Tell me a story."

"Once there was a very evil King . . ." Anna began.

Outside the cave her words were covered by the booming of the drums. The moon glided through the feathery clouds. Below, the sea ran up on the white sand beach at Perseverance Bay and darted back from where it came with the whispered noise of running pebbles. The trade winds swept up the face of the mountain, shaking the dried weeds that clung tenaciously to the steep incline. Back at Hendersen, Johanna was hunched in a round ball on the bed, trembling with fear and planning her discussion with Papa.

Lars was seated alone at the table when Anna entered the

dining room the next morning. "Good morning, Lars," she said. When she pulled her chair back and sat down, Lars did not get up. Anna looked at Johanna's place. "Where is Johanna?" she asked.

"Riding," Lars answered. He picked up a piece of bread and smeared it with guava jelly.

"Riding! Don't tell me Johanna is serious about getting more exercise."

"It's about time," Lars said. "She has gotten much too fat—that is, for such a little one."

Anna poured a cup of coffee from the silver pot in front of her. Lady appeared beside her with a pitcher of cream and a bowl of brown sugar on a silver tray. Anna took some of each and smiled at Lady. "And what of your paw-paw jam, Lady? Have you made some?"

"Yes, mistress," Lady said. "I get it." She moved noiselessly out of the room.

While Lars and Anna ate, Johanna was having her breakfast with Wilhelm over at Bordeaux. "The food *is* better here," Johanna said, cutting into her second egg with her fork. "Mama says it's only because I'm accustomed to these slaves. But you have always had everyone here properly trained. Why, they are so spoiled at Hendersen, they would burn the eggs and think nothing of it."

Wilhelm pushed his chair back and patted his stomach. "Yes, the house slaves were spoiled when Christina was alive. I always said that would happen. And once you've let a slave get the upper hand there is no way of changing him, you can be sure of that." He pushed further back in the chair. "I must get out in the field, Johanna. Some say the land is producing less because we have overworked it. I say it is that the slaves are getting lazy."

"Papa," Johanna put down her fork and wiped her mouth with a white linen napkin. "May I have a word with you?"

Wilhelm frowned. "What is it, Johanna? You can speak here."

"No, Papa. What I have to tell you is of a—ah—it is a dire matter, Papa. And we must be in complete privacy."

"Then come out on the porch. Your mother will not be dressed for another hour."

Once on the porch, Wilhelm pulled a cane-backed chair over next to his rocker. "There, my child. Sit down. You look very warm this morning."

"Oh yes, Papa," Johanna wiped at her forehead with a perfumed handkerchief. "It is much cooler at Hendersen. You get no breeze down here by the sea." She leaned forward and stretched her neck so she could look up to the south. "Fortuna Mountain catches all your wind."

"Yes, yes," Wilhelm mumbled. "Now, my dear, what is it?"

"Well, Papa, I do not know how to begin. You must prepare yourself for a shock." Seeing that her father was curious, she leaned forward and whispered, "I believe, Papa, that Anna is plotting the revolt with the slaves."

"What?" Wilhelm's voice rang out over the plantation. He shot up out of the chair, letting the rocker slam back against the wall.

"Shhhh," Johanna put her index finger in front of her lips. "I told you, Papa, this is an important matter. Do you want to have every slave on Bordeaux eavesdropping on us?"

"They wouldn't dare," Wilhelm shouted. "What's this you're saying?"

Johanna flounced her skirts again. "Now, let me tell you, Papa. Last night—you know how the drums were beating? Well, I was afraid. And Lars, poor thing, had to go out in the field and look for the drummer. Well, Papa, I was so frightened I went to Anna's room. We talked a little—you know, as women do. And let me tell you, some of the things she says are so bad that if the King got word of it, he would have her beheaded!" Johanna leaned closer to her father's scarlet face. "She says that the Negroes are human!" Johanna saw the color ease to a more normal red in her father's face. "And she once told me that she would like to dance with the male slaves." The scarlet color sprang back into Wilhelm's face.

"What! Are you telling the truth, child?"

"Yes, Papa. But wait, let me tell you what happened last night. She insisted on going outside. She said she had a headache. I *know* she was pretending. You know, Papa, I've had so many headaches since my confinement that I *know* when someone has a headache. The symptoms are—"

"Get on with your story," Wilhelm shouted.

Johanna pulled upright in the chair. She carefully folded her hands in her lap and looked straight out in front of her.

"Excuse me, my dear," Wilhelm said, taking Johanna's

120

hand. "I didn't mean to frighten you. It's only that you have me so concerned. You understand that, don't you, my child?"

"Yes, Papa, but you upset me so, I forget what I was saying."

"You were saying that Anna insisted on going outside. What time of night was this?"

"It was past midnight, Papa." Johanna leaned forward again and dropped her voice. "She knew I was frightened, but she refused to stay with me when I asked her to. After she left, I locked the door and got in bed. But the drums were so noisy I became increasingly alarmed. Finally, I summoned up enough nerve to sneak to the window and look out. There, Papa, in the clearing, was Anna—with Bahbu. They were laughing. And then, Papa, you will find this very difficult to believe, she put her arms around that ugly black woman and put her beautiful white face against that ugly woman's black face. She hugged and kissed her, Papa!"

"Ach!" Wilhelm's blue eyes darted back and forth across Johanna's face. "My Anna. What is she thinking of?"

"But, Papa, that is not all."

Wilhelm dropped his fist onto his knee, keeping it clenched. His eyes continued darting around Johanna's face. "Yes, yes, go on," he urged.

"She ran off, Papa. Up the hill. But she was not only running, Papa. She was skipping! She was keeping time to those horrid drum beats. Just like the slaves."

Wilhelm let out a great burst of air in another "Ach!" He leaped up from the chair and paced back and forth on the porch.

"Papa, you'd better do something. Lars says this woman she was hugging is always practicing witchcraft." Johanna struggled out of the chair and walked over to her father. "Maybe she put some kind of spell on Anna. What else could it be, Papa? You know Anna *does* act peculiar. Why, Papa, she is twenty-four. An old maid. Many men have tried to court her, but she always remained aloof. Maybe she *is* sick, Papa."

"She has to be. What other explanation could there be?" He took his daughter by the shoulders. "Have you told your husband of this?"

Johanna shook her head no.

"Then I will ride to Hendersen with you and discuss this

121

with Lars. He will have to decide with me what to do."

Lars was in the lower field when Wilhelm found him and related Johanna's story, almost word for word.

"I cannot believe this," Lars said. "Why would Anna join a revolt against us?" He turned in the saddle and faced Wilhelm. "You don't think that Johanna may be jealous? You know, Wilhelm, your youngest daughter is very beautiful. Maybe Johanna suspects her sister does not marry because she—eh—you know—perhaps Johanna imagines that Anna is enamoured with me."

"Have you given her cause to believe this?" Wilhelm snapped back.

"How could you suggest such a thing? It's only that Johanna *could* imagine such a thing. You know Johanna has not been well since . . ."

"I know. Since her confinement. But why do you think Anna has not let any young men court her? You think it's normal for a woman to reach twenty-four, a woman as beautiful as my little Anna, and not be interested in acquiring a husband?" Wilhelm's eyes flitted back and forth, studying Lars's expression. "And what of her hugging that black wench Bahbu?"

"I can't believe Anna would take part in a revolt against the whites," Lars said. "Johanna may be jealous that Anna is not afraid of the increased rumors. But since Anna was a child, she never showed any fear of the black people. She has never spent much time with them, no more than Christina did—or many other white women on this island have. It's a woman's nature to feel sorry for these people, like they would for any animal. We have never had reason to suspect Anna before. Why do we panic now? It's only because of the unrest on the island that we are wary."

"We can't completely turn out backs on what Johanna says. We must take *some* action!"

"Yes, I suppose you're right," Lars said. "But what? That black wench Bahbu. She's been trouble since the day she arrived on St. Thomas. A planter who buys an Amina is a fool. She was another of my brother's foolish whims!"

"Then why don't you send her to your brother?" Wilhelm said. "Let him have the misery."

"I suppose I could. But Jan will be angry with me if he sees her scars. She is always plotting some witchcraft, and I have beaten her several times."

"And what if he does complain? You don't see him often

enough for it to matter. Come now, you can stand on your own against an old man, can't you?"

"Of course, I can."

"Well, then?"

"She will go and let Jan worry about her witchcraft."

"And that fair-skinned son of hers. What of him?"

Lars glowered at Wilhelm. "What *of* him?"

"Send him too. You know Aminas don't like to be separated from their family. With things as they are, you don't want your slaves stirring up more trouble that could be blamed on you, do you?" Wilhelm's eyes settled on Lars's face. "Or have you special reasons to keep him here?" His tongue darted out and wet his lips.

"He will go, too," Lars said. "I am sick of both of them." He jammed the heels of his boots into the soft belly of the horse and rode up the hill. Wilhelm followed.

When the dust had settled, Tando crept from the rows of cane. Seeing the horses disappear out of sight, he began running. If he hurried, he could reach Bahbu in the high field. She should be there now, giving the slaves their morning food.

"Anna, Anna," Bahbu's whispered voice, laden with urgency reached Anna in the parlor where she was hemming a dress. Anna threw the dress aside and ran to the louvered window. Bahbu's face was raised up to the open slats. "Listen carefully, Anna. I do not have much time. Where is your sister?"

"She is upstairs," Anna whispered.

Bahbu's fiery eyes were outlined by the two wooden slats they peered between. "Your sister has told your father that you are one of us."

Anna gasped.

"Anna, listen. Do as I say. They are going to send us away. A long time ago, before Mary was taken from Hendersen, she told us that Prince would cross the sea—and that his mother would be with him. So we knew before last night. We have been ready. You must guard yourself in our absence, Anna. That is why I have come to you now. Be careful of your sister."

"Bahbu, I cannot bear to think of you and Prince leaving me."

"This is the beginning of the revolt. You and Prince

have looked for this." Bahbu put her hand up to the necklace. "It is said that Prince will kill his father."

"His father," Anna gasped. "I thought the omen said he would kill Lars."

"They are one, Anna."

"Bahbu, how horrible!"

"Good-by, Anna. Be careful of Master Lars."

With these words of warning, Bahbu's face disappeared from between the slats. Anna ran across the room and threw herself on the settee.

"Why, Anna, what *is* the matter?" Johanna entered the room and scurried over to the settee where Anna was sewing.

"Matter, dear sister?"

"Your eyes. Have you been crying?"

"No, Johanna. I think my eyes are getting weak. This fine hemstitching has set them burning."

"Here," Johanna took the dress from Anna's hands. "Give me the needle and thread. Let me do it for you. You know, my eyes are very good."

"You are very kind to me, Johanna. Thank you."

"It's nothing. Now go upstairs and freshen your face. It will soon be time for lunch. We are having a nice chicken stew. You like that, don't you, Anna?"

Anna stared at Johanna's pudgy fingers moving back and forth. All white people are evil, she thought. Why is it that the gods colored me so? She looked down at her arm. The skin was tanned, however, a much richer tone than the sallow white of Johanna's. If only I could color myself permanently, she thought. The sound of Lars's footsteps on the porch interrupted her thoughts. She sat up straight.

Lars did not enter the parlor. Instead, he went up the stairs.

"See," Johanna said, raising the skirt of the dress in front of her. "It's finished. When Lars comes down, we can eat. Lady—Lady—" Johanna pulled herself off the settee and tripped across the room. Anna got up and followed her. Johanna turned around. "Are you sure you don't want to freshen your face?"

"I am very hungry," Anna said flatly. "Let's go eat, dear sister. Doesn't the stew smell delicious?"

Johanna raised her nose in the air, sniffing. "My, it does

smell good. Come along. Lars will be down any minute now."

"Johanna," Lars's voice carried into the parlor. "Will you and Anna wait for me? I have something I must discuss with you."

"We were just going into the dining room," Johanna called back.

"I will not have time for lunch. I am coming right now." He clumped down the steps. "Now then." He strode past them into the parlor. "Come, ladies, sit down. I would like to have a talk with you."

Lars had on a clean white ruffled shirt and tight black breeches. He had changed his boots for a pair that were highly polished. He swiped at the stained corners of his mustache. Anna noticed that the gray hairs took on a darker brown than those that were still blond.

Johanna plopped down on the settee. Anna purposely chose a chair from which she could look at both Johanna and Lars, a brocaded curved-back chair that was deep and comfortable. Lars pulled a caned-back chair up, preferring the higher seat so that his pants did not bind too much.

"Johanna, I will be leaving today for two or three days. Something has come up that I must go to St. John."

"St. John, Lars. What of the drums? What of the revolt?"

"Now, now, little one. Do not let your imagination run away with you. There is no revolt." He looked solemnly at his wife. "Now, my dear," he reached between his legs and pulled the chair closer to Johanna, "I am going to take several of our slaves to St. John. They are the ones who are the cause of the drums. At least I believe this to be so."

"Why don't you punish them?" Johanna said.

"Because I am not entirely sure, Johanna. And I do not want to be unfair."

Anna dropped her eyes. Lars turned around and looked at her. "It is this Bahbu. And her son, Prince."

Anna raised her head. Her calm blue eyes settled on Lars's face. Inquisitively, she raised one eyebrow. From the corner of her eye she could see that Johanna had her startled expression again.

Lars's eyes moved slowly over Anna's face. "Bahbu has been the cause of much unrest here at Hendersen. She has been beaten four or five times for practicing witchcraft, but she will not stop. And her son! He has caused trouble ever since the night of his birth. There are some who say he thinks he is their Christ. Can you believe *that?* Well, you know these blacks are a superstitious lot. But if only a few of the slaves believe it, Prince could make trouble. And his mother, she's an Amina. They are all incorrigible."

Lars noticed that Anna's face remained calm. Johanna must have been wrong, he told himself. Anna does not care about these people. Aloud, he continued. "I wanted to talk with you two women to advise you that I will be gone from the plantation. In case you are worried about being here alone, your father says he will come up and spend the night with you if you desire it."

"I should hope so," Johanna sighed. "I couldn't sleep at night if those drums pounded as they did last night. I was very frightened. Wasn't I, sister?" She put her head coyly on her shoulder and looked at Anna.

"Much too frightened," Anna said. "I went out and spoke to Bahbu. I asked her what the drums were saying."

"You did?" Johanna exclaimed. "What did she say?"

"She said it was her son's birthday and the drums were celebrating."

Johanna slumped back on the settee. Her chin dropped into her neck. "Is that *all* she said?"

"What more do you expect, Johanna?" Anna said, her voice even. "I believed her. In fact, we both laughed about it. I ran up on the hill. The drums didn't sound angry. It sounded like a very happy beat. Don't you think so, Lars?"

"Happy? I never think of those damn drums as sounding happy," Lars replied. "I hate them. The slaves have no right to put a hand to a drum, and they know it."

"Your brother used to let them dance," Anna said. "We could hear the drums at Bordeaux. They sounded happy then. I'm only saying that I think there is a difference in the sound of some drumbeats. We would all be wise to listen. If these people are planning a revolt, the drums most certainly would sound angry."

"You listen to the sound of the drums, Anna," Lars said. "I'll look for the drummer!" Dropping his voice, he said, "Tell me, you aren't afraid to go out at night and talk with the slaves?"

Anna shrugged her shoulder. "I would not be afraid of Bahbu. She is a thin, frail woman, who couldn't hurt me.

126

And she is feeble-minded. Witchcraft indeed! I don't find her frightening. I feel pity for her, that's all."

"Well, then, you don't mind if I take her to St. John?"

"Why should I, Lars?"

Lars raised up from the chair. "No reason. It is just that I like to think of the welfare of my two women. If either of you objected, I wouldn't take them away."

"I'll be glad to see her go," Johanna snapped. She wrinkled her nose. "She is an evil black witch."

Anna remained silent, looking calmly at her sister.

"Come along," Lars said. "You can say good-by. They are ready now. Johanna, have Lady take my baggage out to Prince. We will be going on horseback. I hope to reach town in time to take my boat to St. John before dark."

Johanna and Anna stood side by side at the edge of the clearing. Johanna's billowing red silk dress dragged on the ground. Anna's pale pink cotton dress was shortened so that her ankle-high white shoes showed. She looked like a young girl who had outgrown her first long dress. The midday sun blazed down on their heads.

A group of slaves had gathered together. Now a murmur of voices broke their silence. Bahbu walked into the clearing. Behind her, Prince was walking between other slaves, balancing a large bundle on his head.

Anna stepped forward and moved over to Bahbu. She put her hand out on Bahbu's shoulder and said, in a clear voice, "Good-by, Bahbu. I wish you a good trip and a healthy stay in St. John."

"The drum will sound when we reach," Bahbu whispered. Louder, she said, "Good-by, mistress."

Trying to appear casual, Anna passed by her and moved in front of Prince. She looked up into his amber eyes and held his stare. "Good-by, Prince," she said. Somehow, she managed to keep her voice even.

Anna was so close that Prince could smell the light, flowery scent that was always hers. Her lips were parted, ready to speak again. He ached to pull her to him, to put his lips to hers and stop the words. "Good-by, mistress," he said softly.

The resonance of his voice lingered in Anna's ears. Dropping her eyes, she turned and walked away from him. Behind her, she could hear Johanna's high-pitched voice, "Now you be a good slave for Master Jan, Bahbu."

Anna continued walking, her broad shoulders squared and her head held high. She could not stand the sound of Johanna's shrill voice. She longed to retrace her steps and throw herself into Prince's arms. Prince watched her walk away. When she came to the front steps of the manor house, she moved up them effortlessly. Without looking back, she continued on through the archway and into the shadows beyond.

Unconsciously, Prince's foot moved forward to follow her.

"Come along," Lars shouted. He was in the middle of the clearing, holding the reins of two horses. Prince's eyelids closed. Anna, Anna, I do not want to leave you, he thought.

"You've wasted enough time," Lars said. A whip cracked over Prince's head.

Lars swung into the saddle. Prince went to the other horse and put his hands down so that his mother could step up and straddle the bare back. When she was in place, he put the bundle in front of her. Going back a bit, he leaped up, throwing one leg over the horse and settling astride it. He put his arms around Bahbu and took the reins. His bare heels tapped the horse's belly.

Lars spurred his horse and rode up beside them. "You ride in front," he said to Prince. The group of slaves ran along beside them, calling good-bys. The voices and noises increased as they neared the gate. From behind, Bahbu heard a male voice yell, in dialect, "Prince, we will follow you." And then another, "Do not forget the drum, Bahbu."

Lars halted his horse with a quick jerk of the reins. He turned in the saddle and looked back. The group fell silent, stopping in a scattered pattern behind them. He let his eyes roam from face to face. He turned around and walked his horse out of the gate.

Chapter 11

Jan was awakened by a pounding on the door. In the darkness, he went to the window and called out, "What is it? Who's there?"

"Open up," Lars shouted. "It's your brother."

Lars saw the light flare up in the bedroom. Soon, Jan unbolted the door and threw it open. "What brings you here at this hour?" Jan exclaimed. "Is something wrong at Fortuna?"

"No," Lars said, moving past him. "Nothing important." He looked around. "Where are the lamps?"

Jan beckoned Lars to the door leading to the parlor. Jan went into the dark room. The light from the candle lit up his face, shadowing the deep wrinkles and giving his silver hair a high sheen. Lars noticed that his brother was thinner than he had been a few years ago. And he was very erect. He looks as though he'll never die, Lars thought.

An oil lamp was lit. Flame and smoke shot up in the glass globe. As Jan adjusted the knob, the flame settled down into a straight yellow line. Lars, seeing a decanter and glasses on the high, round mahogany table in the center of the room, poured himself a drink. He took a mouthful, let the liquid roll around his mouth, and swallowed. "Ahhh— you still make the best rum on all the islands. Will you join me?"

"Yes," Jan answered. He moved on to another table and lit another lamp.

Adequately lighted, the parlor came to life. It was a simple room, the furniture all in rubbed mahogany, the chairs all caned. The high, flat ceiling was wooden planked and the floor a dark red tile. Except for the brocaded furniture and rich colored woven rugs at the greathouse on St. Thomas, the room had the same feeling of comfort. Lars liked the room. It suits me, he thought. I'll enjoy it when it is mine. If the time ever comes! He watched his brother sit down in a rocking chair. He is agile, as always, Lars sighed to himself.

"Now, what brings you here?" Jan said. He looked at his brother, seeing him now for the first time in over five years. Jan was not pleased with what he saw. He had seen too many identical red-eyed, puffy faces and the same thickened waistlines on too many planters who enjoyed too much of their own rum.

"To be honest with you, Jan, ever since you left Hendersen, I've had trouble with Bahbu and her son." He took another swallow of rum, looking at his brother over the rim of the glass. Bringing the glass down, he said, "They grieved when you left St. Thomas. And they've never taken orders from me since." Lars watched his brother. Jan's eyes appeared to have become a deeper color with time— or was it the bronze of his leathery skin that made them appear so? Lars went on, "In fact, not long after you left, Prince tried to run away. But he had promise of being a strong worker, so I spared his life."

"That was decent of you," Jan said.

Lars stood up and walked back and forth in front of Jan, looking up at the ceiling. "Look, Jan. I'm not here to make explanations to you of how I oversee Hendersen. Tonight I've brought you Prince and Bahbu. They are incorrigible. I've had to beat both of them repeatedly." He stopped and looked at Jan. "And I'm not a damn bit apologetic for doing it. You don't know the trouble they've caused me." He paced the room. "I decided, with conditions as they are on the islands, that it would be best to bring them here to you. Within the last six months there have been twenty-two runaways on St. Thomas. No matter how firm our laws are, there is a belligerent attitude possessing the slaves of late that is frightening. I don't want the militia running up and down looking for Hendersen runaways."

"No, I suppose having to punish the slaves if they were caught would be distasteful to you, wouldn't it, Lars?"

"Damn it, Jan. I'm not here to argue with you. I brought you those two slaves because I don't want them. And that's that."

"It's just as well," Jan said.

"Aside from that, if this drought we're having keeps up, half the slaves on the island will starve. How are you faring here?"

"Poorly," Jan said. He stopped rocking and took a swallow of rum. "I think it is already too late for rain to save much of the crop. It is going to be a bad year."

"We'll lose a lot of money," Lars said.

"Aside from that, it will make the slaves more restless. If they are well fed, they are happy. Remember that, Lars. If their gardens are ruined, spend money with the traders. Get food to those people if you don't want them to run away."

"Yes, yes," Lars said impatiently. "I'll see that they're fed."

"Where are Bahbu and Prince? I would like to see them."

"Tonight?"

"Yes, tonight. It has been some time since I have set eyes on them. I can still remember how thin Bahbu was when we brought her to Hendersen. Has she fattened up?"

"She will never fatten up. She is as thin and black and ugly as she was the day you bought her." Lars threw his glass up to his mouth and finished the drink. "They had found Mary's hut when I was at the door. I could hear them talking in that savage language." He pulled the lid off the decanter. "If it's all right with you, I'll go to bed now. I would like to leave early in the morning. Johanna is frightened. I have to admit, there *is* something unusual in the air lately. And the drums. My God! Did you hear them last night?"

"I never hear them any more," Jan answered. "I suppose I've gotten accustomed to them. The bed is ready in the south room, Lars. I'll see you in the morning before you leave."

Jan, in slippers and nightshirt, walked out into the night. The house on St. John was closer to the working village than the one on St. Thomas. He liked being near to the factories, mill and slaves. Outside, in the cool night air, he could hear excited voices coming from behind the slaves' quarters. Unlike Hendersen Estate on St. Thomas, here the clearing where the slaves cooked and congregated was back of their huts, affording the slaves a measure of privacy.

Bahbu, squatting beside Mary, looked up and saw a white figure gliding toward them out of the dark. She stared. Could it be Mistress Christina returning? No, it

131

was her master, exactly as she remembered him the day that mistress had died.

Jan was bent forward, picking his way on the earthen path. His long white nightshirt and silver hair were blown back by the wind.

"Master Jan," Bahbu called out. She jumped up and ran toward him. A few feet from him she stopped and dropped her head.

"Bahbu." Jan walked up and threw his arms around her. Then he took her shoulders and moved her back. "Let me see you, Bahbu. Uh huh"—he squeezed her bony shoulders—"you have not changed. Not a bit. Now raise your face and let me see you." Bahbu obeyed. "You *do* look the same," he laughed. Under his fingers, he felt the welts. Bahbu felt his fingers move back and forth over them. "It's good to have you with me again, Bahbu," he said gently.

"It is good to be with you," Bahbu said.

"And what of Prince? Where is he?"

"Here I am, master," Prince's deep voice raised out of the crowd that had gathered. He stepped forward.

Jan looked out eye to eye with Prince. He could hardly believe how strong and handsome the young man before him was. Jan put out his hand. Prince looked at it. He smiled and put his own hand into Jan's. Carefully, Prince squeezed. Jan smiled. The laugh wrinkles around his eyes and mouth were very deep lines. "I knew you would grow into a strong man," Jan said. "But I did not think you would be this big. Here, turn around, let me look at you. You have the broadest shoulders I have ever seen on a man." He let go of Prince's hand and turned him around. Across his back, from the place where his thick neck ran into his wide shoulders, all the way to his narrow waistline, there were the telltale scars of the whip. Jan pushed on Prince's shoulders, moving him around so that they were face to face again.

"Now, then," Jan spoke out loudly, "we have something to celebrate here on St. John tonight." He paused. "Come to think of it, we had better celebrate it tomorrow. Tomorrow," he raised his head and talked to the group that was clustered around him, "you will have a day of celebration. King," he looked at one of the men, "in the morning slaughter a goat. Your only duty is to get the men together and water the gardens. Mary, gather what food you can

132

find. Have a feast. We welcome Bahbu and Prince—they come from Hendersen on St. Thomas."

A great murmur of excited voices stirred up, some in dialect. The word "Prince" was easily discernible.

"Yes, this is Prince," Jan said proudly. The noise increased. "Now, here," Jan called out. "No drums. We don't need Captain Von Beverhoudt bringing the militia."

Mary, standing in the front of the group, nodded her head.

"Good night," Jan said. He turned and walked away from the gathering.

When he came to the front of the slave huts, he saw Lars waiting for him. "What are you doing here?" Jan said.

"I only walked out for some air. But tell me, Jan, what in God's name are you doing, talking so intimately with slaves? You know we're on the verge of a serious insurrection."

"What do you mean, 'intimately'?"

"You lead those savages to believe it's a joke to have the captain of the militia call on you. It's unheard of to confide in slaves, even if you believe such foolish things."

"Listen, Lars, I've watched you, and other planters just like you, until I am sick throughout. I wouldn't blame the slaves one damn bit if they revolted. Each year becomes worse. The prosperous traders send a group of drunken overseers to care for their plantations because they are too rich to dirty their own hands in this soil." He pointed to the parched ground. "These slaves, these savages, as you call them, have sweated and worked and put their lives into this soil to make it produce. They are my friends and I will talk with them in any manner I see fit." His voice rose to a threatening pitch. "Do you understand?"

"Jan, control yourself."

"I am *tired* of controlling myself. I control myself when the council meets. I control myself when I see these poor wretched people being beaten to death at the fort. I have controlled myself ever since I brought you here from Copenhagen. And I am *not* controlling myself any more. Get out of here. I don't give a damn where you go, but get off my land right now."

Lars clenched his fists and watched his brother out of sight. "When you die . . ." He strode off toward the corral.

133

At the hut directly behind the place where the argument had taken place, King and Prince, both with their backs stretched flat against the wall, looked at each other. King nodded his head toward the clearing in the back. "Master Jan is safe," he whispered. The two of them moved off noiselessly.

"It is true what Bahbu says," Prince said. "Master Jan has been colored wrong. He is one of us."

"Of course he is," King grunted. "There are a few on the island who have been colored wrong."

"How many?" Prince asked.

"I do not know. But when we meet in the big field at night, some tell of their masters who are colored wrong. My good friend Christian, slave of Dr. Bodger, tells me his master is a good man."

"You meet often?"

King nodded. "We are cautious. But the white men drink too much rum at night. They cannot catch us." King passed Prince. "Come. I go beat the drum. Mary says to send a message of your safe arrival."

Late the next afternoon, Wilhelm and Victoria rode up to the greathouse at Fortuna. Johanna was sitting on the porch, fanning herself.

"Papa, Lars has returned," she said.

Wilhelm assisted Victoria from her horse and the two of them came up on the steps. "Returned?" Wilhelm said. "He made good time."

"He returned very early," Johanna said smugly. "His dear brother was very difficult again. He made Lars leave in the middle of the night, Papa." She stopped fluttering the fan and leaned forward. "Isn't that dreadful?"

Victoria's busy fingers patted at the bun on top of her head. Satisfied that the loose strands had been tucked back in place, she sat down beside her daughter. "My, everyone is so irritable lately. It must be the drought." Quickly she looked up at the evening sky. It had turned a bright pink from the fiery red ball that hung behind the greathouse. "And no rain in sight." Victoria fluffed and pulled at her skirts until they were suitably arranged around her thin ankles. She opened a fan and shook it in front of her face.

"It's very hot, Mama," Johanna whined. "I wish it would rain. You know how I mind the heat in the summer."

"You are too fat," Victoria snapped at her.

Johanna opened her little round eyes as wide as they would go. "You know, Mama, ever since my confinement I've not been well enough to get proper exercise. What can I do about it?"

Wilhelm, who had sat down on the other side of his daughter, stood up. "Where is Lars? Still abed?"

"No, Papa, he walked over to look in the cisterns. He says we will have to stop watering soon."

"We stopped this morning," Wilhelm said. "If this drought continues, we'll need water for the family. No sense in letting the water get too low."

Lars approached and quickly walked up the steps. "Hello, Wilhelm," he said. "Come sit in the parlor where it's cooler. I'm thirsty as hell." Turning to Victoria, "Good evening, Victoria. Will you ladies excuse us? I have business to talk with Wilhelm."

Once seated in the parlor, Lars poured their drinks. He was saying, "Jan has become even more impossible than before. We both know he spoiled the slaves when he was at Fortuna, but he is even worse on St. John. I can't describe the deplorable conditions that exist there. When I arrived at the fort, the sergeant looked at Bahbu and Prince and said, 'More drummers for Jan Hendersen's plantation, eh?' So you see, Wilhelm, word is around on St. John about my dear brother's lax attitude."

"Perhaps we could get the council to take some action against him?" Wilhelm suggested.

"The council wouldn't take action. There are too many of the planters who are weak-spirited and taken to spoiling their own slaves, thinking that if they are good to the savages it might save their own hides if we have a revolt. And Jan pays a good amount of taxes. The governor would side with him because of it."

"Yes, Jan has always had an eye for good soil," Wilhelm said. "His cane grows by itself, no matter how lazy his slaves are."

"Well, that's not what I want to talk about. I'm concerned about a bigger problem right now. What if this old fool were to turn against me and give his plantations to the company? It has been done before, you know."

"My God!" Wilhelm gasped. "You don't think he's senile enough to do something *that* foolish, do you?"

"Who knows. He's unpredictable. However, I have a plan. When the harvest is over, we will take the family over to St. John for a visit. The women may mellow him. Anna has a very gentle way, and she would no doubt remind Jan of his dead Christina." Lars lowered his voice. "If we handle ourselves correctly, we can mend fences with the old man."

Wilhelm's eyes twinkled. "You're very clever, Lars. And the women would enjoy the trip. Why, my little girls have never been off this island. When they were young, I took them turtle fishing. They were both seasick," he laughed. "I hope Johanna doesn't remember that."

Hearing that Lars would soon forbid them to use water from the cisterns for their gardens, the slaves worked feverishly that afternoon. Three male slaves handled the donkeys, leading them to the cisterns where they filled the copper-lined reed baskets on either side of the animals. Then they filed back to the gardens where six women ladled out the water into smaller containers and moved between the rows of vegetables. The garden was brown. The leaves of the vines were curling up, some already brittle from the burning rays of the sun.

Anna watched the slow process that was going on before her. When a ladle of water was put on the earth, the ground changed color, a jagged dark circle spreading out under the plant. Almost instantaneously, however, the dampness disappeared and the earth returned to a drab, light brown. Only a hard rain could quench this soil's thirst, she thought. She looked up at the sky. Again it was cloudless. The white ball of sun looked harsh against the solid blue around it. Bomba came up beside Anna. Age and hard work had stooped his shoulders so that he was bent over. He stood silently for two or three minutes, watching the women pour the water on the withered plants.

"It's not doing much good," Anna finally said.

"We have done everything, mistress. Every night we loosen the soil so the night water can collect there. But it does not help."

"The dew is heavy here. Keep trying. But I suppose the earth is too dry underneath, Bomba. Oh, why doesn't it rain?"

"We ask our gods for rain. They do not listen." Bomba lifted his face and squinted against the sharp rays of the sun. "They have a reason, mistress. Our food is withering up before our eyes. It has never been this bad before. Not

136

even when the big wind came and broke the plants." He turned his head and looked up at Anna.

She noticed that the whites of his eyes had yellowed with age, his eyes appearing almost all brown now. She put her hand on his shoulder. "Yes, there is a reason, Bomba. In time, we will know." She turned off and moved away from the garden.

The cane fields had never looked so uniform before. The furrows between the plants were clearly defined. She saw the men walking along the ruts, leaning over, their strong bare backs exposed to the sun as they searched for any weed that had survived the drought. She passed by the rows, occasionally waving when one of the slaves looked up. When she reached the top of the high field she stopped and looked out toward St. John, remembering the first time she had come here. It was hazy between St. Thomas and St. John, the outline of the other island being very faint. The sun's rays reflected off the calm sea, creating a thin veil of light that was harsh on her eyes. Anna raised up her arm and waved. "Prince . . . Bahbu," she called out.

It made no difference now if she walked directly to the cave. The top of the rock was just visible from where she stood. Anna looked at it for several moments without moving. I cannot go there without Prince, she thought. She kicked at the ground, covering her white shoes with dust. Sinking to the ground and putting her face in her hands, she burst into tears.

Finally it rained. But the gardens that had provided the slaves with their food had already given up in their struggle to survive the drought. The rain poured down on the hopelessly cultivated plots of land, turning the hard earth to a soft mass of mud that let the remains of the sun-hardened stalks slide down against the wet earth. The majority of plantation owners, reluctant or unable to buy provisions for their slaves, let them run loose at night to forage for food.

Many of the slaves on St. John turned to the Hendersen Estate at night. There, Hendersen slaves shared with them the food their master purchased for his people. But Jan could not feed all of them and, as a result, they all went hungry, including his own. A minimum of one hundred slaves gathered every night in a field at the top of a hill behind Hendersen. Mary worked with them as she had always done. In the center of the clearing she had her

137

small fire on which she was throwing the powders, chickens' feet, and small bits of cloth the slaves had brought for her. Around her, the restless people waited for the gods to speak. Stationed at five or six strategic points, sentinels watched for the militia.

Tonight Mary was mumbling more urgently than usual. Her lips moved in and out over her toothless gums, letting the mutterings escape as a constant hum. Bahbu squatted beside her. Prince stood directly behind them, his arms crossed against his wide chest. He was so hungry he felt hollow. Tonight Master Jan had given them each an extra portion of salt meat. But when it was shared with the others it had not satisfied the gnawing in his stomach.

A chicken's foot was on top of the fire. Prince noticed the thin claws were curled in tight, toward the shriveled flesh on the charred leg. Suddenly it fell through the weakened support beneath it and disappeared.

Mary raised up. She turned her back to the fire and looked out at the shuffling shadows in the night. Her hand raised up. "Hear. The gods say it is very close to the time. Did not they send this drought to make our bellies ache and move us into action?" Her voice rose. "While the white men stuff their faces with food, they turn us loose to starve to death in the field. Look around you at this earth and what do you see? The cane is dead. Our food is dead. And what do we have to eat? We worked this land for the white men. Without us they would not now have the gold to buy their food. That gold is ours—not theirs. We made that gold for the white men with our hands." She put her gnarled hands out in front of her. "With no sugar this year, there will be no gold for them this year. The white men beat and abuse us even when it is not possible to give to them. The gold should be ours. We gave them these plantations. There is not one among us who did not lift the rocks—or carry the water and wood and lime. Then we dug the soil and put in the cane. We pulled the weeds, we cut the cane, we carried the cane to the mill. We ground the cane and made the juice, boiled it and made the sugar and the rum. And when it was done, the white man took it to the dock and got the gold. That is all they have done— collect the gold. Now that we are hungry," she dropped her voice, which cut the night air in a whispered hiss—"they spend our gold on their own stomachs, and let us die in these empty fields."

There was a murmur of angry voices. King stepped up beside Mary. He was a short, stocky man. His muscles were heavy bulges in his forearms and legs. King raised his hand for silence. "Mary speaks the truth. There are those who still remember when you lived in your own villages and ate the food you grew and lived in the homes you built. We did not give it to our neighbor if our neighbor was an evil man, did we?"

The crowd inched forward. "Noooooooo," they moaned.

"Then let us take back what is ours. These plantations. This land. When we have gotten rid of the white man we will live in peace. We will be rich, as they are now. We will share with each other and have enough so that our bellies are never empty."

The crowd surged forward. From somewhere a male voice yelled out, "Let Prince speak." King stepped from beside Mary and moved into the crowd. Prince unfolded his arms and stepped next to Mary. He faced the crowd of shadows.

Prince's resonant voice boomed out over the crowd. "If we are to succeed in driving the white men from the island, our plan must be well organized. When the gods send word for us to take action, we will not have time to repeat our plans. Let me talk of them now. You, King, will send word on the drum. The company's slaves will go to the fort. They will overcome the guards. When the fort is taken, fire two cannon and hoist the flag. When this happens, every slave on St. John will join his brother and kill the white men. Together we cannot be stopped."

"What of the cannon and the muskets?" one voice said fearfully.

"They do not have enough cannon or muskets to kill us all," Prince went on. "It is better for a few to die to save us all than to live on like this. We are agreed on that. So let us hear no more talk of that." He raised his hand, signaling for silence. "Let us remember, we have agreed not to kill the good white men, those who have been colored wrong. Each of you will know when you hear the signal that the time has come. Those of you who have good masters, send them to the sea. Let them take their boats and go off to Tortola. Or to St. Thomas, if they want. When we have captured St. John, when the white men are all driven off, our people in St. Thomas will follow our example. Before the next planting season, every plantation on St. John and St. Thomas will be in control of the black man."

A great noise swelled up. Prince called out, "Stop. We do not want the militia here tonight. Each of you knows your job. The omen may come at any time. And when it does, when you hear the signal, take up your cane knives and rid yourselves of the white men. Go to your plantations now," Prince told them. "We will meet tomorrow night."

Slowly, the crowd dispersed and the shadows disappeared into the night. Soon, King, Prince, Mary and Bahbu were all who remained in the open field.

King paced back and forth before Mary, his every move revealing his impatience. "Why must we wait?" he said. "Our people starve. Another week, another month, and more will die. Why not rise up now and take food from the white men to put in our own bellies?"

"The omen must be fulfilled," said Mary.

"How can you talk of an omen?" King said, "when two small children died today, their bellies puffed with air and their limbs thin as cane?"

Mary rose from the embers of her fire and advanced menacingly toward King. "Without the omen, without the help of our gods, we are nothing. And the omen calls for Master Lars to die at Prince's hand. Master Lars must be on this island—then we will be given a sign."

Prince suddenly broke in between Mary and King. Placing both hands on King's shoulders, he held King's eyes with his own. "Be patient, King," he said. "Have faith in the gods as I do. Master Lars will be delivered here. And I shall kill him. Then the gods will favor us—and the revolt will not fail."

King nodded his head in reluctant assent and the group walked together down the slope to the plantation.

Chapter 12

The militia put out the word that Judge Soedtmann would address the planters on St. John on the morning of September 7, at Coral Bay. The Honorable John Reimert Soedtmann, St. John's magistrate, was the son-in-law of Governor Gardelin. Otherwise Jan would not have troubled himself with the journey. The meetings always end up the same, with the group dividing into two sides. The side I am on, Jan told himself, is too weak to fight the other. What is the sense of arguing?

Sixty-one planters and overseers were gathered on the lawn at the side of the fort. Judge Soedtmann sat on a makeshift wooden stand. On a small table before him there was a neat pile of papers. The group fell silent when the judge hit the table with his gavel and looked up. He spoke out: "I have here before me a mandate issued by our governor, Philip Gardelin, as of yesterday." There was a murmur of voices and the judge waited until they had subsided. "I am going to ask our captain of the militia, John von Beverhoudt, to stand up here and proclaim this mandate." The judge, dressed in a black cutaway coat, tight tan breeches, and elaborately ruffled white shirt, went to the edge of the platform and reached out his hand.

Captain von Beverhoudt, taking the judge's offer, grabbed his hand and leaped nimbly up on the platform. His shiny boots clumped on the boards, shaking the stand. The judge handed him a scroll of several sheets and went back to the chair behind the table. The captain's voice began. "Now hear this. By order of the Royal Council, dated September 6, 1733. The following mandate shall be proclaimed to the beat of drum three times a year." He paused and looked up. Seeing that the group of faces were turned up toward him, he looked back down again at the scroll. He hesitated. He turned and looked up at the wall of the fort. A soldier there began to roll a drum. The captain proceeded in a clear, deep voice.

"One: the leader of runaway slaves shall be pinched three times with red-hot iron and then hung. *Two:* each runaway slave shall lose one leg or, if the owner pardon him, shall lose one ear, and receive one hundred and fifty stripes. *Three:* any slave being aware of the intention of others to run away and not giving information shall be burned on the forehead and receive one hundred stripes. *Four:* slaves who steal to the value of four rix-dollars shall be pinched and hung; less than four rix-dollars, to be branded and receive one hundred and fifty stripes. *Five:* a slave who lifts his hand to strike a white person or threaten him with violence shall be pinched or hung, should the white person demand it, if not to lose his right hand. *Six:* one white person shall be sufficient witness against a slave and, if a slave be suspected of crime, he can be tried by torture. *Seven:* a slave meeting a white person shall step aside and wait until he passes; if not, he may be flogged. *Eight:* witchcraft shall be punished with flogging. *Nine:* a slave who shall attempt to poison his master shall be pinched three times with red-hot iron and then broken on a wheel. *Ten:* slaves shall not sell provisions of any kind without permission from their overseers. *Eleven:* no estate slave shall be in town after drumbeat, otherwise he shall be put in the fort and flogged. *Twelve:* the King's advocate is ordered to see these regulations strictly carried into effect."

The judge rapped on the table, stood up, and called out, "Now then, what have you to say about this?"

"It's about time we had some strong laws to protect ourselves," the overseer from the company's plantation Caroline called out.

"Yes," Peter Kruger shouted out. "Put more fear in their black hearts or we'll never control them."

A thunder of assenting voices filled the air. Jan, his head lowered, pushed through the crowd toward the stand. There, he put his hands up on the platform and swung himself up in front of the crowd. Judge Soedtmann stared meanly at Jan, not welcoming the speech he knew would come.

John von Beverhoudt leaped off the platform and stepped toward the crowd that had surged forward, putting his arms out to indicate they had gone far enough.

Jan did not signal for silence. He stood erect on the platform, his eyes moving over the faces of the men. The voices and scuffling noises faded out. Jan, nodding his head at a planter, called out, "You, Runnels. And you, Kruger," he nodded toward one of the men who had just spoken up, "and Zytsema and Charles and Suhm. *Most* of you. You're starving your blacks. You're too damned greedy to reach in your pockets and pay for food to feed them. You talk about the drought, and the hurricane, and the blight we have right now, but talk doesn't feed the people. They're here on this island, running loose at night, searching for scraps of food like a bunch of starved animals. All of you sit home in your elaborate houses eating the best foods money can buy from your silver and crystal services, while the people who have made it all possible for you are turned loose to die out there." He tossed his head in the direction of the fields behind him. "This mandate is the most sickening thing I have ever heard. Beat them, torture them, strike terror in their hearts. We don't need laws like this. We need to *feed* them."

"Your slaves don't look so fat," Kruger called out.

"Yes," Judge Soedtmann agreed in the ensuing silence, moving to the other side of the table. "What say you about that?"

"My slaves are emaciated because they share the food I buy with *your* slaves. That's what I say about that. All of us planters who are buying food for our slaves have the same problem."

"Jan Hendersen is correct," Dr. Bodger's deep, calm voice interrupted. "We couldn't fatten our blacks unless we bought enough food for all of them on St. John. I buy food. Look at my Negroes."

"We need laws like this and every one of us should support them," Runnels called out.

"Yes—yes—yes," the male voices lifted up, making it apparent that the majority concurred with the mandate.

"All right," Jan shouted out over the voices. "Keep on. You've pushed these starved people to the breaking point.

143

And God spare your rotten souls when you finally see what you've done to them."

"Get that old man off the stand," the overseer from Caroline called. "He buys drummers and witches, not slaves."

"Turn him over to the Royal Council," called another. "He speaks out against the Crown."

Judge Soedtmann moved to the back of the table. Taking up the gavel, he pounded on the table. The crowd fell silent. "Let us have some order here. Hendersen," he turned to Jan, "you've spoken out too often against the orders of our King. But you are an old man, and this time I'll let you off with a warning. Still your tongue!" A pause. "Now, get off this platform and let the sensible planters have their say."

Jan's hands clenched into fists. He dropped his head and turned toward the magistrate. Every face in the crowd was turned up. "Your honor," Jan said evenly, "you have heard the last from me. Of that you can be sure."

The voices sprang up again. The judge knocked on the table. Jan went to the edge of the platform, jumped from the back end of it, and walked away from the gathering.

Early in November, Jan received a letter from Lars saying he would be bringing his family to St. John for a holiday. They would arrive on Sunday, November 21, and depart on the following Thursday, November 24.

The night before their arrival, the drums were silent. No need to stir the militia, Mary cautioned. Soon there would be no militia and they could beat the drums without hiding in the bush. On the hill overlooking the field where the slaves gathered, Mary had called together in private council the eight men who would lead the revolt. There were two from estate Caroline, Christian from Dr. Bodger's estate, King, Prince, and three others from Hendersen. They were all Aminas. Now they were sitting in a circle in the dark field listening to Mary speak in their dialect.

"I do not need to talk with our gods tonight. Master Lars will be here tomorrow. That is their message. Tuesday is a favorable day for us to begin."

All eyes now turned to Prince, who began to speak in measured tones. "On that morning, you men of Caroline will attack the fort. After you have killed the soldiers, you will hoist the flag and fire two cannon. You, Christian, alert your master to leave as soon as you hear the cannon fire. Then take your people and join those at Caroline. Everyone at Caroline and around the fort must be killed. We must hold the fort. You, King, take our people to Judge Soedtmann's plantation."

King nodded. He said, "And I will have his head on a stake for everyone to see."

"This you will take time to do," Mary agreed. "The judge is an evil man to speak out so against our master. Make him die hard, King, for Master Jan."

"And the overseer at Caroline," Prince said. "Be sure you catch him, King."

King nodded. "It will be done."

"The poison, Christian. You have it with you?"

Christian handed Mary a small square of cloth. "It is here. It is very strong, Mary. Be careful."

"I will see to the people from Bordeaux," Mary said. She paused and looked at the packet. "I will put it in their coffee."

Prince looked at each of the men in the circle around him. "Now. You know the plan. We are organized on Caroline, Suhm, Hendersen, Kruger, and Judge Soedtmann's plantations. Once the white men are all gone, we will use Suhm for our meeting place. Do you all understand?" Eight heads nodded up and down. "Tonight we will tell our people that we are ready. The revolt will begin on Tuesday morning. On Tuesday night we will have a drum feast on Suhm plantation. Let every man gather the white men's cows and goats and chickens and take them there. We will not be hungry any more."

"And the gold, Prince. What do we do with it?"

"When we have taken the muskets and cannon, we will need the gold to buy powder. There are Spanish traders who will come. We do not have enough on this barren island to trade with. We will need the gold. The gold will be taken to the greathouse at Suhm."

"Now we go and talk with our people." Mary stood up. The eight men did the same. In the darkness around them, they could see hundreds of outlines. Many, too weak from starvation to stand, were spread out on the ground.

"Light the fire," Mary commanded. Christian ran forward to the large pile of straw and wood that had been collected. He kindled it. The flames leaped up into the air. Mary moved forward until she was clearly visible to all of the people in the field. "The gods sent their final word. Tuesday is the day of the revolt. All of you know who the leaders are. Follow them. When the cannons fire, you will kill the whites. At night we meet at Suhm. There a drum feast will take place. We will have so much food that no one will be hungry, ever again." There were some moans from the people on the ground. "There will be no more suffering. We will be free." Another burst of noise. Mary raised her arms. "Be quiet, my people. When the revolt is over—and the island is ours—we will never again be silenced."

Mary turned her head. "Bahbu, come." From the darkness, Bahbu came into the light of the fire. She moved up beside Mary. Mary reached over and took the amulet into her hand. She raised it up, so the light of the fire shone on it. "Twenty-seven years ago, by the count of the harvest season, the gods sent an omen to me. It is here, in this carving. The gods told me then that the evil white men must be killed. But they gave me a sign, a strong warning that it must be carefully organized. They took my only son away to show me this. But another Prince was given to us and it is he who you will follow tomorrow." Prince came out of the shadows to take his place beside Mary. Still holding the amulet, Mary peered into the darkness at the hundreds of moving forms. "The gods have said that Prince will kill Lars Hendersen. Not one of you but Prince is to raise a hand against that evil man. As the omen has declared, it is Prince who will free us of Lars Hendersen. Then the gods will smile on our revolt."

The next day, Hendersen Estate on St. John was busy with the activities of preparing for their guests. In the kitchen, Bahbu made a beef stew, adding the spices and herbs she had been carefully saving ever since learning of Anna's expected arrival. Mary and Prince stood at a table polishing the silver that had tarnished from long years in a chest.

"It is prettier black," Mary mumbled, holding up a shiny spoon.

"Everything is prettier when it is black," Bahbu said. Her voice held a happy ring. She was anxious to see Anna and could not hide it.

"Everything but Anna," Prince said. "She is the prettiest thing I have ever seen."

"Mistress Christina is the only pretty white woman I ever saw," Mary mumbled. "The white woman's skin is soft on their bodies."

"That is because they are lazy," Prince said. "Anna is not soft. She is like one of us, with strong muscles and a straight back."

"She can carry a pail of water on her head as good as I," Bahbu spoke out. "When she was young, we taught her. Anna was never like a white girl. One time she fell and cut her leg. She did not run home. She ran to me. And she kissed me when I put the pain killer leaf around her leg and told her it would heal." Bahbu looked at Prince and smiled.

"And I could not kiss her, Mary. Mama would not let me. She said if I kissed Anna, I would want to make a baby. And she was right. After the first time I kissed Anna, I could not kiss her any more."

"Then the white men would have killed both of you," Bahbu said. "When we are free, you can make many babies with Anna."

"We will be free next week," Mary said. "It is good for Prince to go out in the field with Anna tonight. He is restless."

"But she will be sent back to St. Thomas with Master Jan when the revolt starts. Who would be there to look after Anna until the slaves in St. Thomas are free and I can go to her?" Prince asked.

"Bahbu can go with her," Mary said. "Your mother is of no use to us. She is too thin to roam the fields and no good with the cane knife, you know that. She is a house slave. She should go back with Anna."

"Did the gods tell you that, Mary?" Prince asked.

Mary hesitated. "No, not yet. But I will ask them. Tonight."

"Mama," Prince looked up at Bahbu. "If Anna and I make a baby while she is here, will you go back to St. Thomas to care for her?"

"Yes."

"Ahh, that is good. Tonight I will tell Anna and ask her to meet me."

Later that afternoon, Bahbu was setting the table in the dining room when she heard the horses approaching. She looked out the window. Master Jan appeared first. Anna rode beside him. Bahbu ran out to the kitchen.

"She is here, Prince! Anna. She is here."

Mary stopped scrubbing a sweet potato. "What of Master Lars?" she whispered.

"I forgot to look. I was too excited when I saw Anna."

Mary glared at Bahbu. "See, you are no use for our plans. Being a house slave with Mistress Christina *did* spoil you."

Bahbu dropped her head.

"Mama," Prince grabbed her arm. "I go. I cannot look at Anna. I cannot hide my feelings. Tell her, Mama, to meet me behind the mill tonight after supper."

Bahbu nodded her head.

"Go," Mary commanded in a sharp voice. "We do not want to spoil our plans because you are in love." Realizing that her voice was very harsh, she looked up at Prince. "I remember when I was like that, Prince." She smiled. "Before Chief died of the fever."

Laughing, Prince ran out the door.

All of the people had dismounted in front of the manor house. King walked up and began to take the luggage up the steps. Watching him move, Lars found it difficult to suppress his anger. He hated the arrogance of King. It was in his bowlegged stride when he sauntered up the steps. If he were my slave, Lars thought, I'd pinch him. My God, it's going to be difficult to hold my tongue.

Standing back for the women to go up the steps, Wilhelm moved close to Lars. "Remember," he whispered, "guard your temper. It's going to be difficult for both of us."

"Come along," Victoria called brightly from the top of the steps. "You two are always chatting. Why, one would think you never saw each other on St. Thomas."

"Yes, yes," Wilhelm said. He moved up the steps. His long legs ached. The journey had been a rough one. They had gone against the sea. He wet his lips. They were parched from the salt water and the sun. "Some of this famous Hendersen rum will taste good," he said loudly as he moved into the parlor.

"Help yourself," Jan said, pointing to the circular mahogany table in the center of the room. "You men make yourselves at home. I'll find Bahbu and have her show the ladies to their rooms." He looked at Wilhelm. "My house slaves are not well trained. An old man living alone does not have much need for this."

148

"Yes, yes," Wilhelm spoke up, his voice cheery. "It's of no importance, Jan. Ahh, I think I can stand that rum now."

From the parlor they could hear Jan calling, "Bahbu—come."

In a short time, from the hallway, "Why, Bahbu," Johanna's shrill voice sang out, "how good it is to see you again."

Anna watched the fiery light flash in Bahbu's eyes as she looked at Johanna and nodded. Anna could feel her heart beat with excitment. Squeezing her hands together in front of her, she said, "Hello, Bahbu."

Bahbu dropped her head. "Hello, Mistress Anna," she whispered.

"Come along, come along," Victoria commanded, returning from the dining room where she had taken the opportunity to inspect it. She lowered her voice. "The house is very small, isn't it, Johanna?" She stepped back. "Go along," she said to Bahbu. "Show us to our rooms."

Bahbu passed the three women. When she was part way up the steps she turned and said, "Mistress Anna, you will have to sleep in the room at the head of the stairs."

"We are not interested in where you put us," Victoria said. "Just *put* us there. My, I'm very warm and sticky. It will be pleasant to change my dress. And my hair. Oh, the wind." She patted her hair.

Bahbu opened the first door. Victoria peeked in. "It's small. But it will have to do."

Anna passed by them. "Thank you, Bahbu," she said. She closed the door and put her back to it. Her heart was pounding so rapidly she thought she could not stop it. Prince—oh, Prince—where are you? she thought.

"Anna—" It was a faint whisper.

Anna gasped. The wide mahogany door of the press was opening. From it, Prince stepped out.

"Prince." She ran to him and threw herself into his arms.

"Anna . . . Anna . . ." He rubbed his hands in her hair "Oh, Anna, you feel good. And you smell good. As I remember you." He dropped his head down and pushed it tight against hers, squeezing her in his arms. Anna raised her face. Her eyes moved over his face. He watched her lips. Not able to stop himself, he kissed her.

"Bahbu." Victoria's voice pulled Anna to her senses. She

could hear the shuffle of bare feet stop outside the door. "There is no mosquito netting here. Bring one." The door down the hall closed.

"How are you going to get out of here?" Anna whispered.

"I go now, while Mama is in the hall. She can say I carried the luggage. I will meet you behind the mill. After supper."

Anna opened the door and peeked out. Bahbu was going down the steps. "Bahbu," she whispered. "Come back."

Turning, Bahbu ran noiselessly up the stairs and entered the room. Anna threw her arms around her and kissed her on the cheek.

Anna stood back. "You look so thin," she whispered. "Have you been hungry?"

"Everyone is hungry here," Bahbu answered. Then, "Prince, if you are caught in here, you will be hung. Come, while those women are in their rooms." She turned to Anna and smiled again. "Anna," she said, "it is good to see you."

When Anna entered the parlor, dressed for dinner, Jan was there alone. He stood up. "Good evening, Anna. You look very beautiful."

"Good evening, Mr. Hendersen," Anna said. She felt awkward.

Finally Jan said, "You remind me of my Christina."

"Thank you, Mr. Hendersen," Anna said. "I have been told that she was a very lovely woman." Anna studied Jan. His silver hair was slicked back, still moist with water. He was clean-shaven and the deep furrows in his sun-tanned face were pleasant to look at, especially around his sharp blue eyes. They made his eyes twinkle. He was amazingly strong-looking for a man his age. Now she knew why Papa and Lars complained of his good health.

"Sit down, my dear." Jan beckoned to a mahogany rocker. "This is the most comfortable chair in the room."

"I thought I might have a walk around the plantation before it gets dark. Would you mind?"

"No, not at all. I would enjoy showing you Hendersen."

"I would be delighted, Mr. Hendersen," Anna answered.

Jan put his arm out. Anna put her arm through his. "We have lots of time," Jan said. "The men have just gone up to dress. They like my rum." They went down the front steps.

"First, let me show you the kitchen. I designed this house in almost the same manner I built Hendersen on St. Thomas. Only smaller. My house is closer to the village out here." He looked in front of them. The factories and slave quarters ran on each side of the clearing. Behind it, raised up on a knoll, was the mill. "The mill is higher up. We don't get as much wind here as we did at Fortuna. Those two ridges over there, channel the wind through the valley. And over here," they walked around to the right side of the house, "I put the kitchen, as I did on St. Thomas."

They came up to the kitchen door. Jan looked in. "Oh, Mary," he called. "Can we come into your kitchen?" He turned back to Anna. "Come along. It smells good in here."

Anna stepped through the doorway. Inside, Mary continued stirring the stew. "Mary," Bahbu spoke out. "Anna is here."

Mary rested the ladle in the pot. Slowly she turned around. Her eyes looked up at Anna. Her mouth fell open. "Aiiii, it is as they say. You are like our Mistress Christina."

"Thank you, Mary," Anna said. "I understand she liked to work in the kitchen."

"She said I was a good cook, better than she could cook."

"And me, too," Bahbu said.

"When I was a little girl, one time Prince and I . . ." Anna stopped. Her face drained of its color. Jan took her arm. "I know that story," he said. "You and Prince would go on the hill and call to Mary and me. Bahbu told me about that."

"You know?" Disbelief rang in Anna's voice.

"Christina loved children. The color made no difference. She played with them, too. What is wrong with that, Anna?"

"Oh," Anna sighed. "If Mama or Papa ever knew. You don't know what would happen to me."

"I know, Anna. That is why I thought we'd take a walk."

"Why couldn't you have stayed on St. Thomas?" Anna said. "Oh, how wonderful it would have been to have someone to talk to. When I was younger I sometimes thought the secret would not stay inside of me."

"Would you like to taste the stew?" Mary mumbled. Before Anna could answer, Mary lifted the ladle. She

151

poured some of the hot broth in the palm of her own hand and sucked at it. Anna put her hand out, cupping it.

"Be careful. It is hot," Mary said.

"It is good, Mary," Anna said. "I haven't had a stew like this since Bahbu left Hendersen. Lady can't cook. She hasn't learned to use the spices."

Mary smiled. It was the first that Anna had seen her do this and she was amazed how quickly the dour expression on Mary's coal black face turned into a pleasing one.

"Do you want a boiled banana?" Bahbu asked.

"No, Bahbu," Anna laughed. "You'll spoil my supper. Then Johanna will complain that I'm ill."

"Come along then," Jan said. "Let me show you the plantation." They turned and left the kitchen.

"What do you think, Mary?" Bahbu whispered.

"She is as you say. She is one of us." She stirred the stew. "She is a big woman, like Mistress Christina. She and Prince will have strong babies."

"Now that you have seen our plantation," Jan was saying. "How do you think St. John compares to St. Thomas?"

"They are very much alike, especially out here in the country. The soil is richer, perhaps. A different color."

"Hendersen on St. Thomas has red soil. It has clay in it. The cane likes it. But the soil here will grow everything. Ah, here, let's sit on the wall." He helped Anna sit down on the stone wall that ran along the west boundary of the estate. Below them, smoke raised up from the kitchen chimney. Other puffs of smoke were rising from around the slave quarters.

"This is my favorite time of day," Jan said. "The workers are in from the fields and there is always an air of happiness that surrounds the plantation. They really look forward to their supper." He paused. Anna was looking at the plantation houses. "Now, Anna. What about the revolt?"

Chapter 13

Anna was not sure she could believe her ears. She stared at Jan. "The revolt?"

"Yes, Anna. The revolt. I never guarded my words with Christina. And I'm not going to do it with you." Jan noticed that she was flushed. She looked very young. "I am an old man, Anna. But I'm not a fool. I know my people. When they are happy or sad or frightened or hungry, they turn to their gods and their drums. I hear them talk, for they have never feared me, thank God, and they are not overly cautious. I know by the tone of their voices, or the way they drop their heads when they are not really shy, exactly what they are thinking. My God, Anna, I've lived my life with the blacks. They are a part of me. Don't you think I know that we are close to revolt? And I know that you are involved, because I have often heard them mention your name." Seeing Anna stiffen, Jan softened his voice. "Don't you realize I know they took Prince to lead them? Don't you think I know that the tempo of the drums has changed and these people are weary of running the fields for food, weary of dying in bondage?" He put his elbows on his knees and dropped his head into his hands. "Oh, my God, why did I ever begin? But a revolt is not the answer, Anna. It will be a useless slaughter of both the blacks and the whites."

Anna turned from Jan and looked down at the plantation buildings. "The slaves outnumber the white men four to one," she said. "Why can't they win their freedom?"

Jan looked at Anna. Amazed at the brittleness of her voice he said, "Certainly you don't want to see these people rise against us?"

"And why not," she said sharply. "I am tired of seeing them treated like animals."

"But Anna, if you care for these people, you would want to keep them from revolt. They will all be killed."

Anna did not answer. Jan walked behind her. Putting his hand on her shoulder, he said, "Why would you want them to risk this, Anna. Tell me."

Anna pulled from Jan's touch. "I thought you were different from your brother and my father. I thought you would be happy to see the slaves free."

They stared hard at each other. "I do want to see them free," Jan said slowly, emphatically.

"Then help them."

"Help who? How many could I help? The majority of the blacks who want revolt would chop off your head, and mine, and every white man's. They're desperate, Anna. I can't help any of them except perhaps my own slaves. And the only way I can help them is to get them off this island before they become involved in it. That's why I wanted to talk to you. You can help me."

"I can't help anyone," Anna said. She moved to the wall and sat down. A long silence and then she said, "I'm confused. I don't know what I'm doing or saying since Bahbu and Prince left St. Thomas." She dropped her head. "I'm lonely at Hendersen without them."

"I can understand that," Jan said gently. "That's why I thought you would try to talk them out of taking a part in this trouble."

"I can't talk Prince out of anything. He believes he was sent by his gods to free his people from the white men. And I believe him."

"Anna," Jan said persuasively, "I know that. But the slaves can't fight the Danish army. They've no equipment. They'll be slaughtered."

"Do you really believe they cannot win?"

"Yes. And if you care about Bahbu and Prince, you'll try to keep them from being a part of any revolt."

"Care for them?" Anna said. She remained silent for a few moments, lost in thought. Then she straightened up and looked deeply into Jan's eyes. "I am in love with Prince," she said quietly.

"Oh, my God," Jan murmured, his voice so low it was a whisper. "A white girl in love with a slave. What chance have either of you?"

"None," Anna blurted out. "That's why I don't care if they kill every white man on earth. I have to be with Prince."

There was a long silence between them. From the plantation the voices of the slaves who had gathered for their supper floated on the trade winds. Jan looked at the slave quarters for a moment. Then he looked back at Anna and said, "It's gone too far for me to stop it. But at least I can take my slaves off this island. And that's what I intend to do. Tomorrow I am taking them to St. Thomas."

"Please don't," Anna implored. "I'll never be able to be with Prince. I'm tired of hiding to see him."

"Stop thinking of yourself," Jan said. "Many lives are at stake. I'm doing what is best for my slaves. And that is that." Seeing Anna wince, he added, "Aside from that, when I'm back at Fortuna, things will be different."

"In what way? Nothing will ever change."

"No, not change. But at least you can live with your secret. If he is killed, you have nothing. Not even the minutes you can have in hiding." He looked at Anna. "You know, Anna, Prince is a Hendersen."

"I know," Anna said quietly. "Bahbu has told me."

"I will do everything I can to help the two of you. It doesn't change anything, really, but it will make your lives a little easier to tolerate." He saw that Anna was thinking about it. He stood up and took her hand. "Come on, Anna. It's time to go back to the house." Quietly, he added, "Do you understand what I'm doing?"

"I understand. And you're probably right. Thinking of Prince being back at Hendersen makes me happy."

"Things will be better, Anna. You'll see. Now, tell me," he stood back and looked at Anna's short dress. "Why are you showing so much of your shoes?" His eyes twinkled. "A planter's lady should be more fashionable." He put his arm out. "But you are so pretty, no one will ever notice."

Taking Jan's arm Anna said, "How could I hide in the cane field in a long dress?" She skipped along beside him. "See, I can run."

Jan laughed. "I'm happy you came here," he said. "And it's going to be good to get back to St. Thomas. Tell me, has Christina's grave been marked well?"

"It's a simple stone, as you ordered. Bahbu had lilies growing there, but they were destroyed in the hurricane."

"We will plant more, Anna," Jan said. Suddenly he stopped and looked at her. "What if we are too late, Anna? What if they plan the revolt tonight?"

"They won't," Anna said lightly.

"How can you be sure?"

155

"Because I am to meet Prince tonight. He wouldn't meet me if he were going to lead a revolt tonight, now would he?"

Jan sat down at the dinner table. Anna, on his right, looked radiant. Her face was flushed, from the anticipation, Jan suspected, of her later rendezvous with Prince. Next to her, Lars rubbed his stained mustache. He looks particularly well groomed this evening, Jan observed. At the other end of the table, Johanna's fat round shoulders held the smaller ball of her head, partially hidden by the tall candles in the center of the table. Jan's eyes moved on to Wilhelm. He was tucking his napkin into his shirt front at his neck. On to Victoria, who sat with her hands folded in her lap. Her mouth twitched. She stared into the candle-light.

"It's good to have people at my table," Jan said. "I have entertained little here. Dr. Bodger and his two sons a few times. That is all."

"St. John appears to be very primitive," Victoria said. "I would die of boredom here."

"We don't have much to do at home, Mama," Johanna said. "Why, you and Papa never entertain. You wouldn't call having us to the house entertaining."

"That council speaks of asking for funds to have a town laid out," Jan said. "At Coral Bay."

"Logical place," Wilhelm said. "Good harbor there. The fort hasn't been well planned, however. If the rumors of revolt . . ."

"Wilhelm," Lars interrupted, "would you pass the stew to Johanna?"

Wilhelm passed the stew. Anxiously, Johanna spooned some on her plate. Wilhelm went on, "How was your harvest this year?"

"We put out thirty per cent of our normal production," Jan answered. "Considering the seriousness of the drought and the hurricane, it was as good as I expected. And Hendersen on St. Thomas, Lars? How did you do?"

"About the same. Not much more rum than I'd use on the plantation in a year."

"Do you still give the Negroes a weekly allotment?"

"My God, Jan. That has been against the law for many years. Do you think I'd give . . ."

156

"I'll have those bananas," Wilhelm called out. "Lars, take them from Anna."

"No, Lars, I don't think you'd give them rum if it were against the law," Jan said. He took the stew from Victoria. "However, a little rum has been good for my Negroes. Especially now, with so many starving. Rum is good for the health—in proper amounts."

"Yes, yes," Wilhelm agreed. "Speaking of rum, could I have a small amount with my dinner, Jan? Your rum is excellent."

"Bahbu, bring the decanter," Jan said.

Bahbu, who had just put a bowl of sweet potatoes on the table, left the dining room.

"Tell me, Victoria," Jan turned to his left, "how have the Moravian missionaries done on St. Thomas?"

Victoria twitched her mouth. "Not well. Mr. Dober couldn't support himself."

"Poor man," Jan said. "I hope he will continue with his work."

"Continue, indeed," Johanna said, still looking around the obstacle in the middle of the table. "Papa says he's working with the blacks, helping them plan their revolt against the white . . ."

"Johanna," Wilhelm snapped. "Pass me those bananas. I'm very hungry."

"My, Papa, you certainly are." Johanna passed the dish and then sat back in her chair. She folded her hands in her lap and stared into space.

Bahbu returned. She circled the table and poured rum into the glasses in front of the men. Lars picked his glass up as soon as it was full and threw it down in one gulp. "More rum, Bahbu. It's still the best rum I've ever tasted," Lars said, taking the decanter from Bahbu and refilling his glass.

"Rumors of revolt are very strong this year," Jan said. "No wonder. So many of the slaves are starving to death. Last week they buried two here on St. John. Are you feeding the Hendersen slaves, Lars?"

"Of course I am. But you know how those devils are. They give away their food to the others who are not fed. I'd use up all the money if I tried to feed the whole of St. Thomas."

"But we're out of food for the slaves, Lars. You know it," Johanna said. "We have been for over a month."

"Oh," Jan said, dropping his chin. "Too much bother to go into the market, Lars?"

Lars took the napkin and wiped his mouth. "You know that isn't so. I had enough food for the month. They stole it. I can't feed the whole island, I just told you that. If they want to steal their supplies to give to their friends, there is nothing I can do about it. I told them I would buy them enough food for their own stomachs. And that I'll do." Lars took another swallow of rum. "It's going to cost a small fortune to keep them going until their gardens are producing again. Let's pray that we have a good crop this coming year."

"Amen," Wilhelm said. "And let us pray our slaves have enough strength to work the fields if we do."

"Your slaves, Papa—"

"Johanna, will you stop interrupting your father," Victoria said. "Look at Anna. Women do not enter into such affairs."

Lars, his eyes beginning to hang heavy, took another swallow of rum. The glass empty, he took up the decanter. "There are strong rumors that our good King has arranged to buy St. Croix from France. With our trade dropping off as it has been in the past three or four years, I think this is a good move, don't you, Jan?"

"No, I don't. It only means that slavery will never be abolished under Danish rule."

"It's been standing idle since 1695," Wilhelm said. "We've proved here on St. John that the soil produces better when it has had a rest. St. Croix is a lush wilderness. If Denmark is going to keep up with the rest of the world with trade in these islands, it's the proper move. You know, Jan, if the vote doesn't discontinue slavery, which it has no indication of doing, why shouldn't the King look to other islands for the Danes? The power of the Danish West India Company would be greatly increased were we to acquire St. Croix." He patted his lips with the edge of his napkin. "I might be tempted to move there myself. The production on Bordeaux is less each year. What say you, Lars? It sounds like the logical way for Hendersen to expand."

Lars put his right elbow on the table. Waving a piece of bread at Wilhelm, he said, "Expand, Wilhelm? For what?" His bleary eyes found Johanna's face. "We have no heirs."

158

Sitting back, he reached under the table with his left hand and searched for Anna's knee. When he found it, it was quickly jerked from beneath his fingers. "One never knows, however, what the future holds. Does one?"

"No," Johanna said.

"How many slaves have you on Hendersen now, Lars?" Jan asked.

Lars dropped his head on his hand. "Let me see. We have twenty-five grown, and seven—no, eight young ones." He lifted his head and added, "At last count. It looks like we might have nine or ten young ones when I get back."

Wilhelm laughed. "I've always said a breeding plantation would be a profitable business. They are, ah, shall we say, fertile."

"Wilhelm!" Victoria exclaimed. "The girls."

"That reminds me, when we are having our cigars, I've a very amusing story to tell," Wilhelm said, looking at Jan. He wet his lips. "It has to do with that big buck of yours, Tando, and one of our wenches. The . . ." Victoria kicked him under the table. "Yes, yes, when the ladies leave the room." He picked up his spoon and ladled the gravy off his plate into his mouth.

An arc of moon hung to the east of the mill. The night sky was dark blue around it. Anna walked around the mill and came into the moonlight.

"Anna," Prince stepped out from the wall. He took her hand. "Come." Together they ran down the black crest of the knoll. On their right, a clump of banana palms made a shaded glen. There they ran, disappearing into the darkness under the broad leaves.

Prince took his cane knife and cut off nine of the leaves and spread them on the ground, making a blanket over the damp earth. "There. Come, Anna, sit beside me."

"It's like the cave," Anna said.

"The gods do not want you to lose your way going home. See?" He pointed upward. "There is the back of the mill."

Anna moved closer to Prince and put her arm through his. "I hate the mill, Prince. It's a fearful thing."

"I hate it, too. It is an evil creation of the white man. King says there are none of them in Africa. When we are free, we will take them down."

159

"When is that, Prince?"

"Come, turn around here." He dropped over onto his stomach. "I will tell you our plans."

Anna listened to Prince's whispered voice. Sometimes the curved, split leaves of the banana palms above them were moved aside by the breeze, letting the patterned moonlight shine in. His amber eyes flashed with excitement. "And on Wednesday, there will be no more white men on St. John. Then we can do the same on St. Thomas, Anna. When that is done, Anna and Prince will not hide any more in the cave or the bush."

"Prince, Jan knows a revolt is about to take place. He is worried about you. He wants to take you back to St. Thomas with us." She threw herself face down in his arms and spoke urgently in his ear. "Let him take you, Prince. Come back with us. Oh, Prince, it's so horrible there without you. No one will know about us, Prince. You'll be safe. Please."

Prince pushed her away and sat up. "Anna. Why would you ask me such a thing. You know I was born to lead my people. The gods picked me to do this. I cannot leave them. And if I could, what of us? We would always have to hide, you know it. What has happened to you? All the plans we made? You know we cannot be together until the black people are free. There is no way, Anna. They would kill us both. You know it."

"But Master Jan would protect us."

"He is an old man. And when he dies, then what? And, Anna," Prince said gently. "What of the babies? When we make the babies, you could not hide that."

"What babies," Anna said leaping to her feet. "We don't do anything to make babies."

Prince laughed.

"I'm tired of your laughing at me," she said angrily. "There is nothing wrong with my wanting you. It's always the same: do not kiss, do not touch, do not come near you. How long will it be before you feel free to kiss me? Must I wait until we meet over there," she pointed upward, "behind your moon and your sun and your stars?" She looked down at Prince, her eyes flashing with anger. "I'm tired of waiting."

Prince sprung from the ground and in the next instant had his arms around Anna, pinning her arms to her side.

Looking into her eyes he said, "Do you know what I am going to do with you?"

"No," she said softly, holding his gaze. "What are you going to do?"

"I am going to place you on this bed of banana leaves, right now, and put a baby in you."

"You wouldn't dare!"

"And tomorrow you tell Master Jan that I am going to fight for my freedom so that I can live with Anna and our babies." As he talked he lowered his weight on one knee and placed Anna on the bed of leaves. Sitting back, he struggled with the rope belt. When it was free he tossed the belt aside and shoved his trousers off his legs. His bare body covered Anna. His lips found hers, pressing hungrily. His fingers fumbled awkwardly, straining to be careful with the buttons on her dress.

Wilhelm stood looking out of the small window in the mill. "Are you sure you saw her with a slave, Lars? You know Anna has always liked to walk in the field."

"Of course I'm sure," Lars snarled. "You think I'm blind?"

"Oh, my God. If it's true . . . Victoria. What will she say?"

"Hand me that rum. We'll worry about Victoria when the time comes." Lars looked out through the opening.

"You've had so much rum now it's a wonder you can see anything out the window. How long have we been here?"

"What difference does it make," Lars said. "You want to catch her, don't you?"

"Her? It's him I want to catch. I'll burn the black scoundrel at the post—alive." He paused. "Why is it that you're so anxious to catch her, Lars? Could it be that she has resisted your advances? Oh, don't look so shocked. I've watched you. I saw you tonight, trying to feel her leg under the table. No, Lars, if what you say is true, it's he who'll be sorry. My Anna will not be harmed. Now, promise me that." He took hold of Lars's shoulder and pulled him from the window. "Do you hear what I'm saying?"

"They're coming," Lars said, pulling away from Wilhelm's grip and running to the wall where his loaded musket was resting. Grabbing it, he ran out the front door

161

of the mill, down the ramp, and then scurried back up to the face of the round wall. Wilhelm followed. Wilhelm's back was flat against the cold stones, inching along behind Lars, when he heard Lars's command, "Halt!"

Wilhelm leaped out. There before him stood Anna. The outline of her pale blue dress and white shoes made her easily discernible. Beside her was the tall, broad-shouldered slave he had seen at St. Thomas. The slave was holding Anna's hand.

"You make a move and I'll shoot you right here," Lars snarled at Prince. "Let go of her hand!"

Slowly, Prince opened his hand. Anna's held on.

"Let loose." Lars raised the gun. Anna opened her hand and let Prince's drop.

"Wilhelm, get me a rope from the mill."

Wilhelm disappeared. In the semi-darkness, the three of them stood motionless.

"Here, here is the rope," Wilhelm puffed, running back to them.

"Tie his hands behind him." Lars held the musket evenly out in front, aimed at Prince's chest.

"Why don't you shoot him now?" Wilhelm said. He struggled pulling the rope in a tight twist. "It'll save a lot of scandal on the island."

"I wouldn't miss the chance of seeing my dear brother's face for anything. This is one time he can't protect a slave without having his own hide strung up at the post. Remember, Wilhelm, the last time a slave dared to fool with a planter's daughter? The ruling in Copenhagen sentenced him to burn at the stake. The law is established. I'll see this one burn too."

"You can't," Anna yelled out. She threw herself against Prince and wrapped her arms around his waist.

Wilhelm shrank back. "Anna," he gasped.

"Anna," Prince whispered. "They will kill you too. Hold your tongue."

From the side of the mill Jan's voice spoke out. "What's going on out here?"

Anna broke away from Prince and ran toward Jan. Throwing herself in Jan's arms, she began to cry.

"Walk," Lars commanded Prince. He followed him with the musket. "If you run, I'll shoot you down, right here in the field."

Immediately, Jan knew what had happened. He bent

162

over and whispered in Anna's ear. "He was looking for you. He went to your room—right after you went out. Be brave, Anna. We must hedge for time. Let me handle this. You be quiet. Don't admit to anything. Trust me, Anna."

"Come up to the parlor," Jan said, his voice calm. "Let's be quiet. There is no sense in having the women carrying on until we know what the trouble is."

"There's plenty of trouble," Lars said. "Wilhelm and I caught this black devil out in the bush with Anna, didn't *we*, Wilhelm?"

"As Jan says, let's go to the house, Lars. We can talk better there." Wilhelm's voice was high-pitched and nervous.

The group moved slowly toward the house. In the darkness from behind the distillery, King moved out into the clearing. His strong legs carried him swiftly to the slave quarters.

He opened the door on Mary's hut and eased himself in. Mary was speaking with the gods. "Quick," King said. "They have caught Prince and Anna together. The white man, Lars, talks of burning him."

"Aiii," Mary cried. She stood up. Her hand darted into the pocket of her skirt. The poison was there. "Tell the council, King. On the drum. We will begin the revolt in the morning. Tell them we cannot wait another day."

"But what of Prince?"

"Do as I say, King. Prince will not die. He was born to lead his people."

The door opened again. Bahbu came running in. "They've caught them, Mary. They are in the house. Prince is tied with a rope. The men are arguing. Lars wants to burn him, now. Master Jan says he will wait until morning so we can all see it. I cannot understand Master Jan. He never before let a slave die at Hendersen, not while he was there to stop it."

"What of Anna?"

"Master Jan is protecting her. Her father is too."

"Master Jan is a wise man. He always told us, Bahbu, that time is very important when it is a serious matter. You see, he gives us time." She leaped forward. Her hand darted out and lifted the amulet from Bahbu's chest. "We will begin the war a day early. King. Go. Sound the drum. Before dawn, we will move against the white men. It is late. We have only a few hours."

"It's only a few hours till daybreak," Lars said, looking at Anna's frightened face. "And then this devil will burn."

Anna held tighter to Jan. The group was standing in a semicircle around Prince. He stood very straight, ignoring the musket Lars held on him.

"Oh, my God," Wilhelm muttered. "I hear the women. What do we tell Victoria?"

"The truth," Lars spit out. "Let her know why her little daughter hasn't married. Huh, Anna?" His red-rimmed eyes looked at her. "Go ahead, tremble against my big brother. The two of you make a good pair."

"What's this?" Victoria demanded, coming into the parlor. She yanked on the belt of her lace-fringed robe. Her mouth twitched. "What's happening?"

"Now, Victoria," Wilhelm said.

"Tell her, Wilhelm," Lars said. "Tell her about her beautiful daughter, laying in the bush with a black."

Victoria screamed.

Over the piercing noise, Johanna's high-pitched voice broke in. "Papa, I told you she was up to something." Johanna put her arm around her mother's waist. "I should have told you, Mama. The men don't listen."

"You mean you knew?" Victoria said. "Why didn't you tell me? Then, hysterically, "I wouldn't have set foot in Hendersen nor allowed her to set foot in Bordeaux if I knew such a thing. She is not my daughter—do you hear —do you hear? Not my daughter. I disown her." Her words echoed about the silent room.

"Calm yourself, Victoria," Wilhelm said. "Now, my dear, we must not let this scandal get out. Lars and I have taken steps to rid ourselves of this black. He will burn. In a very few hours you will see him burn, Victoria."

Victoria's eyes settled on Prince. "I will enjoy seeing it," she hissed.

The hallway at the front door ran between the dining room and parlor. Jan saw Mary standing there. She stared at him for a minute and then padded into the room. "The coffee you ordered will be ready soon, Master Jan," she said. Her voice was flat. She put a silver tray down on the table in the middle of the room. On it was milk and brown sugar.

The boom of a drum sounded out. Lars looked at the window. "What is that?" he yelled.

Jan looked at Mary. She nodded.

164

"It is only a drummer," Jan said. "My people drum every night, since the famine began."

"They would," Lars said. "Mary, pour me a glass of rum. Wilhelm, here, you hold this musket." Wilhelm took the gun. Lars walked to the table and swallowed the rum Mary had poured. "Now, why don't you ladies go back to your rooms?"

"Yes, Mama," Johanna said, in a voice that was unusually firm. "I do not care to be in the same room with *her*."

Slowly, with her arm around her mother, Johanna moved from the room. Mary followed. "Mistress," Jan heard her say. "Could I bring you some hot coffee when it is ready? We have fresh milk."

"How nice," Johanna answered. "Yes, do that. And bring Mistress Bodker some too. You'll have some coffee with me, won't you, Mama? It will be daylight very soon. No need to sleep now. We don't want to miss the burning."

"Dear Johanna." Victoria's voice floated into the room. "I have always said you were such a *good* girl. I don't think I can ever sleep peacefully again—what a disgrace." A pause. "The coffee will comfort me."

Soon Mary went upstairs with the coffee, then padded back down. She came into the parlor. "Coffee is ready, Master Jan," she said. Jan and Anna were sitting now, Anna in the rocking chair, Jan on a straight-backed chair beside her. "Would you like coffee, Anna? It is hot. It will make you feel better."

"Wilhelm, Lars, could Mary bring you coffee?" Jan asked.

Wilhelm sat down. Putting his hands on his stomach, he said, "Yes, thank you. It will keep me awake."

Overhead, there was a thump. Wilhelm looked up at the ceiling. "This has been a dreadful shock for Victoria. I hope she can get some rest."

The drum beat pulsated in the room. Suddenly it stopped, and the room became very quiet. A clock in the dining room ticked. Then, from the distance, another drum beat could be heard. And another—and another.

"Savages," Lars mumbled. Taking his foot, he pulled a chair from against the wall and sat on it. He rested the gun across his knees and looked up at Prince. "You've always been as arrogant as your namesake. We'll see if the flames

165

take some arrogance out of your miserable hide." He laughed. "Wilhelm, bring me some rum."

Wilhelm got up. Mary came into the room carrying a tray with the coffee on it. Putting it on the table, she took up the almost empty decanter of rum and poured some into a glass. She handed the glass to Wilhelm. Taking it, he turned off and handed it to Lars.

Lars threw his head back and tossed the rum into his mouth. He wiped his mustache with the back of his hand. "I've never seen a burning. It will be interesting. How about that, Prince?"

Prince's eyes burned into Lars's. He heard the drums stop. Now the faint tick-tock of the clock was more audible. "Hear that?" Lars said. "That clock doesn't sound as good to your ears as the drums did, eh?"

Mary poured the coffee. With three cups on the tray, she moved in front of Jan. Jan reached out, but Mary turned the tray. He took the cup in front of him, poured milk in it, added three spoonfuls of sugar, and handed it to Anna. Mary held the tray out to him once more. He looked up at her. She did not move, her eyes held his. He took another cup. Carefully, he spooned out three more helpings of sugar. "Thank you, Mary," he said.

She turned away. Then she stopped and turned back. "Master, King would like to see you."

"Ahh," Wilhelm said. "It's getting close to dawn. The slaves are getting up, eh?"

Jan looked at Mary. What was she up to, he thought. He knew they would attempt to rescue Prince. And then what? Where could Prince hide? Jan got up, deciding to go along with their plan. Putting his coffee on the round table, he walked out of the room.

Mary moved in front of Wilhelm with the tray. "Well, well," Wilhelm said, reaching for the coffee. "It smells good." His eyes ran back and forth from the milk to the sugar. He poured some milk in it and then spooned out some sugar. He took a sip. Mary stood in front of him, watching. "Good coffee," he said. He took up the cup and swallowed hard.

From the corner of her eye she saw several figures move in the hallway. "Lars," he yelled out. Standing up, Wilhelm grabbed at his throat. Lars swung around in his chair. Wilhelm sank to the floor, gasping for air.

"Wilhelm," Lars yelled. Mary's foot came up, catching the musket and throwing it off Lars's lap.

From the hallway, King came in, a cane knife in his hand. "Stand still, white man," he said in a deep, serious command.

Lars, caught off guard, stood with his arms outstretched. His mouth fell open. From behind King, two other blacks entered the room. They circled around behind the group. From behind him Lars heard, "Anna, come!" Lar's eyes darted around.

King moved forward. "Stand still!" King yelled in an angry voice.

Lars stopped. The cane knife in King's hand looked very sharp. Then Prince appeared beside King. "Who untied you?" Lars asked, stepping forward. King motioned with his knife, forcing Lars to step back. Then he saw the cane knife in Prince's hand. He looked at the two serious faces glaring at him. On the floor, to one side, Wilhelm was sprawled out.

"My God," Lars uttered aloud, "what is this?" For a moment, he was speechless. Then he opened his mouth and screamed "Jan! get in here."

"Do not call your brother," Prince said calmly. "It will do you no good. He is gone. They have taken him away."

Lars raised his head, looking at the ceiling. It was quiet above him.

"And they will not hear you," Prince said.

"What have you done to them?" Lars demanded.

Prince looked down at Wilhelm's body. Lars's eyes followed his. "You haven't—" Lars said. "By God"—he took a step forward—"I'll have your heads for this—all of you."

Lars stepped back again. It was very silent, with the sounds of the clock echoing in the room. Lars heard a rooster crow. Yes, it would soon be daylight. And then what? Where was Jan? Certainly his own brother would not let these savages attack him. Or would he? Lars's hand rose to wipe his chin. He saw the two men in front of him tighten their grips on the cane knives. Suddenly, Lars jerked around and ran toward the open window.

Behind him he heard Prince yell, "He is mine, King, *mine.*"

Lars felt the powerful hand grab his shoulder. Slammed

around against the wall, he looked up into Prince's face. Now the amber eyes that had always before shown fear or arrogance burned with another flame Lars had never seen. He could feel the knife prodding into his stomach.

"Prince . . . you know I was only jesting. I wouldn't burn you," he said. "Prince, you are my son. I couldn't do that to you. Truly, Prince, you are my son. Do you hear me?" His voice was beginning to become hysterical.

"I hear you," Prince said. As he said each word, the knife jabbed into the soft flesh of Lars's stomach.

"Please, I beg of you, Prince."

"I—am—going—to—cut—your—heart—out."

The words had a beat to them, like the drum. And they were as hollow. He won't, Lars thought. He's only trying to frighten me. He can't, the black devil won't. Oh, my God. Lars saw Prince's arm fly back and come forward. He felt the knife sink into his flesh. He heard his own voice let out. "Ahhhhhhh," and then the searing pain ripped up. "Jan," he choked out.

The name rumbled through the parlor. The knife, now lodged up against Lars's breastbone, was supported by Prince's strong grip so Lars's body could not drop to the floor. Instead, he was slumped partially down, impaled on the knife. His open eyes looked up at Prince. Prince leaned down, close to Lars's face.

"Die," Prince whispered fiercely.

Prince leaped back. Lars's body fell in a heavy heap on the floor. Prince put his foot on the lifeless body and ripped the cane knife from his father's chest.

Chapter 14

Fourteen slaves from the company's estate Caroline walked along the path leading to the fort. Below them an early morning calm had settled on Coral Bay. Peter and William, the two leaders from Caroline, were at the head of the line. In the hand of each man was a cane knife. On top of their arms a bundle of wood had been stacked. In each bundle, buried beneath the wood, were honed cutlasses.

Peter stopped. Each man in turn stood still. "Remember. When we are all in the fort, drop the wood. Take up the cutlasses. There are only nine of them: the lieutenant, the sergeant, and the seven soldiers. But only one soldier will be on guard. You, William, go now to the back of the line. Kill the sentinel when we have passed into the fort. Only the sentinel will be awake. The others will be taken by surprise." Peter turned around and started moving again. His bare feet felt cold from the morning dew on the path. Behind them, the first light of dawn was lifting up into the sky.

The sentinel, sitting in a chair by the closed door, heard a noise. Standing up, he put his ear to the door and shouted, "Who goes there?"

"Negroes, with wood," Peter called out.

The sentinel pushed back the iron bolt and opened the heavy door. "Why are you bringing wood now?" he grumbled. "You brought wood last night. You'll awaken the sergeant."

Peter was silent. The sentinel looked at the line of slaves. "Enter. But be quiet, hear?"

Peter nodded his head. The sentinel stood back, allowing the slaves to pass. As William, on the end of the line, came abreast of the sentinel, he tripped. The wood tumbled from his arms. The astonished sentinel ran forward and put his boot on one of the rolling logs. "You'll awaken

. . ." William's knife came down. The sentinel fell forward. Before the sentinel could recover from the knife wound, William had picked up the cutlass and plunged it into the soldier's chest.

Inside the fort, it was dark. The sergeant, disturbed in his sleep by the noise, pulled the sheet over his head and turned to face the wall, unwilling to come fully awake.

Peter yelled, "Now! Kill the white soldiers. Let them suffer, as we have suffered." He opened his arms, letting the wood crash to the floor. Every arm fell open and the wood pounded down on the stone courtyard. Each slave was now armed with a cutlass in one hand and a cane knife in the other.

The sergeant sprang to his feet. "Sentinel," he barked. "What goes there?" He ran to the doorway. There, to his amazement, he saw a swarm of half-naked black bodies storming the barracks, blades flashing. He ran back into the room and bolted the door behind him. William spotted the slamming door and began to batter it down. The sergeant grabbed his flintlock and leaped from the window. It was a long drop. He landed on his foot and felt it crack. Writhing in pain, he tried to pull himself away from the fort. Before him, black shadows took form. He raised his face. Sweat poured from his forehead. "Help me," he called. The circle of shadows moved closer. The sergeant closed his eyes. Down came the clubs and cane knives.

Inside, the thirteen men had a brief and deadly scuffle with the soldiers who were stumbling around half asleep. More slaves poured through the open gate. Finally there were forty or fifty hunger-crazed slaves rushing through the barracks.

"Hoist the flag," Peter yelled, waving his bloody cane knife. "Go to the cannon. Fire the signal. We have taken the fort. Kill the white men!" He pushed through the crowd.

In the melee, John Gabriel, one of the soldiers, trembled under a bed where he was hiding. He watched the bare black feet pass over the bloody, mutilated bodies of his friends. The calloused, light tan bottoms of their feet were stained red. He closed his eyes.

"Get the overseer at Caroline . . . go to Soedtmann . . . Kill, kill all the white men." The voice carried in to John. Paralyzed with fear, he inched further under the

170

bed. Boom—a cannon went off. John remained motionless. Finally, the three slaves who had hung behind moved out of the room. Boom—another cannon. Then more voices. "To Caroline . . . to Soedtmann . . . Kill the evil white men." Drums sprang up.

Cautiously, John elbowed his way from under the bed. Outside, he could still hear the chanting, crazed voices. He ran to the window. It would be a long drop, but he had to risk it. He hoisted himself onto the wide windowsill and looked out. Quickly, he turned around. Holding onto the wide brick sill, he let his feet drop out of the window. He hung there for a brief instant, then let himself drop. He jarred. Getting on his knees, he knew he had not injured himself. Ahead of him was a clump of bush. Leaning over, he ran toward it. Behind him, the noises were becoming angrier. Kill, kill, kill; kill the white men, pounded indelibly into John Gabriel's brain. There was a boat at Cruz Bay, he thought. If he was careful, he could make it . . . and reach St. Thomas. But he had to hurry. It would soon be light and dangerous to travel. The shadows running off the mountain were taking form. God help me, John Gabriel prayed aloud, looking up at the gray-black sky.

Judge Soedtmann was running around his room locating his clothes. The cannon. Trouble. In the next room he heard his daughter call out. Hastily pulling on his shirt, he ran into the hallway.

"Don't be alarmed, my dear. I have to go, but will be back as soon as possible." He ran down the steps. Only yesterday his wife and three-month-old daughter had gone to St. Thomas with his father-in-law, Governor Gardelin. He thought of them now. He had seen them off on the East Indiaman that had laid off the harbor at Coral Bay.

At the bottom of the steps he stopped. Outside, in the eerie half-light of dawn, he saw many shadows moving around the house. Something was not right. He went into the parlor. From a cabinet against the wall he took out a musket.

The door flew open. "King," he yelled out, recognizing the squat, bowed legs of Jan Hendersen's slave. "Halt!"

King moved into the room. Other shadows pushed in behind him. The voices from outside began to take on meaning. "Kill Judge Soedtmann, King. Kill him."

"He let us starve," another called.

171

Judge Soedtmann dropped the unloaded, useless musket. "My daughter," he gasped. "Please, King, spare my daughter." From above him he could hear her call out. "It has finally come to pass," he told himself as King grabbed his arm.

As he was pulled from the house, blows fell on his head and shoulders. Above the din of voices he could hear his daughter's screams behind him. He tried to shut out the frightened sound. Numb from the searing pain that covered his body, he went limp. King continued dragging him by the arm. The crowd surged up, pushed from behind with such force that they stumbled over him, many of the blows landing ineffectually.

"Stand back," King was screaming. "I have promised his head."

Judge Soedtmann squeezed his eyes together. "Dear God, let it be quick," he thought. He felt the knife at his throat. "My daughter . . ." Mercifully, he lost consciousness.

"Papa, Papa," the young girl screamed. Peter threw her down across her father's body. Holding him, she sobbed. She moved her hand up. It fell into a warm, wet place. Raising her face, she looked at the red mass of jagged flesh where her father's head had been. Her shrill screams pierced the morning air.

"Kill her, she is white," someone yelled. "Kill her, Peter. She is his daughter."

"Kill me, yes, kill me. I beg of you. Kill me," the girl screamed up at Peter, her tear-stained face distorted with shock.

In a towering rage, Peter raised his cutlass. With all his might he brought it down across the white face in front of him, splitting her head as if it were a ripe pumpkin.

Peter turned around. There on the lawn Judge Soedtmann's head was riding on a long wooden pole. Peter laughed as King jiggled the pole up and down.

Five male Negroes formed a circle around the pole. Howling and leaping about, they picked up dirt from the earth and threw it at the white face on the pole.

From the house others came streaming out. Ruth, the judge's house slave, leaped up to the railing of the porch and leaned over holding a crystal glass in her hand. It was filled with a golden liquid. "See, my master. I drink your rum—from your own glass!" She raised the glass.

The rum that she could not swallow ran down the sides of her face, glistening with the sweat that was already there. She threw the glass down on the porch. It shattered, its delicate tinkling noise lost in the roar of the celebration. She ran back and kicked at the headless body.

"Take them out of the way," another yelled. Both bodies were raised. Many black arms stretched up, holding them. Going to the railing, they heaved. The bodies fell, a dull thump against the ground.

The cannon had awakened Dr. Cornelius Bodger. While he was dressing, he could hear his two sons going down the steps. Christian's voice carried up the steps. "Summon your father."

Dr. Bodger went to the top of the steps and called out, "What is it, Christian?" He was still buttoning his shirt cuffs when he heard the noises outside. Hastily, he ran down the steps. Christian, with eleven blacks standing behind him, was at the door. The doctor saw they were armed. "What's the meaning of this, Christian?"

"It is the revolt. We have taken the fort. That was the signal. Come. We have a boat hidden for you and your sons. You can escape to Tortola. They mean to kill all the white men."

Doctor Bodger stepped forward. His two sons moved back, behind him. "You're not serious, Christian?"

"Yes, master," Christian answered. "Only those of you who have been good to your slaves will be spared."

"Christian, our work. We have been working on the medicinal plants and herbs. I do not think of you as a slave."

"I know, master," Christian said solemnly. "But I am a Negro. These are my people. They have suffered much. You have seen it. You have seen the swollen stomachs when they die of the famine. You have seen them die from loss of blood when they have had their limbs cut off. You have seen how cruel the white men are to them. Now, they must die. The white men must die so that my people can be free and feed themselves."

"Christian, not all white men are cruel. No more than the blacks."

"We want our freedom, master. Is that wrong?"

The doctor looked at the forms behind Christian. Their heads were stretched up, listening. The gray light silhouet-

173

ted the outlines but he could not see the black faces in front of him. "No, it's not wrong. But this isn't the way. This island will swarm with troops before the day is out and every last one of you will be tortured to death."

"No, master," Christian said. "We are organized. Before the sun sets on St. John today, the black men will be free."

Dr. Bodger's shoulders went limp. "Then have it your way, Christian. I suppose there's nothing I can do to stop you." He turned around to his two sons. "Go upstairs and dress properly. Put on sturdy boots. We will leave the island as Christian bids us." He turned back. "I suppose I should say that it's good of you to spare us, Christian. I never thought it would come to this." He turned and went up two steps. Holding on to the rail, he leaned around and looked down at the group. "I will be ready as soon as I get my boots on."

Driven into a frenzy by their lust for the white men's blood, a large band of Negroes followed after William. "Kill the white man, kill; kill the white man, kill." A drummer ran along with the group, the oblong drum barrel held in front of him by a leather cord around his neck. His hands pounded down, tapping out a noise that was no deeper than the chant of the voices around it. Now the chant had become their marching song. Inspired, they came up over the crest of the hill and streamed down toward Dr. Bodger's house. They spilled out around the house, surrounding it.

Dr. Bodger's slaves, still on the porch turned to face them.

"Come," William called. "Let's kill the white men. Christian, bring out the master of this estate. We will have his head on a pole."

Christian worked his way through the group in front of the door. William, with a torch in one hand, stood at the bottom of the steps. In the other hand he carried a cutlass.

Christian was tall and lean. He had never labored in the fields. Instead, he had been taken into the household because of his knowledge of the medicinal plants and herbs and there had been working with Dr. Bodger. Christian was respected by his people. They knew he was intelligent. That is why Mary had chosen him as one of the leaders.

174

"William," he said. "It has been agreed that my master and his sons will be spared. They are good people."

"There are no good whites," William yelled back.

"Kill the whites, kill the evil white men," the crowd roared from in back of William.

"Hear that," William said. "Our people do not want them to go free. The white men do not set us free. We have to free ourselves."

William, like most Aminas, was tall. He had worked in the field cutting cane from the time he had been brought to St. John, eleven years ago, and his body was ribbed with muscles. His broad nostrils were still filled with the rotten stench of the ship that brought him here. And his muscular black shoulder still felt the company's brand. Putting his hand up to his shoulder, he said, "When the white man put that iron on my back, I swore to myself I would kill him. And as many like him as I could. This white man is no different than the others." William's thick lips pulled back, showing an even row of white teeth. "I say kill him."

"Kill, kill, kill the white man, kill." The drum began, the chanting started low and deep, then built in volume.

At the top of the steps, Dr. Bodger, with his two sons standing behind him, listened.

"Stop," Christian shouted. "I say you will not kill them." There was the sound of scuffling bare feet on the wooden boards of the porch. The house seemed to tremble from the marching mob that surged forward. Christian stumbled back into the hallway. One of Dr. Bodger's slaves handed him a pistol. Christian leaped up onto the third step. William, still carrying the torch, came through the door, pushed by the mob behind him.

"If you come closer, William, I will kill you. You people," he raised his voice, "do you want to see Amina kill Amina, leader kill leader? No." Christian leveled the gun at William. "But I will shoot you if you come closer."

William stopped and pushed back against the crowd behind him.

"William, we cannot fight among our own."

"If you did not have that flintlock, we would see," William answered. His dark eyes reflected the dancing light of the torch. Dr. Bodger's sons moved back.

"We made an agreement when we met in council, William. I expect you to hold your word. Would you have these people say, for the rest of their lives, that the word of an Amina is not good?"

The people behind William had now fallen silent.

Seizing this opportunity, Christian yelled out, "And who will take care of your wounds today? If you kill the doctor, there is no one to tend us. You think I ask his life to be spared because he is my master? No. If we kill the good doctor, many of us will die because of it. I don't like the white men any more than you. But I am not a fool."

"What about his sons?" someone asked.

"Yes," William said, looking up slyly at Christian. "What about them?"

"Do you think the doctor would save us if we killed his sons? He would put poison in our wounds!"

"Then let the sons live," William spoke out. "We will make them *our* slaves."

Behind him the crowd yelled out their approval. "Yes, let the white men be our slaves. They will cook our food . . . and bring us rum . . . yes, yes, let them live."

William stepped up to Christian. "Then they will live, brother Amina. It is agreed, they will be our slaves. We will spare their lives. And the doctor will take care of our sick."

"It is agreed, brother," Christian said. "Now go. All of you. I will stay. If the others come, I will tell them of your decision."

The drummer's hands began. One male voice began, then the crowd joined in. "Kill the white man, kill; kill the white man, kill." The crowd moved off, their chant echoing through the early morning air.

Dr. Bodger sat down on the top step. Christian walked up the steps to join him. "You were right, master. The black men can be cruel, too. Tonight, if we can hold them off until tonight, we can get to the boat. I am going with you, Dr. Bodger."

"Christian." The doctor stood up. Putting his hand on Christian's shoulder, he said, "Maybe we can help to stop this terrible thing. If we can live through the day."

Peter Kruger, awakened by the drums, was on his way to John von Beverhoudt's plantation when the cannon were fired. As he approached the Von Beverhoudt house he saw John coming out on the porch. Peter reined in his horse at the bottom of the steps and yelled out, "The drums awakened me. I was on my way to summon you."

"I think it's already too late." Von Beverhoudt clumped down the steps. "Come with me to the slave quarters."

Kruger dismounted and ran along beside Von Beverhoudt. When they neared the slave quarters, they could hear Henry, one of the slaves who rode with the militia, talking in an angry voice. They stopped.

"We cannot stop the others, but we do not have to be a part of it," Henry was saying. "Our people cannot hold out against the guns and cannon. Our master was good to us. We were fed. I will not be a part of this revolt. I am staying with Master Von Beverhoudt."

Of the eighteen slaves who had clustered around him there were loud noises of assent and others of dissent. "Come along," Von Beverhoudt whispered, "Before they have a chance to organize, we'll break this up."

"What's going on here?" Von Beverhoudt called as he approached the group.

Henry moved forward. "It is the revolt, master. The drums and cannon tell us it has started."

"Where has it started?"

"They have already taken the fort," Henry said. "Now they will move on to the plantations. Soon they will be here. I am now telling our people they should not join them."

"Join them?" he shouted angrily. "Do you all want to end up with your heads on a stake? By afternoon the governor will have enough reinforcements from St. Thomas in here to kill all of you. Don't be fools!"

The group milled around. Most of them held cane knives or cutlasses in their hands.

"Put down those knives," Von Beverhoudt commanded. The slaves stood still. He walked into the middle of the group. Seizing a cane knife from the hand of a strong male slave, he threw it to the ground. "Now put those knives down," he said evenly. One by one the slaves dropped their arms.

"Master," Henry said, stepping forward. "We had better go to the sea. They will be on us very soon."

"My God," Kruger exclaimed. "My wife is alone. John, where are you going? I'll get my wife and meet you."

Von Beverhoudt looked at Henry. "Are all the slaves in on this?"

"Not all," Henry answered. "Some of them have agreed to stay with their masters."

"Henry. Which slaves? Tell me, man, now! Which slaves have not joined this fiendish thing?"

"The nearest plantation would be Deurloo's."

"That's as good a place as any for us to go right now. They have some cannon there. We could hold out. Peter, go get your wife. I'll ride now and get as many planters as I can to go to Deurloo's. Henry, ride with me. You people," he looked at the other slaves, "go to Deurloo's. And remember"—he searched the faces that were barely visible in the light—"I'll have the head of anyone who puts a finger to a white man. Bring the horses, Henry."

Peter Kruger galloped his horse toward his own plantation. He had many thoughts. His slaves had been particularly hostile the last three or four months. Perhaps he had beaten too many recently. But was there another way to make them come in line? Was Jan Hendersen right? Did kindness and full stomachs make them any better? Urged on by these thoughts, he whipped the horse, getting as much speed out of the animal as he could. Ahead of him he could see his mill. By the time he reached there he could hear the wild noises of his slaves. He leaped off his horse and walked it behind him. Cautiously, he moved around the side of the mill. In the distance, the screams and howls of his slaves increased. When he had circled the mill far enough so that the greathouse became visible, he saw nothing but the bright, dancing flames. Peter Kruger stared at the burning greathouse in utter disbelief.

The fire was still confined to the first floor. The flames leaped out of the windows. Fanned by the wind, they raised up the side of the wooden structure. As the light grew brighter, the dancing bodies took shape. One group carried a woman over their heads. Her arms dangled down, swinging with the frantic rhythm of the dancers who carried her. Her head was rolled on one side, bobbing up and down so violently that her hair shook loose. Suddenly, Kruger realized it was his wife.

He stepped forward. At that very instant, the crowd reached the front porch, which was now ablaze. A drummer leaped up beside them. Peter could see his long arms fly up and down on the face of the crude instrument. The limp body was thrown up in the air. The crowd stood back and let it land on the ground. While Peter watched, too paralyzed by the sight to move, one of the forms moved to

178

each of the four limbs of his wife and heaved her, like a bundle of raw cotton, into the flames. Her white nightdress caught fire, outlining her sprawled body on the blazing floor of the porch. Peter dropped his head. He rubbed his hand through his thinning, wispy hair. The burning form of his wife remained in his closed eyes. The increasing light of the fire made the vision grow brighter and brighter. There was a sickening sweet smell of burning flesh around him. Terrified, he turned and ran.

As Prince entered the palm grove at Deurloo's Bay, he heard the first cannon from the fort go off. He stopped. Somewhere inside this grove Bahbu had led Anna and Master Jan. His eyes were adjusting to the faint light when he heard Bahbu call out, "Here, Prince."

As he moved forward, the second cannon rumbled in the distance. "Hurry," Prince said, running up to them. "The fort is taken."

"Wait," Jan spoke up. "I would like to talk to you, Prince." Jan moved away from the group. "Over here, alone."

When they were out of hearing distance of the women, Jan turned to Prince. In the muted light he could see that Prince faced him calmly. "What of my brother Lars?"

"He is dead."

"And his wife and family?"

"They are dead."

A silence. Jan lifted his chin and stared at Prince. "This, then, is the revolt?"

"Yes, master. It is the revolt."

"I can't blame you for wanting freedom," Jan said. "But it's impossible for you to get it this way. This revolt will only end with all your people killed."

Prince remained silent.

"Prince, listen to me. You've everything to live for. You're a young man. More than that, you have Anna's love."

"And Anna has my love," Prince said. "I have nothing to live for if I cannot have her. But I cannot have Anna as long as I am a slave."

"You can have Anna at Hendersen on St. Thomas," Jan said. "You're my family, Prince. As long as I live, I will do what I can to protect you . . . and Anna. I promise you this."

179

"And when you die? Or when we have a child? You could not fight the white men and their laws. You have tried before." Prince lifted his head higher. "We will have our freedom on St. John and then my people will move for their freedom on St. Thomas. Then Anna and I will live together."

"You *cannot* win, Prince. There are neighbors with great sailing ships with many cannons and soldiers. They will run you down and kill every last one of you. You're not only fighting the planter on St. John. You're fighting many countries who are powerful in these West Indies. Listen to me. You cannot win, Prince. Come with us . . . now . . . to St. Thomas. Come back with us." Jan took Prince's arm. "Please, Prince. Not for me, for Anna."

Prince's deep voice filled the silent palm grove. "I cannot go. I have been chosen to lead my people to freedom. I could not go with you and betray my people. I could not be happy with Anna if I did."

"But it's senseless for you to die."

"If I die, I will have found my freedom."

"And then what will become of Anna?"

Prince put his head back. Above him, through the split palm leaves, he could see the sky. A star remained persistent enough with its flashings to signal through the fading blue-black night. His ears were filled with the soft noise of the sea running up on the sand. He closed his eyes. He was in the cave at Fortuna. The sights and sounds and smells were almost the same. "If I am killed," he said, "Anna knows I will wait for her . . . over there." He opened his eyes and looked up at the sky. "Behind the stars and the sun and the moon." Prince's deep voice was gentle.

"Then make me a promise, Prince. If you know that you cannot find your freedom, burn down Hendersen here on this island. But if you get your freedom, which I hope you will, then Hendersen is yours. If you don't get your freedom, I don't want it in the hands of the company. It would be another mill for another group of slaves who would have to take extra punishment for the ones who revolt here today." Jan put his hand out. Prince clasped it firmly. The two men looked solemnly into each other's eyes.

"I will burn Hendersen down if I see that we cannot win. And you, Master Jan, will you take care of Anna for me?"

180

"You know I will. Now, I will go. Stay here. Bahbu and I will put the boat in the water. I'll send Anna to you."

Prince watched Jan pick his way through the coconut husks. Soon, he heard Anna's footsteps crunching on the husks. "Prince, where are you?" she called.

Prince reached around and took her by the arm. Fiercely, he pulled her to him and wrapped his arms around her. Her cool face rested on his bare chest. His hand moved up and stroked her hair. "I remember, Anna, the first day I met you . . . in the cane field. I wanted to touch your hair then." He dropped his face against the top of her head. "It has never changed." Prince could feel the wetness of her tears rolling down his chest. By the time they reached his belly they were cold. He shuddered, and pulled her closer to him. "Anna, Anna . . ." there was a musical ring to the words he whispered into her ear. "I will be back for you. As soon as I am free. Do not cry." He rocked her back and forth. "Anna, I love you."

A sob escaped from Anna. She pushed from Prince's arms and ran toward the sea. Prince walked along behind her. His bare feet hurt when he stepped on the hard, dried husks that covered the ground. Not a single coconut had escaped the machete in the famine. Now the barren remnants were scattered around the grove.

Bahbu and Jan were standing knee-deep in the gentle surf, holding the canoe. Anna waded out and stepped into the center of the boat. Bahbu nodded at Jan. He stepped in the back. Now Prince was wading out. He took Bahbu's arm and turned her toward the canoe. "Get in," he said.

Bahbu looked up, her eyes questioning. Prince nodded. "Yes, Mama. You go take care of Anna. As you promised." Bahbu raised the leather cord from around her neck, and placed it around Prince's neck. The shiny black carving fell flat on his broad chest. Bahbu turned and pulled herself up into the front of the canoe. When she was seated, she was facing Prince. She raised her head and gazed at her son. No words passed between them.

Anna could feel tears bursting behind her eyes. She squeezed them together. Then she felt the quick surge of the canoe going forward from Prince's strong thrust. The sound of Prince's body fighting against the water as he ran back to shore overpowered the noise of the oar hitting the water. As they glided out, the muffled noises of voices and

181

drums came out over the sea. Anna opened her eyes and looked back toward the island. A pink puff of smoke was rising up from behind a round knoll. As she watched, it grew in color, and an intense red flame shot up into the pale blue sky.

Chapter 15

It was one-thirty on the afternoon of Monday, November 23, 1733 when John Gabriel, the sole survivor of the slave attack on the fort at St. John, ran up the red brick steps of the fort at Charlotte Amalie. "Sound the alarm," he shouted. "Summon your council. There is revolt on St. John."

"Sound the alarm," the sentinel called out in the courtyard. Instantly, a drum rolled. John had brought four people with him in his desperate flight from St. John. The two women, suddenly overcome with the sights and sounds that meant safety, collapsed on the steps, sobbing. The two men followed John Gabriel into the courtyard. The three evenly measured cannon blasts roared out across the serene harbor. "Hoist the flag," another voice yelled.

The street that had, minutes before, been deserted in the heat of the midday sun now became alive. Horses, spurred by their riders, galloped hard toward the fort. From the houses on the hillside people made their way down the brick steps. Charlotte Amalie sprang to life, its citizens pouring toward the protection of the sturdy fort. "Look," a boy called out as he ran, "there are boats coming into the harbor."

In the distance, five or six small boats, three under sail, moved inward. "Revolt on St. John," someone screamed. "The slaves have revolted," another yelled.

A large group of people had already congregated in the courtyard when Governor Gardelin and Mrs. Soedtmann, his daughter, came running up the wide steps. There they stopped and looked at the noisy band of settlers who turned from one to another in panicked confusion.

Sergeant Theodore Ottingen stepped up to the governor. "Revolt on St. John, sir. A young soldier from the garrison there brings the news."

"Get some order in here," the governor commanded.

"Have the council come into my office as they arrive. Where is the young man who brings the news?"

"Here, sir." John Gabriel stepped forward and saluted. He looked about nineteen years of age, and his green uniform was mottled with brown earth.

"Come with me." The governor pushed through the crowd in front of him.

"Wait, Father," Mrs. Soedtmann called. "Please! Has he news of John?"

Governor Gardelin turned to the soldier. "Have you news of Judge Soedtmann?"

"No, sir! I am the only survivor from the garrison. I cannot speak for the lieutenant. He was on his estate at the time of the attack."

"And you heard no word of Judge Soedtmann?"

"Uh, not exactly, sir."

"What do you mean, not exactly?"

The soldier rolled his eyes toward Mrs. Soedtmann.

"What is it," she said, grabbing his arm. "Tell me."

Governor Gardelin put his arm around his daughter's shoulder. "Speak up, soldier."

"The rebels were calling out to one another to go to Judge Soedtmann's estate. I specifically heard them mention Caroline, Soedtmann, and Kruger."

"My daughter," Mrs. Soedtmann sobbed. "She is there with John!"

"And you heard nothing more—if the judge escaped or not?"

"No, sir."

"Come inside with me, my dear," the governor said, leading his daughter through the crowd. "We will have more word as soon as other refugees arrive. He may be among them. Try not to worry."

It took an hour for the council to meet and hear John Gabriel relate the details of the massacre.

"It does not look good for the planters," the governor finally said. "You men take turns, going around the table. Speak up. Let us outline our plans."

William Barens stood up. He had a substantial reputation as a planter. He was also substantial in appearance. His broad chest and thick neck gave him the look of the planter who produced in the field. Barens was dressed in working clothes, a loose jacket-shirt over black trousers and ankle-high leather boots. "We should get the garrison here under arms," he said. "The insurrection could easily spread to St. Thomas. Until we know just how serious things are on St. John, we don't know what their needs are. It is inperative that we take every precaution to protect St. Thomas. If we move too quickly and leave our plantations and town poorly defended, the slaves here may use it to take advantage of us."

"Aye," John de Wint agreed. "This may be the opportunity they are waiting for. Let us get every vessel that is laying off the harbor to come in closer so their cannon can be effective."

"And see that every sailor is armed. We will need every available man if there is revolt on St. Thomas," Barens added.

"Lieutenant Taarbye," the governor said, "give the word that the garrison is to make ready. How many men have we?"

"Ninety-one, sir."

"Then pass the word now." Taarbye left the room. "And you, Lieutenant Stibot, how many vessels are in the harbor?"

"Five, sir. A total of perhaps sixty men."

"Then go and advise the captains of these ships that there is serious danger of revolt on St. Thomas. Ask them to come closer and give us protection."

"Yes, sir."

Lieutenant Stibot opened the door of the council room. A sudden burst of loud voices raised up from the courtyard. The governor stood up. A sentinel rushed to the door. "A planter from St. John, sir."

"Have him enter."

John Runnels pushed past the sentinel and ran into the room. He passed through the circle of councilmen and went to the governor's desk. He put his hands on the top of the desk and lowered his head. Heaving for breath, he shook his head. "You won't believe it, sir."

The governor sat down. Runnels leaned forward. "You've got to send reinforcements immediately. Captain Von Beverhoudt and Lieutenant Charles are doing what they can to fortify Deurloo's plantation. But the odds are overwhelming. There are hundreds of slaves running rampant. They are wild and savage and thirsting for our blood. They've killed in the most brutal fashion every white man they could get their hands on. They've burned down the plantations and looted the greathouses. They have committed the most barbaric deeds a man could think of."

"Calm down," the governor said. "You're near hysteria."

Runnels stood up. He covered his eyes with his hand. "When I departed St. John, there were eighteen men and thirty-six women and children gathered at Deurloo's. They have only two cannon there. They cannot hold out for long against that mob of crazed savages." He dropped his hand and collapsed into a chair.

"Give that man some rum," someone called out, "he's in shock."

John de Wint went to the cabinet and poured a drink. Handing it to Runnels, he put his hand on his shoulder and said, "Pull yourself together. We've got to know what's going on there."

Runnels moved his head back and forth. Staring into space, he said, "If I told you, you wouldn't believe it. Judge Soedtmann—beheaded."

"What?" The governor stood up. His face was pale. "And my granddaughter?"

"Murdered!"

Slowly the governor sank back into his chair. Unheard by the governor, Runnels continued, saying, "And Kruger's wife, beaten and burned to death in her own home. Mr. Beker's three children cut to pieces. The Bodkers, visiting Hendersen estate, poisoned. Lars Hendersen—his heart cut out. Mr. Kint—beheaded."

"What of Jan Hendersen?" William Barens asked.

"I passed him on the sea. He has one of Bodker's daughters with him. The younger one. And a slave. Those of the planters who have escaped have only done so through the efforts of their loyal slaves."

"How did you get this news?" De Wint asked.

"From those slaves who have remained on our side. They hear the drums and tell us what's going on." Suddenly Runnels looked around. He leaped up. "In the name of God, why are we sitting here. Those poor people need help. Let's do something."

"Just a minute," the governor spoke up. "There has been enough savagery for one day." He stood up and looked around the table. "There are over two thousand blacks on this island. Can you imagine what it will be like

186

if they rise against us?" The men were quiet. "None of you have suffered any greater loss than my daughter or I have this day. But we cannot lose sight of our families here."

"Do you propose to abandon those people on St. John?" Runnels asked.

The governor leaned forward, putting his weight on the desk. "No, I do not. But I propose to organize every force we have on this island to protect St. Thomas from insurrection. And then we will assist those on St. John." Governor Gardelin dropped back into his chair. His voice was very low. "Now, who of you will volunteer to organize a group?"

William Barens stood up. "I will, sir."

"Then you may have sixteen of our soldiers. That will leave seventy-five here to protect our town."

"It is not a wise move to send reinforcements to fight the Negroes," Mueller said, leaping up. "We should send enough troops in there with boats to remove the whites. We cannot fight a war on St. John and protect St. Thomas at the same time. The Negroes talk back and forth with those drums. They'll know if we weaken our garrison here on St. Thomas. I'm not for sending any of our troops in there to fight. Let's get those families off the island and wait until we can bring in help from the English or French. We can't spread ourselves too thin or we'll all be killed."

"Aye," De Wint said. "But it is our duty to save those poor people who are at Deurloo's. I'll volunteer along with Barens. We can sail tonight and reach there by daybreak."

"You can't just give up the island to those savages," Runnels yelled. "They'll destroy every plantation on it. What about our investments. Every one of us will be wiped out." He turned, looking at each face. He settled on Barens. "You, Barens, how would you like to lose your plantation here on St. Thomas? There isn't one of you men here who doesn't know what we've gone through to build up St. John. We can't just walk out and give it to those savages. You have to go over there and help us fight."

"What would you propose we do, Runnels?" Barens said.

"Get the women and children off the island. The planters don't want to leave. They'll stay there and fight. Every last one of them. Just get them some ammunition and whatever men you can spare. With enough guns and ammunition we can pick off the rebels one by one if necessary."

"Don't you think the Negroes have gotten arms by now?" Governor Gardelin said.

"Yes. But they don't know how to use them. And they'll run out of ammunition before too long," Runnels said. "Governor, this council's responsibility to St. John is no less than to St. Thomas. Are you going to sit here and guard your own plantations while every planter on St. John is wiped out? What would the King think?"

There was silence in the room. The governor looked up at Runnels. "We'll take a vote on it." He turned to the group of men in front of him. "We have a responsibility to St. John. I personally feel we cannot let the plantations be destroyed without putting up a fight. We could spare one officer and fifteen soldiers from our garrison without weakening our forces too much. If we took, say, one or two loyal slaves from twenty or so plantations, we would not weaken anyone's forces too much."

"Those slaves are costly," Mueller interrupted. "Will the Crown reimburse us?"

"We have a fund that can be drawn on in the event a slave is wounded or lost, according to council's provisions. If we vote in favor of this, that fund will cover every slave who goes to St. John."

"In that case, I see no objection," De Wint said. "There are plenty of slaves on the market today. We can easily replace those we lose."

"A loyal slave is not easy to replace," Mueller said.

"Enough arguing, gentlemen," the governor said. "We will take a vote. Let that settle the issue. All those in favor of the volunteers staying to fight say 'aye.' "

The governor turned his head around the circle of ten men. Runnels watched carefully. Eight nodded assent.

"Enter that count by name," the governor instructed his secretary. "Now, if you gentlemen will excuse me, I'll go break the sad news to my daughter."

Claude Mueller walked down the steps of the fort, holding on to Sergeant Ottingen's arm. Mueller was a short, fat man, and his small feet, shod in silver-buckled shoes, dropped heavily on each step. He was saying to the sergeant, "If you are ambitious, Theodore, this is your opportunity. The King will offer a promotion to any young man who volunteers his services in the face of a sizable Negro rebellion." Reaching the bottom of the steps, he let

188

loose of the sergeant's arm and pulled his cutaway coat into place. "Aside from that, Ottingen, you're one of the few men in the King's service who won't take any nonsense from these barbarians."

Ottingen watched Claude Mueller's mouth. Claude's lower lip was a loose, thick piece of flesh that flopped up and down without appearing coordinated with the words that passed over it. Claude continued, "If we are going to fight, we might as well send the best we can persuade to volunteeer. Why drag this messy affair on forever?"

"Forever?" Ottingen exclaimed. "We can put this rebellion down in a few days."

"Yes, my boy, that we can. Especially if men like you volunteer."

Ottingen squared his shoulders. He was a tall, slender man. His uniform hat was squared low on his forehead, just above his bushy blond eyebrows. Ottingen had a rugged look about his tanned, handsome face. He bowed toward Claude Mueller. "In that case, I will offer my services," he said.

"That's good news," Mueller said crisply. He looked around and dropped his voice. "You realize, of course, that with a victory on St. John, you may be able to command the garrison here in the near future."

Ottingen looked pleased. Mueller went on, "It's only a suggestion, of course. Not that my personal feuds with the Captain have any bearing on the matter. Why—look there. I believe that's Jan Hendersen pulling his boat up below." Claude took a few steps down the hillside. "It is. Come, Sergeant. Here's a planter you must meet. He left St. Thomas to settle on St. John about fifteen years ago. It wouldn't surprise me in the least if his slaves are behind this revolt. He's always given them too much liberty!"

"Yes, I've heard about him," Ottingen said. "Who's the woman with him?"

Claude grabbed Ottingen's arm to support himself. His shoes felt slippery on the brick path that led down to the water. "It looks like the Bodker's youngest daughter, Anna. Yes, she is a beauty. And not married, Theodore." He chuckled. "I imagine she gets lonely out there at Hendersen. Wouldn't you think so?"

"I hope she does," Theodore said, keeping his eyes fixed on Anna.

"The Bodker family was as strange as the Hendersen

family. They kept their own up there in the country," Mueller said. "Jan, Jan Hendersen," he called.

Jan looked up. Seeing Mueller, he dropped his head and continued working the lock in place on the canoe.

Reaching the group, Claude said, "Tell me, Jan, was it horrible?"

"What are you talking about, Claude?" Jan said, without looking up.

"The revolt."

Jan straightened up. "I don't like to disappoint you, Claude, but we missed the bloody part of the rebellion, so I have no details."

Claude's forehead moved down, making his brown eyes frown. He felt a nudge at his elbow. "May I present Sergeant Theodore Ottingen," he said, "of the St. Thomas garrison. Jan Hendersen, Sergeant."

Ottingen squared his shoulders and snapped his heels together. "Sir." He bowed.

Jan saw that the young man's eyes went directly to Anna. "Anna Bodker, Sergeant," Jan said. Ottingen went through the same maneuver again.

Anna nodded.

"I say, Jan," Claude said. "Have you any loyal slaves at Hendersen whom you'd volunteer to send to St. John? Barens is taking charge of the reinforcements. He'll need all the help he can get."

"Loyal to what?" Jan asked.

"Why, to the planters, naturally," Claude said.

"Hendersen slaves have always been loyal, Claude. You know that. They're loyal enough to stick by any planter who treats them right." Jan saw Claude's eyes light up. He went on. "And loyal enough to their own kind that they wouldn't take arms against them."

Claude wiped the sweat from under his lip with a quick swipe of his finger. "You haven't changed any, have you, Jan? If we have a revolt on St. Thomas, I suppose your slaves will be the first to carry you off to Crab Island, huh?"

"I hope they do," Jan said. "In the meantime, why don't you go over there," he nodded to where several other boats were tying up, "and discover the virtues of being kind to your slaves from those people whose slaves carried them off St. John today." He turned his back on Mueller. "Come along, Anna. We have a long journey home."

Jan took Anna's arm and led her past Ottingen. The sergeant bowed. Anna did not look up. Bahbu moved up behind them. When she was next to Claude Mueller, she turned her head and looked into his face. Her coal-black face was somber. In her eyes there was a hard glint, another life behind the surface of them that shot out at Claude Mueller. He felt himself shudder and stepped back. Bahbu moved up the path after the others. Claude turned and let his eyes follow her. The big pad of cloth wrapped on her head made her look topheavy. Her worn blouse hung off her bony shoulders. He saw the telltale scars that crisscrossed her dull black skin.

"What possesses those people," Ottingen said, removing his hat and wiping the perspiration from his forehead. "The young girl and the slave wench look as if they hated us—and the old man was very peculiar."

"The Bodkers and the Hendersens are strange people, my boy."

"What of this woman, Anna Bodker?" the sergeant asked.

"Oh yes. Little Anna Bodker. She moved to Hendersen when Lars's wife had a stillborn baby. Anna was a beautiful child. Long blond curls and those big blue eyes, just the same as today. Everybody thought she'd marry before she was out of her teens. The mother was a pinched-faced little woman whose only interest seemed to be sewing. They say she let this young one run wild through the fields, like the Negro children do. In fact, it is even rumored that she was allowed to play with the Negroes. They say she can sit a horse as well as any man on St. Thomas, and, believe it or not, Theodore," Claude lowered his voice, "they even say she takes her clothes off and swims in the sea."

The sergeant raised his bushy eyebrows and smiled. "*That* I'd like to see."

Mueller laughed. "And so would I. Well, you know, it is difficult to get the whole truth of anything on this island. The planters out in the country, especially on the west, are isolated. I think that is probably what is wrong with the young Bodker girl and the Hendersen slaves. They are just not accustomed to people. Not decent people, at any rate. Apparently Anna has grown up with only Lars Hendersen and Wilhelm Bodker to influence her opinion of mankind. And that, my dear sergeant, by anyone's standards, would make a young gentlewoman a little bitter about life."

"Now that her family is dead, what do you suppose will happen to her?"

"I don't know. But she is fortunate to have Jan Hendersen back on this island. He is a good man. His views are impractical, but he is a good man."

Jan and Anna rode side by side out of the stable. Behind them, Bahbu rode leading the two Bodker horses. When they reached the dirt road, they stopped and Jan turned in his saddle to survey the town. "It hasn't changed much," he said. His eyes turned to the fort. There the Danish flag, braced by a steady wind from off the sea, flew straight out. In front of the fort, horses, goats and people milled around. Then his eyes swept the harbor. The East Indiaman was moving forward, maneuvering into position so its cannon could protect the town.

Jan moved out onto the road and headed west along the sea. From there, several riders were bearing down on them, going toward the fort.

"Stay on the side of the road," Jan cautioned Anna and Bahbu. "We're headed the wrong way today." They rode past the orderly cluster of white and red houses next to the factory. Then past the factory that was strangely deserted today and on into the country. When they reached Bruce Bay, Fortuna Mountain loomed up ahead of them. Jan could see the mill sitting on the flat ridge on the south of the highest point of the mountain. He looked on up at the sun. It was starting its descent toward Fortuna. Now he heard Prince's gentle voice saying, "Over there, behind the stars and the sun and the moon."

Chapter 16

By early afternoon there were fifty-eight Negroes assembled in the clearing at Hendersen on St. John. North of Hendersen, over Cruz, Caneel, and Coral bays, a thick black cloud of smoke hung over the green mountain tops. King, on the summit that held the Hendersen mill, pounded out the message: Come to Hendersen—come to Hendersen, on the drum. The drumbeat was apparently lost in the celebrations on the captured estates.

Mary squatted down at the edge of the clearing. Slowly she got up and walked to Prince. She pointed toward the mountain side. There, outlines of figures moving toward Hendersen took shape. King stopped drumming. Then the noises of the approaching rebel group took over. The drums and voices throbbed: "Kill the white man, kill; kill the white man, kill." In front of the group, several men leaped and twisted and jabbed their crudely made spears up in the air. The people ran down into the gully, up over the mound on which the mill stood, and streamed toward the clearing. Many of the females were dressed in the long billowing skirts of the white women whose homes they had plundered. The men in the rebel group looked to be in uniform, for there was that sameness in their wide-legged, knee-length trousers tied at the waist with lengths of coarse rope. Aside from that, they were bare. Prince crossed his arms on his chest and waited in the clearing.

William was the first to reach the clearing. He pounced in front of Mary and threw a bag of gold at her feet. "We are rich," he said, his voice ringing with satisfaction. The throng of followers moved past William. Some dragged live animals. Others carried ornate pieces of silverware. Three white men, jostled by six guards, were forced into the clearing. Prince saw that it was Dr. Bodger and his two sons. Christian walked beside them.

"Christian," Prince called out. "What is this? I thought you had agreed to free your master?"

"I had to make a new agreement with William," Christian said.

Prince looked around. William was dancing around Mary, howling. "What agreement?" he said, turning back to Christian.

"His life is to be spared if he tends to our wounds. His sons are to be our slaves." Christian carefully watched Prince's expression. Everyone else he had come in contact with today had become so incensed with killing they had not listened to reason. He was not sure of Prince.

"What do you think about this, Christian?" Prince asked.

"I do not like an Amina to betray his word."

"Then why did you make other terms with William?"

Christian looked hard at Prince. He felt that this man before him, their leader, could be trusted. "I made other terms to save my master's life. Our people were excited, worked up. They wanted to kill."

"You cannot have heart to fight with us if we betray you, Christian. It was agreed your master and his sons would be spared. There are no other terms for you to make. Go get four horses, Christian. Ride with them to Deurloo's Bay. When the plantation is in sight, let them go on. You bring back the horses." Prince turned to Dr. Bodger. "I can make no promise what will happen at Deurloo's Estate today. Christian wanted to send you off this morning. I am sorry this was not done."

Dr. Bodger looked up at Prince. "Christian and I were saying, only this morning, that there are good and bad in black or white. You are a good man, Prince. I cannot wish you luck in this rebellion, but I can wish you health."

"It is too bad your skin was colored wrong," Prince said. "We will need a doctor before this is over." He turned. "There is Christian. Now go."

When the doctor and his sons mounted the horses, William, seeing them, ran to Prince. "What are you doing?" He raised his spear toward the doctor. "We will need him. I made a good term with him. The others wanted to kill him. He is alive only because he is going to tend to our wounds."

Anger flashed in Prince's eyes. "*You* made good terms?

194

When we met before the revolt, the terms were made with Christian."

"No white man should be alive on St. John today," William said. "You are too weak to lead our people."

Prince stepped closer to William. "I don't betray my word to my people," he said evenly. "Is that being weak?"

"Our people want his head," William yelled, jabbing his spear toward the doctor again. "Why don't you ask them right now. Here, I'll do it." William turned around.

Prince's arm shot out, grabbing William by the shoulder. He spun him around. "You will not ask them," Prince said. "I have said that they go free. If you object, William, take up a cane knife." Prince let his arms drop to his side. William eyed him carefully. Prince leaned forward, the amulet around his neck swinging free.

William's eyes fell on the carved icon. Slowly, he backed away. "No. We cannot fight." William kept his eyes on the black carved face. "Let them go, Prince."

"Go, Christian," Prince yelled.

The horses moved off around the crowd. Prince was crouched so far forward that he looked as if he would spring on William. "And you get out of my sight," he said. "When you are not so thirsty for blood and rum, we will talk."

When they had reached the crest of the hill overlooking Deurloo's plantation, Dr. Bodger summoned Christian to stop.

"I have been thinking," he said. "You could be of more use to your own people, and to us, if you do go back."

"What!" Christian exclaimed. "They are mad. They are disorganized and crazed. I am sick of my people."

"All of those people are going to die, Christian, if they don't have some sense put into their heads. Their leader, Prince, he seems level-headed. Go back, Christian. When the enthusiasm of this day has worn off, maybe they'll listen to reason. Only a black man can reason with them. Talk with Prince, try to convince him that his people will suffer. By tomorrow the island will be covered with soldiers. Those poor, disorganized people cannot hold out against trained troops. If they give themselves up without any more senseless killing, it will go easier on them."

"And what if they don't give up?"

"Then you can be useful to us in routing them out. If we know their plans in advance, we are better equipped to outwit them."

"I don't want to spy on my people. I'd rather just leave them."

"That's up to you. In a war, you have to decide which side you're on. You are too gentle, Christian, to be on the side of those people you saw out there today. If you come to our side, you betray them no less when you give something to our side."

"I will go back, master. Maybe I can talk some sense to Prince." Christian looked at Dr. Bodger. "I did not realize until this morning, you and your sons are the only people I've ever had. My loyalty is not to the black man or the white man. It is to you."

Dr. Bodger got off his horse. "Come, boys, we have to hurry."

The doctor collected the reins of the three horses and handed them to Christian. Christian's long, angular, black face looked very forlorn. "They will attack you today," Christian said, his brown eyes looking down into his master's.

"Care for your wounded, Christian, as I will for mine."

Christian eased the horses around. He lifted his long, thin legs to the side and let them fall down on the horse. With a sudden burst of speed he rode off.

The revelry at Hendersen had ceased when Christian returned. The people were squatted on the dirt, listening to Prince.

"We have already given them too much time to organize. By now many planters from the south and west of the island have reached Deurloo's who never should have. To win our freedom we have to eliminate the white men first. Then we can feast. Then you can drink rum and eat food and wear their clothes and drink from their glasses. Did you war back in your villages carrying all of this wealth in your hands?" Prince looked around. "No. You go to war with your knife and your arrow—and now with the white man's guns. Look. Look around us. We have only half the number of people we should have to drive these white people off St. John. Where are the rest of them? Back there," he pointed to the north, where the smoke was rising, "dancing and tearing at the people they have al-

196

ready killed. Now take up your arms. We will move those at Deurloo's into the sea. And then the island is ours."

Slowly the crowd rose off the ground. The drums began tapping their chant: Kill the white man, kill. As if they had been suddenly plied with a secret potion, the people began their wild howls and vigorous leaps and turns. "Kill," William yelled. "We want our freedom." He was obsessed again, throwing his spear up into the air and leaping to catch it.

Prince took Mary by the arm. "You stay here. You should be talking to our gods!"

"I am going," Mary grunted. "From the time I was a little girl I waited for this day. The gods will wait until tonight." She tapped her bare feet in time to the drum. "Kill," she mumbled, "Kill the white man, kill . . ." Soon she was hypnotized by the beat and ran along, throwing her arms up into the air, shaking her bony hands and making her mouth move up and down, chanting. Prince trotted along beside her. He had composed his own chant: Soon we will be free, free; soon we will be free.

Lieutenant Charles saw the first of the rebels come over the crest of the mountain and stream down toward them. "Here they come," he shouted. The manor was situated on a knoll and in such a position that they could only be attacked from the front. Here a stone wall gave them some protection. A cannon was mounted on either side of a gateway in the wall. Two men stood ready to assist John von Beverhoudt at his cannon. At the other, Lieutenant Charles and Peter Kruger stood by Carl Iversen. Crouched behind the wall, the other men were spread out evenly. Beside them the women and loyal slaves were ready to reload their weapons. The rebels' late attack had given the planters time to shuttle all but three of the children to a small islet a short distance north of Deurloo's Bay. The three children were in the house.

The eyes of every man were turned toward the mountain side. The drums had increased their tempo to match the running feet. "Kill the white man, kill; kill the white man, kill . . ." the air seemed to shake with the chant and the drums. A white-hot sun blazed down on the planters, making beads of sweat roll down their grim faces.

"Look at this," Von Beverhoudt exclaimed. "And we spent a fortune buying ourselves this rebellion."

"It had to come," Iversen said. "Every time I bought another one of those savages, I told myself it would."

Lieutenant Charles pulled at the tight collar of his uniform and stared at the enemy. "They're better dressed for fighting in this heat than we are," he mumbled.

But none of them took their eyes off the flow of half-naked bodies that was nearing the gully, just below their makeshift fortress.

"You fire first, Iversen," Von Beverhoudt called. "And while you reload, I'll fire. Don't get anxious. Give them a chance to get close enough that each ball will take a good count. We're so outnumbered it's our only hope."

Lieutenant Charles turned to look at his wife. She had her head against the wall. Her eyes were closed. Small chance we have to win against these odds, he told himself. He turned back. In that brief space of time, the rebels were now crossing the field below the summit. Their sharp cane knives and cutlasses glinted in the sun.

"Does anyone here know their leader, the slave they call Prince?" Von Beverhoudt called out. "If we could kill him, it might slow down the others."

"They all look alike," Iversen yelled back.

Dr. Bodger watched Prince race across the area toward the summit. His tan skin made him easily discernible. But none of the other planters would know Prince, for Jan Hendersen had not entertained planters. The doctor put his head down.

"Stand ready, Iversen," Von Beverhoudt commanded. "You other men hold your fire until the cannon is shot."

Now they were coming up the summit. "There's that bowlegged heathen of Jan Hendersen's," Kruger told himself, watching King race with William for the lead. They were eight or nine feet in front of the group who had massed around Prince.

Von Beverhoudt screamed, "Lieutenant, try to get those two men in the front. We can't waste a cannon ball on them."

Lieutenant Charles pulled his pistol from his waistband. Using his left arm for a brace, he took aim at William. The shot was lost in the howls and drumbeats. William fell. The crowd behind him continued. When they reached William, they leaped over the body. Prince saw the hole in William's chest and stopped. William was dead. Mary ran past Prince. "Kill, kill the white man," she cried.

"Iversen. FIRE!"

The cannon shot roared down into the mass of people. The full impact of the shot hit low into the running legs. Six of the rebels fell. Mary eased slowly to the ground.

Prince came up behind her and took her by the arm. "Mary, you are hurt."

"Go, Prince, kill them," she commanded.

"It's Mary," someone yelled. "Mary."

King turned. Seeing Mary on the ground, he ran to her. "Quick, Prince. We will take her to the bush."

Prince and King put their hands together and scooped them under Mary. They ran back down the hill.

Von Beverhoudt fired. Another three slaves fell. The others retreated around Mary.

Iversen watched the tide of human bodies turn off and disappear into the wooded area on the right of the valley. In disbelief he turned to look at Von Beverhoudt.

"We must have gotten one of their leaders," Von Beverhoudt said. "Good thing, too. If they had continued at that pace, we wouldn't have been able to hold them off." Von Beverhoudt looked down the slope in front of them. There William's black body was sprawled out, face down, on the green grass. Behind him three of the wounded who had been deserted in the retreat were pulling on clumps of grass, trying to drag their bodies out of firing range. It was apparent that all three of them had been wounded in their legs.

"Get those devils," Iversen yelled, pulling out his pistol. Lieutenant Charles braced his left arm again and took aim. His right hand jerked from the recoil of the pistol. A scream pierced the air.

"Stop." Dr. Bodger stood up. "Let me go bring them back. They are wounded."

"Are you mad?" Iversen yelled. "We've had enough trouble with them without having to tend to their wounds." He raised his pistol and took careful aim. A shot rang out. Another scream, and one of the crawling forms arched in the air and fell back down on the ground. Now only one was moving. He was grabbing out in front of him with both arms. His legs dragged behind him, so that he looked as though he was rowing his torso down the incline. Lieutenant Charles took aim. He fired. The torso continued its

199

rowing motion. Iversen took aim again. But, before he could fire, another shot rang out. Iversen grabbed his shoulder. "My God, I've been hit!"

Four figures ran into the clearing toward the wounded rebel. Lieutenant Charles yelled, "Take aim."

Dr. Bodger stood up. "Don't fire," he screamed. "My servant is down there. He is loyal to us."

"None of those heathens are loyal," someone yelled. "Kill every last one of them."

Von Beverhoudt raised a loaded musket. Instantly, Dr. Bodger leaped up on the wall. "Don't fire, I said." He turned to face Von Beverhoudt. "Christian is acting under my orders."

Von Beverhoudt lowered the musket. His eyes blazed at Dr. Bodger. "Explain yourself, Doctor."

"There is nothing to explain," he said. "Christian has been trained to heal people, not kill them. You know that."

"John," Mrs. Von Beverhoudt said, looking up at her husband. "You know that is so. Listen to the doctor."

"Am I supposed to let four of those savages escape me because his servant is among them? Doctor, go tend to Iversen!" Von Beverhoudt raised his musket and aimed. A shot rang out. A clump of dirt rose up in front of the figures that were now running with their injured friend lifted up between them. They quickly disappeared into the protection of the wooded area.

Von Beverhoudt lowered the musket. Slowly the planters stood up. The trade winds stirred the leaves of the two palm trees on either side of the summit. The noise made everyone aware that the drums and chanting and shouts of revelry had ceased. In the ensuing quiet, one hollow drumbeat vibrated. The air held the hollow tone. It seemed as if another would not follow, but it did, and continued on. There was, in its solitude, a sad quality about the slow, methodical cadence of the drum. The planters felt it.

"Now those savages will go in there and mourn for their dead," Von Beverhoudt said. He turned and looked at Dr. Bodger tearing Iversen's shirt away from his wounded shoulder. "When you're finished there, Doctor, maybe you'll explain about your servant." He walked back to the cannon. "Don't relax. Those black heathens usually dance and howl for everything, including their dead. They'll work up into another frenzy soon." He looked over his shoulder at the red ball of sun hovering over St. Thomas. "God, I hope reinforcements get here soon!"

"Amen," a deep voice echoed from the group.

Prince squatted down beside Mary. He put his big hand under her head and raised it. "Drink this," he said, holding a cup to her lips.

Quietly, Mary obeyed. Her eyes rolled. "Aiii," she mumbled, "I am weak."

"Christian will have to hurt you, Mary. You will have to be brave."

"What is he going to do?" Mary asked.

"Stop the bleeding."

"How?" Mary whispered.

Prince looked down at Mary's face. Her eyes implored him to speak the truth. "He is going to burn you."

Mary turned her head the other way. There Christian was squatted down, his arm outstretched to the fire. He held an iron into the white heat at the bottom of the pile. She turned her head back. "My foot, Prince. How is my foot?"

Again he stared into Mary's face. "Speak," she commanded.

"It is gone."

Her eyes fell shut and she let out a low groan. Prince reached out and took her hand. He noticed how black it looked against his own brown skin. He raised it to his cheek. "It will not matter," he said. "You do not need your foot to talk with our gods."

"You were wrong to let our people stop," Mary said. "I am an old woman. You do not give up your freedom because of an old woman's foot."

"Our people stopped because they look to you to lead them, Mary."

Mary opened her eyes and turned her head toward Prince. "You are their leader. They know that."

"They know I am the leader that the gods sent. And they know you are their leader that the gods sent before I was born. They have two leaders, Mary. It was shown today when you were hurt. They could not go on without you."

"If only the white man had not taken us from our villages," Mary mumbled, closing her eyes again.

"I am ready," Christian said.

"Wait," Mary whispered. "Have King beat the drum faster. Have Ruth call out to the gods to make me brave."

Hurriedly Prince put Mary's hand down. He went to King and whispered. The drumbeat stopped, then sprang up again. King's strong hands pounded down in a series of rapid beats that vibrated the ground under them. Ruth leaped up. She threw off the scarf that was bound around her head. Immediately six other women appeared beside her. They, too, threw off their scarves. A circle of men ran around the women. They emitted mournful howls that raised up out of the grove. The women moaned. And then the howling and moaning was taken up by the eighty-odd people who were gathered there.

When Prince picked up Mary's hand again, there was a frantic commotion surrounding them. Prince nodded to Christian.

Christian rose off the ground, lifting the rod from the fire. A red-hot ball was on the end of the rod. Quickly he brought it around. "Take off that cloth," he said to the woman who knelt by Mary's leg. She removed the tourniquet. From the ragged wound Christian saw the blood begin to pump out again. Carefully, he aimed the fiery ball at it. Lower and lower he moved his arm.

There was a sizzle, then Mary's scream rang out, blending with the other noises around them. The wound smoked. Christian held the ball in place. There was the smell of burning flesh. Prince felt Mary's sweaty grip on his hand go loose. The drum continued pounding. The howls and moans and occasional frenzied screams continued. Prince held Mary's limp hand for many hours.

By nightfall, Mary was breathing easily. She was covered with a heavy comforter Ruth had taken from one of the other women, and her head rested on a folded white petticoat. Prince put his hand up and stroked the wiry mass of black hair that was standing on end. She had stopped shivering, and now he felt the moistness that had collected on her forehead and hair.

"She is very strong," Christian said. "If she does not get infection, she will live."

Prince stood up and looked at Christian. "I will tell the people they can celebrate. We will not go to Suhm's tonight. Later we will send for the others to come join us here. In the morning we will organize and attack the white men again."

Christian nodded. "Prince, I must talk to you."

Prince looked at Christian's long, thin face. Christian's big eyes were set deep under his wide forehead. In fact, in the dim blaze of the firelight, the wide space over his broad nose looked hollow. "Yes," Prince said, "when our people are settled, I will talk with you."

Prince walked to the edge of the grove where a sentinel stood and looked up at Deurloo's. The feathery leaves of the tall palm trees looked wet in the moonlight. Behind the two cannon he could easily see the outline of the figures that were gathered there. Yes, they would not desert their cannon. How can we fight those cannon, he thought. He had never before seen their effect. It was still amazing to him that so many people could have fallen with a single shot.

"Watch carefully," Prince warned the sentinel. "I do not think they would be foolish enough to come down from there. But do not take your eyes off them. The white men can think of very evil things, you know that."

Prince looked up at the piece of moon. It is shining on Fortuna Mountain, he thought. And Anna. He turned and walked back into the grove. Here fires glowed, casting light up from the ground into the leaves on the trees. Five brighter fires in the distance had animals over them, turning slowly on spits. King was sitting in front of a small fire, leaning against a tree. When Prince approached, he saw that King was asleep, his head slumped down on his broad shoulder. The Hendersen drum was lying on the ground. Prince smiled. King had reason to be tired. A little rum and he'll play that drum all night, he thought. He leaned over and put his hand on King's head. Surprised, King sprang up, holding his big hands out in front of him, ready to fend off an enemy. Prince laughed wholeheartedly. "Would some Hendersen rum make you dance tonight?" he said.

King laughed. The skin on his squat, broad features shone from the firelight. "Hendersen rum makes me dance any time," he said.

"Go, then, have them open the rum. Tell the people to play. Take up our drum, King. Get the others started. And then you dance."

King's eyes rolled slyly at Prince. "I have other things to do. Did you see that black girl from Kruger's? She was a house slave. She is very pretty, Prince. She has full lips— and she is fat. Really fat! She is very nice, Prince. And she is Amina. We will make babies tonight. Babies to grow up in freedom."

Prince laughed.

"And you, Prince," King said. "Is there one you would like?"

"Yes. But I cannot have her."

King shook his head in understanding. "Aiii, Prince. How can you like that white skin? I like my woman black as indigo!"

"Some are colored wrong. They cannot help it."

"The gods have been cruel to them," King said. "That is why I am proud to be Amina. Amina are colored right." He held his short, muscular arm out. "They did not make a mistake with us. Well," King leaned over and raised the drum, "the sooner we start the drum feast, the sooner I can make the baby."

Soon the drums and the wild celebration began. All through the grove, dancing forms circled the fires. Prince saw King. In front of him was a tall, buxom woman who moved her wide hips in an erotic jerk to the music. King's bow legs trounced up and down, his hips jabbing back and forth at the girl. They both had their arms upraised, accenting the rhythm they beat out from their waists down. Their bare feet stirred the dirt beneath them. The girl threw her head back, concentrating on the pulsating gyrations of her hips. Suddenly King lunged at her. She broke from him and ran off into the dark beyond. Prince laughed. King's bowed legs certainly could carry him at great speed.

Christian was leaning against a tree watching the merriment when Prince found him. "You do not want to dance," Prince asked, easing down beside him.

"Not tonight," Christian said. "My heart is too heavy for that. And you, Prince? You do not dance."

"I have other things to think about."

There was a silence between them.

"You think of Anna," Christian asked.

"Yes. I think of Anna. All the time."

Christian pushed himself tighter against the tree. "Do

you feel anything, killing the white men when you are in love with a white?"

"Of course not. Anna is not really white. She is one of us." Prince turned to look at Christian. "Why do you ask?"

"This morning . . . when William wanted to kill the doctor, it made me sick."

"That is only because he is one of the good ones. He was good to you. That is why you spared his life."

"But our people wanted to kill all of the white people. You and I know that all of the white people are not the same, Prince. We say they are colored wrong if they are good. Maybe they say we are colored wrong when they think one of us is good."

"How many white people think a black man is good?"

"Anna thinks you are good. Dr. Bodger thinks I am good. A lot of slaves let their masters escape in boats today. So there must be some good feelings between the two colors."

"Christian. If there are so many good white people, why do they still take us from our villages? There must be more bad ones than good ones. They are always voting on everything. They do not come near a vote to put an end to keeping us in chains."

"I know." Christian's voice was weary. "But it made me sick today to see King throwing Judge Soedtmann's head on the ground and then jabbing it up again. It is very cruel."

"Cruel?" Prince turned his back to Christian. "What of these scars." Turning, he jabbed his finger at the brand on Christian's narrow shoulder. "And what of *that*. They beat us and put hot irons on our shoulders, they chop off our feet and tongues and hands and ears and fingers. When the gods are good to us, the white men chop our heads off and we don't feel the pain any more."

"Our people do not have to act like those white men who have done those horrible things."

"Every black who is here tonight has bitterness in his heart, Christian. Every black who is here wants to be free. I want to be free. I want to be free, Christian, so I can live with Anna. I am a man. I do not want to be a slave to anyone."

Another long silence followed. Mentioning Anna had put

Prince's thoughts in St. Thomas. Christian thought about freedom.

"I would like to be free, too," Christian finally said. "But if I were free, I would still want to follow my studies with Dr. Bodger." His eyes found Prince's. "I cannot kill, Prince. I am no good to you in this fight."

Prince's eyes hardened. "What is this, Christian? What are you saying?"

"I will tell you what it is." Christian moved his face close to Prince's. "I was going to try to stop you from continuing this fight. But you are right. Everyone should be free. Only I cannot kill people. I do not want to be killed either." Christian pushed himself up off the ground. "All I want to do is to continue my work."

Prince leaped up. "What about our people?"

"I was brought here as a child. The only people I really know, the only family I have ever had, is Dr. Bodger."

Prince stood still. "You did not think of this before. Why did you become a leader of our people?"

"I did not know how I really felt until this morning," Christian lowered his voice and looked at Prince. "I could have gone on. Pretending. But I wanted to be honest with you, Prince."

Prince crossed his arms on his chest and paced back and forth in front of Christian. "What do you want to do?" he finally said.

"I want to go back to Dr. Bodger."

"I am glad you told me how you feel. If you have the chance, go. I pretend it is Anna, and I know what you are saying. Anna is my family." He stared at Christian. "But I have to fight for freedom or I cannot be with her."

"If I go back to Dr. Bodger," Christian said, "I will fight beside him. But I promise you, Prince, I will never take arms against you."

"Nor I against you, Christian."

Dr. Bodger sat with his back against the stone wall talking to Von Beverhoudt. "I bought Christian when he was a boy. He always showed interest in the work I did in my laboratory. You know how these blacks are about their bush teas and such. Christian would bring them to me and I often discovered that they were better cures for many things than I had known about before. When my wife had her first heart trouble, he brought a bush that helped her. When our oldest boy cut himself with a cutlass, Christian brought a painkiller plant that really took away the pain. To me, Christian has never been a slave. He is an associate. Christian is every bit as knowledgeable about medicine today as I am. This morning, he was appalled at the crazed manner in which those people came down upon us. And he outwitted the leader, who wanted our heads, as I knew he would. Christian wants no part of this revolt. He cannot kill. Christian is trained to cure people. I asked Christian to stay with the rebels hoping he can talk them out of this meaningless treachery. He will try. And if he fails, Christian will come back here. Then, perhaps, he will assist us in finding out who the responsible parties are, so we can rightfully punish those who deserve it and be more lenient with the others."

John von Beverhoudt got up from the wall beside the cannon and stretched. He was a small, wiry, meticulous man who demanded everything he was associated with to be well organized. He also had a sense of fairness that had struck more of a sense of respect than fear in his plantation slaves. Inwardly, he did not blame the slaves for wanting freedom. As captain of the militia, he'd seen enough of the wanton cruelties many overseers inflicted on their slaves. He always felt that fear of the Negro stimulated it. But Captain Von Beverhoudt did not allow his emotions to overcome his practical side. He had a plantation and he needed slaves to work it. He'd joined the militia to protect his investment. Right now he did not feel very successful in that task.

"Some rewarding relationships have grown between slave and planter," he said to Dr. Bodger. "I know of what you speak. My overseer, Henry, spoke out against a group of his own this morning. There is no way for a man to know how he has gone about getting another's respect, but it is pleasant when it happens." He looked up at the moon. "For such a small slice of moon, it's putting out a lot of light. I hope they wait for daybreak before they attack again. We should have reinforcements by then." He yawned. "Listen to that noise. They should be tired after all the activity they had today." He squinted toward the wooded area. Occasionally a glow of fire broke through the treetops, like a ship's light bobbing down there. His eyes traveled up along the slope leading back to the house. On his right, about a hundred feet from the wall, he saw a

207

movement. He grabbed his musket and raised it. "Who's there," he shouted.

"Christian, slave of Dr. Bodger," the voice called back.

Dr. Bodger stood up and stepped beside the captain. "Can you recognize him if I have him stand up?" Von Beverhoudt asked.

"Yes."

"Stand. Raise your arms."

A tall thin figure rose up. When his arms lifted into the sky, Christian looked like a slender ebony tree trunk on the side of the slope.

"That is Christian," Dr. Bodger exclaimed.

"Come forward. Keep your arms up."

Slowly Christian came forward.

"Christian." Dr. Bodger went forward and took Christian's arm, pulling him behind the cannon. "Tell me. Have you talked with them?"

"Yes, master, I have."

"What do they say?"

"They want their freedom."

Dr. Bodger sat down on the wall. "What fools."

Iversen, with a sling tied over one broad shoulder holding his wounded arm against his chest, got off the wall and came up to Christian.

"Who is responsible for this revolt?"

"Many of them," Christian said.

"Such as?" Captain Von Beverhoudt said.

Christian's shadowed eyes looked at his master. "Speak up, Christian," the doctor said. "We only want to punish the leaders. You can save a lot of the others if we know who the leaders are."

"William and Peter, from Caroline." Christian dropped his head.

"And who else?" Iversen demanded in a sharp voice.

"David from Kruger's."

"David!" Peter Kruger exclaimed. "Wait until I get my hands on him!"

"Yes, go on," the captain said.

"Thomas from Judge Soedtmann's."

"What of the slave they call Prince?" Iversen asked.

Christian raised his head again and looked toward the doctor. "I do not know of Prince."

"He's supposed to be one of Jan Hendersen's slaves,"

Kruger growled. "How many from Hendersen are behind this, Christian?"

"Only the woman called Mary."

"She leads the revolt, Master John," Von Beverhoudt's slave, Henry, spoke up. "I have heard it often. She is a witch. She has powerful medicines."

"A woman, leading this rebellion," Captain Von Beverhoudt exclaimed. "Of course. That's why they fell back today. That old woman they stopped to pick up. Who ever thought a woman would be responsible for this."

"You might know it would be one of Jan Hendersen's slaves," Iversen said.

"That *is* amusing," Peter Kruger said. "Tell me, Christian, I'm curious. Have you heard *why* this woman stirred a rebellion?"

"Yes, sir."

"Speak out. Do we have to pry every word out of you?" Kruger snapped.

Christian turned so that he could see Peter Kruger and looked squarely at him. "Lars Hendersen is the cause of this rebellion. This woman is Amina. She and her mate were captured when they were at war with another tribe. She was the daughter of the greatest witch doctor of all the tribes. Lars Hendersen killed her mate. Later he killed her son, who was his own son. An Amina will go to war if you try to take his freedom from him. To kill his mate and then his child is to ask for a curse."

"What kind of *curse?*" Kruger sneered. He stared at the dark hollow of Christian's eyes.

"A curse on all the evil white men."

In the silence that followed, there was the uneasy shuffling of bodies. Someone coughed.

"Do we believe in this curse?" Iversen asked.

Dr. Bodger stood up. "There is no need for you people to question Christian about what he believes in. We are not holding services here tonight."

"I am only curious, Doctor," Iversen said. "If, as you say, Christian is an intelligent man, I would like to know if he believes in such a thing as a 'curse.' "

"Then answer him, Christian."

"I believe in *this* curse," Christian said. He said the words slowly. They hung in the air.

The drum noises, the howls and yells and screams, rose

up from the grove beneath them. A cloud drifted over the moon and put the group in darkness. Iversen went to the wall. Now a glow of orange light could be seen over the rebel camp. He had to admit, there was something about their drum dances and customs that stirred his soul and created within him an apprehensive unrest. Iversen never heard the hollow tone of a drum at night that he did not feel fear. It was no different right now.

Chapter 17

William Barens commanded the group aboard the company bark that sailed for Deurloo's Bay. There were sixteen soldiers from the St. Thomas garrison. Among them was Sergeant Theodore Ottingen. Additionally, there were nine loyal slaves donated by their owners.

In the distance Barens could see the white line of beach at Deurloo's Bay. The square outline of the house sat on a rise. Behind that, the rounded hills and mountaintops made circular patterns on the night sky. Even by moonlight, Barens could pick out the plots of land that were under cultivation. They seemed to reflect more of the light. The heavy scrub was a black shadow on the island. St. John appeared to be round hills and black shadows.

"It's a great wilderness," Barens said to Runnels. "The rebels have a lot of territory in which to hide."

"Aye," Runnels agreed. "That they do. And they are at home in that tangled shrub. If a white man walked through this bush in those skimpy rags the slaves wear, he would be torn apart by the prickly pear and his skin would be burned and fester from the manchineel. These black hides are tough."

Barens looked up at the sails. They were close-hauled, full of wind, and the ship was well heeled over. "Fortunately," he said, "it's a good night to sail. We should be at anchor within the hour." He looked off the starboard. Going off at an angle to the south was the ship that De Wint commanded. "I hope our timing is correct. We want to unload our men and supplies and get the women and children aboard by the time De Wint and Taarbye are ready to attack the fort." There were seventeen planters and nineteen slaves on the other vessel.

"How many rebels do you think we'll be up against?" Ottingen asked.

"I won't venture to guess. Runnels, here, seems to think

more than two hundred. But I doubt it. They will never get organized into big groups, I'm sure of that. They have no leadership."

"What could these Negroes know of strategy," Ottingen said. "They are probably drunk and roaming the whole island by now."

Runnels looked at Ottingen. "You had better wait to see how we made out at Deurloo's today before you estimate the enemy. Have you looked up there?" He stared at the silhouette of the house. "There isn't a sign of life."

"I've noticed," Ottingen said. He waited a minute. Then he said, "It's a *good* sign. Had those barbarians taken Deurloo's, the place would be ablaze. Or, worse than that, burned to the ground by now."

Prince and King, astride two horses, sat on the ridge behind Cruz Bay. The white sails of the two barks were clearly visible on the sea.

"The one who sails south will come in to attack the fort," Prince said. "The other is bringing reinforcements for the planters at Deurloo's."

"I do not think many of our people are protecting the fort," King said. "Let us hope they have a sentinel posted on the ridge. With all the celebrating tonight, they may not!"

"Until they have had their bellies full of food, they think of nothing else. The mistake was made yesterday. We should have moved on Deurloo's before so many of the planters had a chance to gather there. But everyone celebrated, even the leaders."

"Yes," King grunted. "Giving the white men a chance to get those cannon ready. The cannon are very bad, Prince."

"I do not like it. Each time the cannon fired many of our people fell. I have never seen anything like it."

"It will be worse today," King said.

"Maybe we do not need to attack Deurloo's today."

"What is this?"

"Maybe we can get the white men to come off that hill after us. Why should so many of our people die or be injured by the cannon? If we get the white men to come for us, we will be ready. King, ride to Soedtmann's and Caroline. Put a stop to the celebrating. Tell our leaders

212

that the white men come in boats and we must get ready for them."

"And what of the fort? What if I cannot get enough of our people there in time to protect it?"

"Let the white men have the fort. If they come ashore and have victory, they will believe that we are drunk and celebrating and scattered around the island. Then they will come at us from Coral Bay on our southeast and Deurloo's on our northwest. In between there, we will be waiting for them.

"You are a good leader," King smiled. "It is bad that the other leaders are not with us. They celebrate with the people. Aiii," he mumbled, "the feast began too soon."

"That it did," Prince said. "I am disappointed that our leaders did not hold our people to the plan. To first drive all the white men from the island, and *then* hold the feasts. But they were hungry. I cannot blame them."

Prince, followed by four muscular men who carried Mary on a litter, came into the clearing on Hendersen. In back of the litter five women walked single file.

"Take her into the house," Prince commanded.

"No," Mary called out. "I do not want to go there. Take me to my hut, Prince."

Prince indicated one of the huts with a nod of his head. The procession moved past him. He looked around. What was it that hung in the early morning air, in this gloomy, gray light, that did not seem right? Automatically, he looked up toward the mill. The tapering stone structure was the same color as the drab dawn behind it, appearing as a shadow on the sky. On top of the mill the big blades that yesterday had been locked into position, were now set free. The wind whirled them so fast that they appeared as a circle on top of the mill. The wooden cylinders that moved within the mill click-clacked and rumbled. Unfed, they sent out a loud mournful plea for food. It resounded all over the plantation.

Walking between the huts, Prince came in front of the distillery. Here he saw two barrels of rum on top of a makeshift table. One of the barrels dripped its liquid into the wet, muddy area beneath it. Scattered heaps of powdery charcoal dust still smoldered and sent up a misty haze into the wind. Animal bones, broken crystal, pieces of silverware, and several drums were carelessly abandoned on the ground. He turned so he could look at the greathouse. The square stone house and kitchen were shadows in the dawn. Normally, the blended smells of charcoal fumes and wood smoke and brewing coffee would have reached him. He closed his eyes. He liked going in the kitchen in the morning, to stand close to the fire and drink the hot coffee made syrupy with muscavado and eat the fried corn bread with pawpaw jam. The muscles in Prince's jaws tightened and hurt. He felt his mouth water. Now the heavy odor of rum filled his nostrils. He opened his eyes. The louvered doors and windows of the greathouse were thrown open. Beyond them it was still black.

Everything about the plantation seemed desolate and ugly. Why is it that this place, which is my home, suddenly feels so strange? My home? My family? Without Master Jan, this plantation is not my home. Without my Anna I have no family. Prince dropped his head and listened to the clatter of the mill. So this is what Christian felt. He was sick inside for the things that had become a part of him.

The wind chilled his bare skin. Prince felt himself trembling inside. He pulled up straight, and turned his back on the manor and walked to the slave huts.

"Mary," Prince said softly, squatting down beside her. He lifted her hand in his own. "I have to leave you now. Our people have moved back, grouping between Coral Bay and Deurloo's. We have only a few sentries watching Deurloo's now. We want the white men to come off the hill away from the cannon."

"The cannon are very evil, Prince," she said, looking at him. "You are wise to keep our people from them." Struggling, she raised herself on one arm. "Our people, Prince, they celebrate too much. They are a disappointment to me." She fell back on the straw mat. Staring up at the ceiling, she said, "For all these years, every day our people cry for freedom. And now they stop to play and eat and drink. They must listen to you, Prince."

"Do not worry, Mary. They were very hungry. But now they will listen. Now their bellies are full. I have told King to call a meeting of the leaders tonight. Here."

"You will have the meeting in this hut," Mary said. "I will call on our gods tonight. The leaders will listen to them."

"You are too weak, Mary. The gods can wait."

214

"The gods cannot wait. I am never too weak to call on them. You bring the leaders here."

"Yes, Mary, I will bring them here. Now I will go. Ruth and the others will take care of you."

Mary pressed Prince's hand to her cheek. "The gods will be with you."

William Barens stood at the wall looking down at the wooded area. They had shuttled eight trips with the small boat before the women and children had been safely put aboard. Now the ship was anchored off the islet to the north, sending the small boat in to rescue the children that were hiding there. Barens could hardly believe it. The sun would soon be shining in his face. They had been on the island for over an hour, and he still had not seen a sign of the rebels.

"You were probably right, Sergeant," he called to Ottingen. "I think the rebels have gotten drunk and spread themselves out on every plantation on the island."

"They weren't spread out when they attacked us last night," Captain Von Beverhoudt said. He paced back and forth on the stone floor, his heels clicking briskly. "Had they continued on that first attack, we would have been murdered, all of us. Fortunately, we hit the woman who leads this rebellion. They fell back, retreating with her. Thank God! It was a sight I will never forget."

"Maybe she is dead and they've gone off to have one of their savage rites for her," Kruger suggested.

"Impossible," Von Beverhoudt snapped. "When they mourn their dead they beat those drums frantically. Just listen. There are only a few drums beating in the hills. Nothing frenzied enough for their death ritual."

"We'd better send a group out to see what's going on," Barens said. "Who will volunteer?"

"Here, sir," Ottingen replied, snapping to attention. One by one, seven more soldiers volunteered.

"Ottingen," Barens said, "you'll be in charge of this group. See if you can locate where the rebels are encamped. Try to find out what we're up against. This may be a trap. Be careful."

At that minute a cannon fired, and then another, and another. "Three cannon shots," Barens yelled excitedly. "De Wint's group have retaken the fort." A cheer went up

215

from the planters and soldiers who manned the makeshift fortress on the terrace of Deurloo's house.

"Get a move on, Sergeant. De Wint will secure the fort and send out a party to join us here. With any luck we should be able to put down this revolt very soon. If you can take any prisoners, do so. We need to give the others a lesson. Let them see what is going to happen to them if they don't surrender."

Iversen said, "Let us have a few of those savages. We'll make an example of them that will make the others wish they had never been a part of this thing!"

Ottingen and the seven soldiers left the summit with words of encouragement from the others. "Get those black heathens," one called out. "Bring us a few heads," another said.

When the first muffled gunshot was heard from the southeast of Deurloo's, the planters and soldiers lined up at the wall and stared off into the direction from which it had come. The sun was high above the mountain ridge. The noises increased.

"Sounds as if they met the rebels," Von Beverhoudt said.

"I don't like it," Barens said. "Listen to those savages hooting. Do you think we should send reinforcements, Captain? Maybe our men have fallen into an ambush."

"We can't send reinforcements from here," Von Beverhoudt said sharply. "It's imperative that we hold this summit. If they have ambushed our men, then they will be watching for us to leave the protection of these cannons."

"Look," Iversen shouted. *"Our* soldiers. They're coming back. They have a prisoner."

Iversen and Barens leaped over the wall and went to the top of the summit. Ottingen and his men were running. A tall Negro, his hands tied behind his back, was being prodded by a bayonet one of the soldiers held on him.

"It is one of Soedtmann's slaves," Iversen yelled as they came up the hill.

Ottingen stopped when he reached the flat of the summit. "Ambush," he panted. "Our men who came from the fort suffered heavy losses. At least six dead and twice that number wounded. We heard the rebels attack. Must have been at least a hundred of those savages." He took off his hat. His blond, close-cropped hair was wet. He leaned forward and rubbed the beads of perspiration from it. "We caught our prisoner trying to crawl back to the main group."

"Now, why don't you and your men go inside and rest," Barens said. "This sun is hot. Leave the prisoner."

"With your permission, Mr. Barens, I'd like to stay out here." Ottingen gave a short jerk of his head toward the mountain. "We may be attacked."

"Let's put this Negro on a post," someone yelled. "We'll tie him up and take our time killing him. Those savages will have their spies out. Let them have something to look at."

"A fine idea," Kruger yelled. "Let's get our blacks busy here. We'll put the post at the end of the wall. Right here." Kruger ran to the end of the terrace. "Get him strung up and then I'll have a bit of revenge!" Kruger doubled his hand into a fist and shook it toward the mountain. "I'll brand every one of these heathens we catch with my initial. On the forehead. They killed Kruger's wife, that's what the brand will say," he screamed. He turned around and aimed his fist toward the prisoner. "You'll be the first to carry a K on your forehead. Hear. You people murdered my wife."

The whites of the prisoner's eyes stood out against the dark brown of his skin. His eyes darted to the wall. Kruger saw the prisoner's lips quiver and move in between his teeth. Kruger walked slowly toward him. "So you're frightened, eh? How do you think my wife felt when you savages came at her?" He stopped moving, but his eyes remained on the Negro's face. "You black devil. I'll brand you with K's from head to foot."

Barens and Iversen looked solemnly at Kruger. Ottingen had his eyes fixed on the prisoner. "I don't blame you, Mr. Kruger," Ottingen said in a low voice. "After what these savages did to your wife you deserve the first chance at all of them."

Dr. Bodger stepped forward. "You know, gentlemen," he said, "you have every right to kill prisoners for their part in this insurrection, but it is inhumane to torture them. I don't agree with it. Since we're all in this together, I think we should hold council and vote on the manner in which the prisoners are to be punished."

"Vote," Kruger snapped back. "Did they stop to take a

vote before they beheaded Judge Soedtmann? Or before they threw my wife in the fire. There isn't a torture that is painful enough for these black savages."

The color rose in the doctor's face. "I sympathize with you for your great loss, Mr. Kruger," he said calmly. "But you call these people savages. What are we?"

, Kruger made a fist and took a step toward Dr. Bodger. He spoke between clenched teeth. "And what do you propose we do, Doctor, set him free? You and your sons were the fortunate ones, weren't you? You can afford to be lenient." Twisting his face, he spit on the ground. "I say torture him."

Von Beverhoudt stepped in between the men. "Let's try to remain calm about this," he said, raising his arms to separate the two. "We held council before, and there is no reason why we should not do it now. I say we vote. And you, Barens? You're on the St. Thomas council. How do you feel about this?"

Barens nodded his head. His ruddy face moved from one man to the other. "I say vote."

"Then vote we will," Von Beverhoudt said. "Now, come on, Kruger," he took Kruger's arm, slowly turning him toward the wall. "We'll go over here and hold council. Sergeant Ottingen pass the word in the house that those who want a voice in this should come out."

Ottingen's heels clicked. "Yes, sir." He swung on one foot, nodded at Captain Von Beverhoudt, and then, looking straight ahead, passed Dr. Bodger. Ottingen's boots slammed hard on the stone terrace. The doctor could hear him move briskly up the steps to the greathouse. Every bit a soldier, Dr. Bodger told himself. And an ambitious one.

In a few minutes Ottingen returned. The four planters who followed him squinted against the sharp bright rays of the sun. They looked as if they had been awakened. Their jacket-like white cotton shirts were soiled and wrinkled. One yawned. Looking at the prisoner, he said, "Ah-hah. Our first prisoner, gentlemen. And let's hope it's not the last."

Von Beverhoudt leaped up on the wall and faced the men. Silence fell over the gathering. Twice he made a low noise to clear his throat. Then he said, "We have here a prisoner." His eyes moved from face to face. He had everyone's attention. "I think, gentlemen, that it behooves us, as the planters and soldiers of this island, to maintain

218

the high standards of dignity with which we have settled important issues in the past . . ."

While Von Beverhoudt continued talking, Dr. Bodger turned his eyes to the prisoner. His shoulders were pulled back and he held his head high. And you, Dr. Bodger thought, are trying to maintain your dignity too.

"Now, then," Von Beverhoudt's words came back to the doctor's ears, "we will, first of all, vote on life or death for the prisoner. Those of you in favor of life, say 'aye.' "

"Aye," Dr. Bodger's voice came out. Two others spoke up.

Von Beverhoudt looked around the serious faces. "Then the prisoner will die."

Dr. Bodger looked back at the captive. The expression on his face did not change. His brown eyes stared straight ahead. The muscles in his neck tightened. The doctor knew that he was making an attempt to swallow.

"And the next issue. Is the prisoner to be made an example, for the others to see? Or, is he to be hung and have it done with?"

At once a rumble of voices erupted. "Quarter him . . ." "Stake him out and let him die of thirst . . ." "Hanging is too good for him . . ." "Look what they did to harmless women and children . . ."

Iversen leaped up on the wall and turned to face the crowd. "If we show mercy to this slave," he pointed a finger toward him, "everyone of those rebels," he let his hand swing back, "will think that we are afraid of them. If we don't make an example of *this* one, we might just as well get in those ships out there and give the island over to the rebels."

Suggestions for torture were called out. The men became increasingly louder. They elbowed each other to try to be seen and heard. The prisoner's eyes widened. Above the rope belt holding the ragged, baggy trousers on his narrow hips, his heartbeats fluttered against the taut skin on his muscled stomach. Cornelius Bodger turned away.

The post was erected. A crossbeam was set high, so that anyone on it would not be able to support his weight on the ground.

Then the rebel was tied to it. His long, muscular arms were strapped against the rough wooden beam with stout ropes. His legs, bare from the knee down, hung limply.

His big, calloused feet jutted out about four inches above the sun-hardened dirt.

Outside the wall, in back of the post, a sizable fire blazed. There were three iron rods on the ground. The ends of these rods were in the white-hot coals.

Ottingen watched Kruger lift one of the rods from the fire. On the end of it was a flat bar of metal, about three inches long. When Kruger lifted it above the flames of the fire, it was the color of the yellow-orange ball of late afternoon sun that was hanging over the sea behind the summit. Kruger ran around to the front of the post and jumped onto the sturdy wooden stool that had been placed there. For a big man, he moved with nimbleness. On the stool, he faced the prisoner, who had his head back against the post. Kruger brought his arm up and moved the flat part of the steel toward the rebel's forehead. The prisoner's eyes followed the small red-hot strip of metal that was pointed from earth to sky on the end of the rod. When it was close enough so that he felt its heat, the rebel's eyelids fell closed.

Cornelius Bodger could not keep his eyes on the prisoner. The sizzle of flesh and the agonized scream reached his ears. He winced.

Another terrified scream. Kruger yelled, "Hold still, or I'll put your other eye out!"

Dr. Bodger saw Kruger's arm move toward the post again. And then another scream, and another. Kruger stepped off the stool and let the rod drop to his side. He looked up at the prisoner. "A legible K. I would say. Too bad I got his eye. Oh, well, he doesn't need to see anyhow." Kruger turned away.

Iversen had already lifted one of the rods from the fire. "Let me at him," he said. He stepped up on the stool and aimed the rod at the prisoner's chest. He pushed the rod so that it burned evenly through the flesh and muscles on the prisoner's rib cage. He pulled back. "I only get one brand, to make my I."

Another planter pushed him aside. "Let me there," he said. "Hurry, before I lose the heat." Iversen stepped off the stool. The planter leaped up on it and brought the rod around. Aiming it at the prisoner's belly, he said, "I get two. One for the judge, and one for his daughter." When he pushed the first line on the rebel's stomach, the rebel gave a hoarse scream and then went limp. The following

220

brand was placed without the accompaniment of the tortured noises. The planter stepped off the stool. "Any others here who want to put their brand on him?"

Four of the planters ran to the fire. Dr. Bodger walked out the front gate in the wall and went around to the cross. The prisoner was unconscious. His head was hanging on his left shoulder, the same side where his eye socket was swollen with the angry, raw, slanted welt running across it. His mouth had fallen open. Two of the planters were arguing about whose turn it was to get on the stool. Dr. Bodger quickly raised his hand and let the poison slide from the paper packet into the rebel's open mouth. Putting the empty paper back in his pocket, he grabbed the slave's head and pushed the jaw upward. With his other hand, he slapped his face. "Wake up. Come on, get awake."

"Yes, wake him," Kruger yelled. "We want to hear him scream. Let those other rebels out there hear him. Don't burn him yet, either of you," he called to the planters who held the irons. "Let the doctor get him awake."

The prisoner's one good eye opened slowly. The doctor patted his face and held his jaw up. The rebel's eye looked imploringly at the doctor. Dr. Bodger looked into the one eye. Then the head went limp again. The doctor let it fall, and stepped away. "It is no use," he said. He walked back to the front of the wall. Behind him he could hear the sizzle of the iron. Let them have their revenge, he told himself. That poor man is out of his misery.

As he started up the steps to the greathouse, he could hear Ottingen's loud voice. "I think he's dead! He couldn't take much, could he?" Then the familiar sound of the sergeant's boots clamping on the stone terrace behind him. "Doctor. Wait. I think the prisoner is dead." Ottingen took the doctor's arm. "Come. See if you can revive him."

Cornelius Bodger looked Ottingen in the face. "He is dead," Dr. Bodger said slowly. "His heart stopped beating while I held his head in my hand."

Ottingen's bushy blond eyebrows lowered over his eyes. "Dead. Good God. Why so soon?" His blue eyes searched the doctor's face.

The doctor's eyes met Ottingen's. He said, "Probably a weak heart, Sergeant." Briefly, Ottingen held the doctor's even stare. Then he turned his back on the doctor and marched away.

221

Chapter 18

It was the eighteenth of January. Eight weeks had passed since the revolt had broken out on St. John. News from there was slow in reaching St. Thomas and, therefore, when Claude Mueller sent word to Jan Hendersen that he would be calling at Fortuna on this date, along with Sergeant Ottingen, who had just returned from St. John, Anna and Jan were anxious to see them.

Anna was in the kitchen, making a relish of tamarind, lime, and muscavado. The spicy smell of it attracted three children who played outside the door. They waited for it to be finished and cool enough to be poured into a china bowl so they could wipe the pot clean. Bahbu came up the path, balancing a stalk of green bananas on her head. "Bahnanah, bahnanah," the children begged, dancing around her.

"No bahnanah," Bahbu said. "Not ripe."

The children went back to tossing a calabash to each other. Bahbu padded into the kitchen and swung the stalk of bananas down to the floor. There was a good fire in the oven and the pots of beef and tamarind relish boiled briskly. Anna stirred them, rotating a wooden spoon between the two pots. A strand of flaxen hair had fallen out of place. She pushed it from her face.

Bahbu walked to the stove and took the spoon from Anna. "Too much heat," she said. "You sit down."

Anna laughed gently. "You would have me sitting down all the time, and getting fat, like Johanna was." Nonetheless, Anna went to the chair by the corner table and sat down. A straw basket filled with sea grapes was on the table. "What are you going to do with these sour grapes, Bahbu? When Tando brought them this morning, I thought he was making a joke with me."

"You ride on horseback all day in the hot sun. You are

too white. Your body will get sick. Sea grapes make good medicine for your skin."

"I like working in the field, Bahbu. Don't you think the people are happier now that I am overseeing them?"

"I think they would rather have Master Lars here to beat them than have you get angry and speak strong words to them."

The children's musical patois carried into the kitchen. Bahbu stopped stirring the pots and turned to look at Anna. "The soldier who comes to visit here today likes you, Anna."

"He brings news directly from St. John. It is important to see him."

"It is not good to have a soldier coming to Hendersen. He must be discouraged."

"Bahbu." Anna's surprise escaped in the exclamation. "You are jealous!" She saw Bahbu's serious expression and went on, "You know that a soldier could not replace Prince."

"It is not that."

"Then what is it?"

"It is the baby. Soon your belly will be big."

There was a silence. The laughter of the children floated into the room. "How do you know?" Anna said softly.

"There are signs. Yesterday a lizard came up to your foot when you were picking limes. You are eating very much ripe pawpaw. And you are hungry for spicy food. Your eyes are clear, and your cheeks are very pink. Yes. You make a baby." She stirred the thick tamarind concoction and began to sing in her native dialect. Her high-pitched voice whined a lullaby.

"Oh, Bahbu," Anna laughed. "You know everything. Always." She stood up and walked beside Bahbu. "Prince thought he would be free by now," Anna said. "He has got to be free soon, Bahbu. It will be difficult for me to hide this."

"Do not worry, Anna. I came back to St. Thomas to take care of you for Prince. Until he is free."

There was a noise at the door. Jan entered the kitchen. He came close to the stove to look into the boiling pots. "Something smells very good. Oh yes, your tamarind relish, Anna." Bahbu held up the wooden spoon with some of the thick juice on it. Jan dabbed in it and licked his finger. "Ah. That's good. Just enough ginger."

Anna went back and sat down at the table. Jan followed her. When he was seated, he put his hands up and rubbed his long, silver hair back on his head. "It is better for you to be in here cooking, Anna, than to be out there in the field all day. The Negroes know their work. You do not have to exhaust yourself working so hard." He leaned back in the chair and looked at Anna. "Now do you?"

"I am happy when I am in the field."

"You do get more work out of these people than anyone else could. There is a new, happy spirit on Hendersen, Anna. It's because of you."

"Hendersen *is* different now," Anna said. "But it isn't me. It's you. A plantation takes on a different feeling when a master is of your kind."

"Yes, Anna. I know. But underneath it all, each slave wants to be his own master. On some plantations they are motivated by their fears, hates and pain. On others they are motivated by the necessity to feel equal to their captors. The feeling that I speak about is that you somehow make the slaves feel that they are your equal. They love you and trust you and respect you. And yet, they feel as if they stand equal with you. They have a self-pride in what they do. You give them purpose for every day. We all need that, Anna."

Bahbu shuffled up to the table and put a cup of coffee in front of each of them. It was already lightened with cream and sweetened with muscavado. "The relish, she is finished," she said to Anna. "I put it on the window. I will go set the table in the house. The beef will not burn. I put more water and spices in it." Bahbu walked out of the kitchen.

"Now tell me, Anna, what is your plan with Bordeaux? You know that Claude Mueller is making this trip to inquire of it."

Anna lifted the coffee cup, slowly sipped the contents, and put it back on the saucer. Her voice was very calm when she said, "You do not believe that the Negroes on St. John can win, do you?"

The room became quiet. Jan heard the bubbling noise of the beef stew and the distant voices of the children. He looked at Anna's face. Her eyes met his. "No, Anna, I don't." He saw the color drain from her cheeks.

"I cannot sell Bordeaux," she said. "I could sell the

buildings and the land. But I could not sell the Negroes. I will never be a part of that."

"If that is how you feel, keep Bordeaux. The Negroes know what to do and how to do it. Tando is a good overseer. As long as Bordeaux can make enough money to pay the taxes and feed the people, you will have no problems with it. In fact, Anna, the thing that is different now about Hendersen and Bordeaux is that there is the air of freedom. The Negroes feel free. And they should, for they are part of what we are all doing. Not one of them works harder than you do."

She raised her face. "I am one of them, Jan. I have always been. And now more so. I carry a Negro child within me."

When the impact of what she had said sank in, Jan said, "My God, Anna. We must do something to protect you." He stood up and walked to the window. One of the children ran beneath it and looked up at Jan. "The pot," the child said shyly. He dropped his head, so that his woolly curls looked like a black cap. "We can clean it, Master Jan?"

"We will call you when it is ready," Jan said gently. "Go play."

The child exploded into action. He leaped up into the air and yelled, "Mastah call when da pot she readee." Capturing the attention of the other children, he continued yelling and leaping and showing off for his admiring audience.

Jan turned back and looked at Anna. "I will think of something. It won't be too difficult to outwit these people and their narrow-minded laws. Let me think about it."

"It's my problem. I can't burden you with it."

"Don't be so independent, Anna." He walked to her and raised her face with his hand. "After all, Anna, it is the two of us who are colored wrong."

Anna laughed.

"Now, that's better," Jan said. "For a minute I thought you were going to cry. You looked so sad about your good news. Come, Anna"—he took her by the arm—"it's time you put on a dress. If the men arrive and find you in these slave pants, they'll think I abuse you."

Anna put her hands on her hips. "I think I'm very stylish." She was wearing a pair of the light brown, knee-length pants the Negro men wore in the field. They were so baggy they looked like a short, full skirt. Her clean, long white stockings and ankle-high shoes added an incongruous note to the torn, uneven hemline of the pants.

Jan could not hold back an amused laugh.

"Laugh, Jan Hendersen. How do you expect me to ride in the fields if I must sit sidesaddle? Skirts are not for horseback."

Shortly before noon, just after Claude Mueller and the sergeant had settled down in the parlor with a glass of rum, a dark cloud floated over the hilltop at Fortuna. At first there were large, scattered drops of rain that hit on the ground outside of the open louvered window. Then, swiftly a heavy sheet of water moved over the plantation. Within minutes it had passed and the sun came out again. Sitting close to the window, Anna breathed in the pungent, earthy musk of Hendersen. The smell reminded her of the times she and Prince had crawled through the cane fields with their faces close to the dew-moistened dirt. Once, after a hard, fast rain such as this, they had stood, entranced, above the rock and watched the whiffs of steam rising off its hard surface.

The pleasure of recollection was on her face when Theodore Ottingen said, "The rain has freshened the air, Miss Bodker. I understand you like to ride. Perhaps after dinner we can take a ride together, maybe to Bordeaux." He smiled at Anna. "I like hearty women." His chin set into a firm line, as if no one could dispute his taste.

"It is nice of you to ask," Anna said, pleasantly. "Maybe some other time. I'm rather tired today. Tell me, how is the situation on St. John? Are you close to putting down the revolt?"

Ottingen moved uneasily in the chair.

"Yes," Jan said enthusiastically. "What of the revolt?"

Ottingen put his empty glass down on the table beside him and stood up. "We are not one whit closer to ending the revolt than we were the day it began. We still hold Deurloo's and the fort, but those black devils are still massed in the bush waiting for us to step away from the cannon so they can ambush us."

"Now, Sergeant," Mueller interrupted, "you know your men have captured a good number of those rebels." His lower lip fell open. "You've made a name for yourself, young man. I hear you have more rebels to your credit than any other man on St. John." He paused. "Don't be modest, my boy."

Jan looked up at the sergeant. "Have many of the rebels been killed?"

"Their dead are strewn all over the island. We may very well get the plague. The smell of death hangs heavy in the heat. And yet they won't give up. And we do not have enough men to make an effective drive against them. Their ammunition is getting low. The day before I left St. John they tried to bargain with a planter. Some of their plunder for ten barrels of powder. With proper reinforcements, we could wipe them out. But everyone here on St. Thomas sits back and argues who is to bear the expense. In the meantime, the rebels are ravaging every plantation on St. John. Think of *that* expense."

"The problem," Mueller said, shaking a stubby finger in the air, "is that the Royal Council is trying to place the expense of the revolt on the shoulders of the planters and *we* say it is their fault. We didn't have adequate protection over there. Everyone knows that the fort was inadequately built and miserably fortified. How else could a dozen blacks have massacred the entire garrison? And they expect *us* to put up the money for reinforcements and supplies? Oh no. The company will bear this expense." He raised his finger straight above him, as far as his arm could reach. "Or I shall resign from the council." Putting his arm down, he pulled a lace handkerchief from his shirt cuff and wiped the sweat from under his lower lip. "If it weren't for men like Ottingen here, our good volunteers, those savages would be roasting goat in Deurloo's yard this very day."

Ottingen, who had poured himself another drink while Mueller was talking, spoke up. "If we had another hundred men with arms, we could wipe out every one of the rebels." He put his head back and tossed the drink down like a man who had had a lot of experience in the local tavern. "Well, when council meets tomorrow, I'll make an appeal to them. That is why I'm here."

"Are you appealing for more volunteers?" Jan asked.

"No. St. Thomas won't come up with enough. The planters here are afraid their slaves are waiting for an opportunity to rebel. And rightfully so. Those devils are tricky. I've seen them in the bush. They fight a good battle! We have got to come up with enough money to get assistance from the English or the French. There is a man-of-war in the harbor at Tortola right now. The British were afraid the rebellion would spread there. They might assist us. They could sail into Coral Bay and put eighty troops ashore and wipe out the rebels in a day. It would be a lot less expensive than having the remainder of the plantations destroyed!"

"How many have they destroyed?" Jan asked.

"Too many. Every day a new fire is seen. Hendersen has not been burned as yet. They are using yours and Caroline as their headquarters. You know, I've learned their leader is a woman." Ottingen stuck his chin out and fixed his hard blue eyes on Jan. "One of your slaves."

"Oh?" Jan said. "And how did you come by this news?"

"We have our informers," Ottingen said. "We know their leaders. They say she has supernatural powers. I say she is a black sorceress who should be burned alive—if she doesn't die from her wounds."

Anna tensed. Jan spoke up. "Has she been wounded?"

"The very first day. Her foot torn off by cannon shot."

"I think our dinner is ready, gentlemen," Anna said, getting up quickly from her chair.

Ottingen did not try to hide his surprise at the length of Anna's short white cotton dress. Appraisingly, he moved his head to the side to have a better look at her stockinged legs. Anna raised her head and walked gracefully past him. Ottingen winked at Mueller.

Jan squared his shoulders and stepped closer to Ottingen. He was several inches taller than the sergeant. "Have you something on your mind, Sergeant?"

"No, sir," Ottingen said solemnly. "Not yet."

"Ah, to be young again," Mueller said, stepping between the two men. He looked up at Jan and smiled vacantly. He shrugged his round shoulders. "I don't know whether it's old age or wisdom. I've lost interest in a pretty leg."

Ottingen looked in the direction of the dining room. Anna was standing just inside the doorway, waiting for them. He turned back to Jan and said, "And you, sir? Surely you are not too old or too wise to ignore the beauty of Miss Bodker?"

Jan studied Ottingen. Why argue with him? Anna Bodker was a beautiful woman, and any young man with an ounce of sense would recognize the fact. He knew, however, that if he did not discourage the sergeant, he was going to be a difficult man to keep from visiting Hendersen and pursuing Anna. Ottingen had a way of impressing people that he would not be easily discouraged from important projects.

The three men went into the dining room, and, after Jan had seated Anna at one end of the oval table, he placed the guests on either side of her, and then sat down in his customary chair at the head of the table.

The sergeant and Claude Mueller ate hearty amounts of the well-seasoned food. Claude complimented Anna with almost every mouthful. There was on his round face a distinct look of pleasure. He reminded Anna of her father, except that Claude would, without his sagging lower lip, have a cherubic quality about him. His skin looked very soft and pink, and his brown eyes had, except when angered, a perpetual twinkle.

Ottingen's tight green tunic caused him to sit very erect in his chair. When he had finished the food on his plate, he said, "My compliments, Miss Bodker. I have never tasted a tamarind relish as good as this." He smiled at Anna. His blue eyes softened and gave a gentle quality to his handsome face that Anna had not noticed before. "Any woman who can supervise a manor in this fashion should have a family to enjoy it with."

Anna could feel the color rising in her cheeks. Gratefully, she heard Jan say, "The table must seem very empty to Anna now that so many of her family are gone. It's good to have company."

"I hope I can make some amends on St. John for your great losses, Miss Bodker," Ottingen said. He looked into her eyes again.

Anna dropped her head.

"And what of Bordeaux, Miss Bodker?" Mueller said, wiping his mouth with the napkin. "Is the greathouse open?"

"The house has been closed since my return to St. Thomas," Anna said softly.

Mueller leaned as far over the table toward Anna as he could and pushed out his lower lip. "I was grieved to hear about your family, my child. I do not blame you for wanting to shut out the dreadful memory of the ghastly thing done to those good people." He pulled back in his chair and patted his mouth again. In a voice that he thought was properly sympathetic he said, "Perhaps you would be happier if you disposed of Bordeaux. I believe I could do justice to it."

"I am not interested in selling Bordeaux," Anna said flatly.

"Then perhaps a leasing agreement. Yes, that would be the perfect solution to your problem. After all, Miss Bodker, there is no one to run your plantation. Jan Hendersen has his hands full with Fortuna. I will make you a very tempting offer, my dear." He leaned forward on the table and tilted his head to the side so that he looked up coyly at Anna. "Now, that would relieve your pretty head of any worry, wouldn't it?"

For lack of words Anna sat up straight and looked down her nose at the round pink face that hung over the shiny mahogany table top. With her wide blue eyes fixed on Claude, she raised a spoonful of pudding to her mouth and ignored the question.

How impolite she is, Ottingen thought. She acts like the queen who has raised her scepter and had the buffoon whisked away. Aloud he said, "Perhaps you prefer to have your slaves run loose on Bordeaux and plot and plan an insurrection on St. Thomas?"

Anna looked defiantly at the sergeant. "I beg your pardon."

"Whether you approve or not, slavery is the only possible economic solution to our survival as a colony," he said.

"The tragedy is that you're right," Jan said. "But I have the feeling that Anna will find a way to make the slaves at Bordeaux a happy lot. In ten or fifteen years, when their tongues are still wagging about the Hendersen and Bodker clans, they'll be looking with envy at this woman who will be mistress of these estates. I predict that, Sergeant."

"I hope so," Mueller said brusquely. "But it will most certainly have the tongues wagging when they learn a woman is running Bordeaux."

"Well, gentlemen," Jan said, "I have some news for you to carry back today that will give them something to discuss in the meantime." Mueller and the sergeant turned their faces toward Jan. "Miss Bodker and I are going to be married next week."

From the corner of his eye Jan saw Anna stiffen in her chair. He held Ottingen's eyes. Ottingen looked as if he had taken a low blow in the stomach.

"Married," Mueller whispered. "You? And Anna Bodker? My God, Jan Hendersen! That *will* give them something to talk about."

Ottingen bobbed his head up and down. "It will that," he said in a dazed voice.

Jan sat back in his chair. "Well, now, gentlemen," he said good-naturedly. "You know as well as I do we can't stop the women's tongues from wagging. What else have they to do on this island? They will talk about Anna Bodker and Jan Hendersen in any event, won't they? Ah yes, here are the cigars. Have one." He pushed the box that Bahbu had put in front of him toward Ottingen. Looking at Anna, he said, "Why don't you go and rest, my dear." He smiled at Anna and pushed his chair back.

The sergeant and Claude Mueller automatically stood up. Dumbfounded, Anna looked at each of the guests and nodded. Leaving the room, she could hear Jan's clear deep voice, "At least the women in the village cannot say Jan Hendersen gives more attention to the making of excellent rum than he does to a beautiful woman."

Jan sat down and lit a cigar. Through the smoke, he watched his guests and found himself luxuriating in the quandary in which he'd set them. "You know, Claude," he said, "no one on the island will ever be able to say the Hendersen family did not give them plenty to talk about." He dragged on the cigar. "Just imagine," he let the smoke out, "Anna and I might have a few young ones to keep things going." He grinned smugly.

The sergeant choked.

"Care for some more rum, Sergeant?" Jan said.

"I think I'd better," Ottingen answered. He looked carefully at his host. Jan Hendersen was a virile-looking man. The beating his face had taken from the blazing sun and the tropical trade winds had etched strong character there for everyone to see. "I've heard it said that you are in better shape than your younger brother was," Ottingen said admiringly. "And I believe it."

"He drank too much bad rum in the tavern when he was in his youth," Jan said. He laughed. "I always told him that Hendersen rum and hard work would keep a man in solid condition. And you can see for yourself, gentlemen, I wasn't mistaken."

Chapter 19

On an eastern point of St. John, a rebel scout sat in a palm tree behind the mangroves and was awed at the sight of the man-of-war under sail. He did not need to recognize the English ensign that flew from her masthead to know that this was the fighting vessel the drum from St. Thomas had warned them about. She was a stout, sturdy vessel of thirty-eight guns and ninety men. From his vantage point he saw that her numerous wind-bulged sails propelled the great black hull with such speed that her bow cut the Caribbean, sending an angled spray of white sea water against her. In the blue-gray mist of twilight, he could pick out white and blue uniformed figures scurrying along her decks. The scout eased himself into position on the outer side of the curved tree trunk and, hand over hand, climbed down. Then he took up a drum and pounded out the alarm.

For a week the rebels had been organized and waiting for this attack. Prince counted a total of two hundred and eight able-bodied rebels now divided almost evenly between Caroline and Hendersen. Now that the revelry was over and his people felt the seriousness of their ammunition shortage, they knew they had to rely on close teamwork and the skill of their fighting in the bush to overpower the white men and their guns. The leaders had had ample time to prepare their strategy to meet this threat.

Their plan was a simple one. King and Prince would divide the one hundred-odd rebels from Caroline. King was to have his forces cover the east side of the area behind Coral Bay, where they knew the warship would anchor, and Prince, with his, was to cover the west. They would wait until the soldiers were between them and attack from both sides. The rebels were adequately armed for hand-to-hand combat with cane knives and cutlasses, but their only defense against the guns was now the bow and arrow which had been designed and made by those slaves who were taken prisoner in Africa after having learned these skills. The small amount of ammunition that remained was kept in hiding. It had been agreed upon that it would only be used in the event the rebels would be invaded by a force that outnumbered their own.

Darkness fell quickly on the island, and the Negroes from Caroline quietly prepared to move out into the bush. They gathered in the clearing for Prince's inspection.

Prince stepped into the center of the group and raised his arms. When it was quiet, he said, "David, take six or seven men and scout out the bush in front of us. If you come upon spies from the fort, kill them. We cannot have the English soldiers put on guard." Prince turned in a circle. "The dark fabric you wear is good. Those white soldiers will find out that the black man is not easy to find at night."

David went among the people, selecting the men he wanted as scouts. When a cloud drifted over the moon, it was difficult to distinguish the shadows from the Negroes who moved out into the scrub.

Mary swung herself into the group. In a short time she had become adept with the crude crutches that had been made for her. Squeezing the smooth knobs of the crutches into her armpits, she balanced on one foot beside Prince. The other leg was rigid. Where her foot had been blown off, the flesh tapered into a point over the bone. A puckered flap of flesh that had healed improperly hung loosely beneath the cone of the stump. The ankle and foot that were intact appeared to be too slender, giving a brittleness to her appearance that made the loss of the other foot seem insignificant. The crutches added a sturdiness one would suspect she might need in any case.

"What did the gods say tonight, Mary?" Prince asked.

"The gods say we will have a good night." Her voice was deep, and dramatic, a big voice for the emaciated woman. Varied dialects sprang up, passing the word. "They caution us to stay out of the range of the cannon. By sunrise those soldiers will take to their ship and go." More noisome shuffling. "Be still," she commanded. "Tonight, bring one of the English soldiers, dead or alive, for the gods."

"It will be done," Prince said. "Now we go, Mary. We want to be in the bush before they come ashore."

Mary's bony hand groped on Prince's chest. When she

233

found the amulet, she squeezed it. "Ah, it is warm with life." She dropped the carving. Prince could feel the heat of the wood where it rested on his chest. He moved out of the clearing with a light step.

Prince stared at the ship that was bearing down into Coral Bay. At one glance it appeared as a mass of plump white clouds skimming the black sea. In the next minute, following the sound of whistles and bells and commands that were mysteriously magnified so that stern voices thundered out across the bay, it was as if someone had let the air out of the clouds.

Uncovered, the decks crawled with white specks. "These English soldiers wear white uniforms," Prince whispered to David. By the tone of his voice there was no doubt that Prince considered them to be fools. "Maybe they do not plan to fight tonight."

"They come ashore," David said, pointing. "See."

Four longboats lowered from the brig's davits were on the water. One by one they bobbed toward shore, where they discharged the white dots and then returned to the brig. After two trips each, Prince saw the oarsmen drag the boats on shore. The total number of "soldiers," as Prince called the sailors, was sixty-four.

There were three officers among the soldiers. They could be distinguished from the enlisted men, for they wore blue jackets over their white ducks. Lieutenant Jonathan Williams was the commander. After a labored sprint across the pebbly beach, during which he bruised his knee with the sword that swung from his waist, the lieutenant reached the cover of the palm trees.

Theodore Ottingen snapped to attention and said, "Sergeant Ottingen of the St. Thomas garrison."

"I am Lieutenant Williams. Who is in charge here?"

"I am, sir."

Williams eyed Ottingen. "Oh, very well."

He looked through the tree trunks to the patch of lighter fields beyond them. "With a bit of luck we should have this mess cleaned up by dawn. I've brought you as tough a bunch of sailors as you'll find in all the Indies."

Ottingen suppressed a smile. "I don't think it will be that easy, Lieutenant. The bulk of the rebel forces are divided between Caroline, on this side of the island, and Hendersen, northwest of us. They are damn good fighters in the bush."

"My dear Sergeant," Williams said haughtily, "we were told the rebels are without firearms."

"Yes, sir."

"Then what chance have they against the armed forces of the British Navy?"

"A word of caution, sir, with proper respect for the British Navy. The rebel forces are worthy of regard, with or without firearms. They are at home in the heavy scrub of St. John. There are still small groups roaming around the other plantations, but on the whole they stick close together, relying on their numbers and skill at fighting in the bush to prevent us from retaking the plantations. I do not doubt for one instant that with the assistance of the British Navy we will put down this revolt. But I do not think it can be done in one night."

"Then if you think it is going to be a drawn-out affair, let's get about it. My men have been properly informed of the reward each will receive for enemy captives. They are anxious."

"Come out to the sandy patch of beach, Lieutenant. I'll outline our position." Ottingen moved out of the grove toward the sand, yellow-white in the moonlight. There he squatted down and with a stick drew a rough map. "We are here, Lieutenant." He drew an X. "Coral Bay. The rebels are headquartered here and here." Ottingen looked over at the lieutenant, who was squatted beside him. The lieutenant removed his black hat. Ottingen saw that he had bright red hair, close cropped in front and long in back, where it was pulled into a tight knot at the nape of his neck. He looked young and inexperienced in comparison with the whiskered, rough crew that accompanied him. Ottingen went on, "We should stay in a group and move first to Caroline, here." He pointed to an X. "About half their forces are on this side of the island, preventing attack from our men who are holding the fort. The other half of their group is at Hendersen, over there." He pointed at the other X.

"Caroline, then, is close by," Lieutenant Williams said. "Have they scouts?"

"Yes. And we dispatched our scouts at least two hours ago. They were to advise us if the rebels showed signs of

235

activity. Since our scouts have not returned, I take it for granted that they have nothing to report." Ottingen stood up. "The rebels have no doubt seen your ship. But it takes time to organize strategy for an attack that would be sizable and effective enough to match the strength of the armed forces of the British Navy. Let us move out now, Lieutenant, without giving them that time."

Ottingen and Williams came up over the slope behind Coral Bay. Behind them were sixty-three British sailors and twelve Danish soldiers. On either side of the column was a heavy high tangle of bush. Cactus, tamarisk, prickly pear and serrated weeds were all covered with a lush, dark green mat of sticky, tough vine. The island bush, nest of the night things, was alive with mosquitoes, sand flies and stinging ants. Bugs, roaches, beetles, tree toads and parakeets put out incessant, discordant noises that were disagreeably shrill and piercing to the stranger's ears.

Ottingen raised his arm. The plop of feet quieted so that the cacophony of the bush took over.

"I don't like it, Lieutenant," Ottingen said. "It's too quiet. Too *damned* quiet!" He cocked his head, straining to hear something out there in the direction of Caroline that would ease his unrest.

PLOOM-BOOM, the grave notes of a drum reverberated along with a savage, blood-curdling war cry. At what appeared to be the same instant, the bush snapped, rattled, and shook itself loose into a turbulent life that sent forth the ambushing rebel forces, over one hundred strong.

Not a musket was fired in the ensuing skirmish. The rebels closed in from each side, driving the soldiers and sailors together into a cramped quarter where their muskets were useless. The sailors drew knives and cutlasses, and those who had smuggled ashore their favorite weapon for close combat, the belaying pin, brandished it in the air, cursing to have at it with the rebels.

Ottingen drew his sword. As if he had been dropped from overhead, a tall, light-skinned rebel appeared. The moon shone on the smooth skin of his shoulders, giving it the look of burnished gold. Around his thick neck there hung a leather cord from which a wooden amulet dangled between the bands of muscle on his chest. The Negro crouched forward, brandishing a cutlass in his right hand.

The sudden appearance of the rebel put Ottingen at a disadvantage.

At the same time, Lieutenant Williams screamed, "On guard, Sergeant." Ottingen felt his body being pushed aside. The cutlass swished, followed by a thud. Ottingen was staring at a blue-jacketed headless body on the ground.

"For Mary," he heard the rebel yell triumphantly. Now Ottingen was being jostled and pushed by rebel and sailor alike. African tribal dialects, Danish, and the foreign accents of the English sailors all mingled together in his ears with the impassioned noises of battle. A chorus of voices carried the rebel incantation, "Kill the white man, kill." Ottingen, pressed back, had difficulty holding onto the hilt of his sword, let alone raise it. "Fall back to the brig," he heard an Englishman command.

"Stand and fight," Ottingen shouted.

"Don't be a fool, matey," from someone close to his ear. "We're trapped in here like a bunch of babes in a shark's belly."

On the right side of Ottingen, a sailor was waving a stout belaying pin. He raised his arm. Ottingen let his sword drop and grabbed the pin from the sailor's hand, all the while being carried back. He brought his arms forward and crashed his elbows out beside him, while all around him he heard the dismayed command, "To the brig. Fall back."

Ottingen slammed his elbows into a sailor on either side of him and heard their grunts. They backed from him and were replaced by two more. Now he saw that only three sailors were between himself and the compact group of rebels. The rebels flailed their arms. Moonlight glinted on their sweaty bodies and on the keen edges of the cane knives and cutlasses they brandished. Ottingen pressed toward the Negroes obsessed with the idea that he could inspire the English to hold their ground. All at once the pressure in back of Ottingen gave way. Turning, he saw that the sailors had come upon the top of the slope and were dashing like frightened antelope for the beach.

Luckily for Ottingen, a ball was fired from the cannon at the fort, and the rebels crouched back. A drum rolled. Then another cannon fired. Intimidated, the rebels disappeared back into the bush.

By the time Ottingen reached the beach, the four longboats, each with a full capacity of sailors, were halfway to the brig. The sergeant went to the band of sailors massed around another blue-jacketed officer. "For God's sake," Ottingen's powerful voice thundered out at the flustered sailors, "Lieutenant Williams told me you were the toughest bunch of sailors in all the Indies. Why in *hell* didn't you stand and fight?"

The blue jacket forced its way from out of the circle of white uniforms. "Look here, Sergeant, your governor's envoy led us to believe that a *little* assistance from us would put an end to this revolt. The Spanish Armada couldn't put down that horde of savages." With disgust he threw his head in the direction of Caroline. "We've been tricked. We had to leave our dead back there in the bush. But we have taken our wounded back to the brig—and that's where we're going."

Mary cackled with pleasure, all the while swinging herself around the blue-jacketed torso. A fresh stream of blood oozed from the clean-cut stump of neck. "Ruth, my child, take up a calabash cup and catch that blood. It will make a *powerful* brew." The lieutenant's head was lying, face up, between his ankles. Mary stopped and leaned forward on her crutches to have a look at it. With bent arms, elbows raised up behind her, and her turbaned head dropped low in front of her, she looked like a great black pelican folding its wings in preparation to drop its beak and dive for quarry under the surface of the sea. "You are young, English soldier." She stood up and began walking around the body again. "Aiii. The gods will be satisfied with you."

Caroline was a sprawling plantation. All around the grounds there were now signs of festivity. Fires had sprung up, the drums were pounding, and the rebels were broken up into dancing groups.

As Ottingen suspected, the rebels, seeing the man-of-war set sail for Tortola, had thrown caution to the wind and begun their ritual of thanks to their gods without giving thought to the possibility of any threat from the small band of soldiers and planters at the fort. Now Ottingen and a group of twenty-one men, whom he had organized from the fort, were watching the rebels at play. Ottingen whispered to Corporal Sorensen beside him, "We will spread out, surround them. Now it is our turn to hide in the dark. I will wait fifteen minutes. When we are in position, I will fire the first shot. Then let every man open fire on these devils. God, I hope I can get a shot at that light-skinned rebel who tried to have my head."

"There are a lot of them crawling around down there, Sergeant. We're outnumbered at least four to one."

"But look at them. They're half drunk already. Like a group of children, they have a victory and they run back to play. As we discussed, a swift attack, we hit hard, and then retire to the fort before daybreak. I'm hoping for the light-skinned rascal. But my second choice is that ugly black hag who is so pleased with Lieutenant Williams' poor decapitated body. Now have the men move into position. We have every benefit. Those fires light them up. Pick your targets carefully. Make each shot count."

Prince and King were sitting by one of the fires close to the slave quarters. They faced the fire, their backs to the shadowed bush on the hillside. Close by, Mary and Ruth were busy disrobing the torso of the English lieutenant. King finished a chicken leg, tossed the bone on the ground, and broke off the other leg of the roasted chicken on the straw mat in front of them. "We drove the British off the island in good time," King said, laughing. "And with all the material Mary will get from that soldier," he looked at the headless torso, "we have medicine for the gods that will protect us forever." With one yank of his square white teeth he pulled all the meat off the chicken leg and discarded the bone over his shoulder. Chewing, he said, "Without the cannon to hide behind, the white men do not fight."

Prince nodded his head agreeably. "They are not fighters," he said. "They began crying to get back to their boat as soon as I got this one's head." Prince pointed in the direction of the torso. "I wish they would stop annoying us. They know we will not give them back their plantations. They should go back to St. Thomas and leave us alone. Here. Don't eat all the chicken. Let me have some."

He leaned forward to reach for the chicken when a shot rang out. The whine of the bullet passing over his head came to his ears simultaneously. Prince threw himself on the ground and rolled over toward Mary. "Get in the hut," he screamed at her. Shots whined all around them. The rebels screamed and ran in confusion. Eight or nine ran to Prince and King.

"Damn," Ottingen cursed, losing sight of Prince. He

took careful aim at one of the men in the group and fired. A figure slumped down to the ground.

The rebels formed a protective circle around Mary. Prince and King each took hold of one of her arms and, lifting her from the crutches, ran with her toward a hut. "Put me down. Put me down," Mary protested. Now they were inside one of the huts. From the group at the door came a frightful scream. Another of the rebels fell. "Get away from the door. Stay away from the fires, they give the enemy light," Prince called out. Quickly the group dispersed. Now King and Prince, crouched low, ran out the door and disappeared into the darkness behind the hut. There Prince put his arm out and stopped King. "We have nothing to fight with. Our weapons are still in the clearing."

"Here," King drew a cane knife from his waistband. "Take this!"

"What of you?"

"I have these." King lifted his big hands up in the dark. He curled his fingers, squeezing. "Let me get close enough to the white man. All I need is to get him in my hands."

Prince had to laugh. He knew that King's hands were so strong that a white man could not fight him. "Come." Prince bent forward and ran toward the clump of bush that was behind the huts. King followed.

Ottingen did not see Prince and King run into the bush. He did, however, notice that the skyline directly over the sea was beginning to show a light gray streak. He looked at the soldier beside him and said, "Back to the fort. Look, over there. Dawn. When it's light, we don't stand a chance out here."

Ottingen turned and started to pick his way back through the bush. After a short time he came upon an opening. Here he could see other soldiers and planters breaking out of the bush and running along the road toward the fort. He had just stepped out on the path when he heard the soldier behind him let out a tortured scream. Ottingen turned. In the pitch-black bush he could see nothing. It was quiet in there. Only the occasional chirp of an awakening bird could be heard. But it was too quiet. Ottingen raised his musket and fired into the bush. At once twigs snapped and bush rustled beneath hurried footsteps. The noises moved away. Cautiously, Ottingen went into the bush.

He did not have far to go before he stumbled on the body. Leaning down, he patted the form. The familiar buttons and cloth of uniform met his touch. "Sorensen," Ottingen whispered, "do you hear me?" He shook him. No response. He put his musket down and dragged Sorensen out onto the path. Ottingen let the body go limp on the path and walked around to the side of it. Then he saw the gaping wound in Sorensen's neck. It did not look as if his throat had been cut. It looked to Ottingen as if an animal had torn Sorensen's windpipe out with its teeth. Forgetting his musket, Ottingen ran down the road toward the fort.

Chapter 20

Claude Mueller walked wearily into the parlor of his plantation house. He was dressed in his town clothes: knee breeches and a coat of heavy dark blue velvet, ascot of white, finely embroidered lace, white knee stockings, and black leather slippers with polished silver buckles. His sideburns had been curled into two neat rolls on either side of his chubby cheeks. The rest of his long hair was pulled back, tied with a velvet ribbon at the nape of his neck, so that it hung loose in one curl down the back of his jacket.

"It was very warm in the council room today," he said to Sergeant Ottingen, who accompanied him. "Pour yourself some rum, Theodore." He motioned to the decanter. "Sarah," he called to his wife, "our dinner guest is here. Come, my dear."

Sarah Mueller, a lively, trim little woman in her middle forties, called out from the dining room in a cheery voice, "Dear one. You're home."

Ottingen was glad to be back from the turmoil on St. John to the brightness of the Mueller household. The house smelled good. Sarah's flower garden, under the window of the parlor, filled the room with a spicy fragrance. And the room was pleasing to the eye. The furniture was upholstered in shades of pinks and reds that added warmth to the high luster of the mahogany wood. The louvers of the arched windows were always thrown open, so there was plenty of light and air in the room.

There were spritely steps on the floor, and Sarah came into the room. Sarah's eyebrows were always raised high over her large brown eyes and she had a perpetual faint smile. The combination of these two features made her appear as if everything she saw was surprisingly pleasant. Now, seeing Ottingen, she smiled even more broadly, making him feel that he was heartily welcome, which he was.

"Oh, Theodore, how nice to have you back on St. Thomas." She put her hands up to her face, framing the oval shape of it, and gasped, "My, how handsome you look. That sun tan makes your eyes *very* blue."

Ottingen laughed. "You will never change, Sarah. You know that flattery and good food are the ways to capture a man's devotion. I am devoted to you."

Sarah lowered her eyes. Color came up into her cheeks, giving her a youthful flush in contrast to the graying brown hair that was wrapped in braided circles over her ears. "How sweet of you to say so, dear boy," she murmured. She turned to Claude and, as if noticing for the first time that he was in a heavy suit, said authoritatively, "Here, my dear, let me take your coat. And that ascot. It's much too warm at this time of day to stand on formality." She walked behind Claude and raised his hair with one hand, gripping the neck of his coat with the other. Pulling, she had him out of the heavy coat and threw it over her arm. She waited for him to remove the ascot. Claude handed her the scarf, and then shook his wet shirt back and forth in a fluttering motion. "My poor lamb," Sarah said. "It was a very hot day for council to meet."

"There was no alternative, my dear," Claude said, looking forlornly at his wife. "But now that the company has agreed to bear the expense of getting assistance to the planters on St. John, it's been worth it." Claude unbuttoned his shirt and carefully folded back the starched-stiff collar. "Ah, that's better."

Ottingen handed Claude a glass of rum. Claude thanked him and sat down on a mahogany chair. Ottingen tossed down his rum, made a noise of satisfaction, and went back to the decanter and poured another drink. "It is good to get back to civilization," he said. "For all the difference there is, St. John could be another world. I would detest to be stationed permanently at the garrison there."

"Have no fear of that, my boy," Claude said. "With the reputation you're making for yourself, you'll be able to choose your post. You'll see. I've already suggested to council that a letter of commendation, written on your behalf, be sent to the King."

Ottingen raised his glass and nodded over the rim of it at Claude. "My thanks to you," he said, and tossed the drink down with the ease of the first one. "Now tell me, what are the precise plans of the Royal Council?"

243

"Tomorrow the company's attorney is leaving for Nevis. He has been authorized to make the English a handsome offer. They will not turn it down, I'm sure."

"It is about time. If we could get some troops in there who would stand and fight, we could get this revolt over with. It's a long-drawn-out affair. And a costly one."

"I hear that you were ambushed, Theodore. And what is this they say. Is it true you were so angry you went out the very same night and attacked them while they celebrated their victory?"

"It's true. There is a light-skinned rebel who is one of their leaders. He tried to have my head. And he would have, too, I'm sure, except a young English lieutenant saved my life at the cost of his own. The rebels took the lieutenant's body back to that witch who leads them. Her witchcraft didn't save the rebels' lives when we attacked. We got at least twenty of them. They were all dancing around their fires."

Claude clapped his hands. "Good work, Sergeant. And what of our side? They say we only lost one man."

"That is correct. A corporal. He looked as though someone had torn his windpipe out."

"Torn it out? Impossible!"

"I would say the same, except for one thing." Ottingen looked into Claude's upturned face. "*I* pulled the corporal from the bush. His windpipe *was* torn out of his neck."

Claude's mouth fell open. Sarah came back into the room. Looking at her husband's white face, she said with alarm, "Claude. Has the heat overcome you, dear?"

Slowly, Claude shook his head. "No, it has not." He shook it harder, making his lower lip jiggle. "Why, Theodore, that *is* difficult to believe!"

"What is this you are telling Claude?" Sarah scolded good-naturedly, wagging a finger at Ottingen. "He looks faint."

"It's of no importance," he said. "Women should not be bothered with the details of the revolt. Now, tell me, Sarah, did Jan Hendersen marry the Bodker girl?"

Sarah's eyebrows lifted very high. "Yes. They married last week. *That* is also difficult to believe, isn't it?" Ottingen nodded his head. Sarah sat down on the brocaded settee. "*Very* peculiar things have gone on at Hendersen. I only wish I could have taken that Bodker girl to raise myself. What was Victoria Bodker thinking of to allow her to run wild? They never took those girls to any of the social functions, or made a move to get them out of that wilderness at Fortuna. It's a shame. I think this young one has suffered a sickness of the brain from being alone so much. She is a very peculiar woman. Jan Hendersen is older by many years than her father was. And she is such a young, strong girl. The next thing you know," Sarah lowered her voice and dropped her head, "they will have children."

Ottingen laughed. "That is what Jan Hendersen said they planned to do, Sarah. He said it would give everyone something to talk about."

"Imagine that," Sarah said, "he's the oldest man on the island!" A giggle escaped her.

"Now don't you be naughty," Claude said.

"You know, dear one," Sarah said, "we can always rely on Hendersen Estate to provide us with some gossip. The other day my maid was saying she had heard that the man who leads the revolt, a slave they call Prince, was sired by Lars Hendersen. I don't doubt it a bit. You know Lars was always very crude. He was *much* too familiar with our female slaves."

Theodore poured another drink. "Exactly what did you hear about this man Prince? It is of particular interest to me."

"My girl's patois is difficult to understand," Sarah said, looking sad without her usual smile. "And it was all so confusing. You know, the man who leads them is supposedly related to Lars Hendersen, whom he killed. That would mean he killed his father. And it's rumored he is related to the witch who leads them. I just don't understand it all. It's all so confusing. You know how the slaves gossip about each other. She even said that this Prince who leads them, who killed his father, is in love with Anna Bodker, who just married his old uncle!"

Ottingen turned around and stared at Sarah.

"I don't *believe* that," she said. "No, that's just too much to believe."

Ottingen's eyes hardened. "I don't find that difficult to believe. In fact, it makes sense."

"What makes sense?" Claude asked.

"That the slave who leads them is Lars Hendersen's son."

"Well, that I'll go along with, if you say so," Claude said. "But for the slave to be in love with Anna Bodker?"

245

"For that you could not blame him, Claude, now, could you?"

Claude smiled, an enraptured look, and shook his head.

"No, of course not," Ottingen said. "But the rebel who tried to behead me was unusual-looking. It was moonlight . . ." Recalling, Ottingen lowered his voice. He put his head back and closed his eyes. "His hair was very good, not curly or coarse. And he had fine features, that straight, narrow Hendersen nose. In the moonlight, his eyes and skin appeared to be the same color, bronze or gold." He opened his eyes and brought his head back so that he could look at Claude. "That is what distracted me. That, and a wood carving he wore around his neck."

"What of the carving?" Claude said.

"It had an odd glow. It glistened like a smooth, wet stone would shine in the sunlight."

"It could have been wet with his sweat," Claude said.

"When I got back to the fort that morning, I could not sleep. I thought of that possibility. But no, he could not have been sweaty, for the rebels had been waiting in the bush, idle. It was a particularly clear, cool night. I was comfortable walking through the field in my uniform. He could not have been warm, for he had not as yet been active. If anything, they would have been chilly out there in the bush. You know how the earth cools off at night. All they had on were those ragged, cut-off trousers they wear. But they *are* clever, Claude. They had thought of dyeing their thin rags black so that we could not see them in the bush."

"My word. That *was* clever of them."

Ottingen walked to the window and looked out at Mueller's slaves in the fields below the greathouse. "You know, Claude, if those rebels on St. John had taken Deurloo's the first day, and then arranged with the smugglers for ammunition, I have an idea that the future history of these islands would be vastly changed. The Negro is in his own environment here. He is used to this scorching hot sun and the heavy bush." He turned away from the window and went again to the table with the decanter on it. "I wouldn't admit it to anyone but you, my dear friends, but they have outwitted us at every turn. We even put poison in their cisterns at Caroline. Do you think they drank that water and died? No. And our informers tell us it is their witchcraft that protects them. That's the thing that has given me

246

thought about that glowing piece of wood around this rebel's neck. It was almost as if I *had* to look at the damn thing. A soldier should know better than to be distracted in a situation as serious as the one we were faced with." He poured another drink and held it in his hand. "I cannot help myself. I wonder if we take their witchcraft too lightly."

"Reverend Thamsen would be shocked to hear you speak out in this manner," Sarah said gently. She leaned forward and stared up at Ottingen. "Do you really think there might be something to their rituals?"

"Now, Sarah," Claude said. "You know as well as I do that both of us have, from time to time, discussed the possibility of it. The truth of the matter is that if we were sure there were nothing behind the witchcraft, we would have no reason to prohibit it. Now, would we?"

"Please, dear one, don't talk like that. It makes me very nervous. Sometimes at night, when the drums are beating, I think of it and have to pull the coverlet over my head."

Ottingen threw his head back and laughed. "What are you hiding from, Sarah. Ghosts?"

Sarah shook her shoulders as if she didn't care about any part of the conversation and said, "If you are worried about that foolish thing on the rebel's neck, why don't you ask Jan Hendersen what he thinks? It's his slave who wears it."

"Jan Hendersen is at the blacksmith's today having some barrel staves made," Claude said. "Why don't we ride into town after dinner, Theodore? He might be able to tell you something about it."

"Oh, Claude, you know that Jan Hendersen won't discuss, with anyone, the things that go on at Hendersen," Sarah said. "If it weren't for all the slaves gossiping, we would never hear a thing about Fortuna—or Bordeaux either."

"We're not asking him to gossip," Claude said. "Jan Hendersen has always been outspoken. He might just tell the sergeant something."

"And he might just turn his back on him, too. At least, dear one, prepare Theodore for that."

"That's the most he can do," Claude said, looking up at Ottingen. "Now that he's an old man, there's not as much fight in him. Good thing, too. I imagine he's weary of being laughed at."

"He's a proud-looking man, Claude," Ottingen said.

"Well," Claude said, standing up, "Jan Hendersen has certainly had the last laugh on the island's bachelors by marrying Anna Bodker. Come along, Sarah," he put his hand out and helped her lift up from the settee, "let us have dinner, so Theodore and I can look for Mr. Hendersen. I'm interested in this heathenish carving myself."

Jan had left the Spanish trader that was anchored out in the harbor and was in a longboat nearing the waterfront. Ahead of him the neatly arranged red and white square houses looked colorful against the dark green of the mountain side. "Ho there, Jan Hendersen," he heard a voice call out. Looking up, he saw Sergeant Ottingen standing on shore. Beside him was Claude Mueller, dressed in the long-jacketed blue velvet suit. He now had on a wide-brimmed black hat on which an ornate purple plume was fanned by the trade winds. The feather blew across Claude's face. He whisked it away and waved to Jan.

Ottingen leaned forward toward the boat. "Here, let me assist you." Jan handed him a bolt of muslin, which Ottingen passed on to Claude.

"A gift for your new, beautiful bride, huh, Jan Hendersen," Claude said.

Jan removed his straw hat and sleeked back his long silver hair from off his shoulders. He slapped the hat back on his head and it fell in place, shading his face. "I hear the English did not stay long on St. John, Sergeant," he said.

"No, sir. They did not. Let's hope that this next group will stay to see the end of the revolt."

"Oh. Are the English planning a return?"

"I hope so. The council has authorized funds to entice them. We will know something more definite in a week or two."

Jan reached for the muslin. "Well, gentlemen, it's time I get back to Hendersen."

"Have you time for a drink, sir?" Ottingen said.

"No, Sergeant. Thank you, but my staves are ready and I want to load up and get back to Fortuna before dark." Holding the bolt of fabric under his arm, he looked over at the blacksmith's shop.

Before he had a chance to bid them good-day, Ottingen spoke up. "I would like a word with you, sir."

248

"Oh?" He looked at Ottingen.

"But it is very hot out here in the midday sun," Ottingen looked around. There was no shade on the barren, dusty waterfront.

"Walk along with me," Jan said. He walked toward the blacksmith. Ottingen looked at Claude and shrugged his shoulders, then hurried to fall into step with Jan. Claude, holding his hat against the wind, ran after them.

"I came near to being beheaded the other night," Ottingen said.

"I'm sorry to hear about that," Jan said.

"Yes. Ah . . . it was one of your slaves, I believe. A light-skinned rebel they call Prince."

Jan stopped. Ottingen seized the opportunity to move in front of him and said, quickly, "A strange thing happened. Let me tell you in detail." Ottingen related the incident as he had told it earlier to Claude. In summation, he said, "I felt as if that piece of carved wood had somehow compelled me to look at it." While he had been talking, Ottingen watched Jan's expression and felt that Jan was receptive to the story. "I thought, sir, you might be able to tell me something about that particular carving."

Jan looked into Ottingen's eyes. "Many of them carry objects that are connected with their superstitions, Sergeant. Obviously, this is one of them."

"Then you do not know what this particular one might mean to the rebel, Prince?"

"No, I don't." He held Ottingen's gaze. There was a silence.

"And if you did," Ottingen said in a low voice, "would you tell me?"

They stared quietly at each other. "Perhaps," Jan said slowly. "But I have no way of knowing. I know that this particular carving has something to do with Prince's family. It has been in existence many years. I've seen it often. The expression of the wooden face was different every time I looked at it."

"Have you any idea who carved it?" Claude asked.

"Mary did."

"Mary? The one who leads the revolt," Ottingen exclaimed.

"That's right. Mary carved it." Stepping aside, Jan began walking again.

Ottingen swung around and followed Jan. "The slaves who are loyal to us have great respect for her powers. They say this is why no one informed on her before the revolt, else she would have put some sort of spell on them. Have you ever seen her perform any of these deeds when she was with you at Hendersen?"

Jan raised his head, looked straight ahead of him, and said, as he continued walking, "You have seen the result of her work, Sergeant. She organized a revolt."

"But you said, only the last time we talked, that it was nonsense to believe she was behind the revolt."

"The black man's desire for freedom is behind the revolt. The power she has to lead them is beyond my knowledge. It's something beyond our understanding. Call it what you will." Jan stopped abruptly and turned to look at the two men. His eyes moved from one to the other. "Witchcraft?" The question hung in the humid, hot air. "Who knows?" His eyes settled on the sergeant's face.

"If you think there is something supernatural about the carving Prince wears," Claude said, "stay away from him."

"I'm not afraid of the damned thing," Ottingen snapped. "I was curious, that's all."

"I know what you mean," Jan said. "There is something about the African superstitions that does stir the mind. Perhaps that's its power." He paused and let them think about it. "Now, gentlemen, I have to leave you. I want to be at Hendersen before dark."

The sergeant and Claude watched Jan Hendersen until he disappeared into the blacksmith's shop. Then Ottinger took hold of Claude's arm and turned him toward the harbor. "I believe there might be something in what Jan Hendersen says," Ottingen said. He dropped Claude's arm. "I feel better about it. I'm glad we saw Jan Hendersen today."

"He's a fool," Claude grunted. "By his own admission he lived around that thing for a good many years, watching the face change. And yet he didn't ask about it. I'm disappointed."

"He's a wise old man," the sergeant said. "If he doesn't know, it doesn't have to work on his mind."

"You mean you feel better because you didn't find there was a curse, or some other evil thing attached to the carving?"

"Correct, Claude. And now I don't have to worry about it. I can go back to St. John tomorrow, forgetting that it exists."

Chapter 21

On Saturday, March 6, 1734, Sergeant Ottingen received word that an English man-of-war under command of Captain John Maddox had departed from St. Kitts and would arrive with seventy-one men to reinforce the garrison at Coral Bay.

"It's about time," Ottingen said. "We've wasted three months running around this bush after the rebels."

Von Beverhoudt, who had sailed from Deurloo's to Coral Bay earlier that day said, "If we don't get back our plantations in time for the planting, we'll miss another harvest. Everything has gone to ruin. Our crops taken over by the bush, our cattle furnishing food for the rebel bellies. The council is evasive about the expense of putting down the revolt, while we lose more each day. Now that Barens and I are here, Sergeant, I think we should go ahead with the attack we have planned for tonight."

"I agree with you, sir," Ottingen said. "We've been idle for two weeks, waiting for the rebels to relax. Our scouts say they plan one of those witchcraft things tonight. If we have word that the English are due, you can be sure that the rebels know it too. That's probably why they've called this meeting. Those drums last night. My God, I thought they would never stop."

"Let's hope we can surprise them. They have spies everywhere," Von Beverhoudt said.

"There is not a man at this garrison who knows of our plans," Ottingen said. "We've waited too long for the rebels to get careless to have them put on guard at the last minute. If we have a solid attack on them, it will give us less rebels to worry about when Captain Maddox arrives."

"How many rebels do you think we're up against?" Barens asked.

"One hundred and fifty. We've been able to whittle them down slowly."

"And how many men will we have for our attack to-night?"

"Thirty-five," Ottingen said. The room in the fort was small and musty-smelling. An arched tunnel two feet high, running through the thick stone wall, gave little ventilation. Ottingen put his elbow up on the flat, dusty surface of the window and looked out at a patch of green brush. "Yes, thirty-five. And if we can kill only two of the rebels, Prince and that witch, we may not need the English!"

Struck with an idea, the sergeant turned around to Barens and Von Beverhoudt. "I've got it," he exclaimed. "We'll not go out in force tonight."

"Not in force?" Barens said. "Who would attack them without support?"

"I will," Ottingen said. "Alone. With luck, as a single sniper, I can get either Prince or Mary."

"It's foolhardy," Barens said.

Von Beverhoudt stood up and walked the length of the small room, deep in thought. "I agree with Ottingen," he said. "One of them is worth twenty rebels." He looked at Ottingen. "I consider the woman to be most valuable. She is their witch doctor." He looked at Barens. "What do you say, Barens?"

"Ottingen *is* an outstanding marksman. However, don't you think some of us should support the sergeant? Can you imagine that horde of savages taking out after one undefended man? He wouldn't stand a chance."

"I'll wear one of our slave's clothes," Ottingen said. "And I'll rub my body with mud. If they do discover me, I'll make a run for it. You can have a squad of our men standing ready and cover my escape."

"I will take command of the men who set up the guard for your retreat," Von Beverhoudt said. "And you, Barens, make sure every cannon on the fort is manned and ready for action."

"As soon as it's dark, I'll leave the fort," Ottingen said. "Once I do, no one will go out of those gates except you, Captain Von Beverhoudt, and the men you take to defend my retreat. Let me have an hour before you move out. Then, if you're spotted by a rebel scout, I'll have had time by then for success or failure before he could get back to report."

In the tropics, there is only a brief space of twilight between daylight and dark. At one instant the sun sits on the

253

top of the sea, its rays tinging the sky with purples, pinks and delicate lavenders. In the next, the sun falls into a cavern behind the sea. Night comes over the island like a swift black curtain.

At Caroline, twilight still tinged the sky when the rebel fires were extinguished. Remembering the last surprise attack from the fort, the rebels were on guard. Then it was dark. Thirty-two sentinels moved around the outside boundaries of the estate.

Every Negro in the clearing moved close to the slave quarters. Carrying cane knives and cutlasses, they were tense and alert. In one hut, Mary kneeled close to a heap of fiery charcoal. Knowing that the English were returning to St. John, she was not dismayed by their boldness. Instead, she was determined to arouse the gods to work against the new enemy. She had already fed the fire two thin plaits of bright red hair, four or five strips of blue and white cloth, two fingernails, and four teeth, all cherished pieces of the beheaded English officer. Beside her, a handsome silver bowl held the ashes of his remains. She came up on her knees and raised the bowl, mumbling a feverish incantation. Staring down into the white-orange coals, she tilted the bowl and let the powdery dust spill out into the fire. The heat of the fire blew some of the ashes into her face. She did not take her eyes from the burning coals, for it was there that she would have this last omen now that she was offering the supreme sacrifice of the Englishman. The ashes dampened the fire. Mary felt the heat let up on her face. The edges of the white-orange embers turned to gray ash along with those that were smothering it. Mary's face contorted. She was obviously displeased with what was happening. She shook the bowl. She hissed and made garbled noises.

Suddenly she let the bowl fall on the fire. "Get Prince," she grunted to Ruth.

When Prince came into the hut, Mary was still on her knees. Her arms were limp beside her. Her chin had fallen down on her chest. She was resigned to the curious thing that had happened with her ritual.

"What is it, Mary?" Prince said. Alarmed by her appearance, he fell on his knees beside her. "Speak, Mary."

Mary was quiet. Prince frowned and stared at the graying charcoal. Soon Mary said, "The gods tell us we have nothing to fear from the English."

"Then what is it?"

"The gods told only this. When I asked for a vision of the future, the fire faded and the gods disappeared. It has never before happened like this. It is an omen of death."

"Mary, who will die?"

Mary looked despairingly at the fire. "I do not know. I do not like it." She shook her padded head. "How could the gods be cruel to me? I have given them an offering of great importance."

"Maybe we scooped up too much dirt when we collected the soldier's ashes. That would put out your fire."

Taking Mary by the arm he raised her off the floor. He looked into her sweaty face. "Do not be sad, Mary. You will try again later. The gods will be good to you. They have never turned against you."

Prince knew that she was not encouraged by his suggestion. He put his arm around her waist and helped her hobble out of the hut. "They tell us we need not fear the English. That is important news, Mary. This is what you will tell our people. Nothing else." His voice was gentle but firm. Mary nodded agreement. "Do not worry our people," he said. "And do not worry yourself."

Outside, King brought Mary's crutches. Fitting them into place, she swung herself into the yard.

Sergeant Ottingen crouched down in the scrub. The scratches he had suffered on the arduous journey through the bush made his bare chest and legs feel on fire. Caked mud added to his discomfort. His body crawled and itched. Steeling himself against an instinct to scratch, he remained motionless. Approximately thirty feet from where he was hiding, a sentinel, his back to Ottingen, faced the huts.

A voice came out of the night, from above. "Mary speaks now. See, she is in the clearing." The sentinel moved toward the huts.

Ottingen eased himself out of the cover, cautiously picking a spot for each footstep. As he drew nearer, he could make out the forms of the congregating rebels. But he could not identify Mary at this distance. He had to move down to the huts. Resolved to have his mission accomplished at any cost, he walked down the incline. Ahead of him the murmur of voices increased. His heart thumped wildly. When he was in back of a hut, he leaned against the rough siding and waited for his breathing to become regular.

Mary's voice spoke out. Ottingen was amazed at the

inspiration that trailed on her words. "Many years ago I put a curse on the white men. They will never put us back in chains. Tonight the gods gave me many messages." A pause. In the silence, Ottingen could feel the anticipation of the rebels. It occurred to him that he, too, was hanging on her every word.

"A big ship with many sails, many cannon, and many soldiers will arrive with the first light of dawn. But as we drove away the English soldier before, we will drive away the English soldier again. The gods have promised this." Mary paused. A shuffle of feet and the whispering of voices. Ottingen drew a pistol from his belt and edged around the outside of the hut. Mary continued. "Tonight the gods caution us that we will have our freedom only if we follow Prince. We have but one leader. They do not want us to forget this."

Prince was uneasy. Had Mary seen something in the fire she had not told him? "There are others who can perform the sacred rites to our gods," Mary said. "But you have only one leader."

A shot rang out. Mary's head jerked back and she was flung violently to the ground, her crutches clattering around her.

"Mary," Prince's impassioned voice cut the silence. Stunned, the people moved forward. "Take to the bush and kill the white man," King shouted.

Before he had taken the shot at Mary, Ottingen decided he would risk making his escape on the open path to the fort, instead of hiding in the bush. His decision was correct. As he ran along the path, headed for the security of the armed soldiers in front of him, the rebels behind him plunged into the bush.

The next morning Ottingen and Von Beverhoudt stood on the wide parapet of the fortress wall and listened to the distant drumming. "She must be dead," Von Beverhoudt said. "That sounds like their death ritual. A good job, Sergeant, a good job."

The noises of the drums came in from Ottingen's left. On the right, a steady wind soared over the sea and set up a whimpering sigh where it met resistance against the crenelated stone walls of the fort. Ottingen looked toward the sea. A burst of orange was forcing night off the horizon. His eyes looked hard into the first light of dawn. "The English man-of-war will soon be here," he said.

"Oh?" Von Beverhoudt moved his head, looking at the daybreak. "Do you see it?"

"Not yet. But we'll see it very soon."

Another silence as they both scanned the water. Suddenly, it was there, the man-of-war running downwind toward Coral Bay. Her sails were sheeted out, wing and wing. The seas were up so she rolled easily from side to side and appeared to be waddling forward, waving her fat white arms to the garrison that awaited her arrival.

"My God, she appeared out of nowhere," Von Beverhoudt said. "Why did you expect her this morning? The message gave no time of arrival."

Ottingen put his foot in one of the crenelations and watched the approaching ship in silence. How could he explain to the captain of the St. John militia that he had believed the prediction of the rebel witch, Mary? He had expected the English ship to arrive with the first light of dawn, and it had. Now he expected the English to be repulsed. He took in a deep breath and let it out.

Hearing Ottingen sigh, Von Beverhoudt said sternly, "What is it that has taken hold of you? Your mission was accomplished. You should be elated. Ever since you got back here, you've been staring out into the night as if *we* had taken a defeat, not the rebels. You should be up here with a mug in your hand, drinking to the death of that witch."

"You've got something there," Ottingen said, keeping his eyes on the incoming vessel. "At least she won't be able to inspire those devils with any more of her blasted predictions."

Mary was unconscious. At first glance, her body showed no injury. Removing the heavy cotton scarf that was bound on her head, however, one could see the round mark where a bullet had entered the side of her forehead.

Heavily guarded, the rebels set about their ritual of calling on the gods to make Mary well. Every man and woman danced around the hut in which Mary lay. As the rite grew in intensity, Mary breathed deeper. Through the night she remained in a heavy sleep.

The sky was light gray when a rebel scout arrived and announced that the English ship had dropped anchor in Coral Bay. At once Prince summoned the five leaders in council, where it was decided that the entire force would remain with Mary until she awakened. But Hendersen was a dangerous place for them to congregate, for the planters knew it to be their favorite rendezvous. After a brief discussion, they agreed to try evading the Danish and English soldiers. Thorner's plantation, on the southwest of the island, was chosen as a hiding place. Thorner's, an isolated estate, had been plundered and then neglected because of its inaccessibility.

The sun had risen over the round knoll on the east of Hendersen when the rebel forces moved out into the bush. Numb with grief for their mortally wounded prophetess, one hundred sixty-two rebels walked single file through the dense cover of scrub between Hendersen and Thorner's. The sun's rays seeped into the dewy bush, making an intense, humid heat. Held and magnified by the humidity, the humming of bees and mosquitoes generated an intense sound of jungle life, a drone that overpowered the restrained noises of the barefoot rebels. The sweet, delicate scents of the jungle flowers mixed with the heavy musk of wet earth and rancid rebel sweat.

When the white-hot sun was directly over them, the rebels came out of the bush into the clearing at Thorner's. The open, windswept area lightened their spirits and quickened their steps to the slave quarters. When Mary had been placed on a mattress in one of the huts, Ruth lit a fire and renewed the effort to have the gods awaken Mary from her deep sleep. Quietly, the rebel forces gathered around the hut, some sitting with their bare backs against the wooden siding, others easing to the ground in the area close to the hut. They did not speak. But for the addition of the motionless black bodies, Thorner's plantation was as void of activity as it had been since the day it had been looted over three months ago.

While the rebels set up their silent vigil at Thorner's, Sergeant Ottingen led a mixed armed force to Hendersen. The group was made up of Captain Maddox and fifty-one English sailors, fourteen Danish soldiers, eight planters, and twenty-one slaves.

This was no sneak attack. Under the blazing sun, kicking up a cloud of dust with their vigorous, marching feet, they poured onto Hendersen and fanned out, surrounding the slave quarters. Thrown off balance by the desolation that met them, the assuredness of their advance weakened and they bogged down. Looking disconcertedly at one another, they surveyed the evidence of the rebels' recent departure.

"Sergeant Ottingen," a soldier called out, "in this hut. A fire still smolders. And there is fresh blood on the mattress."

Ottingen ran to the hut and looked around. "Damn," he exclaimed. "They've run!"

"Our bold scheme brought small results, Sergeant," Captain Maddox said. According to the agreement with the Danes, he was to receive five hundred dollars for every rebel captured, dead or alive. Maddox and his men had no political reasons to be on St. John. They had volunteered strictly for monetary reasons. Expecting a fat profit from this particular raid, Maddox could not conceal his disappointment. He kicked at the charcoal embers with a scuffed black boot and cursed under his breath. "And now what, Sergeant?" Maddox said.

"Don't be impatient," Ottingen said, dropping down on one knee to examine the mattress. "By the look of this, I'd say my aim was correct, and that witch took the shot in her head."

"To hell with the witch," Maddox grumbled. "What now?"

Ottingen rose and looked squarely at the captain. "What now? That is what I'm trying to decide, Captain. This isn't the ocean, it's . . ."

"Yes, I know. It's a vast wilderness, where the rebel is at home in the bush, eh, Sergeant?" Seeing Ottingen's jaw set more firmly, Maddox chuckled. "My apologies. I'm impatient today." He grinned. His face, weathered by sun and wind, took on a shy, boyish expression. Maddox's all-over appearance was one of contrasts. He was clean-shaven, and his brown hair was pulled back sleekly into a fashionable knot at the nape of his neck. Yet his large, evenly proportioned features had a tough quality, a seasoned look. "You are the one acquainted with the technicalities of fighting in the bush, Sergeant," he said sincerely. "I'll put myself in your hands."

"Thank you, sir," Ottingen said. "Now, this is what we're up against. We could go out and march through the bush all day. The rebels would stay ahead of us, out of distance, wearing us down. That is, *if* the rebel is in the bush, which I am sure he is not." Now Ottingen saw that Maddox's eyes searched his own. "Could they have moved

259

to another plantation?" he said to Maddox, and then answered his own question. "That makes sense. They have, in all probability, gone off to bury that witch. To pinpoint the exact plantation is the problem. They wouldn't go northwest. That would be too close to Duerloo's. They don't want to risk an attack while they bury her. They could be on any plantation, northeast or southwest of us. Since we are in between, we'll search for them methodically, beginning northeast. Jansen's plantation, over by Caneel Bay, is a likely spot. Yes, that would be more like it."

"Is there time to reach Jansen's estate before sundown?" Maddox asked.

"Yes. If they're not there, it will at least be a good place to bed down for the night. It won't be long before we locate the rebels. They won't quit pounding those damn drums for too long. Between our scouts and the drums, if we don't find them at Jansen's, we'll know exactly where to attack them in the morning."

The sun had gone down behind the sea when Prince came out of Mary's hut. He walked into the group who were sprawled out or sitting on the ground. In a loud voice he said, "Mary still sleeps. There will be no fires tonight. The soldiers will be looking for us." The people sat up and looked at Prince. He continued. "We will fight the soldiers here. But we need time for Mary to awaken. We will not let the soldiers find us until we are ready for them. Now, I want twelve drummers to go out in the bush." Prince crossed his arms on his chest and turned slowly so he could count the men who rose from the ground. When there were at least twelve, he raised his hand. "Enough," he said. "Come with me. You volunteers" —he turned his head so he could look at those who were standing—"come!"

They moved into one of the huts. There King and Peter sat squat-legged on the earthen floor in the center of the hut. Prince motioned the volunteers to sit down. When they were all in a circle, Prince said, "We have decided to fool the soldiers. They will be listening for our drums. This afternoon our scouts brought news that the soldiers have gone to Jansen's." The volunteers looked at each other. "Tonight you will go southeast of them. Make the drumming noises and draw them away from us. Before daybreak, circle behind the soldiers. And then tomorrow night, you will drum in back of them, pulling them back to the north the next day. Stay hidden in the heaviest scrub during the day. In this manner you can run circles around the soldiers, back and forth, until we are ready for them."

"When do you think we will be ready for them, Prince?" Thomas asked.

"When Mary is awake . . . or dead." Prince's words hung in the silence that followed.

"How will we know when you are ready?" another asked.

"By a drum. We will not send a single message until we are ready for you. There are too many of our kind who are spies for the soldiers. When you beat the drums tonight, call on our gods to protect us in the battle with the English soldier. Then the traitors will tell the English we prepare to fight. It will keep the soldiers looking for us. Every night, until you hear King drum, it will be up to you to make the soldiers chase you. Keep four or five scouts out. Do not let them catch you."

"Do not worry," Thomas said, grinning. "The English soldier will make so much noise in the bush we can stay ahead of him." As an afterthought, he added, "And what message will King send?"

"He will tell you to go to Caroline. That will be the signal for you to return to Thorner's. Then we will put up a noise that will point them to us, without any doubt. And we will be ready for them."

For nine searing, hot days the armed forces marched back and forth, from the north to the south of the island, chasing the noises of the drums. At night, exhausted and discouraged, they camped on the plantations where their unyielding search had led them.

Meanwhile, Mary remained in the coma. Often she appeared agitated, breathing irregularly, tossing and mumbling. At other times she went into a peaceful, deep sleep. Patiently Ruth prodded Mary to drink bush tea, raising her head and pleading with her. Occasionally the words sank in, and Mary swallowed according to command, sustaining the tough thread of life that stubbornly clung to her emaciated body.

Just before sunset on the tenth day after Captain Maddox's arrival on St. John the thread broke. Prince was standing in the doorway of the hut, staring into space. The sounds of Mary's labored breathing were all around him. Then the breathing stopped. Prince ran to her side and dropped down, placing his ear over her heart. Slowly, he rose and stared at Mary. Her black skin was a mass of wrinkles over the withered flesh that hung from her bones. Her wiry hair, which prior to her head injury had always been covered by a thick scarf, was white at the temples. And her mouth was open, letting her puckered lips fall in over her toothless gums. Mary looked as though the process of dying had taken her a thousand years.

When the solitary, grave notes of King's drum resounded, Ottingen and Maddox were taking their troops back to the fort. Disheartened by the futile attempts to find the rebels in the last ten days, they plodded along quietly. At almost the same time, they stopped. They looked at one another. Ottingen's bushy eyebrows shot up. He raised a finger. "Now *this* is a different story."

Maddox nodded. "I think so, Sergeant. The southwest. It's been quiet over there."

From the north of them, where the rebel drummers had been in hiding for the day, another drumming sprang up. The hollow tones from the southwest ceased. "See," Ottingen said. "The drum on the south is cautious. It continued only until its message was received. You know, Captain, I think those rebels have tricked us."

"But why? Why haven't they wanted to meet us? They can't hide forever."

"I have no way of knowing what is on their minds, Captain. They have very strange customs. Their rites are beyond my understanding."

"Let's continue to the fort, Sergeant. We'll get some food and rest and take out into the bush later tonight. We've got to find some action for my men. They're discouraged."

Just after dark, a furious commotion of drums and howling voices carried to the fort. Sergeant Ottingen came out of his room and went up to the parapet. Dr. Bodger and Christian, who had been brought to the fort to care for the wounded in the expected engagement with the rebels, were already there.

"What are they saying, Christian," Ottingen said.

"It is the death ritual," Christian answered.

"For whom?"

262

Christian cocked his head. "Could it be?" he mumbled aloud. "Yes. It is. They dance for Mary. They do the death dance for Mary."

"Mary?" Ottingen said. "She died ten days ago."

"Who said so?" Dr. Bodger asked.

"Well, no one *said* so," Ottingen replied. "They were pounding the drums after she had been wounded. We just thought it was their death ritual. I saw her fall. I *know* I shot her."

The black hollows of Christian's eyes came around, aiming at Ottingen's face. Slowly, gently, pausing between each word, he said, "You . . . shot . . . Mary?"

Christian's words chilled Ottingen. He could feel the skin on the back of his neck twitch and crawl. "Don't you *dare* feel sorry for me," Ottingen screamed. Christian stepped back. Ottingen took a step forward, raised his hand, and then, as if an invisible hand had struck his own, he dropped his arm. "I'm sorry, Christian," he said. He turned and moved down the parapet.

"Stay here," Dr. Bodger said to Christian. He went to Ottingen. The sergeant had his head in his hands, looking down. "What is it, Sergeant? You've been led a merry chase in the bush, that I know. But we have all leaned heavily on you during times of stress. It's unlike you to be high-strung."

"I know," Ottingen said wearily. "Maybe I'm exhausted with this ridiculous game of hide-and-seek we've been playing."

"I'm a doctor, Sergeant. I think I can reasonably say I know the signs of exhaustion. These you don't have." He pulled a cigar from his pocket and bit the end off. Spitting it out, he said, "The power of the African witch doctor has to do with the mind." Ottingen raised his head and looked at the doctor. "Don't let it work on yours, Sergeant." A flame flared up. The doctor puffed on the cigar. Aromatic smoke drifted off in the wind. The flame went out. The red ember at the end of the cigar was visible in the ensuing darkness.

"Maybe I am letting it annoy me," Ottingen said. He stood up and turned his back on the doctor. Putting his foot on the wall, he stared out to the west. "Little doubt as to where they are tonight. Just listen to how they cry for their sorceress." He stood up straight and breathed in the

263

air. "All right, Doctor, it won't work on my mind. In fact, I'll make my own prediction, cast my own spell. There is, on the rebel leader Prince's neck, a carving, an idol of their witchcraft. Before I'm finished with this fight, I'll lop off Prince's head and have that carving as a remembrance of my momentary preoccupation with their rituals." Turning toward the doctor, he said, "The best cure I can think of, Doctor, is to set my mind against that which has disturbed it. And how does this sit with you?"

"A good medicine," the doctor said. He looked toward the west. "What a long-drawn-out affair this has become. It appears the only way we will ever live a normal existence here on St. John is to have the head of every last one of them. I yearn for my estate and my work."

"Well, Doctor, it's time I get our men organized and get out there after them. We'll be leaving within the hour."

"Oh? And after a long day in the field? Why tonight?"

"Because I hope that the rebels will think as you do, that we are too tired to go out tonight. If they do, we can surprise them."

"Let's hope you'll be successful, Sergeant. Their leader, Prince, set me free on the day of the insurrection. Later, at Deurloo's, I could have had his life, I'm sure. I wish now I'd taken it. The suffering has been prolonged."

"What is he like, Doctor?"

"It's our loss that he has led a revolt against us."

The advance of the armed forces on the rebels was a slow one. Ahead of them, the turbulence of the death rite grew as they inched forward, hacking at the ground cover. The English sailors still had plenty of energy and swung their cutlasses lightheartedly. After the frustrating, empty search of the last ten days, the howls of the rebels stimulated their lust for a fight and reminded them of the reward in gold for each rebel captured or killed. The Danish planters and soldiers and the African slaves moved forward with high hopes of an end to their four months of harassment from the rebels. Braced by the sounds that guaranteed contact, they passed the night and they were still unspent when dawn broke.

Coming out into a cultivated field at Thorner's plantation, the armed forces stopped for last-minute instructions from their leaders. The plantation was still hidden by a gentle knoll, but by now the din had so increased that every man in the attack force was aware of the enemy and eager for battle.

The field was surrounded on three sides by uncleared land. In the brush on either side of the armed forces, half of the rebels were crouched in ambush, patiently waiting for the armed forces to move forward so they could close in behind them. The other half of the rebel forces lay ahead, hooting and pounding on the drums, luring the soldiers into the trap.

"Over the knoll and at them," Maddox shouted, raising his pistol into the air. Spreading out across the field, the small army advanced.

A band of rebel archers surged out of the bush. At the same time, from both sides, the other rebels sped across the field, so swift and silent that they were upon their foe almost directly behind the stream of arrows that pelted into the aggressors' backs. Confusion broke out. The rebels leaped on their enemy, struggling to wrest away the deadly weapons. Maddox's first shot felled a rebel, and he was about to take another when he heard a fierce noise in back of him, toward the plantation. Turning, he saw the other half of the rebel force, armed with cane knives and swords, pouring down the side of the knoll like a mighty black river.

"Fall back to the edge of the bush and make ready to defend yourselves," Maddox screamed out.

Ottingen, rightfully estimating their situation, took up the cry. "Fall back in a line."

"Fall back," resounded over the clamor of wild hoots and war cries.

The armed forces tried to retreat from the rebels, who, having them in an iron grip, would not let loose. Deftly, the rebels swung their cutlasses and cane knives, spewing blood onto the battlefield.

The Negroes who fought on the side of the armed forces were the first to break free. They retreated to the bush and there fell on their knees. Taking aim to defend their masters, and the soldiers and sailors, they fired random shots at the rebels. The shots were ineffective, but the volley distracted the rebels sufficiently for the remaining troops to break out of the trap and retreat. At the edge of the bush they could not form a line, for the rebels had overcome their momentary fear of the guns and were giving chase.

Now in full retreat, the armed forces stumbled into the bush. The thicket proved to be their salvation. Within it the rebels could not mass together; now the soldiers could make use of their arms. Sensing this, the rebels came to a halt at the entrance to the scrub.

Here, Prince signaled them back. "To the knoll, out of range of their guns. If they come out for another attack, we will use the same trap." He looked around the battle-field. There were four dead sailors and one dead Danish soldier. The wounded had been carried back in the retreat.

"Listen to them run," King cried gleefully. The rebels were silent. The snapping noises of twigs and dried bush moved away from them. "They won't be back, Prince. They've had enough."

"We will be ready for them, if they do," Prince said.

The weakened armed forces had no intention of returning and so continued their retreat to the fort.

Those at the garrison could not believe their eyes when they saw their troops approaching. It was apparent that a ruinous blow had been struck against them. For every three or four men who trudged along the mountain side, there was one who limped or leaned against another for assistance. Their high hopes vanquished, they straggled through the gate into the security of the fort in dejected silence.

Later that night, the Danes held council with Captain Maddox and his six officers.

"I know how weary you people are of this thing," he said, in reply to Barens' effectual plea for the British to remain. "But I have to think of my men. There are not enough of us to put down this rebel group. Four of my sailors killed today. Another twelve seriously wounded." He crossed his arms on the table top and leaned forward. "If you want my opinion, you've got to get at least three hundred troops in here to bring an end to your problem. No, gentlemen, I'm sorry to say that I'm sailing tomorrow. This is not a decision I like to make. But it's the only wise one."

Ottingen's chair scraped on the brick floor as he stood up. "Captain, I would like to extend the appreciation of the Danish colonies to you for the assistance you gave." He put his hands on the table and let his eyes look around the table. "I agree with Captain Maddox," he said sternly. "The English are seasoned fighters. We Danes have never been frail in battle. But we are up against overwhelming odds. There is nothing in our power to eradicate the rebels. If the Royal Council will not come up with the money to get adequate—and by 'adequate' I mean three or four hundred troops—if they can't get us the support we need, we cannot expect every man here to lay down his life in a useless manner. Mr. Barens, let us appeal once more to the council. I think our stand should be that we either get the number of men we need in here to fight the rebels, or we turn the island over to them. Let the council make that decision."

Chapter 22

Following the departure of Captain Maddox from St. John, Sergeant Ottingen and William Barens sailed to St. Thomas to attend a meeting of the Royal Danish Council.

Barens, elegantly dressed in long coat, knee breeches, white stockings, ruffles at his neck, ruffles at his wrists, his blond hair curled in neat rows around his head, was concluding his dramatic appeal to the council. "And if we do not vote to appropriate the funds for a concentrated drive to rout the rebels, I suggest we vote to withdraw our planters and soldiers, and give the island over to the rebels." A silence filled the council room. Feeling that his speech had delivered a strong impact, Barens sat down.

The governor cleared his throat. Pushing aside the long white curls of his elaborate wig, he said, "Let me hear other opinions on this." He looked around the table.

Claude Mueller stood up. "These good men," he said, "have given us hard facts. I move we vote on one issue. Whether or not the council will provide funds for a mass assault on the rebels. Let it be a foregone conclusion that if we vote against it, we vote for withdrawing the Danes from St. John."

"And whom do we ask for this mass army?" De Wint said.

"The French, naturally," Claude said hastily. "Look out there in the harbor. There is a French vessel that can take our envoy to Martinique." Anxious to win the vote, Claude went on, "Let us decide what we will offer the French. Our bookkeeper, here," he turned to John Horn, "can carry our terms."

"And what would you suggest we offer?" Governor Gardelin said.

Claude shrugged. "It's only a matter of judgment to determine a tempting offer, isn't it, gentlemen? But, to answer your question, what difference if we offered them every rebel they capture? The rebels are a loss to us, even if the French don't capture them. But then there is the matter if we should also give up the plantations. Isn't it better to lose only the slaves?"

"Aye," De Wint said firmly.

"Aye" sprang up around the table.

Encouraged, Claude said in a firm voice, "Let us take our vote now, gentlemen." As the noises of affirmation sprang up, he sat down.

Governor Gardelin stood up. "In all practicality, Councilmen, I suggest we empower our envoy to offer four fifths of the rebels, the remainder to be turned over to the company. I feel that we must make an example of some rebels in order to insure our future safety against another rebellion." While the governor talked on, Claude looked slyly at Ottingen and smiled. Even before the vote, it was apparent that the governor and the council were in favor of alloting the funds. The concessions the governor now spoke about were of little concern to Ottingen, or Barens, or Mueller. They knew they had won.

For some time prior to the revolt on St. John, Denmark had been negotiating with France for the purchase of St. Croix. At that time, Louis XV was preparing to support the cause of his father-in-law, Stanislas Leszczyński, in his attempt to take over the Polish throne. Knowing that France was anxious for Denmark's neutrality in the coming war with Poland, a director of the Copenhagen Company offered France 750,000 livres for the island of St. Croix. Shrewdly, he tossed in Denmark's neutrality as an afterthought! The offer was accepted.

Word of the transfer reached the French colonies in the West Indies just before the arrival of the Danish envoy, John Horn, on Martinique. The French authorities, not altogether unaware of the money involved for them in the acquisition of so many slaves but basically pleased by Denmark's offer of neutrality, extended a hand of friendship and greeted John Horn with enthusiasm. On April 8, Governor Gardelin received word from John Horn that the French had accepted the offer of four fifths of the captured slaves and were making preparations to organize a group of Creole volunteers to send to St. John. John Horn estimated that the French would arrive within the month.

Governor Gardelin called a meeting of the council and

announced the acceptance of the offer by the French and called on the planters to contribute one hundred and fifteen of their Negroes to further insure the success of the drive. Claude Mueller was appointed to promote the St. Thomas appeal for slave volunteers. By April 18, Claude had enlisted the services of seventy-one Negroes. He was forty-four slaves short of the goal set by the governor on the basis of five per cent of the total number of Negroes on the island. On this day, Sergeant Ottingen arrived from St. John, to report that a group of forty-odd rebels had made an attack on the militia at Deurloo's plantation, setting the supply magazine on fire. Ottingen estimated that four rebels had been killed, and perhaps a dozen severely wounded.

Visiting the Muellers, Ottingen talked of the attack. "They really surprised the men at Deurloo's. It was such a sudden attack that the rebels were upon them before they could man the cannon."

"Why do you suppose such a small group made the attack, Theodore?" Claude said. "If they had come in force, don't you think they would have taken Deurloo's?"

"I'm sure of it. But this is the way the rebels think. They probably felt that they had to split forces, keeping the main force closer to the fort. We are at an advantage, having the two strongholds on distant parts of the island. In this manner, the rebels keep an eye on each. However, had they massed for an attack on Deurloo's, or if they massed for an attack on the fort, I'd say they could take either of them without too much loss. But the rebels are terrified of the cannon. This group that attacked Deurloo's may have been watching for days for the exact minute when they could make their charge without having to fear the cannon. And I can see how the militia at Deurloo's would get caught off guard. It's tedious to stand by those cannon, chilled by the trades that whip off that plateau in the night and broiled by the sun that pounds down on them all day. They had just gone into the greathouse for a change of guard—and breakfast. Their guards on the terrace entered the house—and that was it!"

"We were fortunate not to lose any men."

"That we were. But the rebels didn't have it in mind to take Deurloo's. They were only concerned with getting the magazine. They probably figure that in this way the cannon are no longer a threat. They will test it, soon, and if they find we cannot drive them off with the cannon, then they will try to take the manor. I've sent some reinforcements and ammunition from the fort. The rebels are in for a surprise on their next attack."

"Let us hope that the French arrive before they make another attack, Theodore. If the rebels had just one good strategist, all of you would be wiped out, just like this." Claude snapped his fingers.

Ottingen walked to the table and refilled his empty glass. "Our garrison is beginning to show the strain. My God, what a dismal life it is, cooped up in that fort. There isn't a man there who doesn't know that the rebel forces could conquer us if they put their minds to it. What a hell of a way for a man to spend his life!"

"Patience, my boy. You'll get a commission out of this and name your own garrison, you'll see. By the way, how do you like the rum?"

Ottingen looked into his glass. "Why do you ask?"

"Hendersen rum, Theodore."

The sergeant sipped it. "It's good."

"And has excellent powers, my boy. Not that you need any of it while you're on St. John."

Ottingen looked at Claude. There was a mischievous smile on Claude's face. Claude lowered his voice, looking around to be sure Sarah was not in hearing range, and said, "If Jan Hendersen can make a girl pregnant at *his* age, think of what it will do for me."

Ottingen frowned. "You mean Anna Bodker is pregnant?"

"That she is," Claude said excitedly. He rubbed his hands, and said, "You heard Jan say that Hendersen keeps a man young. I hope it isn't too late for me."

Ottingen laughed. "You're right, though, that I don't need any of it on St. John. Damn, the rebel women are turning white."

"Turning white," Sarah said, coming into the room, catching the last of Ottingen's words. "Is the sun bleaching them?"

Flustered, Claude forced a laugh. "Ah, Sarah, my love. How is the dinner coming along? Theodore was saying he is very hungry. You know, dear, the food at the fort is tasteless. What have we today?"

"You are getting very absent-minded," Sarah said. She puckered her pink lips and blew a kiss at Claude. "Poor lamb. It wasn't ten minutes ago that you asked." She sat down in a chair and flounced her heavy blue satin skirt. "Have you told Theodore about the latest scandal at the Hendersen Estate?"

"Scandal? What scandal?" Claude said.

"You know, dear one. Anna," she dropped her voice and whispered toward Ottingen, "she is with child."

Ottingen pulled a chair close to Sarah and sat down. "That is not a scandal, Sarah. It's remarkable. And fortunately, there will be someone to carry on at Hendersen."

"There is the possibility of it being a girl," Sarah said. "And if it is, I suppose you two gentlemen will conclude that they will continue having children until a son is born."

"He will if he keeps on at the pace he's going now," Claude said. "An enviable pace, I'd say."

"Claude." Sarah frowned and stared at her husband. He dropped his head on his shoulder and grinned.

"Did Hendersen volunteer any Negroes for St. John?" Ottingen said.

Claude regained his composure. Sitting up straight, he said firmly, "Not a one. He still sticks to the story that his slaves won't take arms against slaves. We can't make him volunteer. It's just as well if we ignore him. Let them sit up there at Fortuna until they go island crazy."

"*Go* island crazy," Sarah exclaimed. "It's a small distance he has to travel. What a disgrace it is that he won't cooperate with us in putting down the revolt. Jan Hendersen has gotten everything from the colony and given nothing to it. And she's following in his footsteps. They come into the fort for services on Sunday, the last to arrive and the first to leave, as if they purposely don't want to talk to anyone. It wouldn't hurt Anna Hendersen to participate in some of the ladies' functions."

"Are her hemlines still as short," Ottingen interrupted.

Sarah laughed. "You cannot fool me, Theodore. You are still taken aback by her beauty, aren't you? Yes, she still wears them too short. As angry as I get with her, she looks like a little girl and my heart warms to her. One of the women was saying that when she and Jan get out past Contant, Anna swings her leg over her horse's back and rides as a man."

"I hate to think of that beautiful woman being isolated out in the scrub with only an old man for company," Ottingen said.

"They appear to entertain each other very nicely," Claude said.

"Claude," Sarah scolded.

Ottingen managed to keep a straight face and changed the subject. "Have preparations been completed for the French troops? The food, the materials for the barracks . . ."

"Everything will be ready. Tomorrow the Spanish traders arrive. When the French get here, they'll find us ready. Our company Attorney is going to St. John to take charge of the captured Negroes. He'll see that they are divided according to the agreement."

"What will they do with our share?" Sarah asked.

"Send them here for trial."

"Trial? They are obviously guilty if they are caught fighting us. What is there to waste time about?"

Claude shrugged his shoulders. "Only a manner of speaking. You know that we won't take time for a prolonged trial. We'll just get them here, find them guilty of treason, and punish them accordingly. It will be a prime example to the other Negroes of what will happen if they try the same thing. When we are finished with the captured rebels, I doubt if any of our Negroes will ever give rebellion another thought."

"I hope not," Sarah said. "Let's hope some good comes out of this dreadful situation."

"There has been nothing good to come out of it yet," Claude said. "But this time I have every confidence that the end of the revolt is in sight. Now, come, Sergeant, let us go have some good food and forget the war."

Claude pulled Sarah to her feet. Sarah looked at Ottingen. "When do you return to St. John?"

"Today. Right after dinner." He put his arm out and Sarah wrapped her arm through his. Walking toward the dining room, he said, "The next time we dine together, the revolt will be over. Then we'll have to find a new topic of discussion."

"We can always discuss the Hendersens," Sarah said, laughing.

"That is a sore subject for Theodore, my dear," Claude said, trailing along behind them. "Theodore's eyes lit up the first day they spotted Anna. It's not easy for a young, handsome man to lose his woman to one not considered proper competition."

"I wouldn't go so far as to say that, Claude." Sarah

turned and looked coquettishly at her husband. "Jan Hendersen is a very handsome man." When Ottingen helped her sit down at the table, she put a napkin on her lap and said, "At the ladies' sewing meets there is a lot of oohing and ahhing when the name of Jan Hendersen is mentioned."

"That reminds me," Claude said, pulling out his high-backed chair. "There is Hendersen rum here on the table today. Help yourself." As soon as he was seated, Claude reached for the bottle himself and filled his glass.

"I've never seen you drink so much rum," Sarah chided. "You must be careful, dear. So many of the planters grow too fond of it."

"Now don't worry your pretty head," Claude said. He sipped the rum and made contented noises. He moved the decanter in front of the sergeant.

"No more today," Ottingen said, smiling at Claude. "I'll wait until the revolt is over."

On the afternoon of April 23, the booming of drums on St. Thomas was picked up by the garrison at Deurloo's. When the sounds moved closer to the eastern end of St. Thomas, obviously being relayed to St. John, Von Beverhoudt doubled the guard on the terrace.

The drum poundings were distinct. From somewhere close to Deurloo's, rebel hands pounded the message on to Hendersen. Von Beverhoudt summoned Henry. "What do they say?" he asked his slave.

"They say that there are two big ships taking on supplies in the harbor at Charlotte Amalie. And that hundreds of armed men are on the ships. And that the ships will sail for St. John."

"Thank God," Von Beverhoudt shouted. *"The French!"*

A shout went up from the other planters. "Stay on guard," Von Beverhoudt called out. "The rebels might try a suicidal attack when they get this news."

At Hendersen, King picked up the message and relayed it to Caroline. As his hands were slamming down with studied rhythm, he could feel cold chills run up and down his bare back. When another drum resounded and he knew the message had been received, he let the drum fall on the ground and ran to the hut where Prince was. "Prince," he gasped, running through the doorway, "what can we do against so many armed soldiers?" Prince, sprawled on a

274

mattress on the floor, stared up at the ceiling. King snickered and said, "Ever since the drums told us that Anna makes a baby, all you do is hide yourself and think. We have bad news today. Get your mind off that white woman."

Prince pushed himself upright, his eyes flashing. "I am trying to think of what we should do. Do you want me to start running in every direction, without thought? Sit down."

"Since Mary died," King grumbled. "We have not had many good messages from our gods. Ruth is not experienced enough."

"She is trying," Prince said. He sat up straight and looked squarely at King. "Why can't we drive these French off the island just as quickly as we drove off the English? The English met us once each time, and then they ran."

"But there are many hundred this time. If we cannot get them in a trap, they will shoot us."

"Not if we shoot them first."

"How will we get ammunition? You talk as if your head is sick today."

"There is one place on St. John that has ammunition. The fort."

King stretched out his hands. "You think we can take the fort with these hands? Do not talk foolish."

Prince stood up and stared down at King. "If we organize all of us from Hendersen and Caroline and attack the fort at night when the cannon cannot see us we will be able to take the fort. And then we will have the cannon to fight off the French soldiers. And we will have ammunition for our guns. We can use the fort for our headquarters."

King leaped up. "You are crazy, Prince! Too many of us will die trying to take the fort. We will not have enough numbers to fight the French soldiers. I do not agree with you."

"There are only fifty men at the fort. The drums tell us that there are hundreds coming on the ships. Why would you rather fight three or four hundred with those hands than risk getting the guns from fifty?"

"If we risk getting the guns from the fifty, how many of us do you think will be alive? Not many more than fifty. And then the soldiers will say, 'Let us kill them in the fort. There are only fifty, and there are hundreds of us.' "

"I know they can say that," Prince said tersely. "But only if they can get ashore on St. John. If we take the fort tonight, how will they get on land to make a camp? We can fire on their ships with the cannon. We can cover the beach with our entire force, killing them before they get ashore."

King shook his head. "I do not agree. It is too much to risk. We are better off trying to trap them. If we stay in a group and try to close around them, we have a better chance." King walked to the door. "Call the leaders, Prince, and take a vote."

Outside the hut the rebels had gathered into a group. The news had circulated and they were uneasy. Prince walked to the doorway. When he was beside King, he saw the faces looking toward him, trustingly. "Then we will take a vote with the leaders, King. But let us move our people from here to Caroline. There we will meet with the other leaders. If we decide to attack the fort, we will be in position to do it tonight." King nodded agreement, and Prince stepped out into the bright sunlight. The people moved closer. Prince raised his arm. "Make ready to go to Caroline. We will leave within the hour. Take with you only your arms. Leave the livestock here. We do not go to feast or dance. At Caroline we will hold a war council. You will be ready to fight tonight if it is necessary." He paused. The grave faces of the rebels remained fixed on him. "Only our scouts will remain behind. We will desert Hendersen."

A silence fell over the group, everyone staring at Prince. From the group a voice yelled out, "What do the gods tell us?"

Prince's eyes moved from face to face. Could he lie to them, tell them that Ruth had received a message from the gods, when in fact she hadn't? No. He could not do that. It would anger the gods, and they would bring their wrath in peculiar ways. He had to tell them the truth. "Ruth has not had a message from the gods," he said in a strong voice. Noises of discontent rose up. "Wait," Prince yelled out. Quiet fell over the people. "You have no reason to blame Ruth. When Mary was alive, she sometimes had to wait for weeks before she had a good sign from the gods. Mary always said that when the gods were quiet, it was a good sign. And since we have not had any omen at all, there is nothing to worry about. Ruth knew how to talk with the

276

gods before Mary died. Mary believed in Ruth. So why can't you people believe, as Mary did?"

The rebels looked at one another. Some shrugged their shoulders, as much as to say, "Why not?" Others looked uncertainly back and forth, unsure of their feelings.

"What do you want to do," Prince screamed out angrily, "hide in the bush, shake with fear, because Ruth has not had an omen from our gods? Do you want to risk losing your freedom because you do not know in advance from the gods that you will win? The gods will be angered by your attitude. They want brave warriors, not trembling mice, to go meet the French soldiers." Prince could see that his words were stirring the people. Brashly he yelled, "Those of you who are mice, go now and surrender to the planters at Deurloo's. Go ahead. Now."

Every face was looking toward Prince. They stood like statues, as if a single movement would show indecision. "And those of you who go as brave warriors, take up your arms and follow me to Caroline."

An earsplitting roar of assent rose up. The rebels spread across the clearing, taking up their weapons and scurrying to get in line. Not a man hesitated.

King walked up behind Prince and put his hand on Prince's shoulder. "The people will follow you, Prince. You are a good leader. When you speak, it is as if you put your mouth against a dying fire and give it air, so that the flame comes up."

It was late afternoon when the rebels who had been at Hendersen reached Caroline. Quietly, they mingled with the rebels who were already there, and received, in return, little fanfare.

Peter and Thomas, with three other leaders, waited at the door of their hut for Prince and King to come to them. By the time they were seated in council, the other rebels were sitting outside, patiently waiting for their orders.

There were seven leaders who met in council, three newly appointed to replace those who had been killed. Prince was standing. The six others sat in a circle on the floor of the hut. Prince looked down at the men. "There is only one way we can take over the island and have permanent freedom," he said emphatically. "We cannot let the French soldiers come ashore." King remained with his head down, but the other five men lifted their faces and stared disbelievingly at Prince.

"How do we keep them from coming ashore, you ask. We need ammunition for our guns. We need cannon to sink their boats when they try to land. We have to take the fort." Casually, Prince crossed his arms over his chest and walked slowly around the men. "You think I speak foolish. Do not forget that I was chosen by the gods to lead you. They would not give this honor to a fool. I speak the words in my heart, words the gods put there when they sent me to lead my people. And I say that a hundred of us, attacking the fort at night, have a better chance than one hundred of us trying to fight three or four hundred soldiers." He stopped and leaned over, peering into their faces. "Yes, some of us will die. But this is the only way to have freedom for those who live. If we take the fort, we can hold off the French soldiers. And then we can take Deurloo's. And then we can buy arms and ammunition from the traders." Prince straightened up and circled the men again, talking as he moved.

"Until we drive all the white men off the island, until we take the garrisons with the cannon, we cannot live as free men. Do you call the last five months on St. John a life of freedom? No. We have been at war with the white men. Why has the war been a long one? Only because we do not have ammunition. We can look back and see our mistakes. Our mistake has been that we are not willing to give up enough lives at one time to take over the fortifications. We have lost just as many, if not more, of our people in these small attacks, and have not taken the ammunition or the cannons or," he raised his voice, "driven the white man from the island." He paused. His resonant voice was strong as he said, "We know that we made out first mistake when we stopped to play and let the white men get organized at Deurloo's. And we made the second mistake when we did not drive them out of there, at any cost. And we made our third mistake when we were feasting, sure of our freedom, and let the white men take back the fort." Prince crossed his arms over his chest again and stared across the room at the wall. "Tomorrow, do you want to say we made another mistake? Letting the French soldiers come ashore? Not *trying* to stop them?" Staring silently over the heads of the men, Prince was an imposing figure. He

278

remained in this position, letting them know he had finished speaking.

Not to be outdone, King sprang up and strutted around the circle, leaning forward so that his face was close to the ear of each man he passed. "How many of us do you think will die tonight if we try to take the fort," he said in a stage whisper, implying that the answer would be too devastating to think about. "Prince speaks of *taking* the fort, as if we will take it just because we attack it. What if we lose? If we do not take the fort, our chance for freedom will be finished tonight. And if we take the fort, then what? We will have lost so many of us, the French can go ashore somewhere else, at any bay, and come across the land and attack us at the fort. We will be so weak we cannot fight off that many men." Prince remained with his arms crossed, staring at the wall. Unexpectedly, King jumped into the center of the circle. He flourished his muscular arms over the heads in front of him, appearing to be driving unseen obstacles from the council room, and said, "To think of taking the fort is to drive away our freedom." In the next instant, as if exhaustion had overcome him, he let his arms drop down. "Prince is my brother. We think the same. We both want freedom. But we do not agree on how to get it." King's magnificent, broad features showed anguish. His sad brown eyes looked toward Prince. His mouth drooped at the corners, quivered as he said, "We will vote." Then he stepped out of the circle, directly opposite Prince.

The arguments finished, Prince and King waited for the five to get up and walk to the side of the leader they agreed with.

Prince could hear the men rising from the floor. He was aware of movement directly behind him. Prince turned. Only Peter stood beside him. They would not attack the fort.

Hiding his disappointment, Prince walked over to King. He put his hand on his shoulder. "Now let us decide where we will go to plan our trap for the French soldiers," he said quietly.

Midmorning on the next day, Prince and King sat in the brush on the ridge above the fort and watched the two French barks unload their cargo. In the cove by the fort there was activity such as the little island had never before seen. Almost a dozen longboats were in the water, shuttling back and forth, teeming with supplies and people. Seventy-four slaves contributed by the St. Thomas planters, thirty-one Danes, twenty-three French officers, and one hundred and ninety-eight Creoles were put ashore. The three hundred-odd men, under the charge of Commander Longueville, were immediately appointed duties. The French officers and Danes, armed with loaded muskets and pistols, set up a cordon around the working crews. Wooden planks, provisions for the army, and ammunition for the supply magazines were quickly and efficiently off-loaded from the boats that plied back and forth from the mother ships.

From where they sat, Prince and King could see the Danish soldiers stand guard by the cannon on the bastions of the fort, ready to cover the landing force in the event of an attack. Before their eyes, the Creoles and Negroes, under supervision of Danish and French overseers, began putting up a barracks in the clearing beside the fort. Voices of command, hammering, marching feet, foreign accents, labored grunts and groans of men toiling under a hot sun, swelled the air around them. It was such an unbelievable amount of activity that Prince stared, gruesomely fascinated, hoping he'd awaken and find it unreal. While he watched, he could feel the coolness of the shadowed palm grove at Deurloo's, the morning the revolt began, and hear Master Jan's prediction of the fate in store for the rebelling Negroes. For the first time since the beginning of the revolt, Prince was fearful.

"I hope, for the sake of my people, that I did not vote the wrong way," King said. He looked over at Prince, his eyes asking for reassurance.

"To watch such an army as this, anyone would doubt his judgment," Prince said. "To be honest with you, King, if I were in the fort and saw so many soldiers coming at us, I would feel trapped. I think you were right. We fight better in the bush. It is where we belong. Come, let us move our people back, away from Caroline. We will put our scouts out to warn us when the soldiers are ready to meet us. In the time between, we dance for the gods, King. Everyone of us had better dance and appease them, make them favor us. We will need their help." He squeezed the amulet. It felt cold against his hand.

Chapter 23

The new encampment for the armed forces on St. John took four days to complete. And then the army was ready to go out in the bush. During that four days, the French had formulated a shrewd plan to wear down the rebels. The fort was on the southeastern part of the island. Their fighting force was divided in half. One half was to go across the island to the north side. Then the two teams would simultaneously begin working in opposite directions, on a westward angle, driving the rebels ahead of them until, eventually, they could corner them on the western tip of the island.

On the morning of April 28, over one hundred and fifty armed men set out for the north side of St. John. They passed a mile east of the waiting rebel forces, who had mistakenly counted on the soldiers' moving from plantation to plantation, as they had before.

A rebel scout reported to Prince that the soldiers were out of range of their ambush, passing east of them. The news confused the rebels, for they could not see the strategy of marching in a straight line through the heavy thickets and over the high knolls when there were no plantations in the path of the soldiers.

The rebel forces came out of hiding and set up another vigil, waiting for the leaders to decide on their next move.

"The foreign soldiers are stupid," King told the rebel council, a contemptuous leer on his face. "They walk out into the bush without a plan. Tomorrow they will walk back again, you will see. If we are fortunate, they will pass our way." He looked around at Prince. "I think we should stay right here. The plantation is surrounded by slopes and bush. Eventually they will walk into our trap."

Prince nodded his head. "I agree," he said. "They will only grow weary from so much walking. If we stay here and wait for them, they will have to come to us."

The rebel forces bedded down for the night, unaware that their stand was practically midway between the north and south sides of the island, a target that would put the armed forces on either side of them at approximately the same time the next day.

Ottingen led the half of the armed forces that moved northwest out of the fort with the first light of dawn. Fortunately for the heavily dressed armed forces, the day proved to be a cool one, and a thick cloud formation protected them from the sun. Ottingen had just come to the top of a knoll overlooking a deserted plantation when one of his scouts approached.

"The rebels are on the other side of that plantation," the scout reported. "They are ready to ambush our men who approach them from the north."

"What luck," Ottingen said. "And now, by God, we'll have the rebels in *our* ambush, for a change." He turned to a Creole who acted as an interpreter between the Danes and the French. "Tell the French officers that the rebels are directly between our forces, just ahead. We will move out now, with speed. No need for caution in the bush."

The rebel forces centered their attention on the men who were approaching from the north. Although they had not, as yet, caught sight of the enemy, they could hear machetes hacking at the heavy ground cover in their path as the soldiers moved forward. Tension built as the sounds continued to grow. Every man and woman held a fixed stance, their nerves stretched taut at the anticipation of contact with the soldiers. And while they stood motionless in the protection of the bush, their every sense centered on the enemy on the north, the other half of the enemy force moved in behind them, undetected, from the south.

Prince caught sight of the soldiers at about the same time that King did, for when he turned to catch King's attention, King was already looking at him. With a hand signal, they alerted Peter, who commanded the other half of the rebels, on the eastern side of the advancing army. As the soldiers moved forward, the rebels spread back, opening their trap for the army to enter.

At this point, the rebel forces were divided in two, ready to clamp the soldiers who advanced from the north between them. A rebel scout scurried through the bush. He was breathless when he finally reached Prince. His mouth moved incoherently.

"What is it," Prince whispered impatiently, harshly. "You fool. You have almost put the soldiers on guard with your dash through the bush."

"Soldiers. Behind us. Many soldiers," the scout forced out between labored breaths.

Prince looked out in front of him. The soldiers were already in the opening between the rebel forces. The path was heavily dotted with multicolored uniforms.

"Aiii," Prince groaned. "It is too late to warn Peter."

Behind Prince, spread out to the west, was his half of the rebel forces, waiting for him to give them the attack signal. Slowly Prince turned around. He raised his arms to the side and with a sweeping motion signaled the rebels to move back. Stealthily picking his way, Prince took step after step, continuing the movement with his arms, watching his people retreat. King waited for Prince to move beside him. "What is it?" he whispered urgently. "You are leaving our people on the other side, cut off from us!"

"We have walked into the lion's mouth," Prince answered. "The soldiers have set a trap for us. There is another army coming up in back of us. We have to move west. It is our only chance. We can only hope that our other force will know and break out to join us. We do not have enough people to meet the soldiers in the middle of their army."

"The drum. I can tell our people with the drum," King said.

Prince hesitated. He looked at the rebels who were still moving back. With vehemence he threw his arms outward, showing them that they were to continue their retreat. Continuing the gesture, he whispered over his shoulder to King, "It is worth a try. You know the soldiers will come after us as soon as they pick up the direction of the drum. But we can probably outrun them. With our forces divided, they will have to spread their interest. It is worth a try, King. You and I will stay behind and send the message."

"No. You go now, take our people back. Move to the west, to Hendersen. I will get there later. The people need their leader."

Knowing an argument would take away precious time, Prince slapped King's back and ran off to join the retreating rebels. King took up the drum. Giving Prince and the rebels a few more minutes, he raised his hand and let it pound down on the taut face of the drum. The first note thundered out above the noises of the advancing army.

"Run," Prince yelled to his people as the drumbeats came up behind him. "We are trapped. Run to Hendersen." The rebels turned. Fleet-footed in the bush, they scurried along, listening to the drum message: Do not attack. Retreat. Do not attack. Retreat. There were three clear messages before the drum noises ceased.

King, hearing the snapping of bush close to him and catching a glimpse of red uniform, let the drum fall on the ground and ran. His muscular, bowed legs carried him easily through the dense cover. Close behind he could hear a volley of gunshots and knew that the soldiers had sight of the rebels. Soon the noises of a great battle behind him. He continued running until the sounds faded and his legs grew tired. When he stopped to rest, he knew that the other rebel group had not fared well. There were tortured screams of such piercing quality they had to belong to the outnumbered rebel force.

After dark, it began to rain. Prince and King sat on the front porch of the greathouse, looking at the deserted plantation grounds. In the gray-black light, the darker outline of factories and slave quarters and mill looked like a ghost settlement. The silence between the two men were accented by the patter of rain on the roof above them and the gush of water that hit the ground on the side of the steps, pouring from a broken water spout that should have carried the precious water to the cistern beside the house. The men had blankets wrapped around their bare shoulders, for the night was chilly, wind-swept, and wet.

After a long period of silence, King threw back the blanket and stood up. "What is it?" Prince said.

"I see something," King said, straining to see through the blackness. He picked up the blanket and threw it over his head. At the same time, Prince stood up and lifted his blanket over his head. Together they leaped down the steps. They ran across the clearing to the distillery. King looked around the corner, toward the mill. Yes, now he could see the outline of forms coming down the knoll. "It is our people. Come!"

Running forward, Prince saw that the group was very

small, perhaps twenty people. "Where is your leader?" Prince asked as he approached them.

"I am here," Peter answered. Coming up behind the group, Peter carried a young woman on his back. Her legs were wrapped around his waist and her head drooped on his broad, bare shoulder. With one arm she held on to Peter's neck. The other arm dangled helplessly at her side.

"Your woman," Prince exclaimed. He took his blanket and wrapped it carefully around her head and shoulders.

"Take the wounded to the house," Prince called out.

Solemnly the group of rebels trudged through the cold rain toward the house, carrying or assisting their wounded. When they were inside, they noticed at once that it was warm. Prince and King had put the storm shutters on the house so that the downstairs could be lighted without fear of the soldiers seeing them. The heat from the candles had provided enough warmth to take off the damp chill.

"Get Ruth," Prince commanded King. "Tell her to bring medicine and other women. Tell them we have many wounded."

Prince took up a candle and ran upstairs. There, he took a heap of linen from a press and ran downstairs with it. The rebels, cold and wet, eagerly took up sheets and pillow cases and dried their bodies. Peter took several pillow cases and ran to the woman on the floor. Removing the soaking wet scarf from her head, he re-wrapped her head with a dry cloth. With the other, he dried her body, patting her face, her shoulders, her arm. When he came to the wounded arm and saw the ragged gap where a bullet had torn through her flesh, he stood up and turned away. Ruth came in the front door. Without speaking, she passed Peter and knelt down beside the woman. First she poured some powdered dry leaf into the wound, and then she placed a patch of green, shiny leaf over the top of it.

By now nine other women had come into the house, carrying herbs and leaves and a pot of hot bush tea. "Bring tea," Ruth said to one of them. And when she had a bowl of hot broth in her hand, she lifted the girl's head and said, flatly, "Drink."

"We must hold council," Prince said.

The council was held in one of the slave huts. There was a small pile of bright charcoal on the floor, in the center of the circle of men. Prince stared into the fiery embers. "Our force is greatly weakened after today," he said. "Tell us, Peter, how many people do you estimate we lost?"

"They have taken or killed at least twenty-five. Those who are their captives will be killed, tortured to death, as happened to the others."

"Do not give us a speech on how they will die," Prince said angrily. "If they are captured, they are dead. That is that. A man cannot go out and fight if there is fear in his heart about *how* he will die."

Peter leaped to his feet. Staring down at Prince, he said, "Because the gods picked you to lead your people to freedom, you think you will not feel pain when you die? Well, you are wrong." Peter's voice raised in volume. "We will *all* die, very soon, at the hands of the French soldiers. There is no escape from them. There are too many."

Prince leaped to his feet. Glowering at Peter, he said, "I *will* escape them. I am going to have my freedom. I am going to live—so I can be with Anna and our baby. I will not let them kill me."

"And how will you stop them," Peter said coldly, "with that wooden carving on your neck?"

"No," Prince shouted. "With my faith in our gods and with my determination to be free."

Peter turned his back on Prince and sat down in the circle. Frustrated, Prince leaped behind him. "You have the heart of a bird because your woman is wounded. You do not talk like a leader of men tonight. You talk like a boy who is afraid of the thunder when there is no lightning."

"No lightning?" Peter yelled back, getting to his feet again. "You did not have three hundred armed men hunting for your life today. You had nothing to take away your courage. I know we cannot win against this many men."

"Then what do you want to do?" Prince said, lowering his voice. "Surrender?"

"If we would all agree to surrender, it might go better on us. They will kill us if we don't. It would be worth a chance."

Prince clenched his fists and took a step toward Peter. "Get out of this hut," he said quietly. "You do not have the heart to be a leader of my people."

"I will go out of this hut. And I will take those people who want to go with me and surrender." He turned and walked out of the hut quickly, not giving Prince an opportunity to say more.

The men in the circle stared silently into the fire.

"Speak up," Prince said. "Are you all afraid? Do you agree with Peter, that we should surrender? Speak up."

King stood up. "I do not agree with Peter," he said. "We do not want to surrender just because we had a bad time today. If we do surrender, they will kill us. And they will make dying as slow and painful as they can. I would rather take my own life if I had to make a decision. And that we do not have to make—not yet!"

"We have met in council to decide how we will fight," Prince said firmly. "Now let us sit down and discuss it. If the time comes when we know we have to die, then we will discuss that. Until then, we will not make mention of it again."

Later that night, Peter, with seven other rebels, left Hendersen Estate. Moving east, a wind-driven rain pounding down on their almost naked bodies, they went to meet the armed forces to which they would surrender.

The next night a rebel scout reported to Prince at Hendersen. "The soldiers move back and forth, one group from the south, the other from the north, pressing toward us."

"Then that means they are divided," Prince said. "If we can attack the groups individually, we have a better chance."

"Today they found out that we are at Hendersen. They bring both forces in from each side tomorrow morning."

"How did they find out?" Prince asked.

"From Peter's woman. They tortured Peter. And her. They promised to save both of their lives if they would tell where you were." The scout closed his eyes and moved his head back and forth. "She told. They burned her from head to foot. At first she would not speak out. But when they tortured Peter, she weakened." He opened his eyes and looked at Prince. "She only did it to save Peter's life. They promised her this."

"And did they keep their promise?"

"No, they did not. After they cut and branded Peter's

skin, they put him on a platform beside the fort. They tied his arms and legs to a wheel on either side of him and had mules turn the wheels. They pulled Peter apart!"

Prince felt his stomach tie into a knot. "He should have died in battle."

"They told the other prisoners that they would kill every leader of the revolt in the same manner."

"They will not kill me in that manner," Prince said, lifting his head and staring out over the scout's head. "I will die in battle, or I will be free. But they will not take me."

The scout rolled his eyes up at Prince, searching in the dim light to see Prince's expression. "There are so many soldiers in the bush it is difficult to move," he said. "Do you want me to go back out there again tonight?"

"No. What sense to that? The soldiers will be here in the morning. Trying to push us back there." Prince threw his head toward the west. "Go join our people. I will soon be there."

The scout left, and Prince was alone. He left his hut and walked vigorously across the clearing toward the mill. At the beginning of the path leading into the wide, arched door of the mill, he stopped. With legs spread apart, his hands on his hips, he stared up at the indestructible building. I wish I could burn you down, he thought. The white man builds a big, ugly machine like you to look down on us. Ugly grinder! You have the same appetite for cane that the white man has for gold. It never ceases. You are the same as the white man. No matter how much we bring to you, you give us pain. You would tear us apart as the white man did to Peter. While he stared up at the mill, the moon edged above its flat top, between the wooden blades, spilling light into Prince's face. Prince's eyes followed the rapid ascent of the pale yellow face. He was reminded that his gods were behind there.

"You, gods of our people," he called out aloud, "help us kill the white men. Help us destroy this ugly machine." Looking up toward his gods, Prince felt himself become calm again, and knew that the gods had comforted him. He turned his back on the mill. A man stood behind him. Startled, Prince threw up his arms, and tensed, ready to spring forward. Recognizing King, he let his arms fall down.

"It is good that you call on our gods," King said, his voice deep and sorrowful. "We need their help."

"You know, then, that the soldiers come here tomorrow?"

King nodded. "And I know how they killed Peter. We cannot let them take us." Suddenly King threw his head back and howled, a low, mournful noise that penetrated the night air. As the howl faded, he called out, "Help us, my gods. Make us brave." He threw himself up in the air, twisting his body so that when his feet touched the ground again he was facing in the other direction. He howled again. And then another leap, landing in the position from where he originally started. When the next howl broke out, Prince's voice joined King's. Together they howled and leaped and gyrated ten times. Then, as unexpectedly as the rite began, it stopped. Both of them stared at the moon.

"Tomorrow we will meet the soldiers," Prince said. "And tomorrow we will kill the white men."

"They are bringing all of the soldiers after us," King said. "We cannot fight that many. We should try to hide from them until they are divided again and attack only half their force."

"We have done nothing but run since they started their marching," Prince said. "Tomorrow we will set another trap for them. At least we are familiar with the land here at Hendersen."

At that minute the moon disappeared behind a cloud. "See," King exclaimed. "The gods frown on it." He pointed to the moon.

The clouds were black and heavy. There was an ominous sign in the vanished moon. The heavens that had just been filled with stars became an endless black void.

"You are right," Prince said slowly. "The gods have spoken against it. We will not meet the soldiers here. Come. We will get our people ready and go out in the bush tonight." His voice was weak, disheartened.

"Where should we go?"

"If the soldiers are coming to Hendersen, we can travel north of Hendersen tonight, and move back east again, behind them."

When the dawn arrived, there were none of the bright pinks and blues that announce a sunny day. The sky remained gray, dismal. The rebels had taken cover in an uncultivated field about three miles northeast of Hendersen. The morning was hazy and damp; the bush was alive with sand flies and mosquitoes. It was agonizing for the rebels to remain quiet on their stands.

Ottingen and approximately two hundred French, Danes, and Negroes arrived at Hendersen, and found it deserted.

"They found out we were planning this attack," Ottingen said to Lieutenant Beaumont.

"But how?" the lieutenant said, shrugging his shoulders and putting his hands out. Lieutenant Beaumont was a tall, lean man with sharp black eyes and features that were almost too fine to belong to a soldier.

"Hell and damnation," Ottingen said. "Their scouts, naturally. Their men take risks ours would never dream of. They have spies in the fort, of that you can be sure."

"Too bad," Beaumont said casually. "The attack will be delayed a few more hours, that is all."

"That is all," Ottingen snorted. "If you'd been hunting for these rebels for as long as I have, it wouldn't seem like such a small matter. I'm fed up with this damnable island."

"Ah-ha," Beaumont said, smiling. "You are short-tempered, my sergeant friend. You need a woman, that is your trouble. Cheer up. Now that the French forces are here, we will put an end to this revolt and you will soon be back on St. Thomas, having your short temper taken care of."

"That's what the English promised," Ottingen said.

"You will see. You will see, my friend. Now, let us put our heads together and think about this situation. If I am going to get the sergeant to his woman on St. Thomas, we better find those slaves very soon." He put his hand on his forehead, as if he were trying to envision the hiding place of the rebels.

"Here's one of our scouts now," Ottingen said. He raised his arm and shouted at the Negro who had been scouting for the armed forces. "Come here. What news do you bring?"

"See," Beaumont said cheerily. "I begin to think and the answer arrives."

The scout, his body glistening with sweat, came up to Ottingen and Beaumont. "The rebels are in back of us. They moved to the northeast during the night. I followed them. They are about two miles from here." The Negro oke with a heavy accent, a sing-song patois that the rench officer could not understand. Beaumont looked at ttingen and said, "Interpret for me. This man speaks a range tongue."

"The rebels are in back of us," Ottingen said.

"Now they are in for it," Beaumont said, raising a ger in the air and wagging it. "Our troops are still back ere. They will flush them out, like a covey of quail."

Ottingen howled out, "Troops. Prepare to drive back to e east again."

"Mon Dieu. What a deep, full voice this sergeant has," eaumont exclaimed. He slapped Ottingen on the back and ughed. "Now that I have put the woman on your mind, ou are anxious to move along, eh?" Beaumont rested his usket on the ground and looked at the gray sky. "I have idea we should leave half of our men here, Sergeant. If e rebels decide to run west again, we will have a wall to op them."

"That's a good idea," Ottingen said. "Let's split them, d have them spread north and south so the rebels can't p through."

When Ottingen and Beaumont had marched to Hender-n with two hundred men, they left behind another hun-ed who were now split in equal groups and in the ocess of marching from north and south, in opposite es, moving westward. So there would be fifty men in ch of the two lines moving westward, fifty in each of the o lines moving eastward, and the main force of one ndred heading directly for the rebels. The island was ing crisscrossed in such a close pattern that it was evitable the rebels could not escape an encounter with e soldiers this day.

After a few hours' march, the main force came to the top a knoll looking over an open field below. "Just above at field," the scout told Ottingen and Beaumont, "in the sh that surrounds it, they wait."

"We go entice them, eh Sergeant?" Beaumont said. "We ll go to the field. Let them come out after us. They will t live long against these guns." He patted his musket.

"What is going to bring them out?" Ottingen said. "They n't come out into an open field."

"I hope the rebel has enough sense to know the French e good soldiers," Beaumont replied. "We have to give em a push, Sergeant, a small push from behind." Beau-

mont scanned the terrain. "See, on the right side of th
field, all bush. You, Sergeant, take fifty of our men and g
around behind them. You put them in our mouth." Beau
mont opened his mouth and bared his teeth.

"Give us plenty of time before you go out in the open,'
Ottingen said. "It's slow traveling in there." He walke
away from Beaumont and passed the word.

As they were assembling, the drizzle of rain increased t
a heavy downpour. Beaumont ran to Ottingen. Flipping
raindrop off the end of Ottingen's nose, he said, "The rai
works in our favor, Sergeant. Hope that it keeps up. Th
rebels won't hear you move through the bush."

"Keeps up?" Ottingen said, looking down at his tunic. "
am so damned water-soaked I won't be able to walk."

"You'll walk. Remember St. Thomas. And the prett
women who are waiting for your return."

Ottingen walked away. His boots were thick with mud
forcing him to lift his feet high off the ground with eac
step. Disgusted, he glared at Lieutenant Beaumont. Th
lieutenant threw his head back and laughed. Ottinge
raised his arm and signaled his group to follow.

Ottingen led his group in a wide semicircle, skirting th
rebels in order to come in from behind them. In th
downpour, their traveling was labored. The rain came ou
of the sky with such force that it hit against the bush an
set up a noise that covered their movement. To Ottingen, i
did not matter that his muddy boots were heavy, or tha
his uniform clung uncomfortably on his body. There wa
the suspense of battle ahead.

When he had traveled quite a distance, he heard fain
sounds of voices to one side, French-accented, and kne
that Beaumont had taken his men into the field. Hopin
that the rebels would center their attention toward Beau
mont's troops, he began the swing to his left, judging tha
he was far enough behind the rebels to push them for
ward. On and on they trudged, boots and bare feet slush
ing against the slippery earth. Ottingen's eyes darte
ahead, warily searching for a sign of the enemy.

But the rebels were not between Ottingen and Beau
mont. One of their scouts had been on the path Ottinge
had started out on and had reported to Prince that th
soldiers were split and planning to surround them. Princ

292

moved the rebels farther back, letting Ottingen swing in front of them.

The swing completed, his men strung out in a line, Ottingen held up his arm and motioned forward, thinking the rebels in front of him.

As soon as the armed force began moving forward, Prince, holding a finger to his mouth for quiet, signaled the rebels to move after them from behind. Scurrying along in the mud, the roar of rain drowning out their footsteps, the rebels soon spotted the backs of the armed men.

Emitting a stupendous war cry, King dashed forward with a burst of speed and leaped onto the back of a soldier. His knife plunged down into the chest of the man and King, his legs still wrapped around his quarry, tumbled to the ground, along with the body.

The soldiers turned, many of them instinctively firing their muskets into the bush as they made the swing. Five or six rebels fell, wounded or dead.

Incensed, the rebels flew through the bush, slashing at brush and vine to clear the way. Their faces were distorted as they crashed through the brush. Their knives and cutlasses waved in the air. Raw courage pitted them forward, wave after wave, onto the line of soldiers.

Prince found himself rushing head on at a soldier who had a pistol aimed at him. Unable to stop, Prince threw himself forward, knocking the pistol from the soldier's hand. The soldier fell backward. Quickly, Prince scrambled forward. He raised his arm and jabbed his cane knife deep in the belly of his foe. The soldier grunted and went limp. Seeing booted feet rush toward him, Prince rolled just as a gun went off. The soldier he had just stabbed took the bullet in his chest. Then he heard King's voice. "Run, Prince. More soldiers are coming."

Prince leaped to his feet and ran after King. They broke through the high growth with such force that they could feel their bodies being stung by the whip of limber green twigs against bare flesh. Other rebels followed.

When King finally stopped to rest, Prince, close on his heels, stopped too. "How did the soldiers get here so fast?" Prince asked. "We had just begun fighting."

"It was not the other half of this group," King said. "It was another force, coming from the east."

Prince looked in the direction from which they had just come. Two rebels were coming out of the bush. He made a quick survey. There were about twenty-five rebels in all.

"Aiii," Prince groaned. "Now we are split!"

"We have got to get back to Hendersen," King said. "We have got to get a drum, so we can signal the rest of our people to meet us."

"Not now," Prince said. "The soldiers will move west again. We will go north, to Jansen's plantation, to get food and water. Tonight, after dark, we will try to get to Hendersen."

Wiping the bloody knife on his baggy pants, Prince tucked it in his belt. "Come," he said to the people around him. "Move silently. We are fortunate that it still rains like this." He looked up at the gray sky, letting the rain fall on his face.

"What if we run into the armed forces?" one of the women said, her voice trembling. "There are not enough of us to fight them now."

Prince brought his face back and stared at the people around him. They all looked frightened, wide-eyed. Prince squared his shoulders and glared at them. "If we meet the soldiers, we fight until we die." He turned away from the group and began leading them north through the bush.

Chapter 24

The twenty-five rebels reached Jansen's estate without an encounter with the armed forces. But when they stood looking at the clearing, each of them hesitated to leave the protection of the bush. Massing around Prince, they were a defeated-looking group of warriors. Their ragged clothing was wet and streaked with mud. Water ran down their faces and hung on the ends of their coarse hair in opaque drops.

"We will stay here," Prince said.

"I know of a cave east of us, by the sea," a young boy said proudly.

A cave, Prince thought. Yes, a cave will be good. But what if we go further away from Hendersen? How will we get a drum? We have to have a drum to signal our people. We can think of that later. Now we have to stay alive. Will we ever get organized again? The soldiers are everywhere. We do not have the opportunity to attack them. And they come at us from every direction. If only the other group of soldiers had not come so soon today. We could have killed most of those we attacked. And now we would be together and able to attack another group. But like this, so few of us, we cannot attack anyone. We can only run and hide.

"Prince," King broke in. "The cave is a good idea. We will be out of the rain. We can take food to it. We can stay there until we get the other people to join us." King thought, how many others are there? And when we signal with the drum, the traitors will tell the white men what we say.

"Yes, we will go to the cave," Prince said. "But first we must get food."

Spotting a banana grove, King broke away from the group. There he found two full green stalks of bananas.

With one on each shoulder, he plodded back to the great-house. Soon every rebel had with him a supply of provisions; sweet potatoes, maize, muscavado, pots of molasses, and jugs of water or rum.

"You," Prince called to the boy, "lead us to the cave."

Over an hour later, when the group reached the cave, they found it a good place to hide. The rebels had to put down part of their supplies in order to climb around the rocky face of a cliff before they entered the cave. After getting all of their provisions inside, they settled down, waiting for dark. The sea swelled up against the rocky coast line below, making a hollow echo against the wall behind them. The walls of the cave were wet, slimy with moss, and salt-streaked. It was not like the cave Prince and Anna had shared back at Fortuna.

When the people had settled down, Prince went to the opening of the cave and sat facing out to sea. He was chilled, shivering. He clenched his teeth so they would not chatter. I am not going to give up, he thought. I will not. I am going to live, so I can be with Anna. If we could only steal a boat. Sail to Crab Island where there is no worry of soldiers. Where there is freedom. I should have made the leaders take the fort. There is so much I should have made the people do. He stared out at the dismal gray clouds hanging over the sea.

"Tonight I will go get a drum," King said. The words rolled around the cave, magnified.

Prince leaped to his feet. "You will not," he shouted. "*I* will go get a drum. I am tired of taking orders from all. I should never have listened to you. We should have taken the fort. What chance did we have once we let the soldiers come ashore? You forget that our gods picked *me* to lead you."

King's mouth fell open, his heavy lower lip hanging down. He looked up at Prince. His eyes showed that he was hurt.

Prince crossed his arms over his chest and turned his back on King. It was very quiet. He looked at the ground swells rippling across the sea, peppered by a heavy sheet of rain. What good did it do to get angry, he thought. Maybe he could get the people together again. Maybe they could drive the French soldiers away. And then what? How many

296

more soldiers would the white men come back with? Unconsciously, he let out a snort of disgust.

With his back to the people, he spoke up. "There is no reason to get angry. But *I* will make the plans. And *this* is what we are going to do. We are going to get a drum. We are going to get our people together. We are going to drive the white men off the island. And then I have a plan for our future." He paused, thinking, no need to tell them about getting a boat and going to Crab Island. They can wait until we are ready to go. Aloud he said, "Tonight I will get the drum."

He heard a rustle beside him. King whispered, "Let me go with you, Prince. It is better if there are two of us."

"The soldiers are moving west. We are behind them. It will be safe to go to Hendersen."

"I want to go with you, Prince," he whispered urgently. "Please."

"If you want to, then you can," Prince said. He remained looking at the sea, stone-faced. Secretly, he was glad that King wanted to accompany him.

Rain was still falling when Prince and King returned with the drum to the cliff above the cave. They sat for hours waiting tensely for a message from one of the other groups. Finally, one drum, then another boomed their messages out into the night.

"A group of thirty-five on the east, led by Thomas," King said, straining to catch each beat. "And a group of thirty north of them. What should I tell them, Prince?"

"We cannot risk having the soldiers know of this hiding place. Whatever we tell them is dangerous. There are too many traitors marching with the soldiers. They will be sure to tell what we say."

Prince and King were quiet. The drum sounds were distinct, magnified by the rain clouds holding the hollow tone close to the earth.

"I have decided what we will tell them," Prince said. He stood erect and crossed his arms over his chest. "Tell them to meet us at Caneel Bay tomorrow night. We have to take that chance."

King put the drum between his legs. Cradling it, he raised his powerful arms. Poised, he waited to catch the cadence of the other drums so he could effectively interject his own message. Then, at the precise minute when there was a pause in the other boomings, King's hands slammed down on the drumhead, sending out a thunderous roar.

They made a peculiar sight, Prince and King, standing on the rocky cliff in the rain, silhouetted against a vast backdrop of rolling sea. The drummer, hunched over the oblong barrel, raised and lowered his powerful arms in a pattern that made the instrument produce a vibrant voice, dominating the night sounds. And Prince, aloof, standing beside him, so preoccupied with the seriousness of the situation that he turned his back on the fact that there could be danger at this precise moment. Neither man altered his position until, hearing the two drums acknowledge receipt of their message, Prince said, "Stop. We go now."

Prince picked his way over the cold, slippery rocks. King raised the drum under one arm and followed along, listening with satisfaction to the other drums.

Henry, slave of Von Beverhoudt, interpreted the drum messages for the men at the fort. In turn, Commander Longueville sent messengers out to the troops who were on the night march, instructing them to report to the fort. The troops scheduled to move east in the morning were told to continue with that plan.

In a meeting of twelve men who had commands, Longueville turned to Ottingen and said, "You are familiar with the ways of these rebels, Sergeant. What do you think of this?"

Ottingen, in a dry, clean uniform, stood at attention and faced the commander. The torches on the stone walls of the meeting room threw a dancing glow on the group of men. The warmth of the room made Ottingen suddenly tired. "They know we will receive their messages," he said, his words coming out slowly. "When Captain Maddox was here, they ran us around the island for ten days, in just this manner."

"Then you believe it might be a game they play with us?"

"It could be, yes, sir. Or, they might be desperate, knowing they have to get together to withstand an attack from us."

"Thank you," Longueville said. He leaned his elbow on the thick-planked table top and rubbed his chin. "I believe they are desperate. However, we will take precautions. Here is the plan. Our two divisions will move east in the morning, as planned. It is obvious that most of the rebels are back up here, north of us. So it won't do any harm to continue the drive. Caneel Bay has the sea on the north. Lieutenant Beaumont, you and Sergeant Ottingen will take your men west of Caneel Bay. Lieutenant Froling, you and your men will go to the south. If the rebels rendezvous at Caneel, as the drums tell us, they will have only one way to get there, from the east. And when they run, they will have only one road of escape, to the east. Those who make it out of there can be driven up the coast line." He twisted his neck, easing the pressure of the high, stiff uniform collar. "Do you men understand?"

"Yes, sir," was the murmur from each man at the table.

Longueville stood up. "Then see to it that your troops get some rest. You will get an early start. I want you in position at Caneel before dark tomorrow. Good night, gentlemen."

All the next day it rained. The dreary hours increased Prince's anxieties about the proposed rendezvous. He sat at the mouth of the cave, staring out at the empty sea. Behind him, the other rebels seldom moved, except, occasionally, one would quietly get up and swipe some molasses on his fingers and stick them into his mouth, or take a raw sweet potato and munch on it. For these people, wanderers at heart, it was an ordeal to be penned up in a damp cave. Toward evening, their silence became unbearable to Prince. Standing up, he turned and faced his people.

"You wonder why I have been so quiet," he said gently. "A strange thing happened to me today that I must tell you about." He sat down squat-legged, facing them. The people looked toward their leader, seeing his massive silhouette against the gray sky and sea. They sat up straight, attentively.

In a strong voice Prince said, "Today I was staring out at this empty sea when suddenly I saw a ship, a big sailing ship. On the ship were my people. The sails were filled with wind and the faces of my people were happy. In the distance there was land, another land, that looked green and fertile. I knew it was an omen." He paused. The people squirmed closer, their faces visibly brightened. Prince continued: "I said, 'Gods of my people, tell me what this means.' A voice, a deep strong voice answered me, saying, 'Those of you who die in battle will take this ship and sail behind the sun and the moon and the stars. Those of you who live, will find a ship and sail away to another island, where there is freedom for all of you.'" Prince's words rolled around the slimy walls of the cave and over the heads of the people and back out across the rain-splattered sea. "So you see, my people, we have nothing to fear. We will have our freedom, whether we live or die. The omen promises this."

Unable to leap and twist in the air, King curled into a ball and grabbed his knees with his arms. He rolled from one side to the other and let out short, deep howls. Instantly companionable voices broke out among the group and there was an air of sudden relief.

Hastily Prince said, "The gods will be pleased that you accept their omen with a light heart and with the spirit to continue the fight for your freedom. Now then"—he stood up—"let us show the gods that we are thankful for the omen. There is no need for us to hurry to our meeting place. The people who come to meet us are coming from the east. They have a long trip. We will not wait in the cave. We will go out and have a drum dance."

Several hours later, the people assembled in a small clearing inside the jungle. There were no fires. Their eyes were well adjusted to the night light so that when the drum began, they had no difficulty forming a circle around the drummer and keeping clear of one another. They leaped, and twisted, and shook their shoulders, hips and arms. The rain poured down on them unheeded. King huddled over the drum, using his body to protect the face of it from the rain. Water streamed down the sides of his neck, around his back, and down his chest. His hands, held close to the drum, were spread so that his thick fingers flopped limberly against the drumhead. On and on they danced, screaming, howling, moaning.

As they became more deeply absorbed in the dance, they fell into a pattern of pairs. Though there were only nine women in the group, those who did not have a woman to face had paired off with another man. Now the beat of the drum was accentuated by their bodies from the waist down. Some dancers jarred their pelvic bones toward their partner's, others rolled forward with a fluid, easy roll, inviting, teasing. These were the suggestive, lusty movements of their fertility dance, symbol of everlasting life.

Prince danced with a young woman whose soggy skirt slapped against her bare legs as she bumped back and forth at him. Towering over her, he tightened the muscles of his buttocks and flung his hips forward so that he almost came in contact with her body at every forward thrust. Prince stared at her black face. Her head was back, her eyes closed, her face twisted with tormented passion.

Having carried the dancers to a reckless peak of excitement, the drummer suddenly stopped. As soon as the drumbeat ceased, the dancers turned their awakened energies to talk of the meeting at Caneel and the ensuing battle.

Thomas, leading a group of rebels to Caneel, heard the familiar noises of the dance and went toward it. When the drum stopped, he threw back his head and emitted a mournful howl.

Prince's head snapped around in the direction from which the noise had come. He raised an arm, cautioning his people to be silent. Another mighty howl rose out of the bush. Prince waited for the low, final note to disappear before throwing back his own head. Rain slapped against his face. He opened his mouth and answered the call with an equally powerful bellow, the lamentable deep bass tone of it rolling over and into the scrub.

Moving swiftly, Thomas' troops slid out of the jungle and hastened into the clearing. Happy at reunion, the rebels jabbered and called out to each other in varied African dialects.

In due time, Prince raised his arm and called out for silence. When the group had controlled their exuberance, Prince said, "The gods have smiled on us tonight. Now we are stronger, and we will go to Caneel Bay to meet our other people."

The rebels fell quickly and quietly into lines near their leaders and waited patiently to begin their march. Prince raised his arm and signaled them back into the bush. As they began to move forward, the roar of musket fire filled the night air. Their other people had already reached Caneel Bay, and an ambush.

Anguished by the sudden volley of guns, Prince screamed, "A curse on the traitor who told the white man where we meet."

Those who stood in the clearing were confused, shaken by the sudden turn of events. They became aware of the torrent of rain that fell on them and shuffled closer to each other for warmth.

"We go to the cave," Prince said to Thomas and King.

"The cave?" King asked, his voice bitter.

"What other choice?" Prince snapped at him. "You would want us to walk into their trap too? It would be like putting a gun to our heads and taking our own lives."

"I would prefer that to sitting in the cave," King said softly. "What kind of freedom is that? We were more free when we were in the white man's chains."

"You are a leader," Prince said sternly. "Do not talk like this. Would you have our people taking their own lives?"

Chapter 25

As Jan rode through the gates at Hendersen on St. Thomas, he could see Anna running down the steps of the manor house to greet him. He felt very tired today. The return trip from Charlotte Amalie had been a very difficult one. It had rained steadily the whole trip, as it had been for several days.

The horse he and Tondo rode and the two mules they led laden with provisions had found the muddy trail difficult to maneuver. And though the first sight of Anna boosted his spirits, Jan soon slumped into a deeper weariness, knowing the news he carried would sadden her.

Anna ran to his horse and took hold of the bridle, halting it. "What news do you hear, Jan?" she said breathlessly.

Jan swung off the horse's back and took the bridle from Anna. "You will catch the fever running around in this cold rain," he said. "Go in the house and put on a shawl." She did not move. He turned and looked into her wide, sad eyes. "You know, Anna," he said gently, "you are heavy with child." He dropped his head. "Look at your shoes. They are caked with mud. Your feet are wet." He raised his eyes again, staring at her face. "Now go into the house and get a shawl. I'll be there soon and we will talk." He put his hand on her shoulder. "Please, Anna."

Reluctantly, Anna went up the steps and hurried into the house. A few minutes later, Jan joined her. Anna eased down on the edge of a chair and pulled the stole tight across her shoulders. "I'll wait for you to change your clothes," she said. "I know the news is not good. It's not your fault. It's you who should worry about getting the fever. You are soaked from head to foot. Bahbu put dry clothes on your bed."

"I will be back in a minute," he said.

From somewhere behind her, Anna heard the shuffle of bare feet. "Bahbu," she called out, "come out here."

Bahbu hurried into the parlor. "What did Master Jan hear?" she said, looking anxiously into Anna's face.

"He has not said anything."

"Our people on St. John are in trouble, or they would talk to us with the drums."

"They could be in hiding, planning an attack."

"No. The last we heard, they were divided. Anna"—Bahbu's voice was gentle—"the long rain is a bad omen, a message from our gods. It tells of many tears. It had never rained like this before."

"Everything is an omen from the gods," Anna snapped. "Your gods. That is all I have ever heard from you. Prince never had a chance to think about anything except that the gods had chosen him to lead his people to freedom. Freedom," she spit the word out bitterly. "If they drove all the white men off St. John, the Negroes would still be chained to their fear of attack. And chained to making the earth produce so they could live. And Prince would be chained to leading his people! Jan offered him as much freedom here as he could have had any place. But no, he could not take it. He had to lead his people. He has never been free since the day he was born. Not only because of the white man, but because of his gods!"

A long silence. Anna heard Bahbu shuffle behind her. "The gods sent Prince to avenge all the pain the white men made Mary and me and all of our people suffer," Bahbu said. "Prince belongs to our people. Now you are angry because you think our gods will take him away from you. If Prince is killed, the black people have suffered the greatest loss."

Anna swung around. Her face was flushed and her eyes sparkled with anger. "And if he dies, I'm not to feel anything, is that what you're trying to tell me?"

"If he is killed, he will wait for you, over there," Bahbu raised her arm and pointed at the gray sky.

"What good will that do me now?" Anna said, hysterically. "What good will it do our baby?"

Bahbu's face was grave. "Stop crying," she said firmly. "What more could the gods give to you than this baby? This baby will belong to you, Anna. I never had a baby of my own." She turned and walked away.

Soon, Jan sat down beside her. "Now then, Anna, let us talk. There are many rumors flying around the town," he said. "But the best of them are not good." He looked at

Anna. "They say the troops have driven the rebels night and day, killing or capturing all of those who get in their way. They are driving the rest to the east end of the island, where they hope to capture the remainder."

"And Prince? Is there word of him?"

"No, none." He sighed. "The leaders will not be allowed to live. By now they know who all of them are. There have been many who weakened under torture and have told everything they know."

"We cannot blame them for that," Anna said.

"No, of course not. Everyone in town says the revolt will come to an end within the next week. Reports from St. John say that each day they capture more. Anna, I don't think Prince can survive."

"Why did Mary and Bahbu think their gods sent Prince to them?" Anna asked.

"Whatever the reason," Jan said gently, "Mary gave him a noble cause when she trained him to believe that a man should stand free. We cannot hate her for this."

"No, I suppose not," Anna said. "Everything about Hendersen brings Prince to my mind and I'm confused. Who can I blame for taking him from me?" She turned around and looked over at Jan. "I try to blame Mary, or their gods, because I'm hurt. But I know I can't really blame anyone. I hope I have a son, Jan. A son who is born with clear skin, so he can be as free as Prince will want his son to be."

"And if he is born with brown skin, Anna? If you have to let him pose and live as a slave child, then what?"

"I don't know," she whispered.

The next morning, Jan came down with the fever. By noon, his face was bright red and his eyes were red-rimmed and watery. By evening, he was delirious, mumbling and tossing in his bed. Long after nightfall, his energy spent, he lay quiet, unconscious against the white pillows. The wild poundings of his heart made the blood vessels in his neck tremble.

Helplessly, Bahbu and Anna watched the poundings weaken as the man's life began to ebb away. At one point he opened his eyes and looked at Anna. His hand reached out and when it found the coolness of her hand, he smiled, a peaceful, contented smile. His mouth worked, as if he wanted to speak and his eyes, now dry and glazed, searched for Anna's blue eyes. She leaned forward and put her ear close to his mouth.

"I go now to my Christina," he said in a feeble, halting voice. He breathed his last breath and let go of life.

"Sarah, Sarah," Claude yelled excitedly, coming into the house.

"What is it, dear one?" Sarah called back.

Claude flopped down in a chair. His short stockinged legs were straight out and his arms hung limply over the mahogany arms of the chair. "Jan Hendersen died last night. The fever. My God, Sarah, there's so much of it on the island."

"Jan Hendersen. He was in town only two days ago. It's this rain, Claude. Everyone is getting drenched from it and catching the fever. Look at you, dear one. You're soaked. Get up. Go change those clothes this minute."

With unusual agility, Claude sprang from the chair. "You think it's the rain?" he asked, as he struggled to get out of his long coat. "Here, help me."

Sarah tugged on the sleeves of the wet garment. "Think of that poor child up there alone at Hendersen. Claude, we have to call on her."

"Not in this rain," he said.

"Claude, dear, don't take your clothes off in the parlor. What will our house slaves think?"

A woebegone expression hung on his face. He turned and looked at Sarah. "Would you prefer that I die of the fever?" he whined.

"Mercy, no. Here, let me pull off those wet shoes. And then you run upstairs and get into dry clothes."

Claude flopped back into the chair, sticking a foot up about three inches off the floor. Sarah stooped down. She took the back of his leg and raised his foot. Taking the pump firmly by the heel, she pulled it off. When she had gone through the same procedure with the other one, she stood back and put her hands on her hips and looked at the ceiling. "While you are dressing, I'll look for that black fabric I have. Now, where did I put it? It might be in the chest up . . ."

"Black fabric?" Claude said. "For whom?"

"Anna Hendersen is in mourning, Claude. I will take her the fabric and make some dresses for her."

306

"Don't be hasty, my dear," Claude said, grabbing hold of his wet woolen undershirt. "You may need it yourself."

"My poor dear one," Sarah said sympathetically. She rushed over and kissed the top of his head. "You go upstairs and get yourself dry. I'll make you a strong pot of hot tea, with a little lime and rum in it. That will take the chill away."

"Are you sure?" he said doubtfully.

"Of course I'm sure. Now go along."

Obediently, Claude went upstairs. Sarah ran to the dining room and pulled out a drawer where she stored her table linens. At the bottom of the drawer she saw the black fabric. She took it and quickly pushed the drawer back in place.

Anna sat staring out in front of her, listening to Sarah give instructions to Bahbu about the sewing. Anna gripped her hands in her lap. Several times today, during the course of the Muellers' visit, she had found herself wanting to cry. They weren't bad people at all. In fact, at one point, Anna found herself almost tempted to put her head against Calude's shoulder and let out the tears that choked her.

"When it is time for your confinement," Sarah was saying as she efficiently cleaned up the scraps of cloth from the table where she had cut the two dresses, "I'll come stay with you. You cannot be here alone. When is your time, my dear?"

"In late October," Anna lied.

"Then I will be here. You can rely on me." She moved over behind the chair in which Anna sat. "Perhaps you'll have twins," she said. She moved around in front of Anna, openly appraising her. "But, no, you're a big strong woman and your dear husband was a big man. You'll have a nice, strong baby, just one." Sarah chuckled. "My personal maid tells me she can predict, before the child is born, if it will be a boy or girl, by the way it is carried. She says if the mother carries the baby out in front, it will be a girl. And if it is well concealed, carried in the back, it will be a boy. All women with child look the same to me." Sarah leaned forward and looked into Anna's face. "How do you think you carry this child, Anna?"

Anna would not be taken in by Sarah's attempt to change

307

her mood. If she gave in, she would like Sarah and Claude Mueller. And if she liked them, she could not lie to them. And if she did not lie to them, her secret might be discovered. Anna dropped her head, feigning embarrassment, and shrugged her shoulders.

Sarah looked at Anna's stony expression. Exasperated, she said, "For heaven's sake, Anna, you must get hold of yourself. I know you've gone through a lot in recent months. But you cannot give up. Why don't you cry? Or why don't you talk? You cannot sit here staring into space for the rest of your life."

Anna moved her head slowly up and looked into Sarah's concerned face. "I'm sorry," she said softly. Then she dropped her head again.

"You poor child," Sarah said. "I'm sorry I scolded you. Would you like me to fix you some dinner? Could you eat?"

Anna shook her head.

"Did I hear someone mention dinner?" Claude said, coming into the room. "I'm hungry, my dear. It's invigorating to walk in the fields today. And what a nice day it is. The sky is always much bluer after a long rain." He went to Anna and bent down, peeking into her face. "Come on, Anna, take a little walk with me. The air would be good for you."

Anna shook her head.

"Well then, I'll sit down here and bring you some cheerful news." He sat down in a brocaded chair. "The militia just rode by, coming from town. Good news they bring from St. John. Last night our soldiers trapped a band of rebels and drove them right into the sea. They leaped off a cliff, at a place called Brim's Bay. Dashed themselves to death on the rocks, that's what the devils did."

Anna looked up. Sarah eased down in a chair, watching him, hanging on every word.

Encouraged, Claude went on. "It will be over very soon, dear Anna. Once we get finished punishing these heathens who had a part in this, you'll not have to worry about your slaves here at Hendersen or Bordeaux. There will never be another revolt, you can be sure of that."

"I don't worry, Mr. Mueller," Anna said.

"Of course you do. Who doesn't?"

"And was there any news from our dear Theodore?" Sarah asked. She quickly turned to Anna and added, "Sergeant Ottingen is like our son. We lost our children in an epidemic years ago, a fever that wiped out many plantations."

"No word," Claude said. "And, therefore, he's in good health. What a brave young man he is. He'll surely get a promotion out of this." Claude dropped his head and smiled coyly at Anna. "When you're over your grief, you must get to know him a little better, Anna. He's an ardent admirer of yours."

"Claude," Sarah gasped. "Not at a time like this."

"Nonsense. Anna is a beautiful young woman. She won't sit up here wasting away forever. There's a lot of living ahead for her."

Anna dropped her head again. "Have they captured all of the rebel leaders?" she said. "The man who leads them, Prince, was a Hendersen slave. He has relatives who would be interested."

"No word of that. So we can assume he's still alive. We would, naturally, hear if they capture that one. In fact, Theodore has vowed to have his head."

"Would you be good enough to let me know if they capture Prince?" Anna said, hoping her voice was properly casual. "You know how these people are, if they don't get news, they'll pound on these drums."

"I'll keep you informed, my dear," Claude said. "I am at the fort every morning when the militia rides out. If there's any news, I'll send it with them."

"Thank you," Anna murmured.

Dinner was announced, saving Anna the necessity of further resisting the Muellers' warm charm, for she stood up and excused herself, saying, "I couldn't look at my husband's empty chair today. I'm going to my room. Enjoy your dinner, please. And forgive me."

"Of course, my dear," Sarah said. "Would you mind if we had a room made ready for us for tonight? I think we should stay over with you, at least for one more day."

"That really isn't necessary," Anna said coldly. Then, seeing the shocked expression on Claude's face, his mouth fallen open, petulantly, she added, "You two are very kind. When my grief is spent, I look forward to having you with me for a long visit. You'll come back during my confinement in October, won't you, Mrs. Mueller?"

"Yes, of course I will," Sarah said. "And I'll leave proper instructions with your maid on how to sew your dresses.

They are both extra wide at the waistband. After your confinement, they can be taken in."

"Thank you," Anna said.

Watching her out of sight, Sarah looked at Claude and raised her hands in a gesture of defeat. "What a strange woman she is, Claude," Sarah whispered. "She looks so soft and tender, so beautiful. And yet, she's as hard as stone."

Claude nodded. "Let us go home, now, dear one. I've lost my appetite."

Chapter 26

Two weeks after Longueville's arrival on St. John, only thirty-eight rebels remained in the cave. Hunted night and day, their number had been diminished each time a party went out to forage for food. Huddled in the filthy cavern, their courage had given out. Except for Prince and a handful, they thought only about the ship that would take them behind the moon and the sun and the stars. Earlier they had pinned their dreams on a ship that would carry them from St. John to another island, perhaps to Crab Island. But now they thought constantly about death.

The imprisonment stretched King's nerves to the breaking point. Once the rain had passed and the blue sky and gently rolling sea beckoned him out into the open field, he could no longer contain himself. "We will hold council," he said on this day, standing up at the mouth of the cave.

Prince, sitting with his back against the damp rock wall, looked up. He was going to contradict King when, resigned to the misery he knew his people suffered, he reconsidered. "Hold council," Prince said.

Irritably, King yelled into the cave. "Would you sit here suffering these miserable days for the rest of your life? I am Amina. I have to be free."

The rebels turned their anguished faces toward King. "We *all* have pain in our hearts," a woman said.

"Then look out at this empty sea," he said in a deep voice. He turned and swung his hand toward the blue water. "What do you see out there?" An uneasy silence. Some of the heads moved in order for them to see out beside the bowlegged speaker. "You do not see a ship to take us away from here, do you? No. The only ship that will take us out of this dirty hole is the ship we put off this shore with our own hands. The ship that will take us up there," he pointed toward the sky, "to the home of our gods." King stared at the people. Many of the heads nodded agreeably. "I do not want to die of sickness, withered up like an old man. I want to die like a brave warrior, while my body is still strong. When I get to the other land, I want to look at my gods and be proud!" More agreeable head-shaking. "Let us go out tonight, like free people. Get food and take our drum and dance. And then, while we have full stomachs and happiness in our hearts, we will get out on the ship that we push from the shore, *together*. As we have fought, let us die."

Thomas leaped up. "Yes," he said in a loud voice. "King speaks the truth. We have lost this fight on St. John to the white man. But we do not have to give our bodies over to them so they can find joy in torturing us, in bringing us more pain." Thomas looked toward Prince. "Our leader would have us sit and wait forever for the white man to leave the island. He talks of finding a boat and sailing to another island. The white man will never leave this island until he has found us. We must cheat the white man. We will let him find us—but only after we have taken the ship to our gods. I vote in favor of it. You people who are in favor, raise your fists."

Prince counted the clenched fists that were raised. Twenty-three. He got up, his eyes moving from face to face. "My heart hurts for you who will sail your own ship from off these shores," he said. "But I cannot make a promise of what will happen if you do not. I will not let the white man have my body to torture, but I am not yet ready to sail on the ship you take. There are fifteen of us who do not vote to go with you. We stay here and wait."

Seeing that Prince was grieved, King moved beside him. "Your heart should not be heavy," King said, his voice a whisper. "Do not let the people see you cry inside. It is not the custom to send our people off to the gods like that."

"I know," Prince said. "I am not only sad that they go to the gods. I am sad that all chance for freedom on St. John is gone. I did not admit it to myself until today, just now."

King put his hand on Prince's shoulder. "I knew it the day I saw the French soldiers land at Coral Bay. Then I was sorry that I did not vote in favor of trying to take the fort. But it was too late."

Prince turned his head, looking into King's eyes. "You are a brave warrior, King. You are my brother. When you take the ship tonight, go with a light heart. Tonight I will be out in the bush, I will dance to the gods for you."

312

King clasped Prince's shoulder. Then, feeling embarrassed by his show of emotion, he went back into the cave.

Before dark, the people filed out of the cave. They went up across the rocks and to the bush with a solid step. King led them to the same clearing where they had held their dance before. Dividing the band of people into groups, he instructed each to bring back food and other necessities for the final drum dance. In less than an hour they were back, dragging live animals, carrying blackened pots and straw sacks of food, lugging puncheons of rum. Fires were lit. Bleating goats were slaughtered. Women cooked bananas, sweet potatoes and maize. The men turned spits, roasting the meat. In some, fear of the journey stirred in their hearts. In others, the solace that their days of pain and fear were nearing an end buoyed them, and they felt blissful. While the preparations for the feast were under way, Thomas was sent out to bring back the hidden bullets and flintlocks.

When the feast was ready, King strutted ceremoniously around the array of food, nodding his head approvingly. He sat down cross-legged on the ground. Instantly, the other people fell around the food and grabbed at it. Cane knives ripped into the meat and deft hands passed or threw chunks of it around the group. With every primitive tool that was available from the jungle, the rebels filled their mouths with food, washing it down with generous swigs of rum.

His appetite satiated, King was the first to rise. He cradled the drum between his legs. Standing close to a fire, his body shining, he pounded the face of the instrument. Never before had King's hands moved as rapidly or his fingers tapped out as many individual beats.

High-pitched shrieks and deep-throated cries went out into the night air. The rebels got onto their feet with a raging passion, quickly getting lost in the dancing.

King hovered over the drum, his hands performing furiously. His muscular belly contracted and released, shot up and down, to the rapid rhythm he created. A grimace stretched his thick, blue-black lips into a straight line across his face, forcing his mouth open as if a soul-rending scream would emit. One of the dancers, passing by the drummer, darted his hand over King's face and threw rum from a calabash cup into King's mouth. That portion which could not be hastily gurgled down, flowed down either side of King's face, lost in the gleaming sweat that twinkled in the firelight.

The jungle quaked and vibrated with furious sounds. Two miles from where they danced, a troop of soldiers heard the violent poundings and shrieks, and marched toward it, their blood freezing as they drew closer.

Finally, King dropped back on the ground, letting the drum fall with a hollow thud beside him. Eyes flashing fire, Thomas pounced on the ground beside him, shoving a jug of rum into King's hand. King drank. Instantly he sprang to life again, and was on his feet. Holding the jug up in the air, he called, "Take up your guns and bullets. We set sail on our ship."

The rebels streaked across the clearing to the heap of guns. Hands shook and trembled, as each loaded a pistol.

Though half drunk, and crazed with the fire of their dance, the rebels suddenly came upon reality. A heart-sickening silence surrounded them as they stood with loaded flintlocks, looking at King.

"Into a circle," King commanded.

With halting steps, the rebels eased down on the ground in a circle. King stood behind them. "Each of you, with your right hand, place the end of the gun over the ear of the one who is on the right side of you," he said.

The circle expanded, the people worming back to make room for their arms.

"Press the gun tight against the other's head. That is right. Now, Thomas. Listen. When I say so, you will pull the trigger of your gun. Then the man who is behind you will pull the trigger of his gun, and after that the one behind him, pull, and continue like this. I will shoot the last in the circle." King paused. "Thomas, go," he said quietly.

King watched the bodies slump, one by one, like the great spinning arm on a windmill. He was amazed at how quickly they sailed off, leaving him standing in the clearing in a hazy mist of gun smoke with a wide-eyed rebel waiting for King to complete the job. The fires flickered and made muted popping and sizzling noises.

King walked swiftly to the remaining man. Placing his gun on the man's temple, he pulled the trigger. As soon as the man slumped to the ground, King took another loaded pistol from his belt. "Gods of our people," his strong voice filled the clearing, "brother has given brother to you. Now I give you my own life."

"Wait."

King turned. Prince stepped into the clearing. He walked directly to King, and took the gun from his hand. "Sit down, beside Thomas," Prince said firmly.

King had to lift Thomas' body to make room for himself in the circle. Sitting down, he let the limp form slump against him. He felt the cold muzzle of the gun above his ear.

"Happy journey," Prince said, and pulled the trigger.

Chapter 27

On the morning of May 27, 1734, Commandant Longueville's two barks sailed triumphantly into the harbor of Charlotte Amalie. A salute from the cannon on Christian's fort roared over the sea. The revolt was over.

At the rail, Ottingen was amazed at the activity on the waterfront. The grateful colonists had turned out in full force, properly attired in their finest, most colorful clothes. The women stood along the wharves waving scarves and handkerchiefs.

Boatload after boatload of smartly uniformed soldiers were pulled up on land by the welcoming hands of the planters. Shouts of praise and tears of happiness poured out from every direction.

Ottingen leaped up on the hard dirt road. The colonists greeted him with an ovation of cheers. He struggled through the happy mob and embraced Sarah, kissing her cheek.

"Oh, Theodore," she cooed. "You are home safely."

Claude patted Ottingen's shoulder. "We'll get some good food into you, m'boy. You look thin."

"I'm dying to give you some news, Theodore," Sarah said. "You'll have supper with us?"

"Yes, of course. I see everyone has turned out to greet us," Ottingen said, looking around.

"No need to look," Claude said flatly. "Anna Hendersen is not here."

"Oh? Why are you so sure?"

Claude leaned closer to Ottingen. "That is the news Sarah has for you," he whispered. "Jan Hendersen is dead. Anna is in mourning."

"What happened?"

"The fever. We have had a bad epidemic, you know."

"But what about Anna? She is all alone up there."

"We offered to stay. She made it very clear she doesn't want company."

"It's not safe for a woman to be isolated up there with that many slaves. Anything could happen to her."

"That girl knows no other life, Theodore. And she's not afraid of the slaves."

"Look, Claude. There are at least fifty blacks up there. We have brought back twenty-four rebels with us. Today they will be tried and punished. There may be repercussions. It's not safe for Anna to be up there alone."

Claude tucked the handkerchief back into his sleeve. "Perhaps you are right. But at least come back for the governor's speech. And what about the party tonight? If you're not there, everyone will talk. You are famous now, Theodore."

"There will be so much revelry tonight, I won't be missed."

"A handsome man like you?" Claude smiled.

"There are hundreds of Frenchmen on the loose tonight. The women will not have time to notice I'm gone."

It was late afternoon when Ottingen rode up to the greathouse at Hendersen. Tying his horse to the post, he looked up on the veranda. Bahbu was at the top of the steps.

"I have come to pay my respects to the mistress of Hendersen," Ottingen said, approaching the steps.

"My mistress is in her room, resting," Bahbu mumbled.

"Tell your mistress Sergeant Ottingen of the St. Thomas garrison calls."

Bahbu disappeared through the arched doorway.

Ottingen went up the steps and leaned on the rail, looking out at the plantation buildings. He particularly noticed that they were not, as he had feared, showing signs of neglect. As far as his eye could see, Hendersen was well manicured. He could see the bare backs of the slaves in the field, going easily about their work.

Hearing rapid footsteps on the stairs, he turned and saw Anna.

"How nice to see you," Anna said.

Ottingen stepped forward and bowed. "I am sorry to hear about the death of your dear husband," he said.

"Thank you," Anna said softly. "Forgive me for not being

317

properly dressed. My mourning dresses are clumsy. I didn't expect company today."

"I'll tell the whole town how shocking it is that the mistress of Hendersen was not prepared to have callers," Ottingen said, smiling at Anna.

"What do I care?" Anna said quickly. She sat down. "What news do you bring from St. John?"

"From St. John? The war is over, Mrs. Hendersen. Longueville has returned this very day. There is a celebration in town as I have never seen before."

"It's over?" Anna heard herself say. "And what of their leader, Prince?"

"Do you feel all right?" Ottingen said, sitting down in front of her. "You look very pale."

"I get faint at times," she whispered. "Now, what was it you were saying about the revolt?"

"It's over. You have nothing to fear of revolt on St. Thomas. However," he dropped his voice and leaned forward, "they will be punishing the rebels we brought back. There might be a few of the slaves here who will retaliate. That's why I have come here today. I don't want you to be alone until it is entirely safe."

"I'm not afraid," Anna said coolly. She straightened up in the chair. "These people would not harm me."

"No, of course not," he said diplomatically. "But you are with child. If you become frightened, there's no telling what could happen."

"You have not told me what happened to the leader, Prince," she said.

"Oh yes, the leader." He stood up and walked to the railing. "I wish I knew. I suppose he was one of those who leaped into the sea. Or maybe his corpse is rotting in the bush."

"You found no trace of him?"

"None." He came back and sat down again. "But you can tell his family that he is dead. There was not a trace of a live rebel when we departed St. John. None could have survived our drive."

"And I suppose you are all very proud of yourselves."

"And why not?" he said. "My God, you have two plantations now. You have an obligation to the colony. I do not agree with treating the slaves cruelly," he said gently. "But they must be treated firmly. The plantations cannot produce without the slaves. And if they were turned loose, then what? They would have to work every bit as hard as they do now to get a living out of this dry soil. They have homes, and food, and someone to care for them on the plantations. Alone they would have to struggle much harder to exist."

"Sergeant, imagine for a moment that you were captured and taken from this island in chains, forced to be another man's slave. Think about it . . . for a moment."

Ottingen shrugged. "But we cannot change what is already done. You have to make some compromises."

"Such as?"

Ottingen stood up. "If you were more interested in the colony's affairs, you could do more good for the slaves in the long run."

"And how would I do that?" Anna said. "They don't have women on their council. No matter how many plantations I own, I could not be heard."

"A woman as beautiful as you could make the council members think whatever you want them to."

"I don't think I am that beautiful," she said softly.

Ottingen laughed. "That's part of your beauty. Now, come, take a walk with me. Show me Hendersen."

"Bahbu," Anna called from outside. Bahbu noticed that Anna's voice was happy. Entering the kitchen, Anna said, "We have company for supper. Set the table for two and make extra food."

Bahbu went on peeling a sweet potato.

"It is good to have company," Anna said.

"He's a soldier. A white soldier. What of the baby?"

A long silence. "I'll send him away. He came here thinking I should not be alone."

"He came here because he is a man and you are a woman. We are not even sure that Prince is dead."

"Prince *is* dead. But even if he were alive, I'm alone. Is there anything wrong with me having a visitor? Must I live my life without anyone else, *ever*, because of loving Prince?"

Bahbu looked up. "You know the laws. You knew them before you made the baby."

Anna sank down on a chair. "But the laws don't make any difference right now. I need someone to talk to. He's only being kind."

Bahbu grunted. She put the potatoes in a pot.

319

"Do you expect me to spend the rest of my life waiting to go behind the sun and the moon and the stars to have someone to talk to?"

Bahbu put the pot over the fire.

"Answer me," Anna insisted. "Is that what you want?"

Bahbu went to the door and looked out. She whispered, "You will get yourself killed if you are not quiet."

Anna pushed Bahbu aside. "Call me when supper is ready," she said sternly.

The oil lanterns brightened the parlor. Ottingen twirled the glass in his hand and stared at Anna. She smiled. He got up and went to the settee. Sitting beside her he said, "This is how I like to see you. When you smile, I melt. When you are aloof, damn, I'm cold."

"I'm in mourning. Do you expect me to walk around smiling?"

"You can't go around scowling for the rest of your life."

"My husband just died."

Ottingen took her hand. "I know, Anna," he said gently. "You've had so much happen recently I suppose you're confused." She dropped her head. "For what it's worth, you're not alone, Anna. I love you, I have from the first time I saw you."

Anna's eyes came around. "You have?"

"Yes, I have." The black dress accentuated her tan. Her eyes were very blue. Damn, she's beautiful. Suddenly he took her in his arms and he kissed her.

"Please," Anna whispered, pulling back. "I'm in mourning."

"I don't give a damn."

Anna threw her head to the side. "Please, people will talk."

"What difference does it make?"

"It makes a difference to me. At least wait until after—"

Ottingen sat up. "I'm sorry." He dropped his head in his hands. What difference did the baby make? He loved her. The baby was a part of her.

Anna got to her feet. "Don't ever do that again," she said sharply. "I'm a widow, and I'm with child. I will not have you mauling me."

Ottingen raised his face. "Look, Anna, I told you. I don't give a damn about anything but us."

"Well, I do! I won't have you making a scandal in the

village. They've talked enough about me in the past. You must stay away from me."

Ottingen stood up. "Is that what you *honestly* want, to be left alone up here?"

Anna's lip trembled. She dropped her face. "Yes."

She's trying to be hard, Ottingen thought. But she doesn't fool me. She wanted to be kissed. I know it. All right, I'll play her game. I'll be patient. She's a lot of woman. It's worth waiting for.

"If that's the way you want it," he said, "then that's how we'll have it. I'll stop by now and then, Anna, until your year of mourning is up. But then I'm coming back to court you." He raised her chin. "Do I make myself clear?"

The third of August was a windless, hot day. The sun's rays struggled through the gray haze that hung over the dry earth. Early in the morning Anna was awakened by twinges of pain. By early afternoon the pains had become regular. Anna sat on the porch thinking back over the last two months. Sergeant Ottingen had been a frequent caller. And Anna had become more and more confused by his attention. What would she tell him if the baby was born white? Could she deceive him, have him believe that it was Jan Hendersen's child? And if the baby was dark-skinned? Could she give it over to the slaves, let the child live in the slave quarters and pretend that it had been born dead? In either case, there would always be fear. The fear that she would be discovered, ostracized, perhaps tortured or killed.

A month ago, after Ottingen had called on her, she had contemplated confessing. For a minute it seemed the solution. If he accepted, then he could share the problem with her. But if not, then what? If he was not as honorable as she judged him to be, if he reported her to the council, then she would be hung. Erasing Theodore Ottingen from her life was clearly the only solution. Ottingen had eased her loneliness, given her dreams about the future. But now that she was in labor, she knew that they had been foolish dreams, unreal. Her baby was going to be born very soon, and her child would fill the gap that Jan's and Prince's death had brought about.

A sharp pain struck Anna's hips. When the pain had passed, beads of sweat poured down her face. She got up.

321

She heard Bahbu in the kitchen. "Come, Bahbu," she called.

Going up the steps, she heard Bahbu's bare feet on the boards behind her.

"It is time?" Bahbu queried.

"Yes," Anna said. "I am going to Master Jan's room. I want my baby to be born in that bed, the master of the house."

When Anna was in the high, four poster bed, Bahbu turned to leave the room. "I bring bush tea, to make the baby come faster," she explained.

The tea did nothing to ease Anna's labor. Hours later, she was exhausted from the pain. With every new pain her head pushed back into the wet pillow. For a long time she felt that the lower part of her body was being crushed by great weights and if she could squeeze hard enough, she would throw them off. Later, the baby became a ball of iron that was hammering to rip through the bruised flesh that held it back.

Bahbu saw the baby's head appear. Up to this point Anna had labored silently. But now, with the head straining to get out of her womb, Anna emitted a series of piercing screams. The baby slid out, face up, between her legs.

Bahbu looked at the child. It was a golden brown. The gods have been good to me, she thought. She picked the child up and showed it to Anna. "We have a boy, Anna," she said.

Anna looked at the brown baby and smiled. Like his father, she thought. Weakly, she raised her head a little to look at the child more. "His name is Prince," she said.

Bahbu spanked the child and it gave out a loud wail.

"When the militia ride through," Anna said softly, "tell them Jan Hendersen's child was born dead, prematurely. Have a grave dug, Bahbu, at Jan's feet. The child will have to go to the slave quarters during the day. At night he will stay with me."

Two days later, Anna heard a horse draw near to the house. She knew that Ottingen had arrived. She followed his footsteps across the veranda, into the house and up the steps.

Looking hesitantly in at her, he said, "I heard about the baby . . . dying."

"Come in, Theodore."

322

Ottingen walked to the bed. "I am so sorry, Anna." He reached for her hand.

Anna pulled away. "Sit down, please."

"Must you always reject affection?" he said angrily.

Anna smiled. "You are always so persistent. I have a story to tell you today."

"Oh? I will listen carefully," he said, humoring her.

Anna closed her eyes. "Once upon a time I knew a chameleon. When the chameleon was small, it lived on a rock here at Fortuna. The chameleon had only black lizards to play with, so shrewdly it turned black. Sometimes it had to go to the greathouse, where the white lizards lived, and then it turned white. The chameleon liked the black lizards best, because the white lizards were really an ugly lot. The chameleon, from being black so much, grew a black heart. And then one day the chameleon fell in love with a black lizard . . ." Anna saw Ottingen's face go cold, but she pressed on, no longer able to contain her secret. "Later, there was a war between the white lizards from the greathouse and the black lizards on the rock. And the black lizard that the chameleon loved was killed. The chameleon grieved. And then one day she saw a white lizard, a handsome lizard with great dash and charm. And, poof, being a shrewd chameleon, and feeling very lonely and sorry for herself, she turned white." Anna opened her eyes. "But she could not change her heart. It was black."

Ottingen's eyes burned into Anna's. "You are a chameleon?"

"Yes."

Ottingen backed away from the bed. "Who?"

"Prince."

"Prince? My God, Anna," he whispered. "Why? A beautiful woman like you. Why would you give your love to a black slave?"

"You would have to begin as the little chameleon on the rock," she said softly, "before the hatreds of the white lizards could affect your love."

Ottingen took another step back. Anna sat up. "Don't look so shocked," she screamed. "Do you think I could love him if he were not a man?"

"A man," Ottingen gasped. "He's a slave, a black slave."

Anna leaned on her elbow. Her eyes flashed. She said firmly, "Anything that the white man does not understand

323

he wants to destroy, doesn't he, Sergeant? Why don't you have me hung?"

"No. No, I couldn't do that. My God, Anna, you have to be mad, as they say." He stared at her. "It doesn't seem real. Just yesterday, we received word that Prince is alive."

"Alive?" Anna sat up straight.

"Yes, alive. He burned down the manor at Hendersen."

"What will happen?"

Ottingen's blue eyes leveled on hers. "I am ordered to St. John to capture him and bring him back." His arms fell beside him. "No, Anna, I'll not give away your secret. But how you can live with it, I don't know." Ottingen turned and strode out of the house.

Chapter 28

At Coral Bay, a captured rebel was led into Ottingen's room in the fort. Ottingen looked hard at the lean black man, amazed to see that he was still healthy and strong after nine months of foraging the bush.

"Whose slave are you?" Ottingen asked.

Stone-faced, the rebel stared at the wall.

"The revolt is over," Ottingen said softly. He swung off the edge of the rickety table and walked back and forth. "You are not going to be punished. Whether you talk to me or not, it doesn't matter. You are going to be sent out of the fort tonight, free." He looked into the rebel's face. "But how free are you?"

No response.

"You are holed up somewhere, lurking in the bush at night. Is this freedom? Is this any better than going back to your plantation, to your owner, and to your family? Yes, I know. You think we will torture you, make examples of you, as we did with the others. No, we have voted against this. The revolt is over. We are anxious to end this thing without more destruction or killing. Do you understand?"

The rebel did not move.

"When you go out of here tonight, go back to the others. Tell them that if they return to their plantations by sundown tomorrow, they will not be harmed." Ottingen started the same easy pace again, his heels clicking on the brick floor. "Yes, I'm offering you a choice. If you go back to your plantations, you'll have your own bed to sleep in, and food to eat without having to scurry like starving beasts in the field at night. But if you want to live like hunted animals, that's your decision." Still no change of expression on the rebel's face. "You have been a prisoner here in the fort for over two weeks. You've not been harmed. We were waiting for the council to hold meeting and decide what to do with you. They voted to pardon you. Now, come, I'll take you to the gate and let you out."

Reaching the doorway, Ottingen stopped. "Tell your leader, Prince, that Jan Hendersen is dead. The woman whose name is Anna is now mistress of Hendersen. He can surrender at Hendersen here on St. John, but he will go back to the plantation on St. Thomas. The mistress of Hendersen has had a child, a son. Tell Prince this." Ottingen stuck his chin out and looked into the rebel's face. Now the rebel's eyelids fluttered nervously. "Do you understand everything I say?" Ottingen demanded. The rebel nodded his head.

Ottingen went out and across the brick courtyard, the rebel following close on his heels. Two sentinels pulled on the heavy doors. Looking at the rebel, Ottingen jerked his head toward the path to freedom. The rebel hesitated, shifting his eyes from the open door to Ottingen and back again. "You'll not be harmed," Ottingen said.

The rebel sprinted through the gate, his tattered trousers flapping as he disappeared in the bush.

The rebels guarded their lair like the hunted animals they had become. For three months the fifteen men and women had avoided capture by crawling through the thickest parts of the jungle in search of food and water. On constant lookout for a boat that would carry them off St. John, they had scoured every beach and cove, over and over again. But the planters who had come back to patch together the ruins of their estates were cautious and every vessel that would float was under lock and key at the fort, guarded by the garrison.

The rebel who had been set free from the fort came to deliver Sergeant Ottingen's message.

"Go back to the plantation?" Prince said. "We have suffered for three months in this dirty hole, waiting to find a boat. Do you think I would walk up to the white man and let him torture me, let him have the satisfaction of saying he tricked the man who led this revolt?" The noise startled everyone. Stiffening, alert, Prince rolled his eyes and listened for the sound of soldier's feet. "The white man be kind?" he whispered. "I am not a fool."

"The white soldier said I should tell you that your master is dead."

"Jan Hendersen, dead?"

"And that the woman, Anna, is the mistress of Hendersen on St. Thomas."

Prince went limp. "Anna, mistress of Hendersen," he said quietly.

"He said you would have to go back to the plantation on St. Thomas. He said that the mistress had a child, a son."

"A son," he whispered.

The rebels were shocked to see their leader's weakness. Several laughed nervously, hiding their mouths, some whispered to each other. Their noises brought Prince to his senses. He rose with dignity. His arms crossed over the bulging muscles on his chest and he drew erect, growing taller and wider, in front of their eyes. His head rolled back, widening his neck muscles. "Gods of our people, you have sent another Prince." He uncrossed his arms and lifted the carving from his chest. Holding it up, he said, "When I see my son, I will give you back this idol. There will be no more curse for my family to follow."

"Do not promise our gods this," one of the women cried out. "The white man *should* have a curse on him forever."

Prince's head snapped around. "This carries a curse on the father of the child who wears it, as well as the curse on the white man. Would you have me die by the hand of my son so that you can have the white man suffer?" He threw his head back again. His lips moved, but his mumbled words could not be heard.

His tribute done, Prince looked solemnly at his people. "I will go back to Hendersen on St. John at sundown tomorrow. I am no longer your leader. Each man will decide what he wants to do. The white man could have set a trap for us. But if not, I will be on the boat the gods have promised, going back to Anna and my son."

Ottingen stood in the clearing at Hendersen looking at the charred remains of the greathouse. The blackened stone base was the only remains of the sturdy house Jan Hendersen had built there. On his left, the mill, its stone face unscarred, was raised up against the pink and lavender evening sky. The arms were poised, promising performance for the payment of cane to its wooden gut.

In back of Ottingen, well hidden in the bush, a rebel leader contemplated surrender. Having made his decision, Prince stepped out. "Prince, slave of the mistress of Hendersen, surrenders," he said.

327

The sergeant whipped around. "I come unarmed," Ottingen said, holding his hands out.

Prince stood straight. Ottingen walked casually toward him. "We Danes are glad to accept your surrender. You will be returned to your owner unharmed." As he drew closer to Prince, he saw the carving that hung on his chest. Purposely, he looked into Prince's eyes, realizing how handsome Prince was. Anna's face flashed through Ottingen's mind. "So you are the slave who led the revolt? Slave of Mistress Anna."

"Yes, I am Prince."

Ottingen looked back at the carving. When Prince's chest rose, the expression of the carved face seemed to change. "I see you wear a good luck charm."

Prince nodded.

"Is this a very special one?" Ottingen asked companionably.

"Yes."

Ottingen stared into Prince's face. "I've always been interested in your witchcraft. In fact, at times I believe in its powers. And what is the power of this charm?"

"It brings death to evil spirits."

"It must have worked for you, Prince. You've done well to survive these last nine months. And it brought you good health, for now you'll live on your plantation with your Mistress Anna."

Prince remained motionless.

"Follow me," Ottingen said. "We'll go back to the fort. Tomorrow I'll send word for your mistress to come to Charlotte Amalie to claim you."

Ottingen stepped past Prince and walked into the darkening jungle.

Chapter 29

Midmorning of August 25, 1734, the Danish slaver *Laarburg Galley* dropped anchor in the harbor at Charlotte Amalie. Before her lines had been made secure, a group of small boats streaked toward her, bobbing up and down on the choppy water.

The boats carried the more enterprising slave traders, those intent on getting to the gunnels of the *Laarburg Galley* where they could inspect the new slaves and fight to place their mark on the best of the lot. Other planters and traders leaned forward on the waterfront, shaking their fists and yelling at those who pulled away.

Amid this confusion, Ottingen's return to St. Thomas was without fanfare. Only Claude Mueller went to the landing below Christian's fort to greet the sergeant.

"Welcome back, Theodore," Claude called. "The *Laarburg Galley* arrived and they say she has lost more than half her slaves. What a waste of money." He looked at Ottingen. "We've had fierce arguments in council. Now that the revolt is put down, the company would try to place the blame on the planters again, saying we were too lax with our slaves. They think they can get us to shoulder the expense. And look at the money that's wasted by the company on these slavers. Only *half* the slaves alive right now of those that set sail on the *Laarburg Galley*. If the company can afford these indulgences, they can come up with the money for the revolt." He threw back his white curls. "Why did I wear this wig?" he said. "It's so hot today."

Ottingen smiled. "Why did you?"

Claude dropped his chin on his shoulder. He looked kittenishly at Ottingen. "You know those Spanish traders show off their finest apparel, Theodore. I don't want them to think we Danes can't afford the same."

There was the shuffle of bare feet behind them. Claude

looked at the line of Negroes moving toward the fort. "They are unchained, Theodore," he gasped, edging closer to his friend.

"Yes, I know," Ottingen said. He watched the surrendered rebels move up the steps. "That's how I got them to surrender. They think they are free to return to their owners. They're due for a surprise when they get inside the fort."

"You're as sly as a fox, Theodore. And that's why you've earned your commission."

"My commission?"

"Yes, Lieutenant." Claude saluted. He arranged his wig curls and yanked at his cutaway coat. "It was signed at the last meeting of council."

Ottingen was pleased but seemed to be in a hurry. He turned from Claude.

"Aha, and who are you looking for, young man?"

"Corporal, bring that suitcase here," Ottingen called. He looked at Claude. "I was hoping to see Anna Hendersen here today."

"Anna? She's in confinement. What a tragedy that was, eh, Theodore?"

"Yes, a great tragedy," Ottingen said crisply. He looked toward the waterfront. "I sent word for her to be here."

"I doubt if she's strong enough for the ride," Claude said. "Not even for the satisfaction of seeing that Hendersen slave punished."

"There," Ottingen pointed. "Look. Beyond the slave traders. See, it *is* Anna."

Anna sat erect, sidesaddle. She held a firm grip on the reins of her black horse as it pranced, straining to have its head. Anna was wearing a black dress and a black veil covered her face. She was so impressive that quiet fell over the traders as their heads turned to follow her. Back of Anna, Bahbu rode a brown horse, astride and bareback. Her thin legs joggled on either side of the horse. When the strange riders had passed, the traders, one by one, fell back to their screaming and shoving.

Anna saw Ottingen and Claude Mueller come up the steps. She reined in her horse by the fort. Neither she nor Bahbu dismounted.

"Good day, Madame Hendersen," Claude said cheerily. He swept off his hat and bowed. His wig curls fell forward. Raising up, he said, "I hope you haven't overdone this. Are you sure you're strong enough for the ride?"

"I am very well, thank you," Anna said.

"I think it will be some time before they get around to punishing these savages," Claude said. "Would you like to ride to my house, Anna, and rest?"

"No, that won't be necessary," Ottingen said brusquely. "Mrs. Hendersen comes to receive a gift."

"A gift?" Claude said, trembling with anticipation. "What is it, Theodore?"

Ottingen opened his suitcase and raised up a round package, its wrapper a dirty white cloth. He held the bundle up in the air ominously.

Fold by fold, Ottingen drew back the cloth, revealing Prince's severed head. The eyes were closed, the skin the color of Fortuna clay.

Bahbu slid from her horse. Going to Ottingen, she reached up and took the head, cradling it in her arms.

Across the waterfront drifted the tireless voices of the traders. Gently, Bahbu raised a fold of the dirty cloth and covered her son's face.

"Here," Anna said, holding out her hand.

Bahbu lifted Ottingen's gift and placed it in Anna's lap.

"Before you leave," Ottingen said, "let me show you something else." He fumbled inside his tunic and drew out the amulet. "I thought I would save it," he said lightly. "Maybe some day I'll have a son. If I do, it will make a nice trinket for him. It's like a chameleon. See?" He twisted it in the sunlight. Looking at Anna, he said, "I think it has a black heart."

Slowly, Anna raised her veil. Her eyes were dry. She looked calmly at the carving. Her eyes moved up, coldly appraising Ottingen's face. "I hope you have a son," she said. "And I think it would be nice for him to have a memento of the revolt on St. John. But I doubt if you would let him wear it. Or, for that matter, if you would wear it. You lack the courage."

Ottingen jutted out his chin. "He'll wear it. And until then, I will." He pushed the carving back into his tunic.

Anna smiled. It was a taunting smile, a smile that said, you would not dare. She dropped her veil.

The mistress of Hendersen and her slave, Bahbu, picked their way through the bargaining traders. In the middle of the road was the line of slaves, shuffling along the dusty road, their cries lost in the din of foreign voices. At the end of the line was a child, unchained, staggering along, numbed by pain and fear.

Bahbu looked at the child, then turned her face up to the sky. The sun was directly overhead, blazing down on the bustling town of Charlotte Amalie, Danish West Indies. Bahbu squinted and looked behind the sun.

Epilogue

Three graves mark the mortal destiny of Jan Hendersen and the two women who were his wives. On each is an eroded stone that shows Anna on Jan's right and Christina on his left. At Jan's feet there is a stone where Anna's son never lay. Two cassia trees drop leaves on the dusty graves.

The stone path to the ruins of the greathouse is now almost covered with Fortuna clay and thorny brush. Chameleons sun themselves on the rocks. The quiet is broken now and then by the bleat of a goat or the shriek of a mongoose. The decay of Fortuna, which set in shortly after Anna's murder, is now complete.

The death of Anna Bodker Hendersen has been the subject of endless stories passed down through generations of natives. A few facts also appear in contemporary government records. A free Negro woman named Bahbu appeared during the hour of first light on August 7, 1739, at Perseverance Estate to beg that the master report her discovery to the governor. She had come into Anna's bedroom, she said, about two hours after midnight to fasten a storm shutter that had come loose. Her mistress lay dead on the great mahogany bed, her head severed.

The boy known as Prince, thought to be the son of Bahbu, was five at the time. Anna had granted him and Bahbu freedom a year after his birth. This fact is recorded in government documents. Anna's lands and holdings were bequeathed to Bahbu, who sold them within a year of Anna's murder. Prince was sent to Spain for schooling, on the condition that he embrace the Catholic faith. It is said that he returned to St. Thomas under the name of Armando Martinez when he was twenty years old, that he remained on the island long enough to buy a quadroon girl, and that he returned with her to Cadiz.

Anna was thirty when she died. The legends say that she

spent the last five years of her life in seclusion and that during her last year she saw virtually no one but Bahbu. It is said that she had become mad. The few who were permitted into her presence described her as strange and of a wandering mind.

There is little agreement on the details of Anna's death. Most say that Ottingen, who had been transferred to the garrison on St. Croix, came back from time to time to see her and had killed her out of unrelieved passion. (Records show that he had arrived in St. Thomas the day of her death.) Some believe that the governor himself commissioned the murder when he learned the true identity of the child Prince. (We must remember the governor's own passion at the killing of his son-in-law and granddaughter by the rebels.)

The most reasonable explanation is the one least often put forth. This is that Bahbu, led not by passion, but by her instinct of tribal destiny, placed the knife gently to the neck of the person she most loved. Underlying this assumption is the fact that the parentage of Anna's child had become known officially several days before the murder. Bahbu, in her own fashion, must have known this. Anna would not have. The black woman, fearing that torture and death would be Anna's fate, may have preferred to commit the act lovingly, with her own hands.

Three women succeeded Anna as mistress of Fortuna. The first died (it is said) of poison several years after she had come there as a bride. Her widower married a humble woman who soon went mad. He was granted permission to return with her to Denmark. The plantation was then sold to a handsome young Dane who came with his bride to take possession on June 17, 1752. Four years later his bride died, it appears by an act of her own will. The owner soon abandoned the plantation, convinced that a malignant presence resided there.

Even today some natives say that the moon and the sun and the stars hang lower on Fortuna Hill than anywhere else on the island.

BESTSELLERS
FROM DELL

fiction

- [ ] ERIC by Doris Lund $1.75 (4586-04)
- [ ] MARATHON MAN by William Goldman $1.95 (5502-02)
- [ ] WINTER KILLS by Richard Coneon $1.75 (6007-00)
- [ ] THE OTHER SIDE OF MIDNIGHT by Sidney Sheldon $1.75 (6067-07)
- [ ] THE RHINEMANN EXCHANGE by Robert Ludlum.. $1.95 (5079-13)
- [ ] THE LONG DARK NIGHT by Joseph Hayes $1.95 (4824-06)
- [ ] SHAMPOO by Robert Alley $1.75 (7808-17)
- [ ] PLEASURE MAN by Mae West $1.50 (7074-06)
- [ ] THE NAKED FACE by Sidney Sheldon $1.25 (4921-05)
- [ ] DOG DAY AFTERNOON by Patrick Mann $1.50 (4519-06)
- [ ] THE BOY WHO INVENTED THE BUBBLE GUN
      by Paul Gallico $1.50 (0719-28)

nonfiction

- [ ] JAMES DEAN, THE MUTANT KING by David Dalton $1.75 (4893-02)
- [ ] MIKE ROY'S CROCK COOKERY $1.25 (5617-04)
- [ ] THE FEMALE WOMAN by Arianna Stassinopoulous. $1.50 (5015-02)
- [ ] MAN KIND? by Cleveland Amory $1.75 (5451-03)
- [ ] CHARLES BRONSON SUPERSTAR by Steven Whitney $1.50 (4561-11)
- [ ] THE JAWS LOG by Carl Gottlieb $1.50 (4689-00)
- [ ] THE REICH MARSHAL by Leonard Mosley $1.75 (7686-06)
- [ ] JOEY by Donald Goddard $1.75 (4825-05)
- [ ] DR. STILLMAN'S 14-DAY SHAPE-UP PROGRAM
      by I. M. Stillman, M.D., and S. S. Baker $1.75 (1913-04)
- [ ] WHY MEN CALL GIRLS by Shannon Canfield
      and Dick Stuart $1.50 (9609-06)

Buy them at your local bookstore or send this page to the address below:

Dell DELL BOOKS
P.O. BOX 1000, PINEBROOK, N.J. 07058

Please send me the books I have checked above. I am enclosing $_____
(please add 25¢ per copy to cover postage and handling). Send check or
money order—no cash or C.O.D.'s.

Mr/Mrs/Miss_____

Address_____

City_____State/Zip_____

This offer expires 11/76